*Also by Matthew Mather*

**Atopia**
*The Atopia Chronicles*
*The Utopia Chronicles* (forthcoming)

*CyberStorm*

# THE DYSTOPIA CHRONICLES

## Book Two of Atopia

## by Matthew Mather

47NORTH

This is a work of fiction. Names, characters, organizations, places, events, and incidents are either products of the author's imagination or are used fictitiously.

Text copyright © 2014 Matthew Mather
All rights reserved.

No part of this book may be reproduced, or stored in a retrieval system, or transmitted in any form or by any means, electronic, mechanical, photocopying, recording, or otherwise, without express written permission of the publisher.

Published by 47North, Seattle

www.apub.com

Amazon, the Amazon logo, and 47North are trademarks of Amazon.com, Inc., or its affiliates.

ISBN-13: 9781477824535
ISBN-10: 1477824537

Cover design by Jason Gurley
Illustrated by Paul Youll

Library of Congress Control Number: 2014934792

Printed in the United States of America

*For Julie, and the memory of Ash House, where much of this was written.*

*And for the boys and girls at the White Horse. You know who you are.*

# Prologue

SEEING HIS DEAD mother making tea in microgravity, a hundred million miles from where he'd buried her in Idaho, was the first thing that ever struck fear into Commander Stockard during his thirty-year career as a space jockey. Even seeing the world flicker like a candle just moments before—the lights of the entire night side of the Earth winking on and off as if someone was flicking a switch—hadn't fazed him.

Startled perhaps, but not scared.

Not like this.

It's just a hallucination, he tried telling himself, cabin fever from being stuck in this tin can for two months. *It's not real.* Keep calm. *Panic is the enemy.* His dead mother smiled, wagging a teapot in the air—did he want some? He shook his head. *No, thank you.*

It had to be the stress. Parking a hundred billion tons of comet ice in Earth orbit was a project of destiny. Seven years ago, when the deep space monitoring network picked up comet Wormwood-P/2058D12, it was heralded as humanity's opportunity to finally—*really*—begin colonization of near-Earth space.

Commander Deng looked at him and frowned. "Still no comms from Earth. What do you think, solar flare?"

Stockard breathed deep. Maybe, but their instruments would have picked up a magnetic disturbance. "Probably more to do with the fight between Atopia and Terra Nova." In the two months since the Comet Catcher mission left Earth, the struggle between these two colonies had climaxed into a full-blown kinetic conflict.

The engine burn had been going on for a minute already. The ship rumbled.

Bits of debris from weeks of zero gravity fell as the ship decelerated. A pencil Stockard left wedged next to a display unit bounced off his suit. He tried to grab it, swearing as he missed.

Glancing at Commander Deng, he could see something was wrong. "Everything all right?" Stockard yelled above the roar of the engines.

She blinked and shook her head. "It's just . . . I think I'm hallucinating . . ."

"Burn complete," announced the system computer. "On target for Wormwood."

Stockard gazed at her steadily. Should he tell her? Fear was contagious. Out of the corner of his eye, in the reflection of the cockpit glass, Stockard's dead mother waved at him from just down the access tunnel. Goose bumps rippled across his arms under the thick layers of his spacesuit.

His mother was waiting for him.

# Part I:
# Limbo

# 1

A DOZEN ARCHED doorways lined each side of the great hall, each twenty feet high and topped with sparkling colored glass. Bright light streamed in. Between the doorways, gold-veined marble columns rose from polished floors to a ceiling frescoed with cherubic angels. An image of God hung over the middle of the room, reaching down to the world below.

It was a virtual projection, one of Jimmy Scadden's private worlds, and it was the first time Nancy Killiam had seen it with her own eyes. She'd heard rumors, but getting into this space had been difficult. You had to be invited. Nancy wasn't, but she'd infiltrated the virtual sensory channels of someone who was.

She was spying from a front-row-center seat.

"Join me if you believe in everlasting peace," Jimmy thundered from a pulpit in front of her, shining in his white military uniform. "Join with me, and you shall never grow old, you shall never die."

It was a psombie recruitment session.

Row upon row of young men and women sat at attention, all of them attending the meeting virtually through pssi—the Atopian poly-synthetic sensory interface. Their eyes and minds were focused on Jimmy. In exchange for unlimited and unfettered access to the Atopian synthetic reality multiverse, Jimmy was bargaining for use of their physical bodies in the real world, disconnecting their minds with a body-lease contract, turning themselves into psombies.

*What was he up to?* Nancy squirmed to stay hidden behind the consciousness of the observer in whom she was hiding. A part of her wanted to burst out and announce to Jimmy that she'd discovered him, but she'd never been good at confrontation, and what Jimmy was doing wasn't illegal. She couldn't go running back to the Cognix Corporation boardroom or Atopian Council, screaming like a child. *Aunt Patricia would have known what to do*, but she was dead. *She's gone. You need to figure this out for yourself.*

Patricia Killiam's passing hadn't just opened up a yawning gap in the fabric of Nancy's life: having one of the founders of Atopia die had opened a vacuum in the power structure of what'd become one of the most potent forces shaping the world—the release of pssi technology. Nancy stared at Jimmy on stage. Patricia had been a central figure in his life as well, but her death didn't seem to be affecting him. At least, not in the ways that made sense to Nancy.

"I have chosen each of you *personally*"—Jimmy nodded to his audience—"to be my representatives in your communities. You are the chosen ones." He paused and smiled. "If, of course, you choose me."

The crowd shifted in their seats. They were here. They'd already made up their minds.

Nancy had known Jimmy her whole life, grown up together with him in the pssi-kid program on Atopia, part of the first generation of children born with limitless virtual reality built into their minds. But this man up on stage wasn't the quiet and efficient Jimmy with whom she'd grown up, the shy boy who had hidden in the labs of the Atopian research centers almost as much as she had.

Jimmy opened his arms to the crowd. "Let me be the one that saves you—saves you from a life of drudgery, from a life of pain, from uncertainty. I can free you from all of this, to a world where your every desire is fulfilled."

With these words the doors to the great hall flew open, revealing dreamscapes beyond. Nancy could only guess what the rest of the assembled glimpsed. Jimmy was using open access to their memories to project fantasy worlds, a combination of where each attendee had felt safest, and of what they always wanted to be. All Nancy saw was her Aunt Patricia, staring back at her from the grave.

"Give me your bodies," Jimmy roared, "and in return I offer immortality."

The reality skin of the hall merged with the fusing realities of the attendees, each of them greeted by a splintered copy of Jimmy who whisked them into their fantasy lands. Nancy released the sensory channels of the person she was ghosting, letting her primary presence settle behind her office desk. Mahogany paneling appeared in her visual sensory frames. Bookcases lined the walls behind her copper-studded leather attending chairs, the Persian carpets underfoot lit softly by green-glass lamps that glowed on the walls.

Cunard, Nancy's digital symbiote—her proxxi—was sitting in one of the chairs. "We should gather more information before we say anything to anyone."

Nancy smiled. Cunard, her protector and counselor, more now than ever before, and never any less of a perfectionist. Then again, he was just a reflection of herself. She nodded, agreeing with him. "Good work on getting me into that meeting."

"What he's doing might not be strictly illegal, but it's certainly suspicious, and it's been hidden from the Atopian Council."

"Or at least hidden from us." Nancy wasn't sure where the fault lines in the newly evolving Atopian power structure were falling. It might just be that she wasn't on a need-to-know list. She felt like she was drowning, unable to get a firm grasp on anything to hold her up. She needed help. "What I need you to focus on is finding Bob and Sid."

"And Vince," added Cunard.

"Yes, and Vince," Nancy agreed. She wasn't sure that they were all together, but they all rushed off just after the fiasco with the altered-reality skin and simulated storms that nearly brought the destruction of Atopia. Terra Nova, a competing off-shore colony in the Atlantic Ocean, admitted to implanting the reality-skin, forcing a closure of the Atopian borders just after Bob and Sid had left with Vince. "Do you think they're trying to find Willy's body?"

"Yes, but something else is going on. Why would they have cut off contact?"

Nancy could see Bob running off to help his friend Willy—with Sid, as usual, in tow—but it was odd that Vince went with them. Never mind that he was three times their age and the famous trillionaire founder of PhutureNews, but Nancy had never seen Vince Indigo rush off to do *anything* in all the years she'd known him when she was growing up. Why now?

"Bob did beg you to go with him," Cunard reminded her. "I don't need to tell you, but his anger is always just under the surface. Hard to say what losing Patricia did to him."

Nancy took a deep breath. Was Bob angry at her? She'd only just caught a glimpse of the old Bob before he left, the one she'd known and loved all those years before his brother had killed himself. For years, Bob had cut himself off behind a veil of drugs, filtering his life through the pain of losing his brother. Nancy rubbed her eyes. I was supposed to be with him, he'd begged me to come, but how could I just take off and leave Patricia's dream in the hands of Kesselring and Jimmy when she died?

Almost as soon as Bob had left Atopia on the passenger cannon, Nancy lost all connections with him, with everyone in his group. They'd completely disappeared off the grid, which was no easy feat.

They had to be hiding on purpose.

But why? Where *was* he?

# 2

"LIFE IS SUFFERING," said a disembodied voice.

The words floated to Bob through a steaming jungle, and he followed them into a clearing where he found a herd of massive, dorsal-finned creatures. Halfway through mouthfuls of fern and bush, they swung their heads to observe him.

"The cessation of suffering is attainable . . ."

Bob looked into the sky, and then down at his hands; four fingers webbed with translucent green skin. The landscape, the animals, the vegetation—it was alien.

"Bob," said another voice, more familiar this time. Bob looked up to find his proxxi Robert standing to the side of the clearing. The animals began lumbering off, crashing through the forest. "Time to get up, Bob."

His proxxi smiled, offering a cup of coffee, and the jungle behind him shimmered. Replacing it were the familiar outlines of Bob's bedroom in his family's habitat on Atopia. Bob shook his head. He didn't need to be babied. Reaching into the reality skin around him, he ripped it down. Sloping wooden beams appeared, the now-familiar ceiling of the farmhouse bedroom in which he spent the last few weeks sleeping. On a high shelf above the door, long-forgotten trunks stood collecting dust, and for the hundredth time he wondered what was in them. Perhaps today he'd have a look.

This end of the farmhouse was turn-of-the-21st-century: wooden-framed construction with soft mineral walls—gypsum calcium sulfate sandwiched between paper—fastened together with formed-metal nails and screws. *Primitive* was the word that came into Bob's mind. The wilderness of reality outside of Atopia was reinforcing the sensation that he'd been cast out of paradise.

On Atopia, his floating island home just off the coast of California, even physical reality was clean, shining, every detail accounted for. The forests up top were perfectly manicured. The corridors below were always polished and shining. Before leaving— before being *asked* to leave—he had only experienced the rest of the world through wikiworld simulations. Now he was out in the wild, with illicit smarticles embedded in his nervous system, and the limited bandwidth forced him into the dirt and grime and specificity of being in only one place at a time. To say it was a new experience was an understatement.

And the constant barrage of hate media didn't help.

When he took off from Atopia right after the *incident*, and then immediately dropped off the grid, the conspiracy nuts were in hot pursuit of Bob and Sid and Vince. It wasn't just the nutjobs, though. The longer their gang remained hidden and off the radar, the more the mainstream mediaworlds were latching onto the conspiracy theories. People wanted answers.

So did Bob.

Propping himself onto one elbow, he rubbed his eyes. "What was that about?"

His proxxi appeared on a floral-print chaise in front of the fireplace in the small room. "What?"

"The jungle with the dinosaurs."

"Dinosaurs?"

Connectivity was limited in rural Montana. Bob had a few dozen splinters—synthetic intelligence bots modeled after his own cognition systems—hunting down leads as they searched through the virtual and real worlds for any sign of his friend Willy's body.

Synthesizing all the information they collected in real-time was impossible through the tiny data pipes they had access to, so his splinters were integrating into his meta-cognition systems while he slept.

It made for strange dreaming.

"You were standing in a jungle with me," Bob continued, sitting upright in bed. "Was it a gameworld? A past construct . . .?"

Robert shook his head. "You must have been dreaming."

Bob stretched and felt through the extra-sensory network of smarticles dusted around the peripheries of the farm. Nothing—no danger, no incursions, not yet.

The dream was fading, the giant creatures sliding into mind-fog.

Robert began feeding Bob a summary of the night's searches. The most significant news was that the Comet Catcher mission had launched from orbit the night before and in two months would be shepherding the Wormwood comet into Earth orbit. Bob scanned the top level of Robert's reports, but there were no new answers, no resolutions. It was going to be another day of waiting. Bob detached his visual point-of-view to see where everyone else was, leaving a fresh splinter to finish chatting with Robert.

Snapping out of his body, his viewpoint rose up toward the ceiling while he flipped his visual system to scan for warm bodies. A housebot appeared through the bedroom door with Bob's clothes for the day. The walls faded and through the transparence the red-outlined images of his friends downstairs in the kitchen appeared, their voices rising into his consciousness as he flitted down to them.

"Sidney *Horowitz*?" laughed Vince as Bob's virtual presence announced itself, pinging everyone's networks while he sat his projection down at the head of the breakfast table. Sid and Vince were sitting at the table arguing about something. Willy's virtual avatar and Brigitte sat across from them, holding hands.

Sid nodded at Bob, acknowledging his arrival, before turning back to Vince. "What's the big deal? It's not like it was secret."

"Horowitz the mastermind scientist!" Vince thumped the table and shook his head. "I just always imagined your surname . . . ah, never mind. It doesn't have a bad ring to it, on second thought."

The main living area, attached to the front of the aging farmhouse, was more of the type of thing Bob was used to on Atopia—lignin-based bio-thermoplastics curving smoothly into an oval dome thirty feet high and fifty feet across, climate controlled as phase-shifting particles in the membrane shell regulated heat and molecular flow across its boundary. Sparrows were nesting at its apex, darting around.

"Want some breakfast?" asked Deanna, busy cooking at the stove. She was an old friend of Vince's, from way back. "I mean, when your body gets down here." She was still getting used to the way the Atopians flitted around their conscious points-of-view. "And since we have all the masterminds at the table now, could you explain to me what happened to Willy's body again?"

Bob nodded, and an angular-armed bot on top of the refrigerator opened itself and handed a packet of gro-bacon to Deanna. Communal eating was just one more in a list of things Bob was getting used to. He glanced at Sid, expecting him to answer Deanna, but Sid was already lost to the world again—optimizing the geothermal regulator under the farm, rearranging the drone scheduling, doing a systems analysis of the mixture of crops in the surrounding fields. Like a chameleon he melted into his surroundings; he'd already added cowboy boots to his usual repertoire of ragged jeans and t-shirts. Bob wished he could lose himself so easily.

"It was my fault," Willy's avatar offered, glancing at Brigitte. "I was trying to make money by splintering my mind into hundreds of pieces, trying to be everywhere at once in the stock markets." He looked at the table. "What I was doing was illegal, at least at the time, so I tried to hide it by rerouting my conscious stream through an anonymous connection on Terra Nova."

Deanna turned to Willy from her cooking and crinkled her nose. "But how did that lead to losing yourself, or I mean, your body?"

Willy forced a grin. "At a certain point I was so widely splintered that I lost track of home base, so to speak, and that's when my proxxi took off with my body."

Deanna frowned. "He *stole* it? I thought your proxxi friends were there to protect you." She glanced at the table of proxxi—Hotstuff, Robert, Vicious, and Bardot—sitting around an identical table in a virtual projection next to the gang.

"That," Bob interjected, "is exactly the mystery. We think he was protecting Willy, but we don't know from what."

"From myself," Willy muttered, and Brigitte squeezed his virtual hand.

"And you have family in the Commune?" Deanna asked. "That's why you want to get in there?"

Willy nodded. "Yeah, my mother. If I hadn't been so stupid, none of us would be here . . ."

Bob shook his head. "That's not true, Willy, there's bigger things going on."

"And this has to do with that virus that infected the virtual reality systems on Atopia, those fake storms that nearly wrecked the place?"

Vince held up a hand. "Sorry, Deanna, as I said before, we can't say more. And we *really* appreciate your help."

She arched her eyebrows and returned to the stove. "All those things they're saying about you in the mediaworlds, you could stop all that just by coming out—"

Vince cut her off. "We just need to get into the Commune."

Shrugging and smiling, Deanna scooped the bacon and eggs onto a plate.

Bob took a deep breath. Nearly six weeks of waiting, a month and a half of letting the dust settle, and this was where they were—still waiting for approval to enter the Commune. Vince thought it best if they all stayed together. The Commune's agents liked things to move slowly during their process. Bob shook his head. "This is such a waste of time." He looked at Willy and Brigitte. "I mean we need to get searching, do something. Not just sit here."

Sid looked up, dragging his attention away from his virtual workspaces. "Hey, calm down, we're all a little itchy from switching to the new smarticles, your body is going into withdrawal—"

"What the hell are you doing optimizing the farm's geothermal pumps?" With his phantom hands, Bob stood up and grabbed Sid's virtual workspaces and pulled them into primary reality for everyone to see. "Shouldn't you be trying to find Willy's body?"

"Hey!" Sid grabbed his workspaces back and filed them away. "I *am* searching for Willy, but there's only so much I can do."

Vince reached out and tried to get Bob to sit back down. "Patience, young man, patience. We have a plan, we'll stick to the plan."

Bob shook him off. "And who put you in charge?" Spinning a splinter of his mind into the fields around the farm, he checked a tripped motion sensor, but it was just a stray buffalo calf.

"In charge?" Vince laughed. "Are you kidding? Anyway, isn't all this what Patricia wanted?"

The poly-synthetic sensory interface—pssi—product release by Cognix had worked as planned. Over a billion users had joined in the first six weeks since its release, but, like many start-ups, operational demands caught up and slowed it down. More important was that it had started to work in its world-saving ambitions. Just two months from release and there'd been no new flare-ups in the Weather Wars, and projected birth rate indicators seemed to be dropping.

"Then why the heck did she send us out here?" Bob shot back. The release of pssi was having the effect that Patricia had created the entire Atopian project for—to push humankind on a new path away from material consumption and into a new world of virtual consumption—but was Jimmy still the threat to the program that she'd imagined?

Bob's body, inhabited by his proxxi, finally came walking down the stairs, but Bob decided to keep his own point-of-view fixed in his virtual self. As Bob's body seated itself at the table, Deanna walked over and dropped the plate of fried eggs and toast in front of it, and Robert, Bob's proxxi, started using Bob's body to eat it.

"I'm done waiting." Bob fidgeted and spun his viewpoint out around the farm again, but then in the corner of one eye he saw his body's hand pick up a strip of bacon. "Hey, none of that!" His body was getting fat from all this sitting around, and bacon wasn't going to help.

His proxxi, Robert, looked at Bob from his own eyes and smiled. "No need to yell." He diverted the bacon onto the floor for Deanna's ever-watchful dog.

"Sometimes, I don't know why I put up with you," Bob fumed at his proxxi. It was intended to be rhetorical.

"Ever wonder if I think the same thing?" his proxxi replied without skipping a beat.

*Because you have no choice*, Bob thought but didn't say.

"I think we're all getting a little stir crazy." Deanna wiped her hands on a dishtowel. "The bots need some help loading lumber, and I need to scan a package in town. How about coming in with me?"

"Sure," mumbled Bob. "I'll flit in when you're on your way."

Deanna rolled her eyes. "I meant you in your body, Bob."

# 3

THE PICKUP TRUCK bounced its way along the gravel road under a clear Montana sky. Bob rolled down his window to get some air, letting his viewpoint escape and spin out above the fields.

Golden fields of summer oats, ready for harvest, swayed in the breeze. Between them, the green shoots of the secondary harvests rose up through their ranks with the winter wheat. Thickets of sunflowers dotted the landscape, alongside clumps of sugar beets in leafy-green patches, barley, and more. The traditional dry land farming of the area had turned wetter and warmer in past years, while much of the southernmost plains had returned to the dust-bowl of more than a hundred years earlier.

Swarms of ornithopter beebots hovered between the swaying wheat and oats, while crawlers and mulebots scoured the ground. The robotic harvesting ecosystem was powered by both the sun and waste organic matter that the crawlers brought back to the hives where it was combusted for energy. The harvest was in full swing, but it wasn't really farming anymore—at least, not like it used to be.

When Bob came outside, Deanna was kneeling, picking up a handful of earth and staring at the horizon. "I often wonder what my daddy would have thought of all this," she said.

A generation ago, a strain of genetically modified crops—which grew sulphuric acid in their stems at the end of the seasonal cycle—had been experimented with to eliminate tillage. The trials were abandoned, but not before the gene jumped into the wild, burning away a swath of America before it was stopped. With traditional farming already on its last legs, a Defense-sponsored program to root out the damage and replant the Great Plains with semi-wild perennial crops began, using robotic drones to tend and harvest the multicrop.

"Did your family own the place a long time?" Bob asked as they drove into town. Not everything was in the databases.

"A few generations of farmers. But it's not like when I grew up here. Nobody left, not the old ones, anyway."

Perennials and robotics had saved the heartland, reducing emissions and erosion, but it had also eliminated the need for humans. Most of the center of America, away from the coasts, became deserted, with herds of reintroduced buffalo again roaming the skeletons of ghost towns strewn across the plains. Food production slid under control of the newly formed Defense Agricultural Division. The Great Plains had become a drone-infested wilderness, and DAD was now feeding the country.

"So were you and Vince, well, were you ever . . ." Bob struggled to find the right words. He'd been itching to ask since they got here, but he was trying to resist his constant urges to pry. Everything about coming out here—hiding, staying quiet, confined to one place and one small group of people—ran against the grain of Bob's character.

Deanna laughed. "Yes, we were. A long, long time ago. I met him when my family sent me to MIT to study robotic harvesting, to try to keep up." She sighed. "And look where that got us."

DAD had been created at the outbreak of the Weather Wars, when maintaining the food supply became a critical national security function—but it also had a darker purpose. The tens of millions of drones used in food production could be repurposed in the event of an attack, from inside or out. As their pickup truck rumbled its way along the gravel road into town, Sid was covering them, hacking into the sensor systems of the thousands of drones that were recording the truck's passage, erasing the image of Bob sitting next to Deanna.

"When did you last see Vince?"

She laughed. "Before three weeks ago—when you all arrived—I hadn't seen or heard from him in more than thirty years."

"And you just took us in when he showed up on your doorstep?" Bob shook his head. He liked Vince, but the man had a way of taking people for granted that rubbed Bob the wrong way.

Deanna turned to look at Bob. "Vince isn't so bad, you know. Sure, he can be conceited, loves to talk more than get things done—"

"Superior, controlling," Bob continued for her.

"Someone's in a bad mood," laughed Deanna. "Yeah, all those things, and wouldn't you be if you were him?" She shook her head. "But you know, he's also incredibly clever, and no matter how shallow he can be sometimes, you'll never find a more dedicated friend. He's not used to dealing with real people."

Now Bob laughed. "That's a problem for everyone from Atopia."

"That's better." Deanna smiled. "And you know what?"

The truck bounced on a rock in the road, knocking Bob into the air. He steadied himself. "What?"

"Ten years after Vince and I last spoke, twenty years ago now—just after PhutureNews started to take off—I received a message from the land registry people that someone bought the deed to my family's farm."

"What do you mean?" Bob had assumed she owned the place.

"When things went bad here, my family lost it after working the land for nearly a hundred years. But someone bought it and put it back into my name." Tears welled in Deanna's eyes. "I never found out who, but I know. That man looks after his own. Taking you in and hiding you was the least I could do."

Bob looked away. He had to admit, Vince was dedicated. He'd spent a fortune already, and he never wavered. Bob turned back and smiled at Deanna. "He is a good guy, sorry, you're right."

Bob released his primary presence again to skim out above the fields. Coming up on the edge of town, they passed abandoned gas stations and grain silos and minimarts. Derelict farmhouses dotted the landscape. Further in the distance, larger, aggressive-looking new developments hugged the foothills. These were massive, a tribute to the new materialism version 2.0 that the explosion of the robotic ecosystem had brought to America. This area of Montana, along the eastern edge of the Rockies stretching up from Yellowstone, was one of the few areas of the interior of America experiencing an influx of new residents, but they weren't here for the farming.

The reason was below, the magmatic upwelling that brought abundant geothermal power.

It was also the reason the Commune was here.

"IT'LL JUST TAKE me a minute to authenticate this package." Deanna hopped out of the truck. "Why don't you follow the bots to the lumber yard? I'll be there in a sec."

Bob sent a splinter to find out what a "lumber yard" meant. Thousands of references opened and he began assimilating the data. He eased down the lever that opened the aging pickup's door, marveling at the mechanics of it. As he jumped out, the robotic carriers clambered out of the bed of the pickup, bouncing the truck up and down on its suspension.

Deanna watched him, amused. "Just follow the bots. They know where they're going." She closed her door.

Embarrassed, Bob closed down the lumber splinter. "Sure."

The quad-bots, nearly as old and dented as the pickup, waited for a cargo transport to pass on the road before running in their awkwardly graceful trot toward a large building down the other side of the street. With a wave to Deanna, Bob burrowed his hands into the pockets of his hoodie and followed them.

It was nearing midday on Monday, and work crews from the surrounding area were stopping in for lunch in the town center. The wide sidewalks, built in an earlier and more optimistic time, felt empty. Trucks and cars competed with robots, legged carriers, and VTOL turbofans for parking spots along the side of the road. Bob scanned the faces he passed, sending splinters to hack and tap into the cameras and sensors nearby to search for anything that might be threatening. Just to be on the safe side, he initiated the identity-theft algorithm from Sid that morphed his ID from one person to the next as he passed them.

At the intersection he stopped and looked up at the traffic signals, the colored lights like ancient semaphores. A knot of workers emptied from a bar at the corner behind him. Bob couldn't help staring at them, forgetting that he was staring from his physical body and not through an invisible ghost in the wikiworld.

"What you looking at, kid?" said one of the workers, the metal elbow of a robotic prosthetic limb poking through the ripped flannel of his shirt. He took a step forward, wobbling back and forth. Both of his legs had to be mechanical as well.

"Sorry." Bob looked down and kept walking.

Many of the people here were mandroids of one form or another, Weather War veterans with wrecked bodies replaced by robotics. As ever, rural communities were providing more than their fair share of fodder for the Wars. Bob shook his head, a faraway splinter scanning the scorched earth around the city.

Something triggered an alarm.

Tensing, Bob flooded his body with smarticles, quickening his nervous system, the world slowing down as his mind sped up. Spinning, he shot backwards a few steps, reaching out to grab a young girl just as she tripped and fell out into the street. A transport growled past just inches from them.

The girl gasped.

More threat alarms triggered. Someone grabbed a weapon in the bar behind him. The emotional constructs of the workers nearby spiked into aggression, and a police camera focused on him. The attentional structure of the whole area zeroed in on Bob.

Reacting without thinking, Bob launched a protective wall into the surrounding digital infrastructure, throwing up one hand with a dozen phantoms that he spun around himself and the girl. Doors and windows rolled closed and locked, and the cars and transports passing in the street skidded to a halt. Overhead, turbofans were redirected away from the area. Screeching white noise filled the audio inputs of people nearby, doubling them over in pain, while he scrubbed the local data and video feeds, firewalling off this section of the wikiworld.

"Stop! Stop!" Deanna yelled, running up the sidewalk behind him. "He's with me."

Still crouching, Bob looked around. He watched Deanna running toward him in slow motion. The person in the bar with the weapon was kicking down the door Bob just locked. Bob scooped the girl into his arms, getting ready to bolt, and then Deanna was there. She leaned close and held him back.

"It's okay, let her go," Deanna whispered into his ear.

With a crash, the door to the bar shattered open and a man appeared holding a shotgun. The gang of workers had disengaged from the white noise attack. They realized where it had come from, and their emotive aggression constructs spiked into directed anger focused on Bob.

"It's okay, Phil, this is just a mistake!" yelled Deanna, holding a hand up at the man with the shotgun. She repeated to Bob, "Let her go, it's okay."

The girl was breathing in quick panicked gasps in Bob's arms. He released her, and with a cry she pushed him aside and ran toward the man with the shotgun, collapsing into his chest.

"You're that Baxter kid in the news," said one of the workers, pointing at Bob. They might be in the country, but they were still connected. Even out here, he couldn't escape the negative media. "We don't want no smart-asses around here."

*Smart-asses.* He meant people using Atopian smarticles. As pssi had spread, so had the pssi-kids. Celebrities in some circles, pssi-kids' ability to infer thoughts, to seem like they were everywhere at once, was as unnerving as it was amazing.

"What are you doing mixing with them, Deanna?" asked the man with the shotgun.

"That's my business." Deanna picked Bob up. "You mind your own." She whispered again in his ear. "Release everything, right now."

Trusting more than understanding, Bob unlocked the windows and doors in the area. Close by and into the distance, their mechanisms clicked and snapped through the silence. The engines of cars and transports in the streets started up again.

Above the hum, Bob heard the man with the shotgun. "You get him out of here."

"NOT EXACTLY THE way to keep a low profile," Deanna joked as they bumped their way back along the dirt road to the farm. "People aren't used to pssi-kids in rural Montana."

Bob sulked in the seat beside her. Reality had a different edge here, rough and wild, and wasn't something Bob could mold the way he was used to. Even a cursory probe of the social cloud showed that almost nobody in Cut Bank was using pssi yet, even as the rest of the outside world had rushed to adopt it in the past weeks. Deanna was nearly the only one in the city even wearing lens displays.

"They're afraid of what they don't understand," added Deanna when Bob didn't respond. "All they have to go on are the lies spread in the mediaworlds about you."

"I saved that girl's life."

A phuturecast sweep had tripped Bob's alarms and predicted her stumbling over a dropped package onto the road, falling right into the path of an oncoming transport.

"I know that and you know that, but they didn't see it. They just saw you running and grabbing her." Deanna sighed. "That was her father with the gun. I know you know that now, but still, you should've looked a bit deeper yourself."

He'd been too quick in assessing and reacting to the threat. He'd failed to parse that the man grabbing the gun was the father of the girl he was rescuing. He could have defused the situation, but instead he made it worse. He made it more dangerous.

"You want to try?" asked Deanna after another mile of silence, nodding at the wheel. Montana was one of the few states where it was still legal to manually drive—in the rest of the country only automated driving was allowed on public roads.

That got Bob's attention, and his mind collapsed inward from the cloud of splinters following the truck. "Yeah, maybe I could get my proxxi to learn it . . ."

"I mean do you want to try it?"

Bob shifted in his seat. "Ah, maybe." But he wasn't sure. He spun back out into his splinters.

After another mile of silence slid by, Deanna smiled and looked at Bob. "One moment you can be like gods, and the next, babes in the woods."

Coming up on the farm, she parked the truck next to the old barn out back. Its graying clapboard sagged under the weight of time. Part of its roof had fallen in. The timbers were rotten.

"Endless reality brings an end to morality, that's what the doomsdayers are saying about Atopia," Deanna said as they climbed out of the truck. The robot carriers in the back started unloading the lumber.

"Nothing is endless." Bob's main subjective, still flying around the fields, brought itself back to the conversation. "If it was endless reality, nothing would mean anything, and that's not true."

"It's not?" Deanna smiled. She was teasing him.

"I'm here for Willy, my friends, and because Patricia asked me."

"But you didn't want to be here, did you?"

Bob looked down. The only place he wanted to be—where he burned to be—was next to Nancy, back on Atopia, but his friends needed him here. "That's a hard question."

Deanna paused and waited for him to look up. "But here you are."

It was time for Deanna to get to work. They walked around the back of the barn and she unlatched its door, swinging it wide open. Something pinged her incoming circuits. Bob waited.

Holding onto the barn door, Deanna smiled. "Looks like one good turn does deserve another."

"What happened?"

"The Commune granted Vince and Brigitte entry." Deanna disappeared into the darkness of the barn.

Bob reviewed the message from the Commune's Reverend that Deanna sent him. "They won't let me and Sid in? Just Brigitte and Vince?" He tried to make sense of it. If this was in response to Bob saving that girl in town, then why wasn't he invited?

A gust of air and dust and hay rocketed out from the barn. Bob squinted and staggered back. The sleek outlines of Deanna's electric jet hovered into view, the setting sun glinting off its polished curves.

"No idea," said Deanna, on comms now. The turbofan's engine ratcheted up several decibels as it rose. "But looks like somebody's watching out for you." Her jet jumped up into the sky, receding to a tiny dot before disappearing on its way into New York.

Deanna was a two-sleeper—a tweeper—dosing up on a cocktail of melatonin and synthetics to sleep twice a day on her three-and-a-half hour commute into and out of New York on her personal electric turbofan each morning and night. The tweeper movement claimed it was natural to sleep twice a day and that this was the way humans used to sleep. The way they went about it wasn't natural, though, tweaking their nervous systems with drugs and electronics.

It made no sense to Bob. Why didn't she just flit into work, using a virtual projection? But this was just one in a long list of things on the "outside" that made no sense. It seemed wasteful, but then all the energy for her back-and-forth trips was sucked up from the ground, from the geothermal generators, and Bob certainly had no standing to complain about anything seeming unnatural.

Bob stared at the spot where Deanna's jet had disappeared into the sky.

A THIN LINE of light hung on the horizon, the remains of the setting sun disappearing as stars began spreading across the sky. Willy had always heard how nice it was to walk in the countryside, that reality was different than flitting in and experiencing it in the wiki-world. Confined in his virtual self now, he was afraid he'd never get to find out. He let his point-of-view spin out around the perimeters, shifting into infrared. In the plains in the far distance, a herd of buffalo scattered at the noise of a passing drone.

Willy was taking an opportunity for some personal time with Brigitte before she went into the Commune. With pssi installed in

Brigitte's neural pathways, even if Willy was only a virtual presence here, to Brigitte he still looked and felt as real as if he was there physically. Still, he was a lucky man that she didn't make a big deal of it. They held hands as they walked down a path leading away from the farmhouse.

"Do you really believe all that stuff Patricia told us about Jimmy?" Brigitte asked. "About him taking over Atopia? That he stole Commander Strong's wife's mind?" She paused. "Do you think he killed Patricia?"

Willy didn't hesitate. "She's dead, isn't she? Isn't that enough evidence?"

"Maybe it was natural . . ."

"Nothing about Atopia is natural. People like her don't die anymore." Willy sighed. "Do you really think it was just coincidence?"

"No, I guess I don't." Brigitte carefully stepped between glowing sugar beet leaves. Genes from bioluminescent houseplants, a novelty fifty years before, had jumped into the wild a long time ago. Now patches of the outdoors, grasses and plants and even some trees, glowed as brightly as the stars over their heads. "It's very brave of everyone to come out here."

Willy kicked his foot along the ground. "They're here because of me, because of my mess."

"That's not true."

"I think it's better if my body stays lost. Something worse might happen if we find it."

"Willy, stop that."

Holding hands, they looked up at the faint smudge of the comet being brought into Earth orbit. It was being billed as the spectacle of the millennium. Where Atopia was trying to help the world flee into inner virtual spaces, supporters of the Comet Catcher mission were dreaming of humanity jumping outward. Either way was an escape from the crush and clutter that plagued Earth.

"I do know that I'm not the only reason Bob is here," Willy said after a pause. "He likes to please people. It's his only fault, if that could be one." He considered his statement for a second. "That plus his temper."

"I know why Bob's upset." Brigitte stopped to pick one of the glowing leaves at their feet. "I know what it means to be afraid for someone you love." She looked into Willy's eyes. "He's worried about Nancy."

Willy squeezed her hand. "It's not just that. You only know Bob as the stoner surfer, but back when we grew up together, he was the star of the Academy. He was Patricia's favorite. He was a couple with Nancy since they were kids."

"Was it what happened to his brother?"

Willy nodded. "To us it seems a long time ago, but to him . . . When Martin committed suicide, Bob blamed himself. Something happened he never told us about. He's angry at himself, angry at the world, and he hid it under drugs, pushing Nancy away, pushing us all away."

They continued in silence, walking to sit underneath an oak tree on a hill overlooking the farmhouse.

"I wish we could talk to Nancy," Brigitte said, breaking the low hum of the drones circling in the fields. "Tell her what's going on."

Willy shook his head. "Any message we send her might be intercepted by Jimmy. It would just make things worse—for her and for us."

Nodding, Brigitte considered. "I bet she's figured out a lot more than you think already."

Willy looked at Brigitte "Have you seen her on the mediaworld presentations? Up on stage, holding hands with Jimmy? Doesn't seem like she's caught on that something is wrong with him."

Brigitte raised an eyebrow. Of course she'd been watching the mediaworlds. "You think you guys are the only smart ones?"

Over dinner, Bob, Sid, and Vince had come up with a plan. Sid made contact with a hacking community in the New York underground who might have leads to finding Willy's body. Now invited, Vince and Brigitte would go to the Commune the next morning, while Sid and Bob would move on directly to New York, hopping a ride in Deanna's turbofan.

"Nancy's not the one I'm really worried about." Willy dug his heels into the earth. "That anger inside of Bob, I'm not sure what he'd do if anything happened to her."

# 4

THE BIPEDAL BUGGY lumbered its way up the soggy mountain trail with Brigitte and Vince crammed together in its tight passenger compartment. The path wasn't maintained, the terrain rough and nearly impassable, but then that was the point—the Commune didn't like visitors.

*This is a wild goose chase*, thought Vince as he swayed back and forth. The Commune—where Willy's mother lived—was the only connection Willy had on the outside. This was the most obvious place to look. Whoever stole Willy's body, they'd be a million miles from here by now. Ten billion people on the planet, and Vince had already spent a fortune combing it for any sign of Willy.

But then again, this wasn't Vince's first goose chase.

At least the future death threats—the unending series of possible future fatalities that plagued him in the past months—had nearly stopped. The imagined futures that pinned him down on Atopia were dissipating the further removed he was from that world. Hotstuff, and the international espionage network she'd set up, had been working hard at containing the future threats. Their efforts paid off. His futures were already becoming part of his past.

On Atopia, the plan to go out and find Willy's body had seemed crucial. Vince craved the excitement of an adventure. But out here, in the light of day, strapped to the back of a robotic crawler as it rocked between the pine trees, with virtual projections of Willy and Hotstuff riding shotgun, it all felt . . . well . . . ridiculous.

Willy's virtual projection tapped him on the shoulder. "Bob's dad left a beacon for him yesterday."

"I thought Sid terminated all communications." Vince turned to Willy. "Aren't we hiding?"

"His dad's getting desperate. He left an encrypted packet attached to a data beacon in the open multiverse," Willy explained. "Bob retrieved a copy yesterday."

"And?" There had to be a reason Willy was bringing this up now.

"Bob opened it. His dad was begging him to come back to Atopia, telling him that they would get all the charges cleared."

In an overlaid display, Vince watched a mediaworld broadcast on the continuing Bob-and-Sid-and-Vince conspiracy: "Why did Sidney Horowitz disappear from Atopia after the attack? We've all heard a lot of theories, but the fact that he and Robert Baxter are friends with Vincent Indigo makes it seem all the more suspicious . . ." Vince cut off the broadcast. He'd heard it a million times already. The newsworlds were predicting more terrorism against Atopia, and every story featured a connection to himself or Sid or even Bob.

Worse was Willy's predicament, and losing his body was just the tip of the proverbial iceberg. Before the attack against Atopia, a warrant had been issued for Willy's arrest for breaching Atopian border security. After the attack, and with Willy's body missing and his virtual presence having fled, the warrant was stepped up to an international one with Interpol getting involved. He was a hunted man.

Terrorists were blamed for the rise in the number of disappearances of pssi-connected users, but this didn't seem to be deterring the public from flocking to it. The media didn't specify who the terrorists were, just that their aim was to slow down the spread of Atopia's product release. The implication was always that Sid and

Bob were tied to Terra Nova. That Willy's body counted as one of the "disappeared" didn't detract the media from lumping him in with the Terra Novan conspiracy theories.

"And Jimmy and Nancy were hanging over his dad's shoulder during the whole message," Brigitte added. "Jimmy was saying that he'd take care of everything, that he and Nancy were worried sick."

"She sure doesn't look worried on stage," Vince said, regretting it even as it came out. Nancy might look happy in the press events and promotion holograms that were promoting Atopia, but who really knew what was going on in the background, what she might have been forced into doing?

But then again, that was exactly the point: who really knew?

Hotstuff frowned at him. "She's been trying to get in touch with us, but Bob blocks her. Of course she's worried. She's thinking the worst."

And the worst could be very bad.

Vince nodded, but his mind was already elsewhere, gathering the last incoming data before their connections were cut off. The trees thinned as they reached the plateau. In a clearing before them a network of dusty dirt roads stretched into buildings and farmhouses that undulated into the distance. Storm clouds gathered over snowy peaks, while cows huddled for protection under ponderosa pines that lined the edges of the farms and forests.

Vince instructed the walker where to stop. "This is it," he announced. Comms would be cut off soon. Inside the event horizon of the Commune, there were no wikiworld feeds, no data streams at all. In a few minutes, he'd need to shut off his feeds from the PhutureNews for the first time in thirty years.

"Don't be so nervous, boss." Hotstuff was done up in safari gear for the trip. "I've got it covered. We'll wait for you here."

With flare-ups in the Weather Wars subsiding, the media-worlds were filling up their empty slots with an unending stream of reports of new apocalyptic cults, and the Commune was the granddaddy of them all. For the first time they caught a glimpse of the shimmering halo that hung in the sky over the Commune. Drones hovered around its perimeter. One skimmed in front of them, its angular curves black and menacing. Behind, almost invisible, floated the aerial plankton, tiny bots that floated on the breeze, their nano-scale rotors keeping them in place. They formed a shell a few dozen feet thick, stretching ten miles around the circumference of the Commune and a mile above it, acting as a giant, electrically-connected Faraday cage that shielded the Commune from any outside electromagnetics and confounded visual and audio signals, as well.

Nearing the outermost road, the walker stopped and squatted.

"I guess this is where we say goodbye," said Vince to Hotstuff as he unhooked himself from the seat and clambered down, stopping to lend a hand to Brigitte.

Not only would comms be shut down, but so would the smart-icle networks in their bodies. They'd been pinged with warnings to turn them off the last hundred yards as they approached the perimeter. This meant Hotstuff and Willy couldn't make the trip. The walker stood up and turned around, making its way back the way they came. Brigitte and Willy began their goodbyes, and Vince turned away.

The Commune was mute on the topic of how they were supposed to get there. Their only instructions were to meet the robotic walker at a specified longitude and latitude along a mountain road. Vince squinted into the distance and then up at the gathering storm clouds. "Maybe the rest of the way on foot?"

"Don't think so." Brigitte pointed to a trail of dust rising on one of the roads coming out from the town center.

It was a horse and cart.

Vince shook his head. "You can't be serious."

The storm clouds churned over the mountaintops, obscuring them, as the buggy and horse neared. There was one driver, dressed in black with a large matching hat. The rolling clouds hit the Commune's perimeter, skidding across its surface to form a dome high in the sky before breaking. The man on the cart motioned to them, urging them toward him.

Brigitte and Vince walked forward. The aerial plankton opened a path in the perimeter wall, and they continued at a jog, running to meet the driver and cart on the other side.

A young man, his cheeks ruddy, pulled up the horses. "Wooooah."

They all stared at each other.

"Come on, don't just stand there." The young man waved at the clouds and coming rain. "We'll be soaked in a minute."

Vince stepped forward. "And you are . . .?"

The young man laughed, holding the reins in one hand while he tipped his hat with the other. "Zephyr." He said it like they should already know him. "Zephyr McIntyre. Didn't he mention me?"

Vince and Brigitte exchanged glances.

"Willy McIntyre's cousin, Zephyr. You're his friends, right?"

# 5

JIMMY SCADDEN LEANED back in his chair. "You have a responsibility."

Nancy looked out the glass window-walls of the Cognix boardroom. Beyond the glittering blue security blanket, a thousand feet below, the leafy green canopy of the Atopian top-side forests swayed in the breeze. Waves caressed the white sand beaches. A paradise, but one in which she was coming to realize she was trapped.

"To who, you?" she replied, turning to face her captor.

"Yes, to me." Jimmy looked around the conference room at Rick Strong, Commander of the Atopian Defense Forces, and Herman Kesselring, the main shareholder and CEO of Cognix Corporation. Dr. Granger sat at a corner of the table, almost behind Jimmy. "To me, to all of us here, to the entire human race."

How easily the words rolled off his tongue. She remembered the awkward Jimmy Scadden of their shared childhood, the one that could barely get a word out. In his struggle to connect, whatever stumbling words he'd managed had at least been honest.

But no more.

"I want—no, I *need*—to go out and find Bob," Nancy insisted. Had Jimmy noticed her infiltrating one of his meetings? She still hadn't told anyone else what she'd found out.

"What we want to do, and we need to do, these are sometimes two different things." Jimmy looked at Commander Strong. "Isn't that right?"

"I agree," said the Commander. "It's too dangerous outside Atopia, especially now."

Jimmy held no direct authority at Board level, but official positions didn't mean much anymore. Nancy wondered again what power Jimmy held over the Board. Perhaps it was the same power that he held over her.

Fear.

"Too dangerous?" Nancy questioned. "For who?"

Jimmy smiled. "For you."

Just two words, and yet so many ways to interpret them.

"It wouldn't look right if you went out and searched for Bob yourself. A bit of a conflict of interest, no?"

Finally, a glimmer of truth.

"I don't need to remind you that he's stolen sensitive Atopian intellectual property," continued Jimmy. "And aiding fugitives."

"Marie is not your property nor Atopia's," replied Nancy. "She was Patricia's proxxi, her property to do with as she liked. And neither Sid nor Bob or even Vince is a fugitive, despite what the media-worlds say."

"Our agents report Patricia's data in Baxter's possession," Jimmy replied. "We have no proof that she gave it to him. He stole it. Of all people, why wouldn't she have given it to you? Why did he run off and hide? Have you asked yourself these questions?"

Nancy nodded. Of course she had. This was a losing battle. "Can we just continue with the situational report?"

"As you wish." Jimmy nodded at Kesselring, who in turn gave a nod to Commander Strong.

Commander Strong glanced at Nancy, and then took control. The primary perspective of the meeting swept into a synthetic space projection.

"As soon as we opened the Atopian multiverse, we had skirmishes erupting between nation-states and corporation-states in virtual spaces that tracked back to assets in the physical world." The Commander began detailing worlds that spun through the attendees' meta-cognition systems, memories, and impressions implanted at required and desired detail in the minds of the observers.

Atopia's fight with Terra Nova was polarizing the world, and this fracturing was limiting the spread of pssi in some jurisdictions. There was some commercial success penetrating spaces controlled by India and Russia, but most of Africa was out of their sphere of influence. None of this worried Commander Strong, but Kesselring wasn't happy.

The release of pssi into the general population was generating unexpected chaos. Most of it was due to things her Aunt Patricia had restricted when she was in charge, but had been included in the release after her departure: emo-porning and uncontrolled neural fusioning were at the top of the list of problems. The macroeconomic models were proceeding on plan, but the social chaos on specific levels hadn't been anticipated.

Nancy stayed quiet while Commander Strong finished his threat report on ownership graphs of corporations controlled by synthetic beings, then a report on a Terra Novan virtual world applying for United Nations sovereign status, but stopped him as he began talking about the *disappearances*.

"Why has there been no special investigation?" Nancy asked. It was almost beyond disbelief.

The biggest problem in the roll-out was customer support, helping people find their way out of virtual worlds they got lost in. Thousands of them were never found, disappeared into the pssi multiverse, their bodies still perfectly healthy, but their minds lost in some inaccessible corner of a virtual world.

"Over a billion people have plugged into pssi in the past two months," Kesselring objected. "Less than one in a hundred thousand is reported as 'disappeared,' as you call it, and from what I've heard, almost all are recovered after a few days. We can't—"

"Have a few people off pleasuring themselves in the multiverse stop what we're doing?" Nancy completed his sentence for him. "How long are you going to stick to that line? From my numbers, the problem is accelerating at an exponential pace." She turned to Commander Strong. "Don't *you* see any connection between this and what happened to your wife?"

The Commander returned her gaze, but she could see his mind was elsewhere. He spent most of his free time in virtual spaces with reruns of his proxxid children. His wife, Cindy, was still in a vegetative state, trapped inside her own mind. Even in meetings like this, he kept a reality skin of a 1940s-era wikiworld pegged around him that reminded him of her.

Jimmy pulled on everyone, bending their attentional matrices back to him. "This is a matter for local law enforcement to investigate, isn't it?" He frowned at Nancy. "And why are you researching this?"

Nancy frowned back at him. "Because it's important."

"What's important to resolve at this meeting is the Synthetic Beings Charter of Rights that you've been championing. It would destabilize the entire economic structure we've worked to build."

Nancy had known this was coming. "Even you must admit that glasscutters and hackers terminating our AIs are becoming a problem; we need clearer laws to deal with this."

"In civil law, yes." Kesselring joined the discussion, thumping his hand on the table. "But not international criminal law. What are you trying to do?"

Nancy was alone in this. It was Patricia's most treasured legacy, and one she promised to try and protect. "When birthing a new AI, there needs to be some international framework for responsibility. As it is—"

"There is a framework, and it's called copyright," Jimmy interrupted.

"I am not going to support a retraction of the Synthetic Beings Charter of Rights."

"SyBCoR is dead in the water, at least as it stands now." Kesselring looked out the window. "You need to be practical."

Nancy laughed. "Practical?"

"Or at least pragmatic." Kesselring looked at her. "Push us, and we can push you."

Nancy stopped laughing. "What does that mean?"

"Don't force us to issue an arrest warrant for Baxter," Kesselring replied. "This could escalate into a national security issue for our partners if we let them know how much information is now in his hands. We have more important things to worry about, no?"

*So it's come to threats and blackmail.* Nancy looked out the window at the white sand beaches, then at the distant stripe of America's coastline on the horizon. Where was Bob, why wouldn't he respond to her messages? Just weeks after Aunt Patricia's death, and Nancy felt like she was failing her, but what choice did she have?

Nancy sighed. "Fine. You have my vote to retract SyBCoR, at least for now."

# 6

BOB STARED AT the Great Seawall of New York at the edge of Battery Park. It was the first time he'd seen it with his naked, natural eyes. If this place wasn't still the financial capital of the world, they would have given up and moved Manhattan by now. Much of the island was now below sea level, the city guarded by an immense system of dikes and seawalls. Money was holding back the sea, but time was a thief and eventually would steal it all.

"We need to wait a little bit longer." Sid slapped Bob on the back. "The glasscutters need to verify us in person."

That morning, Deanna had smuggled them into Manhattan on her private turbofan. Her DAD credentials gave her automated passage through the NYC passport controls. In the meantime, Sid had sent digital copies of himself and Bob to random locations all over the world, leaving forensic breadcrumbs that should be enough to cover their tracks for as long as they needed to stay in one place.

Despite the soggy weather, the Battery was still half-full of tourists, and Bob and Sid wound their way through them. Sid's identity-theft algorithm was stealing the credentials of people they passed, briefly pasting them as their own into the wikiworld feeds. It was hacking the audio and visual feeds in the area, replacing their images with the image of someone nearby, then hopping to someone else as they moved.

They were ghosts in the crowd.

They had come to meet, in person, some members of a glass-cutter guild that said it had leads on where Willy's body might be. Waiting at Battery Park was part of the vetting process. The glass-cutters wanted to verify Sid and Bob in person, sample their DNA using a remote sniffer, to make sure they were who they said they were. Bob couldn't argue with their diligence.

The twilight at the end of the day was gray as the lights of the city lit up the sky, the concrete and metal and glass of the city the same color as the sky and the sea, all of it indistinct from the other in a precipitation that was neither rain nor mist, but something shifting in between.

"So this is New York," Sid laughed, staring into the gray mist. "Been here a million times, but never in the flesh. Can't say I like it better like this. I should go visit Uncle Avi just to see the look on his face—"

Bob grabbed Sid's arm.

"I know, I know, we can't talk to anyone." Grinning, Sid brushed off Bob's hand.

Bob shook his head. "You know who you've always reminded me of?"

"Why do I feel like I don't want to know?"

"Jimmy."

"Seriously?"

"Yeah." Bob smiled. "You guys are two peas in a pod. It's why I talked to him way back then."

Sid smiled. "So I remind you of a psychopath?"

"Not the psychopath part, but the hidden nerd, thinking you're better than everyone else."

"Gee, thanks."

"I mean that in the best possible way." Bob put an arm around Sid, pushing him forward. "Come on, keep moving."

Images of Jimmy hung everywhere around them—on billboards and floating holograms at street corners—part of the ubiquitous advertising campaign for the product launch of Atopian pssi. Beside him in many of the advertisements was Nancy.

Bob didn't overlay a reality filter to erase the images. Filtering reality here felt dangerous. Instead he augmented it, overloading his senses, searching for threats, always on the hair trigger. Fifty feet in the air a self-propelled NYPD gun platform hovered past, and tiny ornithopter drones buzzed through crowds like insects.

A news overlay announced that Atopia had withdrawn support for SyBCoR, led by Nancy.

Sid glanced at Bob, seeing the same news report. "What the hell's going on?"

Bob studied the background of the report. There was little detail, apart from an admission that SyBCoR would undermine the financial structure of the modern world. But there was no way Nancy would've withdrawn support for that without some intense pressure being applied to her.

Seeing Nancy's face hovering above him, worrying about what was happening to her—it felt like a spike was being driven into Bob's head. He escaped by letting a splinter sweep above the bay, sailing over the top of the Statue of Liberty. She was ringed by her own skirt of concrete to keep out the rising waters. Spinning further out to sea, he turned his point-of-view to look back at the twinkling city under the setting sun, extending his view as wide as he could. The AEC—American East Coast—was now over a hundred million people in an unending metropolis that stretched from Boston to Washington.

At the start of the twenty-first century, there'd been only thirty nations of the world's three hundred with declining populations, but now only thirty had ones that were increasing. The humanscape, like the seas and land, was stagnating. Many of the big cities of over a hundred million—Guangzhou, Mumbai, Sao Paulo—had gone feral, their ground levels given over to street gangs. The rich lived in their padded penthouses, part spas and part life-support systems, living out unending twilights in endlessly aging bodies. They said the meek would inherit the Earth, but nobody said anything about the state it would be in when it was time for the handover.

"Really?" Sid said, interrupting Bob's thoughts. "Jimmy? I remind you of Jimmy?"

Bob pulled his main perspective back into his body. "Not happy with that, huh?"

"No, I mean—"

"What I really meant was, you both value intelligence and knowledge above everything else. I think that whatever we find out here, maybe we could use that to tweak Jimmy somehow. Get inside his head."

Sid walked in silence for a few moments. "Oooh, I see what's going on." He turned to face Bob, walking backward. "You want to *save* Jimmy. You don't think he's as bad as Patricia says he is."

"I don't know." Bob wagged his head back and forth. "Maybe, I just don't see him doing all this stuff. He's changed somehow."

"People change . . ."

"I know. But come on, nobody ever thinks they're really a bad person. They always think they're doing whatever they're doing for some good reason. So what's his reason?"

"Cause he's gone bat shit?"

"I'm serious. Ever think that Jimmy is just mad at the world?" But was he just projecting his own feelings onto Jimmy?

Sid considered this. "Still doesn't give you the right to do whatever you want."

"Yeah, but it gives you a reason. If he thinks he was abused by his parents, hard to blame him . . ."

Sid shook his head and laughed. "You'd love a leech if I gave you a sob story about it." He grabbed Bob and pulled him forward. "Move faster, the identity theft algorithm works better with constant motion."

Bob watched the names and details of the people that walked by him pop up into splinters, each one briefly pasting the identity onto Bob. Mr. Brooks, brushing by Bob on his right, had just left his wife and was on his way to his mistress. Peter Lucasis, standing a few feet behind Bob, was probably thinking that he should have never let his girlfriend convince him into getting a cat. All of this was derived from data that was either publicly available or hacked from databases on the fly.

New York was refreshing in one sense—Bob's metasenses felt full again.

Already half of New Yorkers had started using pssi, and Bob let his secondary subjective spin through the mishmash of childish reality skins they were sporting, flimsy virtual realities he could poke a hole through with his phantoms. The more people that shared a reality, the stronger that reality became, but here they were all stuck in their own. Most of them hadn't bothered to change their conscious security settings, and he heard their meta-cognition systems chattering around him like an angry beehive.

Worse were the non-augmented humans. They weren't pssi-aware, but there were enough smarticles floating in the air of New York already that some suffused into their bodies, passively interacting with the environment. They weren't supposed to be active, but Sid's systems could tap into them, sense their nerve impulses to paint a picture of their unprotected minds.

Bob sensed that the man next to him was about to ask him to take a picture. The words hadn't yet formed in his mouth, and he hadn't even really decided yet, not consciously. But the nerve impulses that preceded his decision making were already there.

It was fractions of a second perhaps, but the decision had already been made, and the man wasn't even aware of it yet.

Bob was. Bob waited.

Fractions of a second stretched out in time as Bob quickened his nervous systems in a short burst. "Want me to frame a picture for you?"

The man turned, surprised. "Yeah. Please. Ah, Steve Barker, 06913564."

Bob had already stolen Steve's unique social marker to use as his own identity for the next seconds, but Steve didn't know that. Bob made a show of entering the USM by typing into the air with one hand. Sid stopped and turned to watch from a few paces away. Gathering up his daughter and wife, Steve took a step toward the Sea Wall. Bob stepped back and smiled, framing some stills from the wikiworld and sending them into the man's social cloud.

"Thank you," said Steve's wife, and with a nod and a smile, they continued on their way.

The man hadn't even been aware of the request he was about to make, even though it was preordained by his own chemical nerve signals. It was more than phuturing, more than making statistical predictions based on past events. It was a foregone conclusion, a decision already made before Steve consciously knew it. Was he really making a choice? Did he have a choice? Or was it all an illusion, just preprogrammed? Was all the world just a stage for a play already written?

The wind pushed a break in the clouds, revealing the faint twinkle of some brave stars trying to shine down on Gotham.

"Do you ever wonder why?"

Bob snapped his attention back into his body. Near to him was a man, sitting on a park bench, in a gray raincoat with a hydrophobic shell. The falling mist of rain danced away from him in a veil as the man looked toward the bay. *That's odd.* No hits popped up in Bob's identity algorithms. "Why what?"

The man looked into Bob's eyes, smiling. "A hundred billion stars in this Milky Way galaxy, and a hundred billion more galaxies just like it. Life fills every available crack in this Solar System, and most stars have planets—many of them similar to Earth."

"And yet?" Bob was still trying to get an identity.

"And yet not a peep from anyone out there. Do you ever wonder why?"

Except for the POND data, thought Bob, remembering the mysterious signal from a supposedly extraterrestrial source that Patricia had detected with her Pacific Ocean Neutrino Detector. She'd instructed them to keep quiet about it, but perhaps Bob should release the news. It might even pull society from its downward spiral if the world realized that someone else was out there. But first they needed to decode the data. That's what Patricia asked them to do. What was inside the message might be as important as the message itself.

Bob shook his head, feeling the weight bearing down. He was the wrong person for this job.

The man was still smiling at Bob. "No? You never wonder? You look like you do."

Bob sensed that something had gone terribly wrong. In his mind the Sea Wall before them opened up and the irresistible force of the black ocean beyond came rushing through, swallowing them and everything in its path, sweeping the world away. The vision pulled the breath out of him and he had to lean on the bench the man was sitting on.

The man reached out to steady him. "Sometimes, to look out there, we need to look inside."

The man looked familiar, but Bob's internal systems were sure he'd never seen the stranger's face before. Bob sent splinters shooting out into the multiverse, looking for a recognition point, for any identity associated with his strange visitor. Still nothing. Bob regained his balance and tried to string out the conversation to buy time. "I don't think about it much."

The man retreated and smiled. "You should."

Bob's identity-theft splinters, able to slice through most security blankets in the outside world like butter, were still coming up blank. He felt a phantom pulling his attention away. He turned to find Sid's skewed grin.

"We can go. We've been vetted."

"By who?"

Sid pulled up the lapels on his jacket against the rain. "I don't know. They kept their distance and asked me specifically not to scan for them."

Bob flicked his chin toward his shoulder. "Who's that guy?"

"What guy?" Sid craned his neck to scan the crowd.

Bob turned, but the man on the bench was gone. He rewound his inVerse to replay the conversation, but it was blank as well. There was nothing in his meta-cognition systems or external memories that recorded the event, nothing but what was in his own head. Bob closed his eyes. Had he imagined it?

Sid sensed Bob searching through his systems. "I think you need to get some sleep." He put an arm on Bob's shoulder. "Let's get back to Deanna's apartment."

# 7

RAIN HAMMERED DOWN on the tin roof of the church vestry.

Vince watched the Reverend prepare tea on a side table, a tiny kettle whistling atop a heating pad. The Reverend stooped to fetch a set of china cups and pot from a shelf. Vince looked around. He'd imagined something rougher, something more oppressive—creaking doors, dim rooms, an agonized Jesus hanging from a cross—but the interior was sparse and neat. A water-driven radiator rose up from the wooden floor, filling the space with hissing heat. They hadn't outrun the storm. Soaked, splattered in mud, Vince and Brigitte sat awkwardly in front of the Reverend's desk. Zephyr went next door for dry clothes and blankets.

*So this is what it feels like to be in the middle of a black hole.* The sound of the multiverse silence was deafening to Vince's metasenses. No data feeds, no messages, no information other than what his own mind and body could provide. No Van Eck radiation could get through the shield over the Commune; comms jamming, image jamming, even externally-stored memory jamming of those going in and out. The inside of the Commune was an informational black hole, protected by the American Family Values faction of the Democrats, a neo-wild project of human preservation.

Entering the Commune was passing into another world in more ways than one.

The Reverend smiled at them. "Sorry about the rain." The kettle pinged, and he picked it up and filled the teapot. "Zephyr is . . . well, the boy was late."

"So you're Willy's grandfather?" Brigitte turned to face the Reverend. "He told me so much about you."

"Is that right?" The Reverend wasn't asking, wasn't telling. He picked up the teapot and two cups and placed them on the large desk before them.

Vince heard the tick-tock of a clock in the hallway outside. The wall behind the desk was filled with books, and Vince squinted to read what was written on the spines: several Bibles, Chaucer, Jung, Nag Hammadi, Blavatsky. A painting of a crystal mountain in a desert hung on the side wall. "Don't you want to know why we're here?" Vince asked.

"You said . . ." The Reverend paused, leaning against his desk. "You said you were Willy's friends and wanted to speak with his mother."

"Yes, but—"

"Then that's what you're here for."

"Is she here?" Brigitte glanced over her shoulder at the door.

"She is." The Reverend stood up straight. "I'm going to see where on Earth our Zephyr is with those clothes." Walking toward the door he motioned at the teapot. "Serve yourselves. And don't try activating your smarticle networks." He left the door ajar.

Vince leaned forward for the teapot. "Don't they find it even slightly ironic to be driving horses and carts under a vast nano-bot radiation shield?" He felt some warmth seeping into his hands. "Old man McIntyre must be over a hundred—tell me he's not using the latest in gene modification—"

"I can hear you, Mr. Indigo." The Reverend was in the doorway. "These should about do." He tossed a pile of clothes into Vince's lap.

Walking forward, he unfolded a blanket that he brought around Brigitte's shoulders. She shivered and gripped it around herself, silently mouthing thank you.

The Reverend continued back behind his desk, passing a hand over its center as he sat down. A three-dimensional hologram sprang up over its center, an image of the bipedal transport Vince and Brigitte used on their way up, now threading its way down the mountain trail in the rain.

"We Neo-Luddites aren't against technology. What we are against is the replacement of humans by technology." The Reverend waved his hand, and charts and graphs spread out to fill the room. "DAD now has two robots for every human, and ten times that many if you count synthetic intelligences. We're becoming a very small ruling minority, Mr. Indigo."

Vince did his research before coming. "Weren't Luddites the 'machine destroyers'?"

"Machine destroyers, yes." The Reverend turned the phrase around in his mouth. "But that is not what we do. I think you misunderstand us, Mr. Indigo. We offer our youth an opportunity to connect with nature, work with their hands, and delve into the depths of their humanity before . . ."

The Reverend went silent.

"Before what?" Brigitte asked after a respectful pause.

The Reverend rocked back in his chair. "Forgive my caution. The Commune has enemies, and this business with my grandson William has inspired new ones."

"Father, you know Willy is innocent."

Vince and Brigitte turned to the doorway to see a middle-aged woman with clear gray eyes smiling at them.

Brigitte jumped up. "You must be Willy's mother!" The woman nodded. In two steps Brigitte was taking her hand, leaning in to kiss her cheek. "It's a pleasure."

Willy's mother accepted the kiss but kept her distance. "Likewise, I'm sure."

The Reverend stood and stared at Vince. "So you wanted to speak with Elspeth?"

"Is it possible to talk with her in private . . .?" Vince asked.

The Reverend gestured to the room. "This is as private as you'll be allowed, I'm afraid."

A sense of absurdity overcame Vince—how to tell a mother that her son was gone, but not gone? "We have some disturbing news, and we were hoping you might be able to help us." He looked into Elspeth's eyes. "Willy's missing—or, er, his body is missing."

Elspeth's brow wrinkled. "What do you mean?"

"A few months ago . . ." Vince began but then stopped. A few months ago he'd been living in endless virtual worlds while running from future death threats. How was he going to explain their world to Willy's Neo-Luddite mother?

"Perhaps I could try?" suggested Brigitte.

At a loss, Vince nodded.

"Willy is fine," Brigitte started to say, "so you don't need to worry, but we—"

"I know," Elpeth said.

Vince cocked his head. "You know what?"

Elspeth looked at the Reverend. He met her gaze and nodded. "That he's fine," she replied.

Vince frowned. "And how do you know that?"

"Because he was just here."

# 8

THE TIP OF the Great Pyramid, covered in electrum, hovered in the sky under the hot eye of god. Guardians lined the leafy promenade leading up to the pyramid's entrance. Its base on four sides was surrounded by lush gardens and temples. A priest walked beside Bob as they made their way up the promenade toward the pyramid. "Intelligence is that which creates attachment," the priest said. His face was hidden.

Bob looked up at the Sphinx. It smiled down benevolently, the smooth curve of its nose glistening in the midday sun. "Isn't it the self that creates attachment?"

The priest nodded. "And it is the self that arises from intelligence."

Bob fought the dream. He tried to launch himself into flight to soar above the pyramids and into the desert beyond, but he felt like he was caught in molasses. His feet kept moving along the marble walkway, locked in step with the priest's. Thoughts curled around his mind like sand swirling on the desert wind.

They reached the base of the pyramid and began up the steps to its entrance. The guards parted before them. "It is only through the destruction of the self that peace can be realized," the priest said as they reached the top of the stairway.

With a final glance at the blue sky, Bob ducked his head and followed the priest into the dark tunnel. He had to hunch over and shuffle to get through.

Bob hated small spaces, ever since he had gotten stuck in the passenger cannon access tunnel on Atopia as a child, searching for ways to access the upper levels directly from their habitat. It took hours for rescuers to get him out. Even with his mind able to soar free into synthetic worlds, he'd known that his body was trapped, that the perceived freedom was an illusion.

Between sputtering oil torches, the tunnel was pitch black, leading them down and down. He could only see the shifting shape of the priest ahead. The tunnel eventually opened up into a room that was filled with more guards, and another tunnel led upward from that, larger this time, with a wooden walkway and ropes hanging along its side.

The oppressive weight of millions of tons of stone hung above them, squeezing Bob's mind. "So that peace can be brought to what?" he asked. "To the self?" That didn't make any sense. If the self was destroyed, to what were they bringing peace?

The main chamber opened up before them, and the priest urged him into the room. It was the heart of the Great Pyramid. More priests, their heads bowed, were arrayed around a large stone sarcophagus. Its lid was off, set to one side. Colorful hieroglyphs danced on the walls around them in the flickering torchlight. Bob's pssi instantly translated them, and the stories splintered into his mind—stories of Isis and her husband Osiris, his body quartered and dragged to the four corners, and then his return to life and his betrayal by his brother Seth.

The priests began chanting. A light grew out of a crystal structure within the sarcophagus, rising up to form a shape that hung in space. The shape solidified into a creature that hovered above the assembled. Sobek, the crocodile god, stared at Bob with fiery eyes and said, "It looks like Willy's proxxi is running from us."

The god's face morphed into a green version of Sid.

The priests continued to chant.

"Maybe it's not his proxxi who stole his body," Bob replied.

The confines of the sarcophagus chamber melted into the concrete grays of New York City. Self-driving cars swept by on wet streets. There were no street lights or signals, just a never-ending stream of traffic that melted together at junctions and around corners. Sid had left Deanna's apartment while Bob was asleep, and a splinter, in the middle of a conversation, was integrating into Bob's consciousness as he awoke.

The dreams were becoming more intense.

Sid noticed the arrival of Bob's primary self. "Are you okay?" he asked. "You don't look so good."

"I'm fine," Bob replied. He didn't want to talk about the dreams. "Just waking up. Why didn't you wake me?"

"You needed the rest." Sid smiled. "Besides, you've never been on time for anything in your life. Why so surprised?"

Vince was with them virtually. He'd climbed outside the Commune's perimeter to tell them the news that Willy's body had preceded them there. A projection of Vince's virtual self lounged on a chair, sitting beside Willy and Sid. In the background, multibots were busy setting up the tables and chairs of Herald Square for the day. The square's cover peeled back like a blooming flower as the sun broke through the clouds overhead. The rain finally stopped.

Sid returned to the discussion while Bob assimilated the backstory. "If Willy's proxxi didn't steal his body, then the question is who, or what, did? And why?" He stretched and rubbed his eyes.

"To gain access to the Commune?" Vince suggested. "It's almost impossible to get in there."

"Hold on." Bob slipped his brain into the conversation. "Why couldn't it have been proxxi?" Nothing suggested it wasn't Willy's proxxi who was still guarding Willy's body.

Sid shrugged. "How would he have kept the smarticle network operating in Willy's body while he was in the Commune?" Because all outgoing communications would have been cut off from Willy's mind, was Sid's point. Sid looked at Willy. "Did you have any gaps in your conscious stream?"

"None at all," Willy replied.

It was only when Willy's body left the Commune that access had been granted to Vince and Brigitte. Was it coincidence, or was the Commune part of whatever was happening?

Bob looked around. People walking by kept their distance. They mostly kept outside the information security blanket that glittered in the augmented wikiworld around them. But it wasn't just the security blanket. Vince's phuturing network was also altering their trajectories without them realizing it, keeping them looking away.

Bob and Sid were effectively invisible to people on the street just because nobody bothered to look at them.

Sid's identity-thieving algorithm was active, of course, and Bob's own credentials were constantly shifting, through Rocky, and then Susanna, Bill, Quentin, all of it layered in a time-cloaking algorithm he and Sid had created as kids.

And almost all of the passing people were already on pssi.

A girl approached, walking her dog, and Bob accepted her open reality share, fusing his perception into a bubble-gum-inspired teddy-bear world. The multibots finishing arranging the chairs sprouted lavender fur. Everyone on the street looked happy behind vacant smiles. The girl had virtually fused her frontal lobes with her dog, and they were chatting about what park they wanted to visit.

A woman in a suit brushed past the girl, and Bob shifted into her reality skin. A sleek minimalist world slid into his sensory frames, and a brass-and-glass metropolis rose up out of the teddy-bear world of the girl. The multibots, busy parking themselves under the bright red star of Macy's along the sidewalk bordering the square, shed their lavender fur and became menacing in black.

New Yorkers were early adopters of new technologies, but this might be the last gadget they'd ever install. Bob could already sense psombies passing by on the streets—people whose bodies were under control of someone else while the owners amused themselves in virtual worlds—or parts of composites that fused their neural systems together into collectives.

The pace of cultural change was gaining speed.

Vince rocked back in his chair. "I think this might be a waste of time. Whoever stole Willy's body doesn't want to be found. We should be getting in touch with Terra Nova directly. For God's sake, they're still funneling the communication link into his body."

Bob nodded. Getting in touch with Terra Nova was the next logical step. Ever since the attack on Atopia, though, Terra Nova had been blockaded in the physical and cyber realms. Secure communication from this side of the world was difficult, so they needed to get physically closer. "Way ahead of you," said Sid, uploading the details. Deanna had already arranged transit for them on the New York passenger cannon, to Lagos in Africa.

"What about Sintil8?" Willy asked. His image flickered.

Terra Nova linked the connection between Willy's mind—in his lost body—and Willy's virtual presence here, and they were having trouble maintaining the connection. Bob worried that it might wink out altogether, exiling Willy into the outer reaches of the multiverse.

Vince smiled. "Leave the gangsters to me." His future-altering espionage and counter-espionage network had tentacles reaching into the underworld. "I think it's time we switched gears. I'll be in New York the day after tomorrow. There's not much more I can do in the Commune."

"Perfect." Sid fiddled with his phantoms, uploading data into Vince's networks. "After we pick up some more bootleg smarticles, tonight Bob and I are going to Hell."

# 9

IN THE BLUE daytime sky, Wormwood was just visible to the naked eye. The comet's dust-and-ion tails separated as it neared the sun, turning it into a tiny feathery "v" in the sky. Vince glanced at Zephyr, his chaperone on the hike past the perimeter of the Commune.

They had walked out on foot, two miles each way for some fresh air. Vince had needed to get outside of the Commune's perimeter to get communication uplink, to talk with Sid and Bob back in New York. No comms in or out from under the radiation shield. A splinter of Vince's mind was still lounging on a chair in Herald Square, chatting with Willy and Sid, but his main subjective was back at the edge of the Commune with Zephyr, staring into the sky at the comet.

Vince shielded his eyes from the sun with one hand. "Quite the sight, huh?"

Zephyr nodded, his mouth open, staring up. "Grandpa says people are bringing it here on purpose, that it's one of the signs."

Vince rolled his eyes. *Sign of what?* That people on Earth were doing bat-shit-nuts things like building Communes? But as crazy as what they were doing was, a part of him was fascinated. Below the surface of the Commune was a network of tunnels built into the bedrock of the mountains. The Commune wasn't just an alternate-Amish experiment—it was a fortress for the end of times.

He respected their dedication. More than that, these were genuinely nice people. That was a rare thing in this world.

And he had to admit, he felt safe inside the Commune's perimeter.

When Vince shared that Willy wasn't running Willy's body anymore, the Reverend helped Vince track down what Willy's body had been doing inside the Commune. After talking to the town librarian, they discovered that Willy's body had been reading old manuscripts, ancient copies of Gnostic texts that detailed the Apocalypse. Hoarding ancient texts like this was the sort of thing the Commune was famous for, the prototype for hundreds of copycat doomsday cults that were sprouting up around the world.

"Do you really buy into all that stuff?" Vince asked, still staring at the comet.

"And ye will know the truth, and it shall make you free," Zephyr replied. It was early morning, and the grass underfoot was stiff with the frost of the night before. He turned to face Vince. "Do you know what apocalypse means?"

A drone buzzed past them, darting back and forth to capture motes of spent aerial-plankton that fell like snow, collecting them to return to the recycling center. The rising sun lit up the face of the mountain behind the Commune village in the distance.

Vince shrugged. "Death? Destruction? The end of days?"

"No." Zephyr looked down from the heavens. "Apocalypse is a Greek word, and it literally means 'lifting of the veil.'"

"So something is about to be revealed?" Vince didn't mean to edge his words with sarcasm, but they rolled out that way.

"You might not think much of me, Mr. Indigo, but some of the world's most respected people have joined the Communes."

"Sorry, Zeph, I didn't mean it like that." Vince was well aware of the weekly roll call of new "Communistas"—mediums, celebrities, actors, retired politicians, famous scientists. There wasn't just one

Commune. This one was the largest, but there were dozens around the world.

"Many come to escape, as you did to Atopia. But on Atopia you try to cover the real world—reality skins, virtual worlds, limitless sensory stimulation. The Communes have been trying to cut through that, to see things more clearly."

They'd re-entered the perimeter now, and Vince's virtual reality systems and communications cut off again. He stared at the grass at his feet while he walked, dewdrops from the thawing frost glistening in the slanting sunshine. Going back outside the perimeter and reactivating his body's smarticle network felt like sliding a comfortable sheath around his senses, a plastic version of reality.

Now he felt . . . what?

More alive?

"Make no mistake, Mr. Indigo." Zephyr clenched his jaw and looked into the sky at the comet. "The War in Heaven has begun."

# 10

"HOLY SHIT, SID, what the hell did you do?"

Bob felt like he was dropping into the bowels of the underworld as the elevator sank into the depths. Visions of Cerberus slavering over the entrance to the spirit lands raised a spine of fur on the nape of Bob's feline neck.

"Hell," Sid giggled, "is exactly right."

While New York "above ground" had stayed more or less the same for the past century, New York below was something else. It'd become an endless network of tunnels burrowing below the same bedrock that supported the crumbling skyscrapers reaching into the sky above. Day and night, city-block-long automated earthworm diggers churned through the foundations of Manhattan, burrowing it out.

Hollowing below was cheaper than building above.

Their elevator had arrived just seconds before—a sleek white egg propelled through the pneumatic tube system that fed the Purgatory Entertainment District, deep beneath the streets of Midtown.

"No chaperones allowed," Sid warned. Bio-synthetics, like proxxi, were banned underground after a spate of psombie intrusions. Sid and Bob turned off the connections to their proxxi. You had to be yourself when entering Purgatory.

"We need to fit in," Sid said as the elevator dropped. "If we go to Hell looking straight we'll stand out like sore thumbs. We have to blend in. Consider this camouflage."

Bob blinked and tried to focus. "What do you mean, fit in?"

Sid's usual skin of a battered jacket, ripped jeans, and sarcasm had been replaced with a muscular-looking werewolf. Bob reached up to scratch his head but discovered a paw smoothing down the fur over his long ears.

It was his paw.

Sid patted Bob's head. "I slipped some synthetic-K into your pssi channels and dressed us up for the party."

The plastic walls of the elevator egg shimmered before Bob's eyes. The last thing he remembered was closing off some details with Robert, knowing that he'd have to turn his proxxi off, and then everything went sideways. Sid must have slipped the K into his meta-cognition systems. It wasn't a real drug, more like a virus Sid had infected his networks with. "Turn it off, Sid. This isn't the time for one of your pranks."

The elevator slowed.

"You need to loosen up." Sid's fanged mouth affected his lop-sided grin. "Have a laugh with me, just for a few minutes? When we make the connection, I'll turn it off and firewall a private meeting space."

The egg rotated open.

The yolk of Bob's mind slid out ahead of them, assaulted by the onslaught of the Purgatory entranceway. Pounding music poured out from a maelstrom flecked with distant lightning storms as it sucked the contents of the lobby into the spinning entrance portal.

A zoopharm of creatures thronged the waiting area. Some were in humanoid forms, but many were in fantastical shapes as old school met new in a trendy retro mash-up. Time-shifting faeries spun golden trails of temporal pixie dust in tight curls, while goblins danced aloft with fiery dragons sporting necklaces of shimmering sensory mirrors. In one corner a mass of snakes circled a dancing clutch of witches, and in the other a gang of neon pink babies shared a joint.

Everywhere Bob's sensory spaces glittered and sparkled.

Hundreds waited in the shared pre-party space, and catching a glimpse of a stoned satyr passed out in the corner, Bob realized that for many this was as far as they went.

An uplifted gorilla in body armor poised as bouncer on the metal gangway spanning from the lobby into the black hole at the center of the entrance. Names floated in pssi-space in front of the Grilla, and with a huge paw it pecked them off. The individuals selected, up and down the hallway, sparkled in highlights before being sucked off into the center of the vortex.

"Follow me." Sid grabbed one of Bob's paws. Walking through the crowd, Sid released a weapon of mass seduction that cast a spell of sexual attraction, morphing their skins into objects of desire for everyone they passed based on analyses of likes and dislikes distilled from social cloud data.

Bob watched his mind follow its process, the step-by-step rationalization of the decision to enjoy the drugs for a few more minutes. *What was the harm?* It'd been a long time since he and Sid even had a minute to enjoy themselves. *Just like the old days.* The synthetic-K was settling in nicely. Maybe he could give this just a few more minutes.

Walking up the causeway to the Grilla, Sid announced himself. The Grilla's fur bristled, its nostrils flaring. It was aroused—was it female? Bob could only guess what it saw as they arrived.

"Yeah sure," the Grilla rumbled. Sid made a deal. "Go to Hell, boys."

In an instant they were sucked through the eye of the spinning storm of Purgatory and into Hell.

In reality, such as it was, Hell was a moldy and silent room packed with people. With pssi, though, it pulsed alive in an orgy of sensory stimulation as Hell's professional sense-shifting artists warped the partygoers' realities together with the customized sensory landscapes of the bar.

Each person's sound environment was based on their own musical preferences, merged with the beats and themes spun out from the sense jockeys hovering above the dance floors. Right now they were threading out a high beat-per-minute techno that was fusing into Bob's new wave break beats to birth a syncopated, bass-heavy sound that was just perfect for his wandering mind.

Passing some immortal Goths on the dance floor, the music Bob heard shifted from drum-and-bass-inspired hardcore into industrial coldwave, and then his tunes morphed into freeform happy hardcore as they stopped to watch some pssi-boys and pssi-girls breaking it down in displays of neuroplastic gymnastics on the dance floor.

Sid collected drinks from a bartender and poured one of them into a bowl. Bob lapped it up while Sid surveyed the masses of bodies undulating before him like a raptor hovering above a kill. "Not bad, huh?"

Bob was already licking the bottom of his empty bowl. "Give me the key to unlock this synthetic-K." He shook his head. "This is too much."

Sid's fangs showed at the edges of his smile. "Ask me one more time and I'll unlock it."

The pulsing sensorgy around them thrummed through Bob's senses. He couldn't argue that he wasn't enjoying it. Just five more minutes. He shrugged. "So who are we meeting?"

"They're going to find us." Sid motioned toward some couches in the middle of the dance floor. "Why don't we chill over there?"

Bob began wobbling over. The sense jockey started spinning more down-tempo themes, complete with fluorescent visual traces and a hypnotic aromatic scent that vibrated through the atmosphere.

Bob looked back as he walked, watching his feet leave a phosphorescent trail across the floor. Weaving dancers flashed stuttering optical tracks and strobing fireballs against a black night sky.

He let his mind slide down the rabbit hole.

"Hey, boys," came a voice amid the jumbled colors, "how you doing?"

Bob shook his head. From the melee crowding his visual systems, the image of a young woman distilled itself—or rather, the image of a large pink cat woman.

"My name's Sibeal," she purred. Her tail flicked back and forth, touching Sid.

Bob was collapsed on the couch, swimming in a sensory overload. "Turn off the synthetic-K, Sid, this is too much . . ."

"That might be her," Sid said on a private channel. "Give me a minute."

Bob shook his head. We have to stay together, he meant to say, but Sid disappeared into the crowd.

The sensory overlay of the couches gave the impression that dozens of hands were caressing him, and Bob shivered as he felt it kick in. He pulled his legs up onto the couch in a semi-fetal position.

He could wait a minute.

The pssi-boys and pssi-girls in front of him were putting on a great show, spinning and gyrating as their bodies morphed with the beat of the music. One of them transitioned from two arms to four arms to six and then into a humanoid-millipede form that wormed around a spinning dance move. The dynamics and physics of this multi-legged body shifted perfectly as he morphed from one form to another. The dancer's real body appeared underneath the pssi overlay as the music stuttered, doing its best to mimic the synthetic body's motion that the kid was controlling.

The music stopped and the space filled with a pink mist of ionized vanilla. Bob frowned. Where was Sid? He was pretty sure it had been more than "a minute". The caressing hands of the couch slackened, and applause filled the room.

In the fog Bob saw a familiar shape, standing out of place, but he couldn't focus his mind.

The general announcement channel sounded in Bob's auditory channels. "Let's hear it for SJ Sanjeeve!"

The applause grew louder.

Who was that? The shape became more distinct.

"And now what you've all been waiting for, Atopia's own Kid Pssssssssi–cho!"

A cheer went up through the crowd, and the room dropped into blackness.

"That's Jimmy," Bob said aloud, ripping himself up from the couch's embrace. Or was it? Bob's mind had congealed under the influence of the drugs.

The pink mist faded into a red-orange grayness, and a sub-audio vibration shook Bob's flesh. The ground transmogrified itself into a rippling lake with tenuous wisps of vapor clinging to its surface. As the dancers around Bob shuffled their feet, they sent out waves like they were walking on water. A few of them laughed and began kicking up splashes at each other.

The fog lifted and craggy terra cotta mountains appeared ringing the distant horizon beneath a burnt orange, star-speckled sky. The bone-shaking vibrations of the music mounted in urgency. Through the dissipating fog, the rings of Saturn appeared suspended in the sky, stretching impossibly far up above the dance floor that was perched precariously on its edge. A methane storm cloud was rolling quickly across the horizon, roiling across the mountain ridges as it descended on the crowd.

The dance hall had been patched into the sensor-mote network on Titan, at Kraken Mare near its north pole.

Bob reached out into the familiar hyperspaces that connected him with Sid, but he felt nothing. He tried pinging Robert for help, but realized his proxxi channels were locked down. He sloshed through the methane lake, squinting into the crowd.

The audio wound itself into a keening shriek, and the first globs of methane rain started falling onto the crowd, splashing into the lake, sending vapor shooting upward. On cue, the music dropped into a planet-shaking bass rhythm that sent waves through the lake, toppling boulders down the mountainsides in the distance. The crowd went crazy, bursting into dance, jamming all of Bob's sensory channels.

Where was Sid?

"NO USE TRYING to get any outgoing, mate." The man in front of Sid slapped the smooth bedrock wall to make his point. "No signals get through this." He reached a hand out. "Shaky."

Sid clicked off the synthetic-K coursing through his pssi. The world came into focus. Who was this guy? He studied the close-cropped gray stubble atop the little man's head and reached out to take his hand. No data on him appeared in Sid's displays, no future prediction models, no nerve conduction potentials he could tap into to figure out what was coming. "'Shaky?'" Sid asked. "You mean like 'shaky hands?'"

The man pumped Sid's hand, smiling and crinkling his nose. "No, mate, my name is Shaky."

The guy next to Shaky put out his hand too. "Bunky."

Sid let go of Shaky's hand and shook Bunky's. "Sid."

The girl Sid had made contact with in the main hall, Sibeal, strode into the communal bathroom. "We need to go now!" She shifted out of her reality skin into worn cargo pants, a black tank top, and a grim expression.

A second ago the bathroom had been filled with partygoers, but they'd all exited as if on cue.

Shaky and Bunky's smiles had disappeared as well.

They were the only ones there.

One instant was all it took for Sid's world to change. It took just fractions of a second to realize it was a trap, but it was fractions too late. Sid unleashed a barrage of jamming across all radio frequencies, sending splinters out to hack into the digital infrastructure around him. He logged into the bathroom taps, the hand dryer, the sensory transponders above the sinks, the advertising hologram hanging behind Sibeal, but it was no use.

They had him cold. Flooding his gray matter with smarticles, he quickened, dropping to the floor as Bunky and Shaky reached for him.

There was no way into the open multiverse.

He tried contacting Bob, tried to find a path out to send out emergency beacons, to deactivate Bob's synthetic-K. Sid jumped sideways and bounced off a wall around his attackers. The world slowed down. He twisted and spun. The path to the entrance in front of him cleared. He just needed one . . . more . . . step . . . and then the entrance filled with the hulking shape of the Grilla.

It grabbed him like a rag doll.

Held by the Grilla, the music around Sid transformed into a deep animal growl, his mind filling with images of steaming jungles, splashing blood, and twitching flesh. Sid tried hacking into their smarticle networks, but they were battle-hardened.

Sibeal pulled a shiny black sack out of her backpack. Lifting her arms high she pulled it over Sid's head. He squirmed without effect. Its fabric was laced with metal wires. A Faraday blanket that stopped electromagnetics. The Grilla pulled the sack around him, and Sid felt his connections to the outside world cut off. A black hole opened in the wall of the bathroom, and the Grilla stepped into it, dragging Sid along.

# 11

VINCE LOOKED AT the night sky. A thick carpet of stars hung like a bowl atop the mountaintops ringing the Commune; the bright smudge of the comet was just disappearing behind a peak. Zephyr drove him and Elspeth and Brigitte out past the perimeter again, this time for Elspeth to talk to Willy.

A few weeks had marked the first time Elspeth had seen her son in the fifteen years since she had to leave him on Atopia. Back then, she'd been overcome with fear, unable to stay, but it was a decision that haunted her. Meeting Willy, holding and kissing and hugging him, had been an incredibly emotional reunion. But now Vince and Brigitte were telling her that it hadn't been Willy at all. It was incomprehensible that the person she'd met and shared tears with just days before had been an impostor, and worse, a thief who had stolen her son's body.

Vince was caught up in her shock, shaken out of his emotional slumber. So he made a simple suggestion—why not just come outside the perimeter and meet the "real" Willy in his virtual presence?

He hadn't anticipated the Reverend's swift acceptance of the idea, given their strict stance against synthetic reality technology, but then again, it was his daughter. What were rules if not things to be bent?

Zephyr sat in the cart stoically. Vince could only imagine how all of this was reinforcing Zephyr's ideas of the wickedness of the outside world. Three trips to the perimeter in one day was about as much as the kid could take. He wasn't used to this much contact with the outside world, but it was on the Reverend's strict orders. Vince was taking a walk while Brigitte and Elspeth sat on a blanket in the wet grass under the stars.

Brigitte dropped a packet of smarticle powder into a canteen of water, swirling it around, and handed it to Elspeth. "Drink it," Vince heard Brigitte whisper to Elspeth. "Don't worry, I'll guide you."

What Vince was feeling didn't make any sense. It wasn't one thing or the other, nothing he could put his finger on. It was a combination of things, a perspective that brought the elements of his mind together to create an image that looked familiar—a nagging sensation that one thing fit into another, a square peg that should be a round one if he could just hold it the right way.

He tried to dismiss the feeling, telling himself it was just his mind making patterns from noise, but the more he read into the old religious texts of the Commune, the stronger the feeling became, the stronger the images burned into his mind of creatures with six wings, eyes inside and out, of the eleven-headed Buddha he'd seen in a Chenrezig monastery with dozens of arms.

But it couldn't be possible.

He pushed it into the back of his mind and focused on assimilating his waiting splinters. "Himalayas overtaking Greenland as second-largest reserve of frozen water after Antarctica," went one phuture broadcast, with temperatures in Europe projected to plummet as the Gulf Stream continued to slow.

Part of the mystery around how Willy's body had made it inside the Commune was that the smarticle network inside it should have shut down, and communication in and out should have been impossible. But, somehow, someone had kept the technology working, hiding it from the Commune's sensors. The Reverend said he had no idea how. Vince believed him.

At least one important mystery had been solved.

Vince queried Elspeth about things she talked about with Willy's imposter, intimate details that whomever was inhabiting Willy's body shared with her. Outside the perimeter, Vince uploaded and correlated the information with Willy. Everything matched, down to the last detail. The only entity that would have that level of correct information about Willy had to be his proxxi, Wally—without a doubt, it was Willy's proxxi that stole his body.

Vince felt a new presence bloom into being in the local multiverse. Elspeth. She sat beside Brigitte, now lit by a glowing pssi-halo, her newly-minted metatags hanging in overlaid display spaces around her. The smarticles had infused into her neural system. She was pssi-aware.

"Just relax, breath slowly," Brigitte instructed, holding her hand.

Elspeth's eyes darted back and forth. Her white-knuckled hands gripped the blanket as her perceptions grew sharper and deeper, the informational flow of the multiverse connecting into her sensory systems for the first time. "I'm okay," she replied. "Could you get Willy?"

She didn't need to ask.

"Hey, Mom." Willy appeared from behind a copse of trees nearby. His virtual image glowed alongside a patch of bioluminescent kale.

"Willy?" Tears sprang into Elspeth's eyes. "My baby, what have they done to you?" Forgetting the illusion, she sprang up and ran to her son, embracing him.

Vince looked away, hiding his own tears. He looked at Zephyr, sitting on the wagon, watching the whole strange scene. Zephyr couldn't see Willy, he couldn't even hear the words Elspeth was speaking to Willy in the pssi audio channel, but he watched her jump up and run toward the trees, crying and embracing thin air.

Zephyr didn't bat an eye, his stoic expression speaking volumes—*the outside world was just strange.*

Vince returned his attention to the phuture splinter competing for his attention: Newlandia's application to the UN as the first sovereign virtual nation looked like it was going to happen, while civil rights protests raged in San Francisco from a continued ban on mind uploading research. "Immortality is God's domain," complained the Christian Democrats of America.

A whirring began in the sky and Vince spun his point-of-view into the space above them, zooming in to track Deanna's electric turbofan. It was time for them to get to New York.

"I'm not coming." It was Brigitte, a virtual splinter of her standing beside him in a private communication space, while her body remained sitting on the blanket with Willy and Elspeth. "My place is here, at least for now."

Vince was going to argue, but then looked at Willy and his mother, Elspeth, gripping Brigitte's hands.

"Let me talk to Sid and Bob." Vince started up a virtual meeting space, pinging Sid and Bob, but there was no response. He knew they were at an underground club in New York meeting the glass-cutters. He pinged again. Still nothing. Why weren't they answering? Then the realization: He'd let Bob and Sid go by themselves to a rave club in New York. *I knew I shouldn't have left those two alone.*

He had to make a decision. His gut said no, splitting up even more was a bad idea, but looking at Elspeth gripping Brigitte's hand swayed his emotions back. It might be useful to have someone inside the Commune, and it seemed like the right thing to do. For them, at least.

The turbofan growled, leaves and grass blowing past them as it hovered. Vince sent instructions for it to land next to him. He looked into Brigitte's eyes. "Okay, but you stay in regular contact?"

She nodded.

With a final blast, the turbofan settled into the grass. Brigitte's virtual presence retreated into her body and she waved at Vince.

He smiled back, then looked toward Zephyr. "You take care of them."

Zephyr nodded, tipping his hat. He didn't ask any questions.

Gripping the rungs of the turbofan's access ladder, Vince wondered if he was making a mistake. Grumbling, he swung himself into the cushioned front seat and reached around to strap in the webbing. The clear plastic cockpit enclosure closed and the turbofan began cycling up again, roaring underneath him. With a final wave he bid Brigitte goodbye. The turbofan lurched into the sky and Vince settled into the harness, letting his alpha and theta waves settle his brain for a short sleep on the way into Manhattan.

# 12

THE METHANE STORM on Titan raged, the world a thrashing kaleidoscope before Bob's senses, but he felt something more troubling than Sid's sudden disappearance: other pssi-kids from Atopia were in Hell, and they were searching. The fabric of the local multiverse bent under their psychic weight as Bob sensed them scraping against his identity-theft algorithms. They might be good enough for the world out here, but pssi-kids would make short work of ripping through the thin veil Sid built to hide them.

Bob had to get out of Hell, and soon.

The music roared around and inside Bob. He steadied himself, trying to inhibit the drug coursing through his digital neurons, cursing that he'd let Sid rope him into it. *How could I be so stupid?*

Even before the thought *I need to escape* had fully formed, he left his body behind, jacking his primary subjective past the security systems and into the Purgatory entranceway. He stopped and looked around—the Grilla was gone, and there was no sign of Sid.

While his mind searched for channels out into the open multiverse, his body quickened, flooding itself with smarticles, darting through the dancers back to the physical entrance of Hell. Across the full sensory spectrum of Hell a sharp keening began, a knife that cut through the assembled meta-cognition systems.

Bob sensed it coming.

He threw up walls, started splitting his personalities, splintering himself to hide in every corner he could find.

And then it happened.

Time stopped.

Bob's mind filled with white noise. His sensory channels mushroomed, sliding out of control, squeezing together, blending into each other. The pressure built, vibrating, shaking, and just as the needles began piercing, he heard the screams of the thousands of people in Hell, their minds shredding around him.

Bob threw off one layer after another of his meta-cognition framework like throwing up a stack of bullet-proof vests to stop incoming machine gun fire. He retreated backward in time, and then sideways into any confined information space that wasn't burning. Like bubbles of paint, parts of his mind started exploding in wet pops. He gathered himself inward. What little remained kept probing for escape routes. Finally he slid up the network of the pneumatic tubes and outward to the surface.

Below him, the screaming had stopped, but so had the collective awareness.

As Bob's body raced out of the maze of tunnels, everywhere sagging bodies stared out from blank eyes. Bob spread his identity metatags onto everyone he passed, jacking into their bodies, starting them running in random directions to hide his escape. He began spinning alternate realities, layering and fusing them into the sensory systems of the others, the pssi-kids, slippery eels that slid through the data systems of Purgatory.

Retreating through one world and then another, he found himself running through a burnt and barren landscape with the stakes of tree stumps stabbed into its smoking earth. Ash was falling from a ravaged sky.

"We know you're here," hissed the Hunter, a neural fusion of a gang of pssi-kids he'd known growing up, Daxter and Axel and

Gunner. Now they weren't kids anymore. It seemed they were working for Jimmy, and they were hunting for him.

Bob tried to focus, the world swimming before his eyes. He kneeled down behind a tree stump and began dialing up all the worlds connected to the battle gameworld. One thought remained in the stunted awareness he had left: Get to the passenger cannon. In the real world, a thin slice of his digital awareness skimmed through the wet streets of New York, dragging his physical body behind it like a rag doll on a string.

# 13

*THE TWENTY-FOUR leaders are returning,* said Zephyr. Lightning crackled across the sky behind him. *What do you think happened to Willy?* asked Vince. *He was possessed by a demon,* replied Zephyr. *Don't you believe in demons, Mr. Indigo?*

A jolt woke Vince up.

"It's just the refueling drone." Hotstuff was riding shotgun beside him in the turbofan.

Through the canopy, in the soft glow of the instrumentation lights, Vince watched a drone's articulated arms pull out the main battery pack of their turbofan and replace it with a fresh one. The hop from Montana to New York required an in-air battery drop. The American government didn't use the African space power grid and couldn't refuel via microwave burst in flight like most of the rest of the world.

Vince shook his head and closed his eyes.

The drone held the turbofan like an insect in its legs. The night sky slid by above. Finished, the drone disengaged with a jolt, and the whir of the turbofan ratcheted up a notch. It started climbing back to cruising altitude.

A garbled message from Bob popped up on Vince's messaging systems: "Where's Sid? I can't find Sid." Vince latched onto Bob's message stream, but it was cut off in an eruption of network traffic. Vince's phutures slid sideways. The mediaworlds erupted: *A terrorist attack in the Purgatory Entertainment District, Atopian splinter group responsible. Authorities hunting for suspects.*

The refueling drone cut through the air above them.

Vince shot up in his harness. "What the hell?"

"Don't know, boss." Hotstuff dispatched agents into the New York networks. "Some kind of pssi-weapon was unleashed in central New York, right on top of Bob and Sid's last known location."

Vince's phuturing network was still set in high avoidance mode. Nothing major should have been able to penetrate the protective web surrounding him and his friends, not without some advance notice. "How did this get past us?"

Hotstuff grabbed Vince's primary presence and dragged it into their war room. She spun out a series of scenarios, graphing their interconnectedness. "Being in Commune's black hole generated discontinuities in our future timeline."

Another jolt.

The drone was re-attaching itself. In a secondary display space Vince frowned, watching the drone's insect-legs wrapping themselves around the turbofan.

Hotstuff looked at him, her eyes growing wide. "Vince, watch out . . ."

And then she was gone.

Vince's main point-of-presence snapped from the war room back into his body in the pod of the turbofan. The only sound was the rush of the air past the canopy and the whine of the engine.

The stars slid by overhead.

"Mr. Vincent Damon Indigo," announced a voice over the comms channel of the turbofan. "I am Special Agent Sheila Connors of the Federal Bureau of Investigation. You are under arrest for breach of future confidentiality."

# 14

THREE GEES OF acceleration squeezed Bob into the aerogel of the passenger cannon pod seat, then five gees, then briefly six as it angled up from its subterranean launch tube. His pod launched into free space with a thudding concussion, the air ionizing around it in a blistering tunnel as it bored through the lower atmosphere. His body popped out of the foam seat in the shift to near-zero gravity, the sheen of ionization sputtering out as the pod gained altitude, clearing the densest layers of air on its ballistic flight path across the Atlantic on its way to Lagos.

Escaping New York had been a game of capture the flag, with his body and physical brain as the prize. He started by ducking it into the aging subway system, then a VTOL pick-up and drop-off to the other side of town and quick succession of self-driving taxi exchanges and sprints up and down building staircases while he scattered decoys in his wake. Bob used the predictive policing models of the city to figure out where patrolling drones would be. It was a lot like the games of flitter tag he used to play with the other pssi-kids on Atopia, but this time with life-threatening stakes.

In the twenty minutes it took him to reach and clear the passenger cannon security checkpoints, the NYPD joined the chase. With only seconds to spare, his pod was in the last batch of launches—even in this ultra-modern metropolis, it took time to lock a city down.

Bits and pieces of his mind reassembled themselves at random—secure back-ups of memories and ideas floating back into his brain on the thin data stream. The capsule gained altitude into space. Bob's cognitive frameworks were still fighting off the shimmer of the drug Sid had infected him with. He created a virtual world, shielded beneath an onion skin of encryption, to have a talk with the reassembling bits of his intellect.

*Alone*, was the first thought that mushroomed into his mind, *you're alone.*

Turning inside himself, in a panic he checked the data cube Patricia entrusted him with. It was still there, embedded in the center of his mind. The world he created solidified in his visual channels. A hexagonal chamber appeared with a copy of himself seated against each of six yellow walls. The data cube sat in the middle of the room, a faceted ruby that glittered darkly.

*"Should we tell her?"* the main part of his mind asked. *"Is that what I really look like?"* He stared at the copies of himself staring back at him, blue eyes beneath blond dreadlocks tied back in a ponytail.

*"It's too dangerous,"* replied his cautious self. *"You just want an excuse to talk to her."*

*"An excuse?"* roared his emotional self, a vein popping out in his neck. *"You call this an excuse?"*

*"I agree, we should wait,"* said his lazy side.

His emotional self shook its head. *"You're the reason we're in this mess. Taking drugs? Idiot. The same reason that Martin—"*

*"Hey, stop that."* Bob's inspirational side held up his hands. *"This is a mess, but it's not our fault. We're out here trying to help. We'll get out of this, but we need to plan for the worst. So we should tell her."*

His cautious side remained adamant. *"Patricia said no connections to Atopia under any circumstance."*

"*Sid's gone and we can't find Vince. What difference does it make? This is all gone to hell already.*" His emotional side clenched his jaw. "*Make the connection.*"

"*Let's take a minute and think.*" The main part of his mind considered what the rest of him was saying. "*Who set this off?*"

"*Does it matter? We need to get everything we know to Nancy.*" The face of his emotional facet turned beet red.

His cautious side took a deep breath. "*I guess you're right . . .*"

All the parts of his mind were coming to the same conclusion. "*We'll make contact in the place nobody else knows about.*"

They all nodded. They all knew what he was thinking.

# 15

VINCE LEANED BACK and stretched his neck. "You really shouldn't switch off my Phuture News feeds." It was all that was keeping them safe, he didn't add.

Special Agent Sheila Connors was busy with her remote team. They were firewalling Vince off from the world. She grunted, "You and your friends have been busy."

Connors shared a mediaworld about the terrorist attack in New York. It was filled with images of Robert Baxter emerging from the pneumatic tube system. "A few thousand disappeared, plus six billion future infractions. Half the world is on the hunt for you and your gang."

Vince watched the news report, still working in the background to release his agents into autopilot. Each new security blanket Agent Connors created restricted his outward paths. He only had a few minutes, perhaps seconds.

"Our gang?" Vince snorted. "We had nothing to do with that."

"You're sure?" Agent Connors' tech team continued to jam up the communications channels around them. "So you didn't hack into the phutures of ten billion people?"

Vince paused. He didn't like to lie. "That was for a good reason—"

"And you're not operating an international espionage ring, modifying the future on a massive scale?"

Vince shrugged. "Like I said—"

"There's always a good reason with people like you."

Vince smiled. People like you. Coming from Atopia, Vince felt like an intruder, but it wasn't because of the technology. He felt like an intruder when he watched people, walked by them in the streets, watched them living their little lives. Once he'd been like them, before the wealth, the fame.

Now he was different. He felt . . . what? Sorry for them?

Down below he watched the lights of Atlanta slide by, twenty million of those little people living their futile lives. Maybe she's right, he thought, looking out the window. Maybe I am just a rich asshole. "I'm not going to argue, but you really shouldn't turn off my Phuture News feeds," he repeated.

Agent Connors raised her eyebrows. "Or what?" She was using a version of pssi, and in an overlaid display Vince watched her phantoms cycling through their security controls. Mr. Indigo was hers now, and she clicked off the control of his proxxi.

Vince felt the last of his connections close down. He could still see, but he felt blind.

In the Commune, he had been cut off from his future feeds, but his proxxi Hotstuff was working in the background. And the Commune was a data dark spot. There had been some measure of safety—the dangers Vince couldn't see couldn't see him either. But now Hotstuff was shut down, and out here, in full view of the world, it wouldn't be long until whatever was hunting him would catch up. Watching the last of the lights of Atlanta disappear, he realized they must be on their way to Cuba. Almost the whole southern half had become a gulag for the Alliance.

At least it would be warmer than Siberia.

He didn't need to see fighter drones approaching, didn't need to hear Agent Connors' attempts to argue that they weren't carrying a deadly virus. He didn't need to watch the flames and roar of the attack, the desperate attempts to fight back. He didn't need to see it, because even without his future feeds, he knew it was coming.

# 16

THE GRAY SEAS of the English Channel rolled beneath clouds that hung above it like stains against the sky. The chalk cliffs of the Dorset coast stretched into the foggy distance, and Durdle Door, an oval hole burrowed through the cliffs by the ocean and time, stood above the beaches like a doorway to another world. Smooth rocks, with heads full of seaweed, lay about in jumbles in the tidal pools. In the middle of them, a small boy in swimming trunks, with awkward legs sticking out at angles, was waiting.

"Bob," said a little girl, approaching cautiously. "Is that you?"

The boy nodded.

She dropped her bright orange pail and began running to him.

The boy stood, waving a tiny fishing net in the air. "I figured you would see me here," he said. "And before you ask, I feel fine." The first thing out of her mouth was always, *how are you feeling?* So Bob pre-empted.

It was one of their childhood worlds, where Bob and Nancy came as kids to hunt through rocks, to swim, and explore—a special place that was theirs alone. It was Bob's safest place, even if storm clouds filled it now. Nancy ran to hug him. They sat down facing each other on the wet-seaweed rocks, up to their ankles in tidal-pool seawater.

"What happened in New York?" Nancy asked.

Bob rocked back a little. It wasn't like her to just jump straight into it. "I don't know what happened." Bob saw the explosion of mediaworlds linking him to the attack. He was monitoring the chatter of network traffic searching for him. He'd attached his identity to hundreds of metatags of people leaving the city. It would take time for them to sift through it, hopefully enough for him to get away. "I had nothing to do with it."

Lightning lit up storm clouds in the distance.

"Why have you been hiding from me, Bob? Why are you running?"

A peal of thunder rolled across them.

"I'm not running." He shook his head. "I mean, I wasn't running. It was Patricia who asked me to leave. She sent us out to find Willy's body."

Nancy frowned. "*She* sent you to find Willy's body?"

"I don't know why." That wasn't entirely true. "There's something in Willy's body, something to do with Jimmy she needed us to find out." Looking down, he picked a periwinkle off the rock and inspected it. The tiny creature retreated into its shell. "It's not safe. She made me promise to take you with us, but I failed, I left you behind."

More lightning, and the hollow crackle following it came quicker, louder.

Nancy grabbed both of Bob's hands. "Jimmy's assembling his own private psombie army in cities all over the world. I've seen it. Is that what you're trying to stop?"

What should he tell her? He wanted to tell her everything, how much he loved her, how much of a danger Jimmy was. But what made sense? More than just their lives were at stake. Say nothing, and you might lose her. Say everything, and you might lose her. What was the right thing to do?

"Be careful of Jimmy, he's not what he seems."

Nancy shivered. "I know. I don't trust him, or Kesselring, they're playing power games—"

"He killed Patricia." Bob squeezed her hands. "And his own parents. It's not just politics. Something else is going on."

A bolt of lightning ripped the sky apart behind them, accompanied by a deafening boom.

Nancy stood and pulled Bob to get up. "Let's get inside." Rain started falling. She motioned toward a yellow cabana on the beach.

Bob looked into the pool of water at his feet, the surface rippling in colliding circles as raindrops hit it. A crab scuttled by. Bob felt sluggish, his mind drifting. "I need to go." He handed Nancy the periwinkle, embedding within it the encrypted data that Patricia had left him. It was a risk—it meant the data was returning into the Atopian ecosystem—but Nancy needed to know.

She took it, and leaned in to kiss his cheek. Bob turned and kissed her, then started shutting down the tunnel to the world, but he was weak. It took nearly all of his energy just to hand the data beacon to Nancy.

The crab he'd seen at his feet inched up on top of the seaweed covered rock next to him. It raised itself up on its hind legs, spreading its arms to the sky. Lightning thundered again, and tendrils of electrostatic discharge snaked across the sky to illuminate the white cliffs.

The crab looked at Bob, its mouthparts gnashing. "You'll make a nice bounty, my friend."

Bob's mind was swimming. He logged into his bio-stats. Something was wrong. He'd been physically poisoned somehow.

Snapping his primary subjective out of the sea-world, he popped his viewpoint back into the passenger pod. The milky film of the atmosphere hung over the curve of the Earth, while steely pinpoints of stars hung above.

Nausea overcame him. He retched.

His vitals were way off, his heart racing. A low rumble began. It was the retrorockets of the pod firing. They shouldn't be firing now, somewhere a hundred miles in space over the middle of the Atlantic. The pod was being diverted. Data pipes into the multiverse were shutting down, and, fighting to remain conscious, he made another copy of the data he'd given to Nancy and sent it out in a sealed beacon.

If Sid was still out there somewhere, he might find it.

Blackness descended.

# 17

"I HAVEN'T HAD any contact with Bob," Nancy lied.

Jimmy was sitting in a chair behind a huge desk, facing away from her. They were in the palace of his elaborately maintained private universe. He stared down the length of a long reflecting pool which divided his manicured gardens, stretching to the horizon. Ornate moldings, gilt in gold, framed frescoes of angels in the ceilings. Thick velvet curtains draped lead-glass windows. "Did he tell you anything?" Jimmy turned to look at her.

"I told you I haven't talked to him since he left." She shifted in her chair. "I'd tell you if I did."

Jimmy smiled. "I'm just finding out whose side you're on." He looked at the ceiling. "Of course you understand it would be treason if you had contact."

"Treason?"

"And hid the contact, I mean."

Nancy felt her cheeks flush, but in this projected space her face remained stone-still. "I don't believe 'treason' is an offense described in the Atopian constitution."

"You know what I mean. Anyway, enough, I was just asking." His smile grew wider. He turned to Dr. Granger. "Please continue with the summary of operations."

Dr. Granger was sitting in an attending chair with a pile of reports in his lap. He smiled at Nancy and then began unpacking his presentation. Charts and graphs started filling the shared display spaces above Jimmy's desk.

"Happiness indices are at all-time highs in places where pssi has spread through the population," began Dr. Granger. "Crime is dropping, and business productivity and profits are sky-rocketing at companies that have adopted the pssi-suite. A complete success." Dr. Granger stopped and looked at Nancy. "The Infinixx distributed consciousness app is the most downloaded sensory interface."

This was Nancy's own creation. She took a deep breath. "I still disagree—"

"The Board's decision is final," interrupted Jimmy, staring into his gardens.

Nancy hung her head. Instead of forcing new users to create their own memetic structures, using their own memories, they'd instead adopted a cookie-cutter approach. They were pre-formatting people's expanding minds. It made it easier to access their thoughts, but the public didn't seem to mind. Or even notice. They just wanted the endless reality.

Jimmy argued for a backdoor to combat viral reality skins, like the one that nearly destroyed Atopia. Nancy was able to hold him back in the general release, but in each jurisdiction there were secret deals going on, allowing governments to peer into the minds of the population. *If people had nothing to hide, then they had nothing to fear*, went the line of reasoning that Jimmy kept putting forward. And everywhere that pssi was released, the people were happier than ever—happy, but living in dreamworlds.

"The subsea computing facilities are on track," continued Dr. Granger, and began detailing the self-replicating data ware-houses being constructed under sea floors, using seawater for cooling and powered by geothermal generators. It was a vast computing organism growing into the crust of the Earth to make virtual space for the billions of personal universes being created within the pssi multiverse.

"Any progress on the legal front?" asked Jimmy halfway through Dr. Granger's run-down on the computing facilities.

More graphics spun into their shared spaces. Anti-trust suits were being brought under control, and key patent litigations against Terra Nova continuing.

"And what happened to Patricia Killiam's personal research projects. The POND, for instance?"

Dr. Granger shrugged. "She terminated that before she passed."

Jimmy turned to the two of them. "I was talking to Nancy."

Nancy's attention was elsewhere. "Pardon? The POND?"

"The Pacific Ocean Neutrino Detector," Jimmy said. "Don't tell me you don't know of it."

Of course Nancy had heard of it. "But I don't see how that has any—"

"Everything has relevance, Ms. Killiam. Your aunt shut that project down just before she passed, and the data from it is missing. I'd bet that Baxter took it, and I'd like to know why. He's a prime suspect in the New York attack, and we need to know what's going on."

Jimmy paused. "His terrorist actions were designed to halt the spread of pssi, to incite fear in the consumer population." Over a thousand people's minds had been wiped out in the New York attack, a thousand people now vegetative psombies. "He's continuing your Aunt Patricia's campaign against us."

Nancy could sense she was on thin ice. "I don't believe she was working against us." And the attack in New York wasn't what was slowing down the release. Half of the billion new users of pssi were displaying signs of tech-induced schizophrenia, and even the AI-run tech support channels weren't enough to sort out all the problems.

Jimmy rocked his head back and stared at the ceiling. "Then who was she working against?"

Nancy stopped herself from saying, *you*. "I don't know, Jim, you know more than me."

Jimmy looked at her, squinting, and then slowly returned his gaze to the reflecting pool.

# Part 2:

## Heresy

# 1

"WHERE AM I?" Sid was still stuffed in the black sack, his connections to the outside world cut off. After being dragged out of the bar, he'd been thrown over the shoulder of the Grilla. In stops and starts he was carried, pushed, and dragged down one tunnel after another, deep into the bowels of New York.

They'd stopped for a few minutes. It seemed like this was the destination. Sid used inertials to track every inch of the path down. By his calculations they were three hundred and sixty-two feet under Third Avenue and Forty-Second Street. He knew exactly where he was. Sid's question wasn't about spatial coordinates—he just wanted to know what they'd say before he crushed them.

"Do you want the good news or the bad news?" Sid recognized the voice as Bunky's, one of his kidnappers from the bathroom.

In an overlay some scant details appeared as his internal pssi displayed what it had so far: British birth origin, Somerset accent, blood vessels on the surface of facial skin indicating probable history of alcoholism. In another situation it seemed like someone he'd enjoy meeting. Sid played along. "Bad news, please."

The Grilla dumped him onto a chair, ripping the cover off him in a motion that nearly flayed the skin off his arms.

"A martyr, I like that," Bunky said. "The bad news, my friend, is that you're completely fucked."

Sid blinked and looked around. His sensory system gathered information at the same time as his extrasensory one did the same, hacking into any networks nearby. He was in a large cavern, roughly hewn from black bedrock. Naked fluorescent bulbs dotted wet-streaked walls. Gaping holes led outward. The cavern was filled with a shanty town of tin roofs and lopsided structures that filled the floor and climbed the walls. Halfway up one side of the walls, at the mouth of one of the tunnels, Sid was seated on a terrace, surrounded by his captors.

"Now the good news." Shaky, his other kidnapper, smiled at Sid. "You're in a pub. The White Horse. I mean if you've got to be fucked, might as well be in a pub, right?" He cackled at his own joke.

Sid's internal systems were piecing things together. Both Bunky and Shaky were at Battery Park when he walked around there with Bob. His inVerse plotted their paths from recordings, mapping their paths backward in the recorded wikiworld.

A serving bot dropped a pint of beer in front of Sid. "Yeah, I know I'm in a pub." He picked it up and took a swig.

One of the first things he hacked into, in the seconds since they removed the cloak, was the food and drink system of the establishment they were in. Sid had ordered a beer. In fact, several beers. More plunked down in front of Shaky and Bunky. They roared with laughter.

Shaky slapped Sid on the back. "You're all right, mate!"

On the opposite wall of the cavern, directly ahead of Sid, two tunnel openings yawned open, like two giant eyes staring at him. Mesh netting held back loose rock near the entrances, while white tubes wormed their way around the mouths. Metal ribs lined the tunnels, flanked by fat packets of cabling that snaked into the distance and disappeared into the darkness. Clunking up through each of the tunnels were large construction mechanoids.

Bunky saw Sid looking at them. "No need to worry, just our better halves come to get us for work."

Sid wasn't worried. He was trying to crack into them. A construction mechanoid on the rampage would give these assholes something to think about.

"Afraid we can't hack into those," said Vicious, Sid's proxxi. Only Sid could see and hear Vicious. Between them they were spinning out a range of escape scenarios—flooding the tunnels with water by opening a sewage drain, carbon monoxide poisoning from jamming exhausts, a blinding flash of floodlights followed by a power failure. A combination of these might give Sid just enough time.

Sibeal, the girl from the bar, sat down on a bench next to him. "Before you do anything you might regret, let's have a chat." She grabbed one of his phantom hands in synthetic space. "And no, I don't want a beer."

Sid readied his attack vectors. "So what's this about, then?" It didn't matter. Whatever the reason, he was about to unleash a very unpleasant learning experience on them.

This was a den of phrackers, 'cutters, and underminers. Sid knew their kind. He was their kind. The underminers were really just construction workers, tied to whatever local mob affiliates they had to be, but the 'cutters and phrackers mostly worked for the Asian gambling syndicates. They knocked out corporate AIs, shifted the future timeline to try and shift odds, struggling against the future regulators who were fighting a losing battle to make sure the future is what it was supposed to be.

Sibeal rolled her eyes, and in an overlaid display Sid was surprised to see a knot of phantom limbs spread out from her, uncoiling into the hyperspaces where he was readying his assault. One by one, his strings of control were cut.

"We're friends," she replied. Sibeal wrapped the cut strings around him, tying up his virtual hands. She smiled. "In fact, we're fans."

"That's right, mate," said Bunky, raising his beer.

Sid glanced at his proxxi. Vicious shrugged. There was nothing he could do, but this didn't seem threatening either. Sid turned to Sibeal. "If we're friends, then why the kidnapping routine?"

Sibeal shrugged in pssi-space. "There wasn't time to explain. We had to get out of there. Your friend unloaded a massive synthetic charge in that bar."

Who were they talking about? "My friend?"

Sibeal opened a channel and shared her mediaworld reports. "Over a thousand people lost their minds, Bob was right in the middle."

"If we hadn't gotten you out of there . . ." Shaky made small explosion gestures with his fingers, as if his mind was blowing. "You should choose your friends more carefully."

Sid assimilated the mediaworlds and frowned. "There's no way Bob had anything to do with this. I was with him the whole time." *Not the whole time.* They must have snatched him too. "Where is he?"

"We thought you might know." Sibeal watched for Sid's reaction. "He's gone off grid. There's one heck of a bounty attached to him." She paused. "And you, too, for that matter."

In augmented space, Sid's proxxi nodded. So that was what all this was about—bounty hunters. He could guess what they wanted. His friends. "I can't help you."

"If you help us, maybe we can help you." Sibeal spun a new information packet into Sid's networks—a data beacon. "We found something your friend left behind. Want to have a look?"

He was on dangerous ground here. They had kidnapped him, yet claimed to be friends, then admitted they were bounty hunters. Nothing in the logical chain made him think he should trust them, and yet his gut told him he could. He was the one that had contacted them in the first place, and he needed as much information as he could get. He could let this roll. Whatever happened, he was confident he could outsmart them if it came down to it, but it might be useful to give the impression that he was in it for the money as well. He nodded. "But we split any commission?"

Sibeal glanced at Bunky and Shaky and they both nodded. "Sure," she replied.

In the background their networks began handshaking the reputational matrix of the deal. Sid hoped it wouldn't come to that. He was tracking the hundreds of identity tags that Bob left behind in his escape, multiplying these by the thousands of exit points and the dense transport network.

Bob could be almost anywhere in the world by now.

# 2

THE PRIEST WATCHED the young man in the next cell. So young, and yet he couldn't ignore the signs. He looked out through the rusted bars of his own cell, shuffling his feet along the stone floors, looking for just the right angle. Yes, there it was, hanging in the blue sky, its tails spreading as it grew. There was not much time.

The young man groaned.

"Water?" asked the priest.

The heat inside the mud walls was oppressive under the relentless midday sun. The young man's eyes fluttered then opened. His breathing was heavy and ragged. His lips were cracked. "Yes, water, please," whispered the young man.

Reaching under the folds of his thobe, the priest produced a leather bladder. He extended his wiry arm between the bars of their adjoining cells.

STILL COMING TO his senses, Bob blinked. His meta-cognition systems were coming back online, but his neural load of smarticles was low. How long had he been out? He didn't know, but he needed a refill. He didn't have enough in his system to reach out to the satellite networks: he had no GPS or tracking information. Bob's eyes darted around the room, collecting information.

His internal systems were busy mapping his immediate environment.

The man in the cell next to him smiled, revealing a mouthful of blackened teeth, and he held up a leather pouch. Water sloshed within it. Bob studied the man: faded keffiyeh headdress, deeply creased face of battered leather, watery eyes laced with cataracts.

Bob's pssi posited an origin for the man: Bedouin.

It was near zero humidity and over a hundred and thirty degrees. He had to be in the Sahara somewhere. It was within the range of the launch energy of the passenger cannon pod when he'd blacked out.

Taking the bladder from the Bedouin, Bob mumbled, "Thank you."

He lifted himself up on one elbow and drank. He'd never been this dehydrated before. His biostats were all over the place. Heat stroke was setting in. Just raising himself up brought a wave of nausea.

"Slowly," urged the Bedouin, his palms up. "Drink slowly."

Bob looked at the bladder of water, then the dusty floor. The Weather Wars had wreaked havoc on this corner of the world. There were rivers of water in the sky just as there were rivers of water in the ground, and weather tech was enabling rich countries to divert all of it. He took another swig from the bladder.

His proxxi, Robert, was still locked out, and Bob flexed his phantoms into the empty hyperspaces around him. Barely anything for them to hold onto, just the faint chatter of a cellular voice network at the edges of his senses. He let loose a splinter to see if it could burrow through, but its cognitive strength, like his own, was thin at best.

"'Where am I?'" the Bedouin said. "'Who am I?'" He smiled. "Yes, very good questions."

He seemed able to hear what Bob was thinking. Who was this old man? Or was he asking Bob to think about his own identity?

He was certain he was in northern Africa, but then again, as the old man's face swam in his visual fields, whether this was "reality" was another question. His body might still be in the passenger pod, while his awareness secreted away in a virtual world.

The aches and pains felt real enough, but how to verify that he was in base reality—the identity world? The only sure-fire way would be to kill himself—if his awareness snapped into another time and place, back in his body, then this world and space wasn't real. But if nothingness came afterward, then the world he was in, or rather had been in, was real—and there was no possibility of return. And of course, he didn't really know if nothingness came after death, either.

It wasn't an experiment he wanted to try quite yet.

Reaching inside his core with a phantom, he punched his Uncle Button, the hardwired fail-safe built into the deepest layer of the pssi operating system that snapped your consciousness back into your own body.

Nothing changed.

*This must be it, then.* Best to leave that final escape route for another day.

Taking another swig from the leather bladder, Bob leaned higher against the wall of his cell, feeling the straw embedded in the mud bricks prickling his back. He leaned over and inspected a wound on the side of his leg. Whoever snatched him had cut out his subcutaneous patch of smarticle reserves.

He had been in this area of the world once before, on a family holiday. His father hired a guide to take a sensor-scanner out into the Western Desert between Egypt and Libya. Some of the earliest Christian churches, from the first century, were in the ancient oasis towns that dotted the basins of the Sahara. There wasn't much detail in this area in the standard wikiworld, and hiring a guide to physically visit with the sensor enabled his family to flit in and "be there" from Atopia. The trip had been a gift from his father to his mother. She was a devout member of the Atopian Christian society, the Eleutherous.

Bob messed the whole trip up by missing the outings, and if he did make them, by heaping scorn on the idea of religion and poking holes in any stories the guide told. He ended the whole project by jamming the sensor with his dimstim traffic. It was an accident, but his mother had been quietly crushed by his thoughtlessness.

Thinking of his family, his stomach knotted.

He always found a way to mess things up. Barely two days after leaving the security of Deanna's place, and already everything had fallen apart. Why had Patricia put this on him, trusted him?

Then he remembered that he gave Nancy a copy of Patricia's data cube. Now he wanted to take it back. Maybe she hadn't found it yet.

"Life is suffering, young man," said the old man, watching him.

Bob looked at him. Life is suffering. "What do you mean?" He handed the water pouch back, letting his hand touch the old man's, just enough for a few smarticles to transfer from Bob's skin.

"It is obvious you are suffering." The old man tucked the pouch back in his thobe.

With a sweep of his phantoms across virtual workspace controls, Bob logged into the dusting of smarticles on the man's skin. Measuring skin potential was an old method of lie detection.

"I'm stuck in a jail, shouldn't I be suffering?"

"But suffering isn't necessary."

It was working. Bob was getting a baseline measurement of the man's skin tension. He switched tracks. "How did I get here? Were you here when I arrived?"

The old man looked up, opening the palm of his hand to the ceiling. "You dropped from the sky in a flaming chariot, as it was prophesied."

Bob groaned internally. Not another doomsdayer. "How did I get in the cell? Who put me here?"

Nodding, the old man narrowed his eyes. "Four men, one of them old Toothface."

His skin potential remained steady. He was telling the truth. Bob studied his face. "Are you with them?"

"No."

No reaction. Nothing that Bob could infer from the man's body language or facial markers or skin potential indicated he was lying. Bob relaxed slightly.

"And where are we?"

"Near Siwah, the town is several miles away. Just the four men are here, and us."

Bob decided the old man was telling the truth. "And why are you here?"

The old man laughed. "For seeking the truth."

Without an outside connection, Bob had to rely on his internal wikiworld maps. He did a quick flyover of the models of the maps and terrain he had, but there wasn't much resolution. He stood on his bunk and pressed his face against the metal bars of the window. Looking back and forth through the window, he reconstructed as much of a three-dimensional map of the area as he could, trying to correlate this with his internal maps.

He needed more information.

Bob looked around the sandy floor, searching, and there, in a corner, he saw a scarab beetle. Walking over he picked it up, blowing the dust off it, lifting it up to his mouth.

The old man watched, his eyes growing wide.

Spitting on the beetle, Bob gently began rubbing it. The old man frowned as he watched Bob massage the insect. Slowly, over several minutes, some of the smarticles in his saliva worked their way into the creature and suffused into its nervous system. Bob made a connection, opening up a sensory space that morphed into the beetle's. Looking up, he could see his own grotesquely large face peering down, could feel the beetle's terror. Calm down, he told it as he took control of its motor neurons, I'm a friend.

Bob's body put the beetle back on the ground, and his mind began scuttling off in it.

# 3

IN THE RECESSES of the shelves behind the bar, Vince watched cockroaches dart between dirt-encrusted bottles, their antennae waving in the darkness as they waited. He could only imagine what it must be like upstairs. "Could we get a room?" he asked, wishing he hadn't.

The bartender leered at them. "I could get you a fresh one."

"Yeah, that would be . . ." For a second Vince thought he was offering a clean room, until the jab in his ribs from Agent Connors. *Ah, he meant a fresh girl.* "No, this one's fine." He turned, winking at Agent Connors, taking in the scowl on her mud-and-blood splattered face. "Just the room."

There were a few regulars sitting at the bar, eyes staring straight ahead, their thoughts not on the future but the past. Vince wished he was one of them.

Two days ago they crash landed in the bayous of Louisiana. Spinning on impact, Vince's turbofan bounced off Agent Connor's aircraft, lessening the blow. Within seconds Vince extricated himself, amazed to be alive, and was running off through knee-deep water when his conscience hit him. He returned to pull the unconscious Agent Connors out of her cockpit, then splinted her broken leg before she came around. Slogging through the muck, he managed to find a small patch of dry ground.

For two days they struggled to stay alive out there. Once Connors regained consciousness, she made attempts to get in touch with her support teams, but they weren't responsive. This area of Louisiana was on the fringe of government control. Vince didn't stop her trying. He figured whatever the charges were, he was better off fighting them in court than fighting off whatever was in the swamp.

Connors tried to establish her control over the situation, but Vince had tossed her weapons into the swamp when she was unconscious. Vince didn't like guns. That turned out to be a bad idea. Their arrival brought scavengers of all kinds— garbage drones, swamp people, animals. While the machines and humans gave them a wide berth as Connors hurled verbal threats at them, the alligators weren't as easily dissuaded. Neither were the cottonmouths, deadly poisonous snakes that crawled everywhere.

Even with all that, the biggest problem became water. The standard-issue med kits in the turbofans didn't contain water purification tablets, and drinking the raw bayou water would bring on diarrhea or worse. As the day waned on the second night, battered and thirsty, with hope of rescue evaporating and the gators getting braver, Connors gave in. Vince managed to flag down some good old boys out hunting, and they'd hitched a ride into New Orleans.

The bartender in front of Vince curled his lip. "No rooms available, mister."

Vince frowned—the hologram outside said vacancy, as well as the online feed. "But your—"

"Did I stutter?"

New Orleans had been abandoned for a generation, at least officially. Doubly doomed, it was sinking while the oceans were rising, battered by wave after wave of monster hurricanes. Ninety percent of what used to be the city was below sea level, swamped, the old levees having long given up. Without the finances of New York to hold back the oceans, what remained of New Orleans had long gone feral.

Vince was about to argue when he felt another jab. Agent Connors flicked her chin toward the media hologram floating behind the bar. Vince looked up to stare into his own eyes. An image of his face was floating in the middle of the broadcast. "The former founder of Phuture News, Vince Indigo, indicted in federal courts today on conspiracy charges, is reported dead in a crash—"

The bartender glanced at the hologram. "Like I said, no rooms. Don't want my place wrecked in a raid."

"—New Orleans has been quarantined by DAD in a reported viral outbreak—"

"Should just throw you to them," growled a man hunched over his beer beside them. Black goggles covered most of his face, a sharp metal spike protruding from one eye. His leather vest was open to the waist, revealing skin laced in red welts of scars.

"Mind your tongue, Sledge," barked the bartender. "We don't give anyone up to the farmers, but that"—the bartender looked Vince square in the eyes—"don't mean I want you here." He rubbed stubble atop his head, then reached under the bar and threw something at Vince. "Now get out."

Vince recoiled, half expecting a grenade, but it was a first aid kit. "Thanks," he mumbled. He followed Agent Connors to the door. She was limping on her broken leg—well secured in a fast-cast— but their infected wounds were more of a problem.

Exiting the swinging saloon doors of the bar, they were hit by a wave of sweetly-putrid humidity and an explosion of noise— Bourbon Street. Officially New Orleans might have been abandoned, but unofficially, it was a backwater playground. The surrounding ten-block area was one of the few that remained above the high tide line, the swollen Mississippi swallowing the rest. Masses of revelers thronged the street, thousands of matchsticks rubbing shoulder-to-shoulder in the powder keg of the ancient Latin Quarter. Pounding music poured out from the sense-shifting doorways of bars and nightclubs.

"I think we should just drop her and run," said Hotstuff, materializing beside them in a halter top and shorts.

It was a thought Vince had wrestled with more than once, but whatever was chasing him was hunting Agent Connors now as well. When she tried to radio in, her credentials were revoked. She had no response at all. The enemy of your enemy could be a friend, and right now, after losing track of Bob and Sid, Vince needed all the friends he could get—and besides, he was confident he could ditch her pretty quick the moment he didn't need her.

"I'm going to remind you again that you're still my prisoner," Agent Connors said. A hulking mandroid, more machine than human, stumbled into her and she swore, shoving it away. Turning, it laughed, reeking of alcohol, and spun back into the crowd.

"And maybe I should tell this crowd that you're FBI."

Drones hovered overhead, hawking the newest synthetic drugs, skinshops, and real-human-meat kebabs—delicacies left over from body mod surgeries. Human-animal chimeras—of course Grillas, but also frog-faced thugs and reptilian conmen—hung in doorways between the mechanoids and humanoids. Flashes of New Orleans' past forced themselves into Vince's sensory frames, reality skins that were being pumped out as hard and fast from the bars almost as furiously as the music, and all of it drenched in alternating stench-waves of sweat and urine.

Pain shot through Vince's back. "Can we stop for a minute? Get a drink?"

Agent Connors nodded. She didn't look any better than Vince felt.

That being said, Vince felt as comfortable here as Agent Connors was uncomfortable. Louisiana was where his family originated. He smiled. The world still needs lawless places. He always liked a good party. Even if the world burned down around this place, people would still be coming here to celebrate, and to hide. The world needed criminals just as much as it needed heroes—and anyway, the difference between a criminal and a hero was more often a matter of timing than moral compass.

At least, he hoped it was.

# 4

"SILICON GONE WRONG, 'bad glass,' get it?" Sibeal was trying to explain why her group was called the glasscutters. "We hunt down bad glass, errant digital organisms." She looked at the ceiling. "But I wouldn't call them criminals. Really they're just misguided pieces of code."

The White Horse was bustling at the end of a busy day for the undergrounders. The main bar, of curving polished mahogany, was packed two deep with people ordering pints, their arms high, waving at the bartender. The plush carpeting underfoot smoothed the hubbub of voices, and overhead lighting reflected from polished brass banisters and the mirror-lined walls.

Sid was running background simulations of escape routes, creating ever-more-elaborate systems and models of the networks around him. "Whatever works for you," he replied to Sibeal, shrugging. Most of his attention was on a simulation where he was uncorking beer kegs to hide a dramatic escape. It'd become more of a game than a serious undertaking, and Sibeal was forcing him to maintain his primary presence with her. Really, he was sulking.

"Doesn't matter what name you attach to a thing," rumbled the Grilla, sitting across from Sibeal. It lifted a tankard of beer as big as Sid's midsection to its lips. "If it's done badly, it's responsible."

Sid looked at him. "So if a lion eats an antelope, we should book it for murder?"

The Grilla slammed its drink down. "Want to start into the Africa jokes?"

Sid almost fell out of his chair. The Grilla's nostrils flared, and anger seemed to swell it double in size. "No . . . I didn't mean . . ."

The Grilla's hackles eased down. It turned to Sibeal. "Still need me?"

She shook her head, and the Grilla gulped down the remains of its beer and stormed off.

Sid eased back to the table. "Testy."

Sibeal watched the retreating Grilla. "That's Furball, by the way. He's cuddly when you get to know him." She looked back at Sid. "Only his friends call him Furball. Best for you to stick to his name—Zoraster."

"Zoraster? Seriously?"

Sibeal nodded. "So is it a deal?"

She wanted Sid to get Willy to talk to her. Sibeal's glasscutter guild had tracking information on Willy's body—there was a huge bounty—and she was offering to share it if he'd introduce her to Willy, get his primary subjective down for a chat. This was the reason the glasscutters had initially contacted Sid. She figured that if she could talk to Willy directly, she might be able to figure out where his body was.

Sid doubted it, but didn't see it doing any harm. Despite the massive resources they exhausted, the only thing Sid and his friends had managed to confirm was that it was Willy's proxxi that stole his body. Hearing that the glasscutters had a lead was the first real bright spot.

Sid wasn't even sure what the mission was anymore. Bob had disappeared, was maybe captured, maybe worse, and the same for Vince. Sid had a very thin list of options. Throwing in with bounty hunters seemed morally questionable, but then Sid based decisions on what made sense to get to the objective, and not on the shifting sands of morality. And he didn't have other options. Something was better than nothing. "Sure," he replied. "I'll get Willy down here."

"And I want to see what's in that data beacon, just me, strictly private," Sibeal added.

Sid and Vicious were having trouble unpacking the data beacon Bob left for them. Bob had been careful, wrapping it in layers of shared-memetic encryption only Sid could decode, and it was taking a long time to unwrap. And why would he share whatever he found with her? At the very least, this was more leverage he could use later. He picked his beer up. "I don't think so—"

Two giant metal hands crashed through the walls of the bar, ripping through brick and mortar, tearing a hole. Sid and Sibeal barely flinched. Bunky's face appeared in the gaping ruin. "This here's a workingman's pub, none of this fancy-dancy stuff . . ."

The reality skin Sibeal and Sid were sharing slipped away like paint dropped in water. The rusting corrugated tin roof of the real White Horse appeared over them. Bunky was standing on one of the hands of his construction mechanoid, back from work. Shaky, of course, was next to him, and smiling just as goofily.

A serving bot slapped two beers down in front of Bunky and Shaky, and they roared in laughter. Beers from Sid had become something of a ritual. "I do like this guy," Shaky said to Bunky. They picked up their pints, and Sibeal walked over to greet them.

Sid leaned back and looked around the cavern floor from his view from the White Horse two stories up. He noticed there was an Eleutherous meeting hall to one side, and more Grillas had arrived, working on the diggers and constructors in the pits below.

Before being abducted by one, he'd never seen a Grilla up close and personal before.

Animal-human chimeras, bred for combat in the Weather Wars, Grillas were yet another ill-considered ambition with unintended consequences. Animal-human chimeras had been around for a long time, starting with pigs grown with human organs for transplants. It was only a short step for some researchers, less averse to chimeric tinkering, to experiment with human voice boxes and frontal lobes in male silverbacks.

The world had been in a moral uproar until the first reports of the raging silverback battalions, in full battle armor, ripping their opposition to pieces in Weather War battles high in the Himalayas. After that, the moral tide turned into a debate about sending "our boys" into battle against them. Almost overnight, all sides had their own Grilla units.

Even unaided by an exoskeleton, a combat Grilla could dead lift two tons, scale forty-foot walls, and if all other weapons systems failed, rely on a fearsome set of fangs. They were famous for having bad tempers, but then again, if you sprang into existence to discover that your Creators were human assholes, you'd be pissed off, too.

In this high-speed-evolution world, after a few years robotics became cheaper than Grillas, especially when the larger costs—urban ghettos filled with creatures returned from the wars, half-accorded rights and civil unrest, long-term health and safety issues—became obvious. They'd now been banned from urban centers, an entire generation of a doomed race, and relegated to places like this.

But cost was only half the story.

The human mimicry of synthetics and bots was one thing, but looking into a Grilla's eyes, you couldn't help but feel like you were peering into your own soul—and humans reserved a special hatred for things that reminded them of themselves.

# 5

"JUST BE CAREFUL of him," said one of the men.

Must be the one the old man called Toothface.

Cranial gene-mod therapy tended to induce hyperdontia when done badly. The man's head was grotesquely mushroomed on one side and a second and third set of teeth had grown in over his first. He wiped drool from his mouth with the back of one hand. Making it worse, he had a shabby reality filter fixed over top of it all, a transparent overlay showing off the large brain that had grown inside the shell of his expanded skull.

Then again, part of what Bob was seeing might be an artifact of the sensory mapping.

He was struggling to make sense of the scarab beetle's neural pathways, trying to wrest control of its six legs from the still-skittish owner. The beetle tried to scurry back under the door, but Bob held it firm, edging it forward.

Bob had a splinter working to correlate the view from the thousands of lens in its compound eye into something understandable to his own visual cortex, but the experience was unnerving. The image of the men in the room ballooned, as if he was looking into a carnival mirror, slowly coming into focus but then distorting again, the men glowing in the infrared-shifted spectrum of the insect's vision.

"When is . . ." one of the other men said. His lips kept moving but the audio feed slipped into garbled static. Bob tunneled down into the tibiae of the beetle, the thin cuticle ear drum located on its front legs. Instead of trying to interpret nerve packets at the end of the trachea, it might be better to go straight to the timpani. It worked, and the sound information normalized. ". . . so will be here the day after tomorrow?"

"Yes," Toothface replied. "The kid's neural load is bleeding out fast. The priest is dangerous, he knows—"

The priest, Bob thought, looking at the old man in the cell beside his. So the old man was a priest.

The terrified beetle managed to override Bob for a second and shifted under the doorway, garbling the sound again. Bob steadied it, sending soothing impressions into its primitive awareness, trying to match his brain's gamma frequency waves to those of the insect's optic lobes.

Not for the first time, Bob wished he had his proxxi there to help him. Robert was still locked out. Something happened in the event under New York that warped his pssi interface.

"—just stay out of that room," continued Toothface's voice after a second or two. "Keep him isolated. Is that clear?"

The other men nodded. Bob noticed a clutch of keys on one of their belts. Toothface sat down at a wooden table in the middle of the room while one of the men went to fill a kettle from the well outside.

"The forty-year war is nearing its end," said the Bedouin to Bob. "They're getting desperate."

Bob held the beetle steady, shifting his primary awareness back into his body. He'd ghosted into insects before, but beetles had undergone an explosion of radial evolution that resulted in a bewildering array of sensory systems. He had never inhabited a scarab beetle before, but he was getting the hang of it.

"The Weather Wars, you mean?" Bob replied to the Bedouin.

Depending on what you defined as the starting point, the Weather Wars had been going on about that long. But how would capturing Bob have anything to do with that long-drawn-out conflict? Bob looked at the old priest more carefully. They said he was dangerous. How?

The priest shrugged. "Attach what names you like."

There were no digital or network systems in here, no listening devices, so nobody could hear them. This was more to protect them than me, thought Bob. No way for him to escape digitally. Everything about this place was as primitive as possible, including the physical locks. He had to get those keys.

"The star with two tails is rising in the morning sky again," the Bedouin added. "Gog and Magog are unshackled."

Bob stared at him. The main danger this guy seemed to be was to himself. He played along. "So this is it, then, the end of the world?" In an overlaid display, his insect-mind watched the men in the other room pouring tea.

"Not the end, a rebirth." The Bedouin looked out his window at the sky. "But yes, it will be the end of this world."

"And that's a good thing?"

The Bedouin sat down on his cot. "I am not excited, not afraid, but embracing, accepting." He took a deep breath. "The world must be cleansed. Our suffering must be brought to an end."

Despite his disdain, a part of Bob could understand what the priest meant. He'd been sheltered on Atopia, but much of the world was a horrible place, plagued by war, disaster, famine. The pattern was repeating. After enslaving the natural world, humans were now enslaving the endless virtual worlds and creatures they were creating. It wasn't something Bob thought about much, protected and isolated on Atopia, but coming out into the world was changing his perspective.

The men in the next room laughed, and Bob sharpened his awareness in the beetle.

"No more dirty desert after this," Toothface said. "With the money we get for this kid."

"If he's so dangerous, maybe we should just cut him up into pieces," laughed one of the men, pulling a cruelly curved knife from his belt. "Just to be sure he doesn't go anywhere."

Toothface liked that and slapped the table, all of them joining in laughter. "Maybe we should," he said gruffly, and the laughing stopped.

Letting the beetle slip back under the doorway, Bob looked at the priest through the bars of the jail. "Is there anything bigger than a beetle I could get my hands on out here?"

# 6

THE MAN IN front of Vince held onto the bars of the balcony railing as if they were the bars of a cell. "Buddy, you got some smarties? Just a little," he begged, "just a taste."

Not a man, realized Vince, staring into the desperate face, but a boy, emaciated with that same hollow look all junkies shared. "Sorry—"

"Please, I know you have some, I can sense them." The boy reached through the bars and grabbed Vince's arm.

"Hey!" Vince pulled away, and the boy jumped back, rubbing the fingers he'd touched Vince with into the back of his neck. He'd swiped a few of Vince's smarticles onto his fingers, and was rubbing them into the spot closest to his pleasure centers, trying to eke out a tiny jolt of endorphins in a fantasy world.

"Should just give the kid what he wants." Agent Connors yawned.

Smarticles, the tiny neuro-reactive engines that powered commercial pssi, were a controlled substance internationally. In the big cities, Cognix was giving it away for free, hooking a populace that would pay for it later. This place, however, was outside any legal-licensed jurisdiction, which meant having *real* smarticles was illegal—though that didn't mean everyone wasn't copying them.

And they definitely weren't free.

"Not going to happen," Vince replied.

Money wasn't the problem. Sid had created their own private smarticle stash for their gang, to shield them from prying eyes. Vince swallowed his in a time-release capsule that had attached itself to the inside of his small intestine. He didn't want them getting around. They could be used to track him.

"So what's our next step?" Vince asked Connors.

Two bloodied and ragged people leaning on each other blended perfectly into the melee of Bourbon Street, lending them a cloak of invisibility, but everywhere they went for a room, they were turned away. Of course the bars were open twenty-four hours, so they still had somewhere to go.

"We wait." Agent Connors settled herself into a corner beside Vince.

Vince leaned back and closed his eyes. She might not have any connections here, but he did. He sent out some bots to test the local underground. Hotstuff was feeding him threat reports, his mind cycling through images and situational reports.

He watched a pack of pickpockets, a gang of neurally-fused teenagers that were circling through the crowd, prowling. Even in the short time they'd been there, Vince had watched a breathtaking progression of trending memes moving through the crowd, evolving hourly, new forms morphing from old; an influx of new machines, neural formations, virtual worlds, reality skins.

True mind-uploading was beyond current technology. Research into it was banned in many places—mostly on moral and legal grounds, and on religious ones in America—but the distinction was blurring. The meta-cognition frameworks of most "people" were outweighing their meat brains. The logic behind the original bans, clear just years and months ago, was becoming irrelevant as pssi permeated the population.

When the turbofan went down, he'd assumed he was going to die. They were too high, it was too fast, they had no protection from his networks. The survivability matrix was nil. In the flames and noise he'd closed his eyes, waiting.

And then nothing.

When he regained consciousness, it was quiet, just the sound of bullfrogs groaning in the darkness. He was soaked, twisted together in the metal and plastic wreck. He didn't feel anything. Relaxing into what he assumed was his coming death, he closed one eye, looking at the stars in the sky, then opened it and closed the other. Two working eyes. Pausing, he tried wiggling his toes—and no spinal cord injury. Gingerly pulling himself out from the wreck, he'd checked his body for gaping bodily wounds. None of those either.

Amazing.

On closer inspection, he found some wounds to one leg, a cut clear across his face, but nothing major. Just seconds before he'd been at peace with death, and now, it was like he was reborn. He expected he would be horrified, in shock, after a traumatic accident where he was injured, almost killed, but it was quite the opposite. Vince had been overjoyed, ecstatic, hopping around in the swamp examining the mangled turbofan, marveling at it. He cheated death once again, and this time by himself.

Vince opened his eyes and looked at Agent Connors. She was asleep.

"She's pretty, isn't she?"

Vince looked up to see Hotstuff, her eyebrows arched as she stared at him.

"Huh?"

"Whatever." Hotstuff was streaming him summaries of the threat reports. It wasn't much—they didn't have much network access—but then again, there wasn't anything to report either. It seemed that cutting him off from Phuture News had also separated Vince from whatever was chasing him.

"Any questions?" asked Hotstuff.

"Um, no, this looks . . ." but Hotstuff signed off and faded away without letting Vince finish his sentence. He frowned.

"I think your proxxi is jealous."

Vince turned to see Agent Connors smiling at him, her eyes half open. He forgot that he had opened his pssi channels to her and she was able to see his proxxi. He had wanted to be sure that she had the same situational data he had. They were in a dangerous spot.

"Of you?" snorted Vince, shaking his head and returning his attention to the nearly empty threat reports.

"The second we get out of here, make no mistake, you're going to jail," continued Agent Connors. "So don't get any ideas."

Vince looked at her. "Me? Ideas?"

Agent Connors rolled her eyes before closing them again.

Hotstuff popped back into his visual frame, sitting across the table from him. "There's someone coming," she whispered.

Before Vince could ask, Hotstuff sent him the report. An Ascetic was walking toward them. So his feelers had found something. Vince spun a viewpoint outside, watching the crowd of partygoers part like the Red Sea around the advancing figure—a stump of flesh suspended between six spindly metal legs, gliding spider-like across the ground.

Vince kicked Agent Connor's leg under the table, and she jolted awake. He spun the information packets on this Ascetic into her networks.

"Mr. Indigo, I presume," the Ascetic hissed directly into his head. It wasn't speaking. It had no mouth. It closed the last few feet of distance by lifting itself up on its hind legs to bring its head even with their balcony.

"Yes." What was he supposed to say? There wasn't any use running.

"I have someone who wants to meet you," continued the Ascetic, the naked slab of its body hanging in space in front of them. Skin was grafted across its face, pulled taut; no eyes, no ears, no mouth. "Someone you've been wanting to meet."

"We're not going anywhere," whispered Agent Connors.

The Ascetic turned its body toward her, revealing a large, square cross emblazoned on its flesh. "I am deaf, but I hear all, I am blind, but I see all. Ms. Connors, do you see?"

Sheila's face went pale. "What do you want?"

"It is not what I want," hissed the Ascetic, just a voice in their heads. "But what you want."

# 7

"WE DON'T HUNT people." Sibeal looked up, considering her statement. "Or, we don't hunt humans. You're our first."

Willy's primitive avatar flickered. As the Alliance—America and Atopia and its allies—blockaded data pathways to Terra Nova, there wasn't enough clean bandwidth getting through for him to project something more sophisticated. It was becoming obvious they were planning some new action against Terra Nova, but the mediaworlds, and even Phuture News, remained quiet.

"You're not hunting me," said Willy's avatar after a pause. "Just my body."

Sibeal nodded. "Not really even your body—we're hunting your proxxi, Wally, who's stolen your body."

Even Sid stopped for a moment to contemplate just how weird this situation was. He'd convinced Willy to come down and talk to the glasscutters, but his signal was getting weak. Even if the signal from Willy's body was being routed through Terra Nova, his virtual presence wasn't allowed inside it, and transmissions from Terra Nova weren't allowed outside in Allied space anymore. His awareness was being squeezed into the thin cracks of the multiverse in between.

Willy's avatar remained static for a few seconds, and just when Sid thought the connection had been lost—"I'm not sure Wally is responsible," came the audio stream from the avatar, but its lips didn't move. "He might be doing what I asked, or what he thought I asked."

Sid had filled everyone in, about Willy telling his proxxi to keep them safe, no matter what, when he was running his illegal business.

"So you're saying it wasn't him?" echoed ReVurb, the phracker—phuture cracker—Sibeal invited to be part of her team.

Sid didn't trust phrackers. Even if they weren't telling the truth, they could engineer the future so what they were telling you became true. They were slippery. Only a small part of a phracker was in the present. Most of them hung around in expensively maintained alternate future realities that spun outward from the present moment in time. The other parts of them sat in the past, winding through post-factual worlds that could have happened if different decisions were made.

"I'm sure it's my proxxi that stole my body," Willy replied. "But I'm saying he's not responsible."

"Because you set him on this course?"

After an even longer pause, Willy's avatar nodded. Sibeal and ReVurb had been interrogating Willy for a good hour already.

"So me and Willy have held up our end of the bargain." Sid stretched his phantom limbs. "How about you show us what you know?"

Sibeal looked at ReVurb, who nodded, and data packets were sent into Sid and Willy's networks. Sibeal pulled their primary subjectives into a view of the American east coast from a hundred miles up, overlaying the names of cities and districts.

"Each of these," Sibeal explained, pointing toward red dots that appeared one by one, "are suspected points of entry by Willy's body into the AEC infrastructure."

"Suspected?" Sid frowned. "But I thought you had something concrete—"

With a stuttering breath, ReVurb pulled himself into the present. "He's invisible in the zero timeframe, we can only derive his appearance by second-order artifacts in the positive and negative—"

"I get it," interrupted Sid, assimilating the data they'd sent him. They couldn't observe Willy's body directly in any data feeds, only a derivative of him in the past and future, like the wake of an invisible boat. Even so, Sid should have been able to see it.

"There's some very strong glass at work here," added Sibeal, "like nothing we've ever seen before."

A light bulb went off in Sid's head. "And the only reason you saw any of this was because Willy came into the underground."

"Right, we have our own sensor networks." Sibeal pointed at the city centers of New York, Philadelphia, Washington, then spun the globe to indicate other points of contact in London, Paris, and Istanbul with the trail fading in southern Asia. "This is as much as we have."

"So where am I now?" Willy asked. "Do we have an end—"

His avatar flickered and then dimmed. Sid swore and dove into his workspace, trying to route alternate connections for Willy's mind. In fits and starts, the avatar began to reappear.

"I'm doing everything I can," Sid said to Willy in a private space. With Bob gone, Sid felt responsible for Willy. It had become a personal point of pride to outsmart the Alliance filters, to keep the data coming so Willy could stay with them, but his pride was melting into fear for his friend. Sid didn't have a lot of friends.

"I know," Willy replied. "I'd better send you some information Vince sent me—"

Sid nodded, sensing some data packets arriving, and just then Willy's avatar completely disappeared.

Before Sid could give chase, ReVurb blocked his exits into the data pipes out of the underground. "Don't bother, it's hopeless."

"We do have some news—would you like the good or bad first?" Sibeal said after they let Sid work in futile silence for a few seconds.

"Why do people keep asking me that?" Sid didn't wait for an answer. He was still working in the background, but he knew Willy wasn't coming back. He'd had enough with the bad news. "Okay, good news this time."

"It seems Mr. Indigo survived the crash. We've located him in New Orleans." ReVurb smiled. "At least, that's what they're going to announce in the news tomorrow."

Vince was the granddaddy of the phrackers, although he was on the other side of a line that was increasingly thin. Now he was indicted, he'd practically joined their ranks. Probably something Vince, in his position, should have seen coming. In all cases, ReVurb seemed to be happy about it.

Sid waited. "And the bad?"

"The Ascetics have taken him."

*Well at least he's not dead*, and then quickly on the heels of that thought, *but he might wish he was if they couldn't get to him soon.* "Anything new on Bob?"

Everyone there—Sibeal, ReVurb, Bunky—shook their heads.

Sid's proxxi pinged him, dragging his point-of-view into a workspace world. "What's so important?" Sid grumbled. Vicious opened up a display. Before his avatar disappeared, Willy sent them some documents that Vince had forwarded him.

Willy's proxxi had been reading religious texts at the Commune. Vicious did a statistical analysis on the texts and one line stood out, something scrawled in the margins, a line Vicious couldn't find any contextual links to: "The beginning of man, where time stops in a thousand tongues." What the hell did that mean?

# 8

MOLEHILLS BECAME MOUNTAINS, at least from the point of view of the beetle Bob struggled to keep control of. The blanket of stars of the deep Sahara, thick enough for even an insect to imagine it could reach up and touch, hung above him in the sky. Moonrise was coming. He had to hurry.

Two legs forward, two legs back, two other legs forward, first two legs back. Just keep the rhythm, Bob kept telling himself. He couldn't see it yet, but even without a three-dimensional overlay map, the beetle's keen sense of smell was homing them in to the garbage pile.

*Come on, you love this smelly stuff,* Bob urged to the beetle's small mind. But the beetle knew: here there were predators.

The beetle topped a tiny crest of sand, each grain the size of a boulder, and the town's garbage dump came into view. It was pitch black, but in the insect's infrared-shifted vision the garbage glowed with heat against the cold desert floor. Within the glow, something shifted, something brighter, and then another.

The rats were feeding.

The beetle's legs backpedaled, quivering, but Bob pushed it forward.

Bob's smarticle count was low, and keeping a communication link at nearly a half a mile was pushing his limits. Soon he would be empty. Already he felt the symptoms of withdrawal—his tweaking neurons, the buzzing itch on his insides that couldn't be scratched.

I'm sorry, Bob wanted to tell the beetle, I need help. I need you to sacrifice yourself for me. He wanted to explain how this was the only way. But how to explain that to a creature, any creature, that their time must come to an end so that yours could continue, that there was some other good that required their death.

But there was no time for that. Bob pushed and pushed, ignoring the keening terror in the mind he was sharing. The looming pile grew larger, and then one of the warm red patches stopped, the saucers of its eyes turning toward Bob-beetle. In an instant it was over, the rat darting in and snatching the beetle from the desert floor, the beetle's fear for an instant eclipsing the brightest of stars overhead.

And then nothing.

Bob's telepresent link went blank, but he waited, maintaining the connection to the smarticles in the beetle's body, which was becoming a part of the rat's. The transfer was incomplete, but an image began forming. Mammals were much closer to home, much simpler to inhabit. Bob-rat now looked up from the garbage pile, tasting the remains of beetle shell in the back of his mouth.

Rubbing his eyes, Bob withdrew his primary subjective back into the jail cell and looked around. In amplified low-light he surveyed the walls, watched the priest sleeping in the cot in the cell next to him, and listened carefully to the snoring of one of the men in the front. Nothing had changed, so he slipped his consciousness back into the rat.

The smarticle density was too low for Bob to control the rat's nervous system entirely, so he had to be selective. He tweaked the rat's keen sense of smell. There's something delicious in that structure up the road, was the message Bob implanted. The rat froze, its head swiveling to the horizon, and then it was off, scurrying toward the jail.

# 9

"SO HOW DO you like jail?" asked Vince, taking a gulp from his beer. He wasn't too concerned about the Ascetics. They were criminals, if ones built around a quasi-religious cult centered on self-denial. He understood criminals, and it was always just about the money—it was never personal. Anyway, he was the one that contacted them. More distressing was his inability to see the future since Agent Connors' team took away his Phuture News access. The lack of control was an itch he couldn't scratch.

Connors leaned over the railing of their room's wrought-iron balcony, inspecting the exterior wall. The noise of Bourbon Street echoed from several stories below, while the whine of electric VTOLs spun through the black skies. She leaned back in and turned around. "Is that supposed to be clever?"

"I mean," Vince mumbled, "just wondering if you're having any insight into what it feels like yourself." He smiled. "It's just a question." Flopping down onto one of the two beds, Vince placed his beer on the center console and began playing with the room's controls, but nothing activated. He frowned and gave up. "No matter how much the world changes, you know what stays the same?"

Sighing, Connors bowed her head. "What?"

"Beds!" said Vince, slapping the one he was on. "All this technology, all this change, and beds are pretty much the same thing as five hundred years ago, I'd bet."

Connors leaned out over the railing again. "You're like a seventy-year-old kid, you know that?"

Vince frowned and then smiled. "I'd bet a million dollars I know what you're thinking."

"A million dollars is about what you spend on a pair of shoes, isn't it?"

"You know what I mean." He took a sip of his beer. "You're thinking, with one good leap I could just make it over to that next balcony." He took another sip. "There's no need to look out there. Hotstuff mapped the walls, exterior features, interior corridors."

It was about a thirty-foot vertical drop onto concrete. Connors sighed. "But you don't want to escape?"

"Not question of want, we're in their territory. I've gone through thousands of scenarios, and the best one is to sit tight. We can negotiate our way out."

She turned to him. "You know what I think?"

He sat up and smiled. "What?"

"I think you want to be here."

"Want to be here? If I don't get out of here, I could lose a couple of hundred-billion dollars." With the charges filed against him, he could stand to lose more than just Phuture News. He could end up in jail. A real jail, where he wouldn't be able to escape into simulated reality. A confined concrete cell. No future, no movement, no control—the thought made Vince ill. He put his beer down.

Connors laughed. "I'm sure you can tie up the courts for years. I bet you have cash squirreled away all over the place. Characters like you always have escape routes planned."

That was pretty accurate, Vince had to admit. He nodded and picked up his beer again. Hotstuff, sitting in the corner, raised her eyebrows. Vince slouched into the silk pillows, inspecting the gold-flecked wallpaper and brass lighting fixtures above his head.

Connors gave up on the outside. Leaning on the balcony railing, she turned to Vince. "So you said I had it wrong?"

"Yeah."

"How so?"

"We were trying to do the right thing when I breached all those future confidences." Vince sensed that doing the right thing was what drove Connors forward.

"And what was this thing?"

"We found out that Cognix was hiding some test results on pssi."

"I heard about that. So that was you guys who forced it out?"

Vince shrugged. "Didn't quite work out like that, but we pushed the issue."

"Interesting." Connors considered this. "And you don't think your friend Robert Baxter had anything to do with the attack in New York?"

"No way." Vince shook his head vigorously. "He's a good kid. Can be a bit of a flake . . ."

Connors smiled. "And this coming from you?"

Vince smiled back. Finally, a sense of humor. "Bob's one bright kid."

"Not just a kid, a pssi-kid," corrected Connors. "It's hard to know what they might be capable of. They're . . ." She paused, searching for the right words.

"Not human?" Vince offered. "That's not true. They're just like us, but slightly more advanced. People 2.0."

"If you say so." Connors pressed her hands together at her chin. It was her thinking pose. "And you know Baxter this well how?"

"From surfing together."

Connors' head sagged and she snorted. "Surfing together. Wow."

Vince sat upright in the bed. "You can tell a lot about a person from surfing with them. Board meetings, we'd call them, sitting in the swells and chatting. Bob has a lot of friends. That says something about someone."

"Sure. A lot of criminals have a lot of friends."

"Funny." He put his beer down. "I'm being serious. The way someone lets other people get up on the waves, helps out if there's a problem. He's a straight shooter, nice guy, whatever you want to call it, but he didn't unleash some weapon that hurt people. Of that I'm sure. His worst crime is being a little nosy."

Connors paused. "I heard he's a drug addict."

Vince stared at her. "And did you also hear his twin brother killed himself?"

"Yeah, I did . . ."

"So give the kid a break."

Connors pushed herself off the railing and came into the room. She sat down on the bed opposite Vince. "And what about Sidney Horowitz. Do you think he had anything to do with that reality virus that nearly wrecked Atopia?"

Vince didn't answer as quickly this time. "Naw. Sid likes to think of himself as a rebel, likes to play pranks, even get up to some mischief, but he's a good kid, too. A bit of a loner, but a good kid."

"Forensics said his digital fingerprints were all over that thing."

"Maybe, but it wasn't Sid that unleashed it."

"You sound awfully sure." Connors narrowed her eyes. "What aren't you telling me?"

Vince finished off a last gulp from his beer. He put the empty bottle down. "What do you mean?"

"Makes you look awfully suspicious to jump off Atopia right after someone sabotaged it, then go and hide. If you guys had nothing to do with it, what are you doing out here?"

Sighing, Vince picked up a pillow and fluffed it, then stuck it behind his back and leaned against the headboard. "I'm not sure how much I should tell you." Patricia had given them strict instructions to keep this to themselves. If nothing else, Vince liked sticking to a plan.

Agent Connors pointed toward the locked door. "We should be working together to find a way out of this. I know you have more information than you're telling me."

"Work together?" Vince threw his hands in the air. "Find a way out of this? We are only in this because of you." He swung his legs off the bed to face her. "And I should help you for what, so you can drag me to jail? I saved your life."

Connors didn't flinch or back away. "Someone's got a quick temper."

"You come out of nowhere, try and snatch me out of the sky. You know nothing about me—"

Agent Connors held one finger up in Vince's face. "Oh, I know you."

"You know me?" He looked at the ceiling and then back at her. "Why don't you tell me, then?"

"I know you stole Phuture News away from your business partner when you started up."

Vince stared at Connors. "You know nothing about that." He took a deep breath. "Want me to describe you?"

Connors shrugged.

"Let me see," began Vince. "Workaholic, never married"—one hand shot up—"wait, married to the academy. That's you." He rocked back a little. "I bet your dad was a cop."

Connors' face remained impassive.

"Yeah, that's it. Trying to live up to Daddy, always needing to prove yourself. That's why you tried to snatch me out of the sky. All this drama. You need to prove yourself."

"Not bad," said Connors quietly. "But I know you, too."

"Oh yeah? Try me."

"Just another rich asshole who thinks he's above everyone else."

# 10

"FOR THE MONEY, of course," replied Bunky.

Sid volunteered to help Shaky and Bunky repair one of the construction mechanoids. Melodies of a Lynyrd Skynyrd song echoed from a hundred years in the past. The music filled the virtual worlds Sid was building for the simulations. He had never heard the song before—a tribute from another time to an Alabama homeworld—but it was growing on him. Bunky picked it.

"I mean, it's not just the money," Shaky added, "it's our jobs, like, you know what I mean, mate?"

They were trying to explain to Sid why they'd kidnapped him. On Atopia, money had never really been a motivator. It was just something that existed, in the background, secondary to the grand experiment that was Atopia. With unlimited access to synthetic reality, who needed money to buy things? You could just spawn as much of anything you liked, at any time, and perfect health was an unspoken part of the deal. On the outside, however, all these things he had for free on Atopia—the smarticles, unlimited multiverse access, skins—cost money.

"It wasn't really about kidnapping you, mind you." Bunky clapped Sid on the shoulder. "We were just securing you. The money was supposed to come from the bounty for catching Willy's proxxi."

Sid was discovering the extent of the obsession with money and material luxury that filled the collective conscience outside Atopia. "Yeah, I got that."

He was building virtual-world models of the rotator cuff joint of Bunky's construction mechanoid, trying to fix a broken seal. Bunky and Shaky were riding along with him, in toy-balloon avatars attached to his consciousness as he spun through his virtual worlds. Sid looked up to see Bunky-balloon smile, a big grin with one front tooth broken in half.

"Do you not get your tooth fixed because of the money?" Sid asked.

Health care was the other fixation. Elective gene modifications could double life expectancy for the rich, but even basic health wasn't always guaranteed for the poor. Atopia's pssi technology was being applied across the systemic injustice like a numbing salve to treat a mortal wound.

Sid wasn't philosophical by nature—that was Bob's domain—but it was hard not to ponder the more time he spent out here. He understood that the basics of economics had moved from products to services, and were now moving to trading information for the purpose of self-advantage in the purest form of the idea. What exactly the "self" referred to was the new problem. The definition of a "person" was losing coherence in the face of synthetic intelligences, neural fusioning, and the expanding cloud of information that made up a person.

Shaky-balloon roared out laughing at Sid's question. "Ha, no mate, Bunky here is deathly afraid of anyone drilling into that thick slab of a skull!"

Bunky-balloon glowed red. Sid smiled.

"Almost done," Sid said, shifting attention away from Bunky. "Can you see the array?"

Sid tried splintering the solution sets to Bunky and Shaky, but their external meta-cognition frameworks were childlike. Instead he began flipping through a series of images, showing each option visually.

Bunky and Shaky nodded as one. "Yeah, sort of," they both replied. If Sid didn't know better, he would have suspected they were neurally fused, but he knew they were just best friends.

The simulations were set in motion, and Sid spun the most likely scenario, a hollowed-out view of a giant robotic arm rotating in a three-dimensional space around Shaky and Bunky's perspectives. Sid chuckled. They weren't the sharpest cheeses in the drawer, but they had no problem understanding complex geometries.

"What's it like, like?" Bunky asked.

Sid was deep into modifying his virtual-world model. "What's what like?" It was the first time he'd gotten to work on repairing a complex robot first hand.

"Being a pssi-kid—isn't it kind of freaky, like? Is it true you don't see any difference between the real world and virtual worlds?"

Sid paused. If you'd asked him that question a few weeks ago, he'd have agreed. His virtual worlds were as real as the reality he experienced on Atopia. But reality on Atopia wasn't the same as out here. "Yes and no," he replied as he fiddled with his model. "It's not easy to explain." An infinite number of alternate universes, and pssi as the backdoor to crossing the threshold—on Atopia it made sense, but here, the dream was fading.

"I'll tell you one thing," Bunky said after a pause. "You're like a bloody god to these glasscutters."

Sid smiled. "Could have fooled me."

"Naw, he's right," said Bunky. "Sibeal practically squealed when you contacted her. She's got some serious fan girl going on."

Sid ignored the praise, spinning the newest simulation into the hyperspace around their points-of-view. "So what do you think?"

Shaky-balloon frowned. "Not bad, but . . ." With a jittery phantom limb—he wasn't good at adapting his nervous system in virtual spaces—Shaky grabbed the projection and squeezed, popping them back into real space. Sid, Bunky, and Shaky were standing next to each other on a gantry above the construction mechanoid's shoulder.

". . . I like things I can touch with my own two hands." He banged the rotator cuff joint of the mechanoid with a hammer and laughed. "If you see what I mean."

"And I"—Sid spread a dozen of his phantom limbs around his body like wings—"like things I can touch with my own twelve."

Bunky laughed, and Shaky bent down to the mechanoid and began banging away, hammering at the joint.

"After all my simulation work, really?" Sid shook his head as he watched. He turned to Bunky. "So you two are Midtown miners?"

Bunky nodded. "New York central branch of the worldwide Urban Miners Association. We staked out Midtown years back, prospecting seams of urban ore under the streets."

"And that makes you money?" Sid asked, trying to get into the flow of their thinking.

Bunky smiled. "Amazing amount of comatose stock down here—obsolete infrastructure, buried pipes, cabling, old landfill. We piece together old maps, way back to the 1850s all the way into mid-twenty-first century, mapping the city underground, and then dig it out, sometimes with city planning permission—"

"—but most of the time without!" laughed Shaky, kneeling beside them with a crowbar jammed into the mechanoid's shoulder.

"Did you know"—Bunky paused, his eyes narrowing—"that a bin of electronics waste is a hundred times richer in precious metals than the finest wild ores dug from virgin soil?"

"Didn't know that."

Shaky stood up, satisfied with his work. "But the best is in the gutter."

"This one's mind's always in the gutter," Bunky joked, slapping Shaky on the back.

The arm of the construction mechanoid swung up and down. Whatever Shaky had done, it worked.

"What I'm talking about," continued Shaky, "is street sludge. We filter it from the sewers. Platinum group metals—palladium, rhodium—plus gold, silver from medications, industrial effluent, better than the highest grade—"

Bunky elbowed him. "Enough, he knows, this is the great all-knowing Sidney Horowitz." He winked at Sid. "Time for us to get to work, mate."

Without warning, the construction mechanoid's digger-hand swung in and scooped Sid up. Of course Sid's proxxi, Vicious, saw it coming, and angled his body to sit into the hand at just the right instant, recognizing this as a "friendly." At the same time, Bunky and Shaky were hoisted into the riding compartments of their respective mechanoids, and with a low whine the other digger bots and worms in the pit whirred into life.

Bunky looked over his shoulder at Sid. "We're off to see what your friend Willy's body was up to in the underground."

Sid nodded. Willy's body had been pinpointed stopping at specific locations. The underminers were going to see what it'd found so interesting.

In a few crunching strides, they were off down the tunnel leading from the repair pit. The smaller digger bots and worms followed behind. Where Sid's neural system had plastically adapted to control his phantom limbs, Bunky and Shaky had trained theirs, through years of hard work, to be neurally adapted into their diggers and mechanoids, like learning to play a piano. Their tools and bots were as much a part of their bodies as their hands. Sid watched them disappear around a curve in the tunnel.

"Don't even think about it."

Spinning on his heels, Sid turned. The Grilla, Zoraster, emerged out of the blackness of one of the service tunnels to his left. Sid hadn't even known he was there. In augmented space, a glittering security blanket sparkled around Zoraster. It was hiding his digital signature in the local wikiworld. In real space, the beast seemed to appear silently from nowhere.

Sid felt a noose around his phantoms in pssi-space, choking them back. Zoraster was pinning them. Sid had started sliding into the cracks of the digital infrastructure in the tunnels, looking for ways up and out. It was habit.

"There's a reason you're not getting access to outside networks," said the Grilla, tightening the virtual noose it threw around Sid. "Want to guess why?" The Grilla dropped twenty feet from the service tunnel to the pit floor, effortlessly, without a sound, its hulk looming over Sid. "I don't trust you."

"I've told you everything I know." Sid backed up a few steps. "I even got Willy down here to talk with you."

"You might think you're making friends, that you've got these underminers and 'cutters wrapped around your little finger," Zoraster rumbled, "but trouble follows you and your friends."

"But I told you—"

The Grilla shoved Sid back against the cold stone wall. "Save the sad story. Your friend Bob disappearing, you left all alone, your friend Indigo tracked to the Ascetics, goddamn gangster freaks." Sid could feel the Grilla's heat, his breathing like the bellows of a locomotive. "You're good at sneaking around, Horowitz. You know what Grillas are good at?"

Sid trembled. Where he'd been able to easily anticipate what Bunky and Shaky would say, even Sibeal and ReVurb, he had no idea what this Grilla would do. He shook his head.

The Grilla turned and stalked away, jumping and swinging up the pit wall. "Killing," Sid heard it growl as it disappeared into the blackness. "That's what we were built for. Killing."

# 11

HE HAD NO choice. Bob had to kill the man in order to escape.

He'd run through hundreds of simulations after bringing the rat back into the jailhouse and sneaking it up to the man's chair, using its little hands to slip free the keychain. With his low smarticle count, maintaining control over the rat was draining.

Bob was exhausted.

He slipped some of the rat's smarticles into the guard by getting it to lick his hand. The guard was asleep, but his theta and alpha waves frequencies were shortening, his sleep lightening. Bob tried his best to push the man's mind back down, but his circadian cycle was completing its daily loop, the Earth's spin pulling this place back toward sunshine. The animal was awakening within. Daylight was coming, and there was only a half-hour gap between shift changes.

Bob had to hurry. They were coming for him. Who "they" were he didn't know, or at least didn't know who they were working for, but the likelihood of his situation improving was dwindling as quickly as his smarticle reserves.

The guard was asleep against the door, and there was no way to ensure getting out without risking his raising an alarm—except to kill him. In Bob's weakened state, knocking him unconscious would be unreliable and noisy, as would trying to slip into his mind and take control.

He slipped into the rat's consciousness. Pull, little friend, pull, he urged. The rat dug its incisors into the fraying rope, dragging the keychain under the wooden door. Its body strained, and then pulled free and started toward Bob, the keys jangling as they skidded across the stone floor.

Pulling his awareness out of the rat, Bob got up from his cot and looked around the room. The priest was awake, sitting rigidly upright, his eyes luminous saucers in the reflected moonlight. Bob reached down between the bars of his cell and the rat backed up onto his hand, bringing the keys. Setting the rat on his shoulder, Bob reached around the bars and slid the key into lock, then creaked open the door to his cell. Barefoot, he padded across the cold flagstones, his heart thumping in his chest.

Fear, that predator that lurked in the back of the mind, was shaping Bob's mindscape, morphing his dreams of the future, coloring the ghosts of his past—fear for himself, fear for Nancy and his family, fear of the unknown. He wanted to curl into a ball and retreat into one of his fantasy worlds, but he couldn't. They were counting on him, even if they didn't know it. He couldn't fail. Not again.

His throat parched, his tongue sandpaper, he opened the door to the front office and peered through. Combining the rat's visual input, staring from his shoulder, with his own, he built a low-light and infrared model of the room. The man's janbiya, a curved dagger, sagged on one side of his sash. Everything was still where it should be. Everything was set.

Could he kill a man? He didn't want to, but really, he just had to plan it. Outside the window, a thin light was dusting the horizon. The man stirred.

Bob let go.

He released his body into a pre-programmed routine, his quickened nervous system sliding the door open, stealing silently across the floor. In an instant his hand grabbed the man's knife, unsheathed it, and then just as quickly drove it through the man's jugular, slicing it into the back of his neck between the third and fourth cervical vertebrae. Bob severed the man's spinal cord in one motion.

The man's body jerked, and blood sprayed Bob's face, spurting out on each heartbeat. The man's eyes opened wide, just inches from Bob's, the man's mind surfacing from a dream world for one final moment. Inadvertently Bob connected into some of the smarticles the rat had transferred into the man. It wasn't much of a connection, but enough to sense the void of the unknown opening below the man's mind, the fear swallowing him, falling, falling.

Bob snapped back into his own mind and stared into the man's dead eyes.

"Come," hissed the priest, behind him, and then in the open doorway. "We must hurry. They will be here soon."

Bob was frozen, immobile. He couldn't move. This man had been in the way to Bob's freedom, to the safety of his loved ones. Bob hadn't had a choice, had he? He needed to sacrifice this man for the greater good, and it wasn't as if his captor was innocent.

Nobody was.

Bob inhaled the sweat-smell of a body whose mind was gone, but whose biological systems were still toiling through their final, futile metabolic processes. He'd killed a million times in his gameworlds, felt hot blood splash across his face, but this was different.

"Come!" urged the priest, now outside the doorway.

Bob regained control of his body, pushing himself off the guard. Reaching down he grabbed the man's water canteen, and then stumbled out the door into the cool night air. The sun was coloring the horizon, the stars washing from the sky.

# 12

IT WAS A night of fitful sleep.

Vince gave up while it was still dark. A nice hot shower would help get his brain cycling. He quietly stole into the bathroom, then turned on the water and stepped into the stall. He closed his eyes and let the water pound against his sore body. He could have stood in the shower forever, letting his mind wander. He was the one that had reached out to the local gangsters, but since they'd been sequestered in this room, he had no idea what was going on. He assumed they'd just want some money, but maybe he assumed wrong. Taking a deep breath, he pushed the temperature selector to its coldest setting and exhaled. The icy water blasted against him, and he gritted his teeth and counted to thirty. If that didn't wake him up, nothing would.

After his shower, Vince went onto the balcony to watch the sunrise over the waterlogged metropolis, the ruined buildings of the city rising like ghosts through a blood-orange fog that burned off as the sun gained in the sky. The hours passed. Connors sat on her bed, and Vince on his, in silence through most of the muggy day, listening to the sounds of catcalling and drunken arguments outside as Bourbon Street came back to life.

It was a lot of time to think.

"You're wrong," said Vince finally as night began to fall again.

Connors had her eyes closed. "About what?"

"I haven't cared about money in a long time."

She laughed. "Probably because you have more than you can spend in a hundred lifetimes."

"You know what I mean," muttered Vince. His entire empire was probably being expropriated as they spoke. "The reason why I'm here, to answer your question of yesterday, is to help a friend."

"There's always a reason." Sitting up in her bed she turned to him. "You committed crimes, Vince, you stole the future information of billions of people, made it public." Pressing her face into her palms she asked, "So what was so important, seeing as you want to get it out? Why did you do it?"

Vince paused. He pulled a pillow into his lap. "Do you know what it's like to see the future, to see everything in the future, when the only thing you want is in the past?"

"Regret, you mean regret." Connors rubbed her face. "I know regret."

He swung his legs off the bed and turned to sit and face her. "So if you know so much about me, where was I born?"

"Boston."

"Brothers and sisters?"

Connors cocked her head to one side. "None. A spoiled only child."

Vince smiled. "My favorite baseball team?" Not everything was in the databases.

"Yankees."

He had to hand it to her that this answer wasn't obvious. Vince looked at the floor. "What was my mother's nickname for me?"

"Indy."

Perhaps obvious, but this was from before the days that machines recorded every breath a person took. It was time to get the rubber to the road. Vince's eyes narrowed. "Why did I fake my own deaths?"

"Everyone said it was a game," replied Connors, but before Vince could pounce she added, "but I don't think so. I don't think those were fakes, I think someone was trying to kill you."

"If you thought someone was trying to kill me, why were you hunting me?"

"Because you broke the law."

"Then why did you shut off my Phuture News feed if you knew it might be dangerous?"

"Because I wasn't sure."

Vince shook his head but smiled. A risk taker. "And now you are?"

"More than I used to be." Connors swung her feet off her bed and turned to face Vince. "You said I don't know anything about the situation. What situation? Maybe I could help."

Vince's network ran through a dozen short-term simulations. A bit of truth couldn't hurt. "My friend, Willy McIntyre, had his body stolen."

"I heard about that. So that was why you were at the Commune?" The mediaworlds were only too aware that Willy's grandfather was the Reverend.

"Yeah," Vince replied, knowing it was only half the truth. Could he trust her with what they'd found out about Jimmy Scadden? It would only endanger her life.

Connors didn't look convinced. "So why did these Ascetics come for us? What is it they think you're looking for?"

Vince looked away. He didn't want to tell her that he'd contacted them "I don't know."

"Uh-huh." She rubbed one eye. "Okay, then, what can you tell me about these Ascetics?"

How to explain the Ascetics? A global Russian-origin mafia running illegal body-mod shops, synthetic drugs, emo-porn, and prostitution in all its ever-expanding forms. They controlled the darknets, private worlds unreachable from regulated spaces. "They're like the Hell's Angels of the cyber world—"

"I'm not stupid. I mean, what can you tell me about this chapter? Who are we facing?"

A tough question. The Ascetics weren't something you could just query. Initiation required sacrifice, a ritualized destruction of the physical, cleansing body and mind through modification into an ascetic form. The basis of darknets was anonymized content and access, so the Ascetics anonymized themselves in the physical realms as well, removing—arms, legs, faces—identity.

"This one is heavily tied into Vodoun," said Vince.

Connors frowned. "Voodoo," he added, "that's what they call it here, from Vodoun in West Africa, hoodoo in other places."

Hotstuff was feeding Vince updated situational reports every few minutes. She pinged him an alert: they were coming. He made a deal.

Getting up off the bed, Vince got up and faced the door. "This sect controls the Spice Routes, the darknet data pipes that transit illegal . . ." He paused, reconsidering his words. ". . . or rather, morally challenging goods and services."

"Morally challenging?"

Vince looked at her and smiled. "Columbus was a slave trader, and you have a holiday for him." He tensed. It was almost here.

Connors frowned. "Why are you standing there?"

"I said I would go if they promised no harm to you," he replied quickly. "They know you're FBI, it's all out in the open, but I still have some pull, some hidden—"

Before he could finish, the door crashed open and an Ascetic slid through, a silvery web of thousands of legs shimmering beneath a tattooed black torso and white-painted skull.

"It's time, Mr. Indigo," reverberated its voice in their heads.

"For what?" grunted Vince, forcing back its intrusions into his mind.

The Ascetic's body undulated across the floor, its mass of shimmering legs winding into the center of the room while its torso twisted between Vince and Connors. Black peacock feathers sprouted out of its back. Its blank face looked at them, laughing silently. "Time to find what you've been looking for."

# 13

THIS WAS JUST what he had been looking for.

Bob relaxed into the sun lounger. Sighing with contentment, he brought the ice-cold mojito back to his lips. Dappled sunlight fell across him through the canopy of palms overhead, and a cool breeze blew in over the ocean. He studied the droplets of condensation forming on the sides of the glass, the shredded mint leaves pinned under the ice cubes, and then took another sip.

"Would you like another drink?" Nancy asked. She was standing beside him in a yellow wrap-around, the shadows of her bikini just visible beneath.

"No thanks, sweetheart."

Nancy's shadow swept past him. He raised one hand to touch her, but she was gone.

"There is always another," said a voice of gravel, the words clattering through the air.

Bob sat up and took off his sunglasses, squinting into the brightness.

"And another, and another." Someone sat on a chair nearby, obscured by the shade of a bush. His face was dark. Bob couldn't make him out.

Bob holding up one hand to shield his eyes from the sun. "What?"

The owner of the voice pointed skyward. "The star is falling from heaven to destroy a third of all things."

Bob put his drink down and looked up, rubbing his eyes. Something was in the sky—the comet—its tails spreading outward from the sun, the tip nearly touching it now. "That's no star. The Comet Catcher mission is bringing it into orbit."

"This world ends, and another begins." The man behind the voice retreated further into the shadows. "Don't you want an end to this suffering?"

"What suffering?"

"What suffering?" The man laughed. "What suffering indeed."

Bob's mind filled with a dozen, then a hundred, then a thousand images of burned earth, slaughtered animals, smoking landscapes, dead seas. "Would you stop?"

"Smoke has engulfed the world once more." The man leaned forward. "The Dajjal had returned, Gog and Magog arisen—there is only you who remains."

Bob's vision swam. Only me who remains. "Stop talking! Please stop talking . . ."

The man leaned into the light. It was the priest. The greens and blues of the ocean patio drained into the endless seas of sand that surrounded them. Bob found himself staring into the priest's face, into his creased wrinkles and dark eyes.

"Can we focus on practical things?" complained Bob. "I'm getting tired of—" He stumbled, sending a cascade of sand down the face of the dune whose ridge they were laboring along. Ahead, wave upon wave of sand disappeared into the distance, starkly lit by monochromatic moonlight.

"I wasn't saying anything." The priest turned and began walking again, his footsteps sure and measured. "You were muttering nonsense. I just asked if you were all right." The rags hanging around the priest's withered frame flapped back and forth with each step.

"You were just talking to me." Bob staggered forward. "I was trying to relax, and you were talking. Why won't you just let me be?"

Nearly a day ago, in the early morning twilight of their escape, they put several miles of trackless desert behind them before the alarm was raised. The priest led the way, to a secret oasis, he'd said, somewhere hidden.

Somewhere safe.

"You hide in the worlds in your head," murmured the priest. "For this small suffering"—he motioned at the sand around them—"you throw this world away for another."

Bob's skin was blistered. Even in the cool night air it was burning. When they escaped, the morning sun had climbed and climbed into the sky, and he had no protection. He'd heard that a Bedouin could walk for a hundred miles through the open desert, but hearing about a thing was different than experiencing this scorching hell. He could almost feel the frail bubble of his immune system failing as he tracked the ultraviolet-radiation damage to his skin cells, commandeered his autonomous nervous system to retain moisture, watched his neurological signals scatter as he dehydrated. And so he retreated into the private worlds in his head, leaving his body in low-power autopilot to follow the priest.

"Why do you care?" Bob followed the priest footstep by footstep. "All you talk about is the end of the world."

After escaping, he'd fed the rat to a Nubian vulture. He watched it tear the shrieking creature apart and gulp it in down in pink lumps. He had no choice. He needed information. By flitting into the vulture's mind as the rat's precious smarticles transferred into it, he got a sense of the magnetic fields in the area. Bob sent the vulture aloft to map out the terrain to the south.

Of course Toothface chased them, sending out drones into the sky and sandbots to climb through the dunes. Using the vulture, soaring high in the sky, Bob weaved between the searchers. The priest was a master at finding hollows, places to hide, disappearing as if he weren't even there. They walked, ran, and scrambled to hide all day under the relentless sun.

All the water was long gone. Bob closed up the pores in his skin to keep every molecule of water he could in his body. This acted to heat his core more, raising his central body temperature. His body and brain were frying and on the verge of total neurological failure when the setting sun finally brought relief.

The priest didn't even turn as he spoke, his words carried to Bob on the sirocco, the never-ending wind that blew through the deep desert. "What's your idea of Nirvana?"

Bob whispered from between cracked lips, "Heaven?"

"Perhaps. It literally means extinction, like a candle being snuffed out."

Bob wasn't sure what was worse, the heat, the priest's mouth, or the wind—none of them ever stopped. The wind was a biting aerial sandpaper that wore down the skin and stung the eyes, filling them with grit and gunk. When he closed his eyes, Bob saw the face of the man he killed, the life draining away, felt the way his hand had stuck to the dagger, glued there by the man's blood.

"Have you seen the signs?" asked the priest.

Bob groaned. He shouldn't have followed the priest. They were heading due south—that much he could infer from the position of the stars in the sky—but his internal data systems were failing. Soon he'd have to rely on his meat-mind, and he was worried about what was left in it.

The priest walked on, gliding across the sand as Bob trudged behind.

"Soon all will be revealed—the apocalypse—one thing changing into another, the world spinning into a vortex . . ."

"You mean the singularity?" It was a popular topic with the doomsdayers.

"The singularity, the apocalypse, the revealing, all different names of the same thing," replied the priest. "Vishnu, the destroyer, and Shiva, the rebuilder, different faces of the same reality—all avatars of the same being."

Bob was beyond exhausted. "How much further to the oasis?" Maybe he could pinpoint his location.

"It is not the destination that is important," answered the priest, "but the journey."

Bob stopped, leaning over, his head spinning. "I'm grateful and all"—he looked up at the priest—"but could you please stop with the metaphysics lessons?"

The priest stopped in his tracks, balanced on the knife edge of the dune whose ridge top snaked before them into the distance. "This is a fine line we are treading." He motioned toward the inky blackness to their left and right where the dune slid into the depths. "On both sides the abyss. You are from Atopia, yes?"

This old Bedouin nomad probably heard that from Toothface. Bob nodded, expecting more religious nonsense.

"Jimmy Scadden must be stopped."

Despite the heat, the hair prickled on Bob's arms. "Wha . . . what?"

"I am not some old fool." The priest stood up straight. His body seemed to tower over Bob. "I live in this world too. I am, like you, a prisoner trying to break free." His eyes glowed in moonlight. "And I know things you do not."

"What do you know about Jimmy?" Bob took a few deep lungfuls of air. Had he miscalculated this old guy? "Tell me about Jimmy," he managed to gasp out between labored breaths.

"All in good time." The priest leaned over and put a hand on Bob's shoulder.

Bob felt a soothing calm.

Turning, the priest continued. "We have a long journey."

"How much—"

"It is not the destination," interrupted the priest, "but—"

"Yeah, yeah, I get it, the journey."

The horizon to his left was beginning to lighten, and their pace quickened as the flaming sword of the sun began to rise again.

# 14

FLAMES FROM FIRES atop abandoned buildings reflected in the dark waters as Vince raced across the submerged streets. Pregnant clouds hung overhead, threatening rain, and tendrils of smoke crawled between the abandoned buildings, the smell acrid like burned flesh. Vince gulped huge mouthfuls of air, his eyes tearing up as he stared straight ahead and gripped the frame of the battered aluminum airboat.

"Indigo," shouted the small man driving the boat, and Vince looked away from the murky waterscape rushing toward them. "Your name, yeah?"

"My family used to farm it down here, generations ago." The small man wasn't an Ascetic. Vince guessed he was a worker on the sludge farms, making extra on the side driving taxi boats at night.

The man nodded. "Oh, I know."

The noise of the engine, just inches behind Vince's head, was deafening. Did he hear that right? "What do you mean, you know?" he yelled back.

"I know you from here."

"I'm not from here, I'm from Boston," shouted Vince over the roar of the airboat.

Shaking his head the man looked out into the darkness. "Oh no, you from here, otherwise, we wouldn't be goin' where we goin'."

Vince paused. "And where is that?" In the background, Hotstuff was plotting possible paths and destinations, gathering as much information as she could.

The man smiled up at him, his gold teeth glinting. "The fires of Saint John been burning bright every night since solstice this year." The whites of his eyes seemed disconnected from his face. "Tonight is a big night, big honor, boss. You be in the brule zin, the kanzo, you be a hounsi 'fore the night is out." He started cackling and slapped his knee with his free hand. "Or not, or not. We going to pon-shar-train."

Reaching down between his legs, the man pulled up a bottle and took a swig from it, then offered it to Vince.

"No thanks," mumbled Vince, but the man held the bottle up. "NO THANKS!" he yelled this time.

The man shrugged and took another drink himself, muttering in a language Vince's automated translators couldn't decipher.

"Pontchartrain," Hotstuff said, sitting in front of Vince, the rushing wind ruffling her virtual hair. She spun a local map of the area into a display space, collapsing the probability spaces. "He means Lake Pontchartrain and the Saint John ceremonies—"

"I know," said Vince. He remembered the ghost stories his grandmother used to tell him of the old country where she grew up, a parish not far from where they were now. Half-remembered, these childhood memories ballooned into cartoonish dimensions of ogres and demons that inhabited the swamps.

Thousands of people gathered on the shores of Lake Pontchartrain each year to celebrate old Saint John. Whether he was the same John of Patmos as John the Baptist was disputed, but here it didn't matter—here they were one and the same. Spinning through the networks nearby, Vince saw they were gathering there today, a giant party was assembling. More than parties, though, these were ceremonial gatherings—voodoo gatherings, and Saint John's was the most important.

Voodoo. Vince reconsidered and leaned close to the man. "What's that you're drinking?"

"*A trompe*," the man replied, picking up the bottle and offering it to Vince.

"Vince, I don't think you should . . ." Hotstuff started to say, but Vince grabbed it and took a drink.

Warm and sweet at first taste, *a trompe* seared into Vince's gullet, a warm fire spreading from his neck to his stomach. He took another big gulp, and then another, coughing, waiting for the alcohol to steady his nerves.

"Bokor gonna get you, you keep drinking that," laughed the man, taking the bottle back.

"The Saint John fires are . . ." Hotstuff started a detailed situational report, but Vince was only half-listening.

All his life, Vince had been running from the past; the past of his family, the past of his own life, even the suffocating past of the world. He escaped into the future, became the master of it as a way to run and run, but now he was being dragged back to his roots, back to the past he tried so hard to erase.

How had he ended up here? With his phantom hands he pulled up a workspace, dragging his point-of-view into a recording of his inVerse from the crash landing. His own recollection was fuzzy, the noise and confusion, loss of oxygen when the hull of the turbofan had been breached. But there, he saw himself taking control, programming a controlled landing near New Orleans. It wasn't just coincidence—part of him wanted to be here, going back to the beginning when he thought his end was coming.

"Vince!" Hotstuff yelled, tugging his mind out of the fog.

Shaking away the inVerse recording, she grabbed his viewpoint and spun it above the airboat. Vince watched himself, white knuckled, gripping onto his seat frame. Soaring higher, ahead he saw a massive bonfire rising up out of the water, surrounded by an undulating mass of people.

The fires of Saint John were burning bright, and they were almost there.

# 15

CRUEL FIRE BURNED in the sky.

There was nowhere to escape, not even virtual worlds. Bob's smarticle reserves were gone. It was just him, in his own head, for one of the first times in his life—and more than anything, he desperately wanted to get out.

That inner voice. Sometimes suddenly, sometimes gradually, Bob would become aware of the words he was listening to, that no one else could hear; telling him, guiding him—judging him. Not his proxxi, not the clipped memetic static that flowed into his meta-cognition systems. It was now the voice of his mother: "Stay out of the sun, Bob, you know you need to stay out of the sun . . ."

He looked at his arms and laughed. "I can't, I can't get out." New blisters formed under the old in his peeling red skin. He took off his shirt and wrapped it around his head in an attempt to stave off heat exhaustion, but now his body broiled, his flesh cooked under the flames from above.

"Keep moving," urged the priest, ever ahead, dragging him along. "It is not far now."

Bob laughed.

They were being hunted, but the hunter wasn't Toothface anymore. Fear was stalking Bob now, the fear of death, the knowledge of that ultimate predator that kept his feet moving beyond exhaustion, gnawing him away from the inside out until all that remained was a shell. He didn't believe the priest, but then the choice came down to moving or dying.

He kept moving.

One step after another. His tongue swelled in his mouth, his brain felt like it was bursting against his skull. Each step took concentration and effort as his legs cramped up. He wanted to lie down. To sleep. *Just focus.* One step, and then another, and another.

"Look!" The priest pointed over the top of the next dune, then he disappeared.

On all fours, Bob scrambled to the top of the ridge, and then, kneeling in the sand, began laughing again. This time it was for joy. In the distance he saw a wall of sand and rock, and before him a trail that led down. Oases in the open Sahara were massive depressions, descending hundreds of feet below sea level into the desert floor where the water table, even here, still flowed in places. A mile or two away stood a small knot of palms, a patch of cool green in the blinding sand.

Water—there had to be water.

His pain gained some meaning, and Bob dragged himself to his feet, stumbling through the sand. The copse of trees remained stubbornly distant. *Is it a mirage?* But gradually, step by step, the palms grew. Then he was among them. The priest called to him, beckoned him to a well. Bob staggered over and dragged a bucket up out of its depths, splashing water onto his face, laughing and drinking.

"Slowly," the priest instructed, standing above Bob. "Do not drink too much, too fast."

Nodding, Bob sank down against the mud and stone side of the well. We can rest here, he thought, we are safe. Then something twinged. Something wasn't right.

"You feel it," said the priest, not asking. "Free your mind, let go . . ."

One of Toothface's sandbots was approaching. Bob saw it in his mind's eye, the mechanical cockroach cresting one dune and then another, tracking its way toward them. It didn't know they were here, it was scouting, but soon it would know.

How did he see it? Bob blinked and looked at the priest. The smarticle count in his body was zero, he had no internal computing resources or extra-sensory networks active.

The priest nodded. "Use me, release your mind."

Too tired to question it, Bob relaxed into the stone wall of the well, closing his eyes. The image of the sandbot became more vivid. It wasn't far now. He sensed its internal networks and signaling systems. Worming his mind into the sandbot, he flexed, feeling it shudder.

"Do not destroy it," said the priest, "divert it, send a signal that we are not here. We become invisible."

Nodding, Bob logged into its memory core, adding a false sensor reading. The sandbot turned, satisfied it had swept the area, and crawled off in another direction.

"Good, very good," the priest commended.

Bob took another drink from the bucket he still held in his hands.

The priest stood over Bob. "We can rest until nightfall, but you must eat. We need you stronger."

Closing his eyes, Bob scanned the area. Date palms, but these had been scavenged by insects. Perhaps he could eat palm shoots? He took another sip from the bucket. Opening his eyes, he watched a scarab beetle scurry under a pile of palm leaves.

"Yes," said the priest, "you must eat."

The beetle emerged from under the palm leaves and stopped, and another joined it. Slowly they began moving toward Bob and the priest. More joined them, a procession that crawled up to and onto Bob. Lying inert, he looked at them, and then picked one up, held it near his mouth, and licked it. Then he popped it into his mouth and bit down, tasting the bitter flesh squirt between his teeth.

Bob opened his mouth and the beetles began crawling in.

He feasted.

# 16

THE SPACE AROUND Vince buzzed with insects, both natural and artificial. Quick, syncopated beats of metal drums filled the air, rising and falling in rhythm with a mass of dancers. The houngans—male voodoo priests—dressed in garish costumes of red and green, sang above the drums, leading prayers. In the center, a massive bonfire. An effigy of Saint John was burning, his flames leaping into the sky.

A patch of soggy ground rose up out of the waters and the airboat, its engine cut, slid silently aground. Lake Pontchartrain didn't really exist anymore, it was just another part of the Mississippi delta, but the past drew people to this patch of swamp, St. John's Bayou, that was once a part of Pontchartrain's shoreline.

Drones circled in the darkness, and pontoon boats filled with revelers dotted the waters between floating fires. From the jumble of music and hoots of laughter echoing, not everyone was here to get religion. This was a big party for all comers. Or perhaps the party was the religion.

"Mr. Indigo, this way." An old woman was waiting for them, standing at the edge of the water with a Grilla hunched ominously behind her. She beckoned to Vince.

A mambo, a voodoo priestess, thought Vince, looking at her flowing white robe. She seemed genuine in her enthusiasm. Vince took another pull from the *a trompe* bottle, feeling its fire in his throat. He walked to the front of the boat and took her offered hand.

"Why am I here?" asked Vince as he jumped down, landing ankle-deep in mud. In the background, Hotstuff was keeping their guard up, searching for threats.

"It is the night of *kanzo*, Mr. Indigo." The mambo's eyes sparkled in the firelight. "When the loa pick the tribe."

Vince stepped forward out of the muck onto slightly more solid ground. He knew what the *loa* were—voodoo spirits, but not deities, more like intermediaries to God.

"This is your journey," she added, leading him into dancers that swayed back and forth with the drum beat.

The crowd parted, revealing a knot of young men, their eyes seeing but not seeing, faces painted white, deep in a trance-like state. The priestesses, their white robes flowing, circled the men, chanting. In augmented space, the reality skins of the assembled fused into a phantasmagoria of monsters and demons that swayed above the dancers. Vince's vision blurred. He thought he saw a lougaroo, the crocodile werewolf of Louisiana-swamp legend, appear and then disappear though the crowd.

Vince looked into the fire that towered before him. The flames of Saint John. It was John who was supposed to have spoken to God in a cave on Patmos—one of the Greek islands—where he'd written down Revelations and the Apocalypse was described.

"We need to get out of here," hissed Hotstuff in Vince's head. He turned an eye inward. "I think she wants you to go through the houngan ceremony . . ."

One of the boys near Vince convulsed, then stood up straight. The mambos near him shrieked and parted to create an opening. Through the opening Vince saw a bed of red-hot coals spread from the base of the fire along a line that led to a fiery portal. A black cauldron sat at the end closest to him, filled with a bubbling liquid.

The rhythm of the drums gained in urgency. The boy staggered toward the cauldron.

"You see," said the old priestess, again by his side. "The *loa* taking possession, the spirit will protect him."

Did they want him to witness their rituals? The Ascetics here were intimately tied into the local religion. He had no choice, nowhere to run, his fear matched by his fascination. Vince watched a pattern of stars emerge from the fire.

The boy stood at the rim of the cauldron. The drums built their way into a crescendo. Without warning, the boy leaned over and plunged both arms into the boiling oil.

Hotstuff cringed. "That oil is nearly six hundred degrees, there's no way his biological systems could—"

But Vince wasn't listening anymore. The collage of stars from the fire took shape, arranging itself into a diamond-weave of gold. The lougaroo appeared in the crowd again, its crocodile face leered at him, but then fear flashed in its eyes as a hulking figure divided the crowd in front of Vince.

Pulling his arms from the boiling oil, the boy held them aloft, undamaged, and the crowd erupted in cheers. The drums were furious, their beat disappearing into a cacophony of noise. Behind the fire, its image undulating in waves of heat, Vince saw a bull being led by its nose ring, standing knee deep in water.

The boy took a tentative step forward onto the red hot coals, and then stood on them, leaning forward and walking toward the fiery portal. On the other side of the fire, a spider-legged Ascetic mounted the bull, a blade flashing in its robotic limb. It reached down and ripped the blade across the bull's neck. Blood poured out and the bull dropped to its knees.

Vince looked back from the fire. The hulking figure loomed over him, the star pattern burning in its forehead, a flaming sword in one of its hands.

"Don't resist," whispered the priestess in his ear.

"Vince!" Hotstuff yelled. She tried to take control of his body, to move him away to safety, or to override his sensory systems, but it was no use.

The dark figure reached and grabbed Vince. He didn't flinch. Down, down, the figure reached, blackness enveloping Vince, and then the figure went inside, disappearing into Vince's body.

The priestess's eyes grew wide. "Papa Ogoun!" she hissed, staring at Vince, backing away from him.

Vince felt a presence inhabiting his body. His mind flashed forward in time, and he watched himself walking across the coals, his body traversing through the fiery portal in the fire and emerging unscathed on the other side. Then his mind flashed backward, into a jungle where great green beasts stood between towering ferns.

"Vince!" screamed Hotstuff. "I don't know what—"

He plunged his arms into the boiling oil. He didn't remember walking to the cauldron, but he felt no fear. The boiling oil felt as cool as a mountain stream, and the fires of Saint John beckoned him, the carpet of hot coals an oasis of tranquility he wanted to swim in.

And then the screaming began.

Bright flashes and orange fireballs erupted in Vince's peripheral vision. The spirit in him retreated. Looking down, he was standing barefoot in the coals. He looked up. The rising heat distorted the image of a military mechanoid that stalked toward the gathering from the darkness. Overhead, bursts of fire as aerial drones exploded.

Vince's defensive networks came back online, and in augmented space a three-dimensional situational report blossomed into his awareness.

"Nice to see you're back," Hotstuff gasped.

She threw up defensive shields in the informational spaces around them, hacking into the control systems of the attacking drones. Allied forces were attacking. A ragtag of opposition was surging in from the outlying swamps and New Orleans itself, but they were overmatched. A small blip at the center of the display was the location of Vince's body, dead in the middle of an angry swarm of attacking drones.

"We need to get moving. Vince, can you hand me back kinesthetic control?"

Blinking, Vince nodded, his mind reaching into itself to reconnect with his motor control neurons.

The knot of attacking drones intensified in the situational display. "I don't think there's a way out of this." Hotstuff attempted to surrender. "They're not accepting any comms . . ."

Vince felt oddly calm. Looking up into the sky, a shape moved and grew. A giant eagle—no, a drone, its wings sweeping like a bird's—swooped over the fire. Its talons extended and latched onto Vince, snatching him away into the night as a thundering explosion enveloped the fires of Saint John.

# 17

A MASSIVE QUARTZITE crystal rose hundreds of feet out of the limestone landscape surrounding it, and Bob and the priest stopped in its shadow to rest. Over the aeons, the wind had etched the limestone bedrock beneath the sands into fantastical forms that sprang from the desert floor like alien sea creatures. Dunes sat hunched upon this bedrock, stretching into the distance as they slowly sailed their lonely courses, their hulks propelled by the same unrelenting wind that shaped this place.

"The War of the Sons of Light against the Sons of Darkness began long ago," said the priest. Bob was half-listening. "The White Rider has appeared once more. Your Jimmy Scadden."

Bob nodded, too weak to argue. So now Jimmy is the Anti-Christ. But not everything out of the priest's mouth was nonsense. He was more connected to the world than Bob realized. He knew a lot about Atopia. More important, though, the priest had access to a synthetic reality technology that he was letting Bob channel. Bob had never experienced the Terra Novan systems, not first hand, and this had to be some variant. There was more to this priest than met the eye.

And without him, Bob would already be dead.

"We can't head into Egypt," Bob whispered between cracked lips.

Egypt was the only one of the African countries that wasn't a part of the African Union. It was officially neutral, but fell more under the umbrella of the Alliance, and therefore more under Atopia's sway.

The priest leaned against the wall of crystal and stared into it. "There are a series of oases leading into Egypt, it is the easiest—"

"I can't go that way," Bob croaked. "Is there a way toward central Africa?"

"There is a way, but you'd die if you went yourself."

Venturing into Egypt, in Bob's current state with this bounty on his head, was as good as giving up. There had to be more like Toothface out there. He was hunted now. He needed to get into friendly territory—it was his only chance—but he couldn't expect the priest to risk his own life. Bob needed to get into the African Union and get in touch with Mohesha, Patricia's old friend on Terra Nova. She knew he was coming. She could help.

Or should he just give up? This was way beyond anything he ever imagined. He didn't know what the right thing to do was anymore. But then the angry voice in his head, *You can't fail again.*

"Just tell me the way."

# 18

SID PUT HIS pint down. "The Devil and God got into a big fight over that."

"Over what? Responsibility?" Sibeal snorted.

Sid wagged a finger at her. "What I'm saying is that God giving free will to humans is what got the Devil so upset." He smiled. "Or at least, that's the story."

They were arguing at a table in the White Horse Pub deep under Midtown. A half-finished burger sat in front of Sid beside three empty pint glasses. Leaking runoff from new construction rained down onto the corrugated metal roof, and all levels of the pit and cave walls were abuzz with the chatter and clatter of machinery. The pub smelled of stale beer and mech-grease.

Sid found himself using his reality skins less and enjoying the grittiness of the "real" world the more he stayed underground. He reached out with a phantom limb to tweak the serving bot for another beer. A bit more than a week, and he was already a part of the scenery, just another regular. Of course, Zoraster was never far, the Grilla shadowing him wherever he went.

Sibeal wasn't one to be interested in theories without some practical application. "So you're saying that if something is pre-programmed, then it's not responsible?"

"If you had no choice, would you feel responsible?" Sid replied.

"I think responsibility and accountability are different. No matter what, if you do something, you're accountable." Sibeal took a deep breath. "So who won?"

A serving bot placed another beer in front of Sid. "Who won what?"

Most of Sid's attention was splintered into an array of workspaces where he worked with his proxxi on cracking the data beacon Bob left behind. Sibeal constantly pestered Sid about the beacon, so Sid had made a deal: if she granted him access to outside data pipes, he'd give her a view into what was inside the data beacon. This outside access was promised despite the objections of Zoraster, who felt a better option might be to simply bury Sid at the end of a service tunnel and be done with it.

"This fight between God and the Devil," Sibeal said.

Sid picked up his beer and frowned. "You know, I don't know." He took a sip. "I guess it's a constant battle."

"And do you think we have free will?"

Sid took another sip. "I think there's a more important question."

"And what's that?" Sibeal was working with Sid to crack the beacon, so, like Sid, only half of her attention was at the table.

Sid smiled. "Do you feel like you have free will?"

"Come on." Sibeal shook her head. "Are you being stupid on purpose? Of course I'm making choices."

"Then that's all that matters."

In a splinter he always had tracking the Grilla, Sid saw Zoraster growl and shake his head. He was eavesdropping, shadowing Sid, sitting in a corner of the pub out of sight. Sid smiled and ordered him a beer—he knew a conversation like this would set the big monkey off. A second and a half later, a serving bot slapped it down in front of Zoraster. He grabbed it and sucked half of it down, glaring at Sid.

Sibeal poked him. She found a match for one of the beacon's encryption keys. Sid nodded at her, impressed, and accepted the key. It was good work. "So you and your glasscutter friends hunt machine intelligences—do you think they have free will? Like you think you do?"

"Are you asking if I feel guilty for hunting them down?"

Sid took a sidelong glance at his proxxi, Vicious, who was working beside him in their virtual workspaces. "Yeah, I guess I am. It's one thing to hunt a person—they have rights, due process—but a synthetic intelligence? Terminated at whim . . .?"

"So we're the bad guys?" She withdrew her splinters from their shared workspaces. "These are virtual worlds with virtual beings, Sid. And if I have no free will, as you say, then how could I feel guilty? Want to talk morality?"

Sid watched a pattern emerge from the virtual workspaces they shared. He threw his primary presence in to take a closer look.

"Nothing to say?" Sibeal demanded.

"Forget it, I was just messing around." In the virtual workspace, one encryption key was fitting into another, the chain enclosing Bob's data beacon opening up.

"This is such a load of horseshit!" roared a voice that stopped both Sibeal and Sid in their tracks. It was Zoraster, lumbering up from his table to confront them. "You two, dancing around each other like teenagers in heat."

Sibeal frowned at him. "I don't know what you're talking—"

"Your little crush is putting us all in danger," he growled, pushing aside two tables. "We should have turned this worm in for a reward days ago. Now the heat's on, the feds are breathing down our necks. We already got what we needed, why are we waiting?"

Sibeal stood to face the Grilla. While she stood just a foot shorter than him, he was four times wider at the shoulders. "Don't you want to find the truth? If what Sid is telling us is true . . ."

Sid told them everything he knew, what Patricia Killiam told them about Jimmy Scadden, stealing peoples' minds, corrupting the pssi program from the inside out. He didn't have proof, though.

"The truth?" Zoraster grabbed Sid by the back of his neck. "The truth is that we have no idea what's inside that data beacon, and you're granting him outside access to share it. You know the kind of trouble this could get us all in?"

Sid squirmed to get out of Zoraster's grip. "It's a risk for me, too. I have no idea what Bob put in that beacon. I'm being totally open with you, and the second we open that thing, either you'll see I'm lying or you'll get your proof."

Zoraster picked Sid up off the ground as if he were a toy. "You're making your responsibilities ours."

"Put him down!" Sibeal yelled.

"And here you are," Zoraster continued, ignoring Sibeal, "chatting about free will and responsibility—a slippery fish with a silvery tongue. In the real world, you do something wrong, and you're responsible. It's that simple. Time to own up, fly boy."

Sid dangled in the air, staring into Zoraster's face. "But what is the 'real world?'"

"This"—Zoraster banged the pub tabletop, knocking over the empty glasses—"is the real world, my friend. Screw it. Enough is enough." He turned, Sid flying through the air on the end of his arm.

"I don't think so," Sid whispered.

Zoraster snarled. "What did you . . ."

The outlines of the pub and pit walls shimmered.

". . . say? . . ."

The world around them reformed, and Sid and Sibeal were standing on the floor of a repair pit, several tunnels down from the main den. Now Zoraster was the one suspended in the air, twenty feet up in the tight grip of a construction mechanoid.

"What the . . .?" He squirmed, then roared, the sound echoing down the tunnels.

Sid laughed. "Really? You expect me to be here for a week and not crack into everything? Overpower your synthetic immune systems, hijack your realities? You might think you've been watching me." Sid smiled. "But I've been the one watching you."

"Let . . . me . . . down!" Zoraster flexed, straining in the grip of the mechanoid. Its metal fingers shuddered, but did not give.

"Calm down, you big monkey."

Sibeal's eyes grew wide. "You really shouldn't call him a—"

Sid put one hand up. "We've cracked the data beacon. Who wants to see what's inside?"

At that, Zoraster quit wriggling.

"Outside access first," Sid reminded Sibeal.

"Don't do it," Zoraster growled, but it was too late.

"Your security blankets are bullet proof, right? Both outgoing and ingoing?" Sid asked Sibeal. There might be something nasty inside.

Sibeal nodded.

Dangling the unopened data beacon in a private virtual world, Sid reached out to grab the exit key from Sibeal. In an instant he was out, spinning a part of his consciousness—chaperoned by a splinter of Sibeal—to soar above New York while he reconnected his meta-cognitions systems with his outside search agents. At the same time, Sibeal opened the data beacon, spreading its contents across the walls of a secured space.

"My God," she whispered.

Sid left a good chunk of his attention matrix with her. From what he saw, most of what Bob put in the beacon was data from Patricia Killiam that Sid had already seen. At least this would confirm his story, hopefully calm the Grilla down. He watched Sibeal as she absorbed details of Jimmy Scadden's probable exploits on

Atopia; killing his own mother, killing Patricia Killiam, trapping the wife of Atopia Defense Force's Commander, Rick Strong, in a simulated reality suicide.

"What's in there?" Zoraster grunted. He wasn't plugged into the data stream.

Sibeal looked at Sid. He shrugged, *why not*. Something tugged at Sid's awareness, and a mediaworld broadcast opened up around him: mushrooming explosions, a wave of attack drones descending onto a submerged city. "Why didn't you tell me?" New Orleans had been attacked.

"Nothing we could do." Zoraster relaxed as he assimilated the stories about Jimmy. "Could you let me down from here?"

The mechanoid's hand opened up, dropping Zoraster to the floor of the pit.

They hadn't found Vince yet, Sid saw as he scanned the media reports, so maybe he escaped. Or maybe they captured him. Or maybe he was dead. Nothing in his networks gave any indication of where Bob might be. As the number-one suspect in the Manhattan attack, a manhunt was underway by nearly every police agency on the planet, but so far, it seemed nobody had any ideas.

Sibeal grabbed Sid. "What the hell is this?"

Sid was busy dropping agents into the Louisiana networks and digging into the New York passenger cannon logs. "What?"

"This Pacific Ocean Neutrino Detector data."

The POND? Sid had heard of it. It was one of Patricia Killiam's pet projects. "It's a planetary scale neutrino detector that Dr. Killiam embedded on the floor of the ocean—"

"I know what the POND is," interrupted Sibeal. She grabbed Sid's primary subjective and dropped a stream of data into it. "But what is this?"

Sid's mind did a double-take. He redirected part of himself to see what Sibeal was freaking out over. The POND had detected something in the neutrino flow it was monitoring—a message or transmission. He tried to understand the script of physics that came next, but it appeared the message emerged from another universe, or, at any rate, not from a terrestrial source.

"Aliens?" Sid mumbled, trying to get his head around it. Bob never told him anything about this.

From the logs, Patricia terminated the POND project right after the message was received. While the translation systems weren't able to decode the content, a contextual pattern had emerged. It wasn't just a message—it appeared it was a warning, and one directed specifically at Atopia.

"I've never seen this before," said Sid. "I'm as surprised as you are."

Sibeal began running her own translation memes through it. "Can this be real?"

For once, even Zoraster was silent.

The back of Sid's mind tickled, and he reflexively shoved away whatever it was, trying to focus on the POND data. Then it tickled again. He swiveled his attention outward. In an instant, he began shutting down his external networks and cutting off the agents he'd instantiated in Louisiana. He closed down the world with the data beacon in it.

Sibeal turned to him. "Why'd you do that?"

"Something in that data beacon we just opened, it's alerted Atopia."

A composite of pssi-kids, ones that Sid grew up with on Atopia, just turned their attention his way. He'd sensed them in the bar the night of the attack in Hell. Bob had warned him about the danger of exposing the private data on Jimmy Scadden. It was what had gotten Patricia killed, and why they had to escape from Atopia.

But Sid hadn't appreciated just how dangerous it could be.

"Something got out," Sid said. "The second that data on Jimmy was decrypted . . ."

Now that the can of worms had been opened, he suspected the whole Midtown den was in danger. There was no telling what Jimmy might do to anyone who knew his secrets.

He was afraid they were about to find out.

# 19

HIGH OVER THE Gulf of Guinea, the coast of Africa a thin line on the horizon, a drone began dispersing decoys, dropping them toward the distant speck of the Terra Nova platform. The viewpoint dropped down, following the warheads as they spiraled in, and then the inferno of the Terra Novan slingshots began to fill the air with superheated plasma. The simulation halted, and the shared reality space of the meeting morphed into streams of financial data and mortality statistics that ballooned into the attendees' meta-cognition frameworks.

It was a joint planning meeting between Atopian and Allied staff, held in virtual space. The meeting's presentations spawned into alternate realities that stretched forward and backward in time. The simulations grabbed each attendee's consciousness as needed to explain what needed to be understood. Questions were raised and answered in private meeting spaces that popped in and out of existence.

The senior staff of Allied Command was present with their senior staff. Their black-and-red uniforms composed a full two-thirds of the circular conference table in the meeting world created for the event, with the other third made up of the Atopian representatives. Jimmy Scadden presided over the whole thing, conspicuously outfitted in his military whites.

Nancy Killiam excused herself, pulling her consciousness into the identity space of the conference room. Taking a deep breath, she leaned forward and put her elbows onto the polished mahogany table. She buried her face into her hands, rubbing her temples with the heels of her hands.

Jimmy noticed her retreating. "Is everything all right?" He began calling the meeting to the last point, dragging the focal point of everyone's mind back to him.

Nancy stared at him, wondering how much he knew. Bob had been in a passenger cannon pod, arcing high over the Atlantic, when he reached out to her. He'd dropped her a data beacon before he'd cut off contact, but she hadn't told anyone.

"If you have any more information, now would be the time." Jimmy smiled.

"No," Nancy replied coolly, "I have nothing new."

This was mostly true. She hadn't decoded the beacon. It was too risky. For now.

One by one, the meeting participants inhabited the bodies sitting around the table. In the background, around the peripheries of the room, the merged realties of the simulation worlds continued to evolve, like a shifting veil of rain.

"We all have personal relationships with Vincent Indigo, Robert Baxter, Sidney Horowitz, but this is how traitors work," Jimmy added. He knew she was thinking about Bob. "They use you, your history together—"

This was both dangerous and patronizing. She shifted the latest tracking reports into the meeting's informational spaces. "Thank you, Mr. Scadden, but I'd point out that it was you who had the last contact with Robert Baxter before he left Atopia, in fact suggesting that he leave, if I remember."

Everyone was at the table now, and they were listening to his exchange with Nancy.

Jimmy blinked. "Yes, but—"

"Robert Baxter and I were friends," she continued, "but he is a part of your family."

Jimmy turned to the rest of the meeting. "I'm quite sure everyone knows where I stand."

"I think that it is quite clear where everyone stands," said Commander Zheng, head of Allied Command, looking at Jimmy. "*Except* you."

The Alliance had grown increasingly aware of the disproportionate influence Atopia was wielding as pssi spread into their consumer populations. While it had sided with the Alliance, in the past Atopia had never formally joined.

"You know my condition for joining the Alliance," Jimmy replied. He brought a series of Terra Nova attack simulations to the center of the meeting space.

The Atopian council had done its best to downplay the near-disaster of the Terra Novan reality skin, to limit the damage to its brand and upcoming product release. In this they'd almost succeeded too well. Nobody on the outside believed Atopia had been in mortal danger. The impression was that it had all been a kind of extravagant corporate espionage between these two competitors as they rushed to release their products.

The Alliance had been willing to go along with blockading Terra Nova in the physical and cyber realms, but Jimmy was pushing for an all-out kinetic attack with full Allied support. The varied conflicts of the Weather Wars were finally subsiding, and an attack against Terra Nova would constitute an act of war against the African Union.

Jimmy looked around the table and smiled. "The Great Peace is almost upon us, ladies and gentlemen. Terra Nova is all that stands in your way." He turned to Zheng. "It is your choice."

The Alliance needed Atopia. Very little would stand in its way of dominance if Atopia joined them, but if it switched sides, or went its own way . . .

Zheng stared at him, his jaw set for a long moment. Then he nodded.

# 20

THE MAN WITH the ax paused, waiting for the screaming to stop. The earth was muddy from a rain shower, but the fast-moving clouds overhead cleared a patch of blue sky and the sun just managed to shine into the grassy courtyard between the farmhouse and barn. With a whimper, the screaming abated. Satisfied, the man balanced a log on the chopping block, squared his feet and swung his ax back—but then paused again.

A line of birch trees shimmered against the backdrop of the dark forest that rolled up into foothills of the Ural Mountains, and someone appeared. A man, of slight frame and tentative step, peering toward the farm. Hesitating, the newcomer hung back.

The broad-shouldered man raised his ax in salute. "Mr. Indigo! This way!"

He motioned toward a patio set against the back of the farmhouse. Then he returned his focus to the log—still balanced on the chopping block—and swung back his ax again, looping it around to neatly split the wood in two. The ax stuck into the chopping block, and the man left it there, pausing to wipe the sweat from his brow with the back of one arm. He pulled his dangling suspenders up around his shoulders and walked up to the patio.

◆◆◆

VINCE CONTINUED WALKING toward the farmhouse. It was a synthetic space construct. Just an instant before he had been walking through the Louisiana swamp that the eagle-drone—that rescued him—had deposited him into. Someone dragged his primary subjective into this world. So he continued walking to see what they wanted.

He checked back with Hotstuff.

"All good here," she replied to his query. In an overlaid display he watched her continue to slog through the swamp with his body. "Somebody's hacked your subjective channels. I could try to get it back—"

"No," said Vince, still walking toward the farmhouse. "It's fine." The man ahead of him was motioning again, inviting him to come and sit on the patio. There were no metatags, no background data feeds on either this world or the man, but Vince could guess.

"So," said the man loudly as Vince neared. "You've been wanting to see me." The man laughed. "In a manner of speaking."

The thick Russian accent was surprising. No automated translation, but the man wasn't a native English speaker. This just confirmed Vince's suspicions. "Wanting to see you might be an exaggeration, but yes, I've been looking for you." Vince reconsidered his statement. "Someone asked me to look for you."

The man on the patio nodded. "Dear Patricia Killiam, a victim of her own creation. A certain tragic poetry, nyet?"

The screaming began again, a soul-tearing screech from the barn, and Vince stopped on the stairs leading onto the patio.

"Pay no attention to that," said his host with a wave of one hand.

An image materialized in Vince's display space of a man bound and gagged. He was naked, his body laced in welts and old scars, but his face was obscured with black goggles, a large spike protruding from one eye. Vince frowned. "That's—"

"—Sledge," continued the broad-shouldered man. "Yes, the one you met when you first arrived." Sledge began screaming again, some unseen agent twisting his body in agony. "He was the one who contacted the Federals, led them to the Saint John ceremony. Led them to you, in fact. We're just teaching him a small lesson in loyalty."

The image of Sledge faded, but the screaming remained. Vince braced himself and continued up the stairs to the patio. The man stood and extended one hand. "How rude of me. My name is Mikhail."

Vince shook his hand. What were the rules of conduct when meeting a notorious gangster? Probably erring on the side of caution was advised. Vince scanned reports from Hotstuff on Mikhail: rose up through the ranks of the Russian mafia in the late twentieth century after starting a career in Stalin's security apparatus. Some even hinted that he'd been a tank commander in the Red Army's defeat of the Nazis outside Leningrad, the battles in which he'd probably lost the first parts of his own body. The best guess was that he was now just a brain in a box somewhere, but exactly where, nobody knew. He was one of the oldest people alive—if the term could really be applied to him anymore.

"Some call me Sintil8, but I think we can dispense with facades, Mr. Indigo." He let go of Vince's hand and motioned for him to sit down opposite him at a rough-hewn wooden table. "And before you ask, Connors is safe. We are directing your proxxi to her location now."

Vince surveyed the area. His threat assessment systems had no information. Vince was reduced to using his meat-mind, and he strained, his inner voice looping through warnings. Looking behind him, nobody was visible, nothing apart from the trees and mountains behind the dirt trail that led out of the farm. Then again, he was only seeing—only sensing—what Mikhail wanted, allowed, him to see. There was no getting around the fact that he was entirely at the gangster's mercy. Vince half-shrugged and took a seat.

"Drink?" asked Mikhail, and without waiting for an answer summoned someone inside. "Aberlour is your favorite, yes?"

A mandroid, this one a stump of flesh suspended on two thin metal legs with matching arms, appeared with a bottle of scotch and two tumblers, setting them down between the two men. It made to leave but Mikhail raised an arm.

"Susan," said Mikhail to the mandroid, "I'd like to introduce you to Mr. Vincent Indigo." He paused, smiling. "But I think you might have already met on Atopia."

The mandroid—Susan—turned to Vince, attempting a smile with the scarred remains of her mouth. Red photoreceptors glittered in the back of her empty eye sockets. "A pleasure, Mr. Indigo," she said, her voice a rasping electronic signal that entered Vince's consciousness from behind.

Vince squinted, staring back into her skull-face. Yes, Commander Strong introduced him to this mandroid when they were working on deciphering the storms threatening Atopia three months ago. He reached out to shake her hand, feeling cool metal. She turned, releasing his hand, and disappeared back into the farmhouse.

Mikhail poured the scotch into the tumblers, watching Vince. "So you are searching for William McIntyre's body, yes?" he asked, handing one of the glasses over. Raising his own, he nodded, *cheers*, and took a drink.

Vince stared at Mikhail. He'd imagined tracking down Sintil8 and sending an agent to gather information from a distance. This was much more intimate. He didn't think dissimilating would help. It was time to lay the cards on the table. "Yes," he replied.

Mikhail raised his glass again and drank. "Good."

Vince considered the drink in his hand. If Mikhail wanted to kill him, he'd had ample opportunity, and anyway, he reminded himself, this was a synthetic projection. He took a sip. It tasted like Aberlour. Vince settled into the chair. "Did you help Willy's proxxi steal his body? Smuggle it out of Atopia?"

Mikhail pursed his lips. "Yes."

"How did you get it out without leaving a trace?"

"Susan was there, with others, of course." Mikhail smiled. "And the Spice Routes—the darknets—even Atopians needed their secrets."

Vince nodded and took another drink. At last, some progress. "Okay, so then why?"

"Because he discovered something very useful to me."

Vince studied Mikhail's face. He'd been one of the most powerful opponents of Atopia from the very start, lobbying to have access to the brain's pleasure pathways removed from its protocols. As one of the greatest purveyors of pleasures in the physical world, and arms dealer to all sides of the Weather Wars, the organizations he worked with stood to lose a lot of money when Atopia launched itself into the world.

"You mean Jimmy Scadden stealing people's minds in the pssi system?" Vince asked. "Were you hoping to use that to stop its release?"

"Perhaps." Mikhail cocked his head to one side. "But there was more to it than that."

Vince took another sip from his scotch. "And what was that?"

Mikhail nodded. "Why Jimmy committed these acts."

"And why did he?"

"That is something we are going to find out together, Mr. Indigo." Mikhail sat back in his chair with his drink.

"Together?"

"I don't think we'll find Willy's body otherwise. Not in time, anyway."

"For what?" Vince asked, and then it struck him. "Wait, you don't know where Willy's body is?"

Mikhail shook his head.

Now things were making some sense. Bob had the information from Patricia. Mikhail needed them, needed their help to get what he wanted. "Okay, I get it."

"Good."

"So now we're working together, what is it that Willy's proxxi has that is so important?" Vince didn't really expect him to answer, but wanted to see what he'd say.

"Mr. McIntyre's body holds the key to something I have been searching for a very"—Mikhail looked skyward—"very long time. When I was a young man, I fought against the Nazis."

As Mikhail spoke, he uploaded data packets into Vince's meta-cognition systems. It was better to show than to tell. Images of burning villages flashed into Vince's display spaces, place names and dates flooding his short-term memory. The playback switched to a bleak wooden shack, of bodies stacked one atop the other.

"I was captured, interred in one of their POW camps, and did what I had to in order to survive."

Vince watched an image of an emaciated young man, missing an arm, walking through a pack of SS officers. They were smoking and chatting, laughing, oblivious to the intruder in their midst as he lifted cigarettes and packs of chocolates from their pockets.

"But they soon learned of my . . ." Mikhail paused. "Let's say, special skills."

An image filled Vince's mind of the same young man, strapped to a wooden board, his head pinned back and probes inserted and clipped to him, the room filled with oscilloscopes and electronic devices.

"In weakness, I turned on my own. I became a part of the evil."

Now the young man was wearing an SS uniform, his cold eyes watching a stream of people being ushered into gas chambers.

"The Nazis were obsessed with the occult. Aryan is a Sanskrit word—Iran literally means 'land of the Aryan.' Did you know that?" Mikhail arched his eyebrows.

Vince shook his head.

"Hitler's prized possession was an ancient Buddhist statue from the Indus Valley, carved from a meteorite. He claimed it contained the ultimate power over reality and death, the fountain of everlasting youth."

Vince saw an image of the statue, enshrined on an oak table in the middle of the Berghof.

"That didn't work out too well," Vince muttered.

Mikhail ignored him. "It was the real reason he started the Nazi space program and planned moon bases—to search for more of it—for the exotic crystals it contained. Some secret societies called it Vril, but there have been many names."

"Why are you showing me all of this?" asked Vince.

"I know that you've studied the ancient manuscripts." Mikhail sat up and leaned into the table, looking straight into Vince's eyes. "Whomever understands this message shall never die. Does this sound familiar, Mr. Indigo?"

Vince nodded.

"The Gospel of Saint Thomas." Mikhail went on: "When you make two into one, when you make the inner like the outer and the outer like the inner, and when you make male and female into a single one, when you make eyes in place of an eye, and hands in place of a hand, then you will enter." Mikhail paused. ". . . the last word is untranslatable. These texts were dug up in Nag Hammadi at the end of 1945. I was part of a team that found them."

"Can you get to the point?"

"Connect the dots," replied Mikhail. "Have you ever heard of the Voynich manuscript?"

The Voynich manuscript. Vince had heard of it, but didn't know what it was. He instructed Hotstuff to search their internal data files.

"But you have seen the Buddhist statues, the ones with many heads and hands."

Vince nodded. Like the ones he'd seen in the Chenrezig monastery.

Mikhail leaned back from the table. "Your Mr. Jimmy Scadden is not just a madman, but I think influenced by something I've seen before. Willy's body contains the key to unlocking the secret."

Vince just stared at him. "What secret?"

"Toward the end of the Second World War, I fought with the Afrikaan units with the Rommel, the Desert Fox. Our units were destroyed by the Allies, but I escaped capture. I met someone out there."

An alert wailed in Vince's audio channels. Mikhail scowled, summoning a graphic that hovered over the table.

"It seems our friends aren't done yet." An image of drones skimming the Louisiana bayous spun into the space between the tables. "We need to cut this short and send you back to Connors." He stood up.

Vince held out one hand. "Wait. Who did you meet?"

Mikhail stared at Vince. "I think you just met one at Pontchartrain." Mikhail began deconstructing the world they were in, the mountains and forests collapsing to an interior point of space. "There are those that walk among us that are not of us." He uploaded a document to Vince as he vanished. "The Nag Hammadi texts weren't all that I found."

# 21

THERE ARE NO atheists in foxholes. Picking up a fistful of hot sand, Bob watched it pour through his fingers, just like the grains of life felt like they were being sucked from him and into the scorching air. He squinted into the sun. There are no atheists stranded alone in the middle of Sahara, either.

Then again, he wasn't alone.

"The mind creates suffering as a natural product of complex processes." The priest was always walking ahead of him, leading the way. "Nothing can really be said to be 'I' or 'me,' we are all one." He fixed Bob with his black eyes. "You need to get up."

*This suffering isn't shared*, Bob wanted to scream as he pulled himself back to his feet. But the priest had to be hurting as well, and Bob was the one who had insisted they come this way, out into the deep desert. Even a Bedouin had to feel this heat. It wasn't just the heat. With zero humidity, every molecule of water on the inside of his body wanted to get outside. Bob desperately wanted to rest, to dig his way into the cool sand beneath the surface, to bury himself. Please make this wind stop. It was eating into his skin like a blowtorch.

"We need to keep moving," the priest insisted.

So far they had connected with two oases, stopping at each to fill their canteens and themselves with as much water as they could. And to eat, but Bob tried to forget this. He steeled himself and plodded off behind the priest. Each breath felt like it was burning his lungs, as if the oxygen within it were on fire. They were nearing the top of a sand dune, hundreds of feet high, and on each footstep he would crunch through the stiff top layer of sand, his foot sinking underneath.

Toothface was still hunting them. From time to time a drone would appear in the immense blue sky, or a swarm of hunting bee-bots would buzz at the peripheries of his consciousness. Each time, the priest would hide them in the folds of the desertscape.

"How much farther?" He'd been out of water for a day.

"Not much more now." The priest returned a few steps to support Bob, pulling him up to the top of the ridge.

Bob laughed, and would have cried if any tears were left in him. He'd hoped to see another gaping hole into the bowels of the Earth, dark cliffs guarding a hidden sanctuary of palms. But all that greeted them on the other side was an endless sea of white dunes, riding all the way to the horizon.

"Come." The priest held Bob's hand. "Follow my voice." He led the way down. "There are many kinds of intelligence, just as there are many kinds of suffering. It seems a hopeless, endless cycle, but one that can be broken . . ."

Bob closed his eyes and tried to follow, but his legs buckled, spilling him down the side of the dune. In his mind he tried to get up, but his body remained still, his face to the sun, his eyes closed.

The priest knelt beside him in the sand, his hand on Bob's shoulder. "We are close. Not much further now."

But Bob couldn't will his body to move.

Bob had never really contemplated death before. On Atopia, it seemed like something that happened to other people, in some remote parts of the world, like catching malaria. *How did I arrive here?* There was the story, and then the story of how the story was told in his head, and then there was the story of the parts that were left out. Why had Patricia asked him to do this?

Opening his eyes, he saw the comet hanging in the sky next to the sun. I'm not afraid, I'm just so tired. And then the voice again in his head, the anger, telling him not to give up, to get up. He pushed himself up on one elbow.

The priest loomed over him, blotting out the sun.

Bob's mind circled around and around. I must exist in other universes. So my echo will live on. It doesn't matter. Suffering is worse than just letting go. Oblivion is peace. His body slumped back into the sand.

"Don't give up yet." The priest was close, his breath on Bob's cheek. "Open yourself to me, there is still hope."

Bob closed his eyes and took a deep breath, feeling the mind of the priest near. Open to me, the priest asked again, and Bob released, feeling the spirit of the priest flow into him.

"In the oceans, when you were surfing, do you remember?"

"Yes," Bob replied, his mind floating.

"Your little friends, the plankton, you summoned them to support you if there was danger."

Bob remembered. Those bright days on Atopia seemed endless. Carefree days he spent surfing with his friends, but he was always careful. He always kept a bloom of plankton nearby that he could summon up out of the depths, millions of tiny creatures that could, together, support his body if he was sucked into the depths.

"Call to them," urged the priest.

Bob felt his mind spreading, his consciousness skimming the tops of the sand dunes. He tried calling out for help, but there was no response.

The priest was cradling him in his arms. "Let go and call again."

Bob's mind sank further, seeping into the desert floor. And then a tiny reflection, a small chirp in the vastness of mindspace, followed by another. And then a roar.

"You see? They come, they hear you."

Bob opened his eyes. He saw only the burning eyes of the priest nested deep in the creases of his face. Bob's mind was thundering now, but around them it was quiet, just the hiss of the sand in the wind.

The priest smiled. "Wait."

Something fluttered in Bob's peripheral vision. He turned his head. An insect circled and then dropped, landing on his arm. It stared at him, its antennae waving, it wings flexing. It was tan, with long legs, and looked like a grasshopper. A desert locust. It continued to stare at Bob, bending its hind legs to preen its wings. Bob turned to see another locust land on the sand next to him, and then another. Soon a cloud of them were buzzing around him and the priest.

Over the tops of the dunes, a murmur grew into a roar, and as the swarm descended upon them, Bob felt the relief of the sun finally dimming. His initial revulsion was replaced by joy at the sweet coolness of the insects' wings on his skin. The swarm enveloped Bob, tens of thousands of them digging beneath him. At their urging, he rose up out of the sands on a writhing mass. Up, up, they pushed him, the swarm rising with his body, and then became airborne, carrying Bob's body into the sky, westwards, toward the beating heart of central Africa.

# 22

SPANISH MOSS HANGING from the live oaks swayed in the breeze, and a woman, leaning over a crashed drone, looked up. Insects were buzzing, swarming, in the muggy late afternoon heat. Looking around again, the woman rolled up her sleeves and gripped a wrench between her teeth. She ducked her head into the access hatch of the drone.

At the edge of the water nearby, Vince peered around the trunk of an oak. He was caked in mud, soaked, after pulling himself through the bayou. "Connors?" he called out.

The woman's head shot back out of the access hatch, and she grabbed the wrench from her teeth, brandishing it as a weapon as she turned. She squinted. "Vince?"

Nodding, Vince hobbled out of the water and started across the grass. The drone Connors was working on had crashed next to an old barn. A rusted propane tank sat beside it, its green paint peeling as if it were a slow-motion chameleon blending into the forest.

Vince stopped and tried to shake off some of the mud. "Yeah, it's me."

Hotstuff was walking beside him, her virtual projection as pristine as Vince was filthy. She rolled her eyes. "See, I told you we should have gone around."

"I wanted to find her," Vince replied in a hushed voice. "Why don't you make yourself scarce, see if you can log into that drone?"

He pointed at the wrecked mess Connors was working on. It must have been damaged in the attack.

"Sure thing, boss." Hotstuff sashayed up across the grass and faded from view.

"I'm still plugged into your proxxi channels." Connors shook her head. "I can hear you talking." She turned from squatting on the turbofan air intake and hopped down to ground level. "So what happened to you?"

If she was happy to see him, Vince had a hard time seeing it. He plucked a piece of mud from his cheek. "Had to wrestle a 'gator or two back there coming through the swamp—"

"I mean when they took you? Where did they take you?"

"Some voodoo ceremony."

Connors smiled. "And did they stick any pins in you?"

Vince smiled back. So she was glad to see him. "Naw, they left that for you." He paused. "I met Sintil8."

Of course Connors knew who this was, but she surprised Vince by turning around to return to the drone. He closed the last few feet and leaned against the airframe. "Aren't you going to ask me what happened?"

Connors had half of her body inside the access hatch. "Pass me the knife." She reached out one arm. "And no, I'm not going to ask, not unless you tell me the truth."

Vince spotted a blade with tape wrapped around it. He handed it to her. "I'm telling you the truth. He wanted to know what we were doing here."

"Uh-huh." Connors grabbed the knife and leaned further into the drone casing. "Mikhail Butorin doesn't just talk to anyone. Why the hell would he want to talk to you?"

"Aren't you happy I made it out?"

"I don't think it's any coincidence."

"What? That you're happy?"

Even from inside the cowling Vince could hear her snort. "No, I don't think it's any coincidence that you made it out, or that you magically found me here." She pulled herself from the access hatch and stared at Vince. "I'm getting the feeling that I'm a pawn in something"—she shook the blade at Vince—"and I don't like it."

They stared at each other.

"I've already told you what this is about. Trying to find my friend Willy's body."

"And why would Mikhail have any interest in that?"

"Because . . ." Vince took a deep breath, wondering how much he should tell her. "Because Willy's proxxi found out something about Jimmy Scadden, maybe enough to derail the entire Atopian program."

Connors' eyes narrowed. "And what was it that this proxxi found out?"

"We don't know, that's why we're searching for him." He looked at the drone. "What are you planning on doing with that?"

Tapping her knife against the aluminum shell, Connors stared at Vince. "You expect me to believe that we just crash-landed next to New Orleans, and you randomly met with Butorin who just *happened* to be looking for the same thing you are?"

Vince shrugged. "Okay, it was me who contacted him. I thought he might be able to help us."

Connors smiled. "See? That wasn't so hard, was it?" She uploaded some schematics into Hotstuff. A three-dimensional model of the drone appeared floating in space between them. "This one is Alliance military hardware; I've got all the tech-specs. Should be able to rewire it for manual control, get us out of here."

"Need some help?" Vince asked. Hotstuff was already helping Connors on the software side.

She grabbed a wrench and shook her head. "My brothers and I used to rebuild these all the time when we were kids." Turning, she stuck her head back into the access panel. "Why don't you go and see about some shelter in that barn." She pointed with the arm that wasn't in the access hatch. "Get cleaned up. There's some water purification tabs I scrounged, some food."

A light rain started falling, and it looked like worse was on the way. Shelter was a good idea. Vince started up a private comm network with her while he walked to the barn. "Brothers? I didn't know you had brothers."

In the shared space that he'd opened up, she replied, "You never asked."

The barn was in the process of being reclaimed by the encroaching swamp, and the knotted arms of wisteria vines engulfed it, dragging it back into the embrace of the earth. Vince kicked clumps of grass and weed away from the bottom of one door and pulled it, hearing the crack of rotten wood as it opened. "You're right, I don't know anything about you. Are you religious, Connors?" Inside it was dim, and his visual systems switched to low-light imaging. The interior was piled with junk—discarded aluminum furniture with legs sticking out, a rusted claw-foot bathtub, jumbled piles of wood. Vince stooped to pick up the body of a plastic doll, and then spotted its head nearby and picked that up as well. He tried reattaching them.

"My family was Catholic, but it never appealed to me," Connors replied. "Too much fire and brimstone. Why, are you?"

Vince carefully stepped his way through the junk. Looking overhead, he was relieved to see that the roof seemed intact. "No." Some planks near a far wall looked like they were in good shape, and he went to have a look. "Or, I mean I wasn't."

"What do you mean, you weren't?"

Gingerly, Vince reached down to pull up one of the planks. He remembered his grandmother's stories about always checking under the seat in an outhouse. Black widows and brown recluse spiders would just love a pile of wood like this. He inspected the timber he picked up. Covered in cobwebs, but it was straight and dry. "Did you know that Buddhists think that people in the past—the very long past—were basically immortal? And that the Jataka stories from India, written down thousands of years ago, talk about an infinite number of parallel universes, side by side, and that we create reality with our minds?"

"You know," replied Connors after a pause, "I did not know that." Her mind was obviously elsewhere as she tried to figure out the drone controls.

"Ever wonder why the prophets describe epiphanies as 'out of body' experiences?" Vince continued. "That when they talked with God, they felt like they were moving into another world?"

"I don't know—because they were talking with God?" Connors emphasized the last word. Her sarcasm was obvious even through the virtual comm link.

Vince shoved aside debris with his foot to clear a wide patch of earth to make a fire pit. He worked in silence for a few minutes.

"Where's this coming from?" asked Connors.

Vince picked up a rusted tricycle and inspected it. "When I met Mikhail, he was talking about Iran, about how the old Nazis were obsessed with it."

"Seriously?" The avatar Connors was presenting in the shared discussion space frowned. "That's what you talked about?"

"She finally believes something I say, and then she can't believe what I'm saying," mumbled Vince under his breath.

Satisfied he had enough space, he started laying down several of the thicker planks, and then put the rest cross-wise on top of them to create a platform. "Have you ever seen those images of Buddha with the multiple arms and heads? Like when Vishnu tries to impress the Prince in the Bhagavad Gita and takes on a multi-armed form?"

Connors grunted as she pulled out a circuit board. "I don't know what prince you're talking about, but yeah, I've seen the Buddhas with the arms and heads. What does this have to do with anything?"

"You're going to laugh."

"Try me."

Having finished building the platform for sleeping on, Vince looked around for anything that they could use as a cover. The sun was going down. He sighed. "Doesn't all of this sound a lot like pssi? Multiple phantom arms sprouting out with splintered minds, out-of-body excursions into other worlds—humans on the verge of immortality?"

He was right. Connors did laugh. He couldn't blame her.

"Mikhail also mentioned the Voynich manuscript—have you ever heard of it?"

"No, I have not."

Hotstuff pinged Vince that they had finished what they could on the drone, and that Connors was on her way inside the barn.

Vince uploaded the data he had on the six-hundred-year-old Voynich manuscript, and images of naked nymphs, unrecognizable plants, astrological diagrams, all written in an unknown alphabet, flooded the shared display space between them. Translation tools hadn't been able to make sense of it, but they did confirm that it contained coherent information. None of the plants or animals were anything that had existed—at least, not in this world. In their shared space, Connors looked at it and sent Vince another frowning emoticon.

"When I was running around a few months back, trying to save my life from whatever future threat was trying to kill me," Vince said, rummaging around in a pile at the back of the barn, "I spent a lot of time decoding ancient texts. I'm sure I saw something in there."

"In where?" Connors was leaning against the frame of the open barn door.

"In the past. The end of ordinary reality is the start of the merger with the divine for Buddhists—so my question is, if we've reached the end of ordinary reality with pssi, what exactly would we be merging with?" Speaking of miracles, Vince found a metal case filled with what looked like tablecloths. He pulled one out and held it aloft. They weren't even that moldy. They'd make great covers.

Connors nodded. "I think what you need to merge with is a good night's sleep."

Climbing back through the scattered junk, Vince tossed the metal case on the floor. It was going to be cold. They'd better get a fire going soon. "Maybe you're right."

"Anyone want to chat with the outside world?"

Hotstuff materialized sitting on a cross-beam above their heads. She was back to wearing battle fatigues. No sexy outfits anymore.

"You got it working?" Connors asked.

Hotstuff nodded. "Main avionics are shot, it ain't getting airborne, but we can get comms working. A clean channel right into the main data trunks in the sky. But you've capped the connection on this side."

Connors nodded and smiled. "Didn't want you guys escaping."

"So you're going to contact your government buddies?" Vince looked down at the floor. "Last time you tried that, they flattened half of Louisiana."

"There are still some people—"

"I think it's time to give me a chance, no?"

"Are you kidding?"

"Do I look like I'm kidding? Look, you can chaperone, throw a security blanket around me, whatever you want."

Connors lifted her hands to her face and rubbed her eyes.

Vince held his arms wide. "I've got a lot of friends, Connors, in a lot of places."

"Okay," Connors conceded, "we can try it your way. But I remain in control of the connection."

Smiling, Vince nodded. He wondered if he'd be able to get in touch with Sid or Bob, or perhaps the Commune and Brigitte. He hoped someone was still left out there.

While Hotstuff and Connors began setting the parameters of the communication link, Vince retreated inside his head to look at the texts Mikhail gave him. Like the Nag Hammadi libraries, they appeared to be ancient pre-Christian Gnostic, but it was like nothing he'd ever seen before.

The texts were written in precursor of Aramaic, so Vince's automated translators were having a difficult time making sense of it, but in the Book of Pobeptoc an impossible passage popped out at him: "Wal lie body is where the flesh eaters live."

*The Book of Pobeptoc.* Was he seeing things? How could it be possible?

# 23

A SEA OF green sludge sat fermenting between rolling mountains of sand under a sky dotted with distant clouds. In a hollow between the dunes, on a dusty peninsula that jutted into the blooms of algae, was a shanty town of corrugated tin and mud brick. Everywhere was garbage. At the side of a putrid stream in the middle of the town a man in ragged jeans was sprawled out, shirtless, emaciated, and covered in sores.

"Wake up, young master."

Bob opened his eyes to find the priest looking down at him, cradling him in his arms. The smell of rot and decomposing flesh nearly made him gag. He spat out a mouthful of water.

"Slowly." The priest brought the cup to Bob's lips again.

Taking a deep breath, Bob blinked and leaned his head forward, taking a sip. He was leaning against a wall of rough concrete blocks, in merciful shade. In front of him, a pig was rooting through a mound of plastic bags in a pool of water, and further, several young boys were stooped over, stepping through the muck, searching. One of them kicked aside a robot scavenger, pulling away a tin can for which the bot was going. The boy made a face at the bot and it scurried away. He deposited the tin can into a sack slung over his shoulder.

"Can you stand?" the priest asked.

Bob wasn't sure. *How did I get here?* Closing his eyes he tried pushing himself up, and, trembling, his body responded, but only just. "Give me a minute."

The priest nodded and offered more water. It spilled around Bob's beard. Beard. Bob reached up to feel his face. It was covered in shaggy hair. It was the first time he had ever grown facial hair. It itched.

"We need to keep moving," whispered the priest, looking toward the knot of children hunting through the islands of garbage in the stream. "You still want to get into the African Union, yes?"

Bob nodded. Across the filthy river, standing above the corrugated tin roofs, stood the local microwave array that received and transmitted to the space power grid. Africa was leapfrogging ahead, replacing old-style infrastructure with more efficient ideas like the matter-net.

"Then I have someone for you to meet."

Clenching his teeth, Bob groaned and tried his body again. Pushing against the concrete wall, he inched his way to his feet. "Let's get going."

Holding Bob's hand to steady him, the priest led him along a path at the side of the stream, past stinking piles of plastic bags and eel bones and shredded packaging. They walked through an opening under tarps, held aloft by haphazard wooden poles, onto a dusty street between mud brick houses that leaned unsteadily into each other. A scooter buzzed by, honking at Bob as he nearly fell into it. The boy riding double on the back turned and gave Bob the finger.

Bob stared at the trail of blue exhaust following the receding scooter. "Where are we?"

"Goudjoul, on the side of Lake Chad." The priest adjusted his grip on Bob, then looked up into the sky. "Or at least, what used to be Lake Chad. We have crossed the great divide."

Images flowed into Bob's mind, information pulsing through the connection with the priest. Goudjoul was a small frontier town between the Allied and African Union territories, on an island in a sea of algae on the border of Chad. Lake Chad used to be a vast inland sea, but all that remained was a puddle of green—it was the only place on Earth where the species of algae outnumbered the species of animals. Bob followed the priest's eyes up and saw the comet hanging in the sky, ever larger, its tails spreading ever wider. The critical thing was that they were on the other side of the Sahara desert, on the fringe of sub-Saharan Africa.

"Come," urged the priest, motioning toward a crowd gathering in an open square ahead.

Bob felt something sticking to his leg and looked down. A leech had attached itself. He reached down and yanked it off, leaving an oozing wound.

The priest saw his look of revulsion. "Parasites make up the majority of life on Earth." Grabbing the leech, he held it in front of Bob's eyes. "Do you hate them? Do you see yourself? Humans are the greatest parasites of all."

He threw the leech into an alleyway and kept walking. The lesson was over.

In this place a ragged, half-naked man aroused little curiosity, and Bob stumbled behind the priest. *Am I hungry?* He wasn't sure. Everything felt like a dream, the images before his eyes flat and two-dimensional. He eased through the crowd like a ghost, sensing the people around him. People walked by him, the men in cloaks, the women in burkas, hidden from view, but not hidden from Bob.

On Atopia he took for granted, like breathing, the speeding up of consciousness, the ever-expanding meta-cognition systems fueled by the machines, but here, the humans were so slow. He could sense the neural potentials flowing through their bodies, anticipate their movements, know their intentions before they became consciously aware themselves—he could almost hear their thoughts flowing through them.

In the few people who were connected to the pssi multiverse, Bob was intercepting the thoughts and images flowing through their external cognition networks. The memplex here was shallow and homogenous, the allowed external-thought patterns restricted. They were free to think what they wanted in their meat-minds, but the digital minds here were forced open to the local council. They were regularly cleansed of unclean ideas.

The Atopian network was present here, nudging itself into this crack in the side of the African Union. There were a few people using pssi, but there were more that were renting it. Spinning into a viewpoint that hovered above the bazaar, he picked out the psombies, the minds of their owners given free access to the multiverse play worlds in exchange for lending their physical bodies to Cognix Corporation.

Bob and the priest stayed well clear of them.

Something else he stayed out of was communication networks. He could have reached out into them, but he was in unfamiliar territory that was crawling with Atopian access points. He had to remain invisible.

Up ahead was a laamb wrestling match. This Senegalese sport was the biggest in Africa, almost the biggest in the world, and every town had its local contests on weekends. A thickly-muscled man sat scratching in the dirt, his eyes wide, and his neck muscles taut. He was speaking to the spirits, the *loa*. This area was under heavy influence of *voudon*, the ancient religion that spread from here into the Americas hundreds of years before.

The crowd grew denser. Bob began noticing the deformed and injured scattered throughout. The Wars were fueling massive death tolls in central Africa, and starvation and plagues were driving people into the cities, at least those who could afford it. Despite the amputations and injuries, there were no mandroids here. The area was too poor to support the robotic ecosystem that outnumbered humans elsewhere. If the African Union was a rising superpower, here in the fringes it was still grindingly deprived.

A young boy caught Bob's eye. He was sitting on a tree stump, his withered arms and legs curled up into his body at awkward angles.

"Hi," said Bob in Chadian Arabic, the words flowing from his mouth.

The boy looked up and managed a pained smile, flies buzzing away as Bob reached out to touch him. Flitting into the boy's nervous system, Bob discovered the source of the deformation—a demyelinating nerve disorder brought on by malnutrition. Simple enough to fix, at least in the short term. Bob concentrated, letting his mind flood into the boy's neural system. He began restructuring the grey matter. He wasn't used to the technology the priest infused into him, but it was superior to Atopian pssi in many ways, even as a novice.

Bob smiled, releasing the boy, and continued walking into the crowd.

THE STRANGE MAN'S touch felt like cool water running into the boy's veins. The pain disappeared, and the boy's arms and legs unfolded. He smiled, leaning over to put his feet on the ground. Reaching up he pulled on his father's hand, who turned to look down in amazement at his son, standing on his own feet for the first time in years.

The man cried in disbelief and began calling to his wife and friends. The boy stared silently at the disappearing silhouette of Bob. The crowd at the edge of the laamb wrestling circle was frenetic, screaming and thundering with the ongoing fight. Bob had to force his way in, past the men preparing themselves, their eyes, not seeing. He found the priest talking to two scruffy military men.

"Transportation into the African Union, no questions?" said a gaunt man dressed in threadbare khaki fatigues, an aging AK-47 slung over one arm. He was talking to the priest.

The priest nodded and pointed at Bob.

The man's eyes lit up. "Ah, yes, yes." He turned to speak to another man in fatigues beside him. They both nodded. He turned back to Bob. "This is danger. Will be expensive. Much risk."

"You will be rewarded," the priest said. "I will make arrangements."

Staring into Bob's eyes, the man smiled with a mouthful of broken teeth. "At the main dock, tonight, just before the sun goes down."

"Sure," Bob replied, trusting the priest knew these men.

The gaunt man continued to stare at Bob.

"Do I know you?" Bob asked.

The gaunt man laughed. "We are all friends here. Good, we will see when the sun goes down, down by the docks."

With a roar from the crowd, one of the wrestlers pinned the other to the ground. Bob heard the crack of breaking bones, earning another roar. The laamb wrestling match was over, and the crowd began dispersing.

Bob stood in place, in a daze. The men in fatigues were gone, the priest was gone. Something nibbled one of his fingers. He looked down. A goat had wandered up to him. It bleated and nudged him again, looking up at Bob with its slatted-pupil eyes. Bob sensed its fear. It was lost and hungry.

He was lost too.

Bob reached down and petted it. He decided to care for it, find it some food, some shelter. He'd always had a soft spot for animals.

They were simply non-human people, with the same abilities to make conscious decisions, grieve and worry and love. And this went both ways; in humans, there was also the beast.

Then again, looking down into the animal's eyes, even if he fed it and found it shelter today, what would happen to it tomorrow? The animal was a bag of bones, its fur mangy. Perhaps a quick end, to stop its suffering, was better.

AN UNDULATING CARPET of green stretched to the horizon. It glistened under the setting sun. The African Union began somewhere over that horizon, and Bob was close, finally on his way.

The AU was the second axis of world power behind the Alliance of China and America. A deep distrust of the old world and colonial powers ran deep, a distrust that ran into the bloodstream of anything African. The AU was commissioning its own aircraft carriers, at-sea platforms, and south-south trade outstripped north-north for the first time in history: the distance of Lagos–Rio was half that of New York–Frankfurt. It was also the first jurisdiction to grant full human rights to certain uplifted animals, the Grillas.

Bob settled into his seat of the wooden longboat, its gunnels worn with time and sweat. An ancient internal combustion engine, probably from an even more ancient car, was fixed to the back of the boat, its drive shaft extended and attached to a propeller. The engine roared, the driver standing high in the back like a gondolier, cutting a path forward with the boat through the algae.

"I can come as far as the border," said the priest, sitting just ahead of him. "There is a transport waiting. Beyond that, I cannot. Just as you have enemies outside, there are those in Lagos who hunt me."

Bob nodded. He couldn't ask for more than that, knowing how much he missed—feared for—his own loved ones. He hoped it wasn't too late.

Once they cleared the ragtag collection of boats in the harbor, the driver gunned the engine. Bob had never seen a gas-powered one before, and he watched the fumes pouring out of it and into the naked atmosphere with a morbid fascination.

They were smuggling him past the legal check points up the Yoba River and into Nigeria. The paramilitaries arranged a drone transport from there through the exclusion zone. An outbreak of nano-goo a decade ago had forced evacuations and a tactical nuclear strike by China on its own failed site in the Gobi desert, so replicator factories now had to be physically firewalled off from the rest of the world. The exclusion zone around Assembler City outside of Lagos was the best way to get in without anyone noticing.

Turning, Bob squinted ahead, westward, into the setting sun. Something was dead ahead of them. *What is that? A forest?* Something was casting long shadows across the pond-scum surface, but whatever it was, as the boat approached, it parted, moving aside to create a path.

The driver throttled back the engine.

It was people, hundreds of them, standing naked, knee-deep in the shallow water with their arms outstretched. The webbing between their fingers glowed green in the light, and folds of skin stretched from their arms to their bodies—a Greenie colony, people bioengineered with photosynthetic engines in their epithelial mitochondria.

They fed off sunlight.

The boat glided through them. Bob turned to watch their faces, their eyes closed, impassive. He saw the lignin-thermoplastic shell of their habitat burrowed into the side of the dune island behind them. There had to be a deep-core thermal generator in there. It was expensive to maintain a colony like this—nothing about it was natural—and just around the corner there was grinding poverty and suffering.

Bob shook his head, looked away to stare back into the setting sun.

# 24

"ROBERT BAXTER AND Sidney Horowitz," said the news-world announcer, an elfin girl with a deadly serious face, "friends or accomplices?" She paused for dramatic effect. *"Or BOTH?"*

An image of Atopia floated into the display space of the splinter Sid had following this thread. "And how are they related to the disgraced Vincent Indigo? The greatest personal financial loss of all time, over a trillion dollars gone with the collapse of his empire . . ." The social clouds tethered to the story erupted at mention of a trillion dollars: "Can you imagine?," "What was he thinking?," "Serves him right," "Did they find him yet?," followed by a chorus of, "Who cares . . ."

Most of it was just noise, but one thread led into an interesting aside: a ride through the pneumatic tube system under New York with the reconstructed mind of one of the party-goers injured in the attack on Hell. It was new information, and the splinter encoded this into a memetic ping to catch Sid's primary attention. Sid added this to other data being collected. It seemed that Bob had been heading for the passenger cannon on the day of the attack. He sent agents to conduct a deeper forensic sweep.

In another newsworld, an image of the glowing skyline of Manhattan's financial district floated into view, followed by a view of three-dimensional tunnels underneath it, layer upon layer, millions of conduits. A panel of media pundits, in severe black suits, weighed in: "Sidney Horowitz is still definitely in Manhattan, and the NYPD is asking anyone with any information . . ."

Sid had heard it all before, a million times in a million media-worlds, but listening to it still sent dread tingling into his fingertips. Worse, he could only imagine what his mom was going through. *But this is what I always wanted, right?* A rebel, fighting for a cause, fighting for his friends. Sid nervously tapped his phantoms and dove into restructuring the airflow mechanics of the tunnel systems.

His bravado was wearing thin.

Pressure was coming down on the Midtown den. The underground was a collection of misfits, and to their credit—with the authorities bearing down—they were coming together. But not all the parts fit, and not everyone was happy. It wouldn't be long until someone gave Sid up.

"You all right, mate?" Bunky asked, noticing Sid on the media-worlds again. The inky blackness of an access tunnel stretched out ahead. Sid was riding shotgun in Bunky's mechanoid.

Retreating a chunk of himself into the physical world, Sid looked at Bunky in the dim red light. "I guess." he replied. Since the attack on New Orleans, it was anybody's guess what would happen next. The phrackers were busy modifying future timelines as best they could to try to deflect the attention from Sid, but their efforts were starting to be noticed. It was just adding to the incriminating evidence.

A flashing door appeared in the rock wall ahead. They were on their way to a materials testing lab with the rocks they collected at the spots where Willy's proxxi stopped in the underground. They didn't find any machines, didn't see anything unusual, so they dug out some samples from the surrounding rock to test.

Bunky smiled at Sid with his broken, toothy grin. "Mate, we've got your back. Don't worry."

The access door opened ahead of them, and Bunky's mechs began unloading the samples.

Sid smiled and retreated to his inner worlds, monitoring the stream of data from his splinter network. "Was the police action in New Orleans a step too far?" echoed one newsworld. He spun through some splinters monitoring the physical world: "A winter hurricane? Depression in the Caribbean looks like it will build into category four and hit the east coast in January . . ." He moved his attention into a different newsworld. "Central Africa reports a huge locust swarm that swept through the desert and into Chad . . ." This last newsworld story was so unusual that it pricked his attentional matrices. When was the last time a spontaneous locust swarm moved through the Sahara? He filed the thread for closer inspection.

"The Synthetic Beings Charter of Rights has been derailed by Nancy Killiam, the heir of the founder of the SyBCoR movement itself, the late Patricia Killiam . . ." another story began, which flowed into, ". . . glitches in the Atopian synthetic reality system, or ghosts in the machine? We talk now to . . ." which streamed into, ". . . tens of thousands more disappearances reported by independent sources . . ."

Sid smiled. Like a frog sitting in water heated to a boil, the public was barely noticing. At first the disappearances had been explained away as system problems, then psychological ones, but what Sid suspected was Jimmy's excesses were getting difficult to hide.

". . . but Jimmy Scadden, head of conscious security for Atopia, says that terrorist actions related to Sidney Horowitz . . ."

Sid's smile evaporated.

Going through his list of projects, he checked the decryption agents working on the POND data, to see if the mysterious messages from a parallel universe could be unwound into anything intelligible. *Nothing yet.* He felt a familiar phantom pulling his consciousness, and his smile returned. He didn't resist.

Coming back into real space, his proxxi, Vicious, was disgorging his body from the mechanoid and onto the terrace of the White Horse Pub. He tweaked the serving bot for a round of beers and slid himself into a seat between Sibeal and Zoraster.

"Anything new on the POND data?" Sibeal asked right away. It was a hot topic in the pub.

Sid shook his head.

"I'm sweating like a glassblower's asshole!" whooped Shaky as he sat down on the other side of the table with Bunky. The serving bot slapped a beer down in front of him and he grabbed it up.

Sid turned to Sibeal. "Anything new on your side?"

"Some bad glass out there." She spun some data into a private workspace with Sid. "Like nothing I've ever seen before. What do you make of it?"

Sid slid a part of his mind in to take a look. "Doesn't look like it was doing anything wrong."

"Did you see how it was mutating? And it's not attached to any human tags—"

"Come on, it wasn't doing anything." Sid felt annoyed at the way she always targeted machine intelligences. Maybe he felt like he had to stand up for his proxxi, Vicious, who was sitting across from them in his virtual projection.

"Yet," Sibeal replied.

Sid put his beer down. "I'll bet you're happy SyBCoR got slammed."

Sibeal frowned. "SyBCoR would make my job a lot easier, if you want to know. The big AIs hide inside corporate structures so even if they kill people, it's hard to get the shareholders to stand down."

"Worse than people?"

"At least if they had civil rights and obligations, the playing field would be evened. And it was your friend Killiam who killed it, and I bet it wasn't on moral grounds."

The argument wasn't really anymore whether the machines qualified as "people" philosophically, but more about the economic chaos from granting billions of machines even basic civil rights. The rise of Atopian pssi was, in theory, supposed to buffer this effect by moving economics into virtual consumption.

"Anyway, machine intelligence is different," added Sibeal. "I don't know why—"

Sid knew she was about to get into the statistical inference versus biological debate. He cut her off. "Do you understand why you do things?"

Sibeal looked at him defiantly. "Of course."

"There's a difference between rationalization and reasoning. You do things because you want to, because a set of reasons put up afterwards always make it fit. Reasoning is just an illusion—"

"You're going to talk to me about illusions? You're the master of illusions."

"Exactly."

"Kids, kids," Bunky interjected. "Come on now, we're here for a nice pint." He raised his glass and grinned. "And those results are coming in from the materials lab. How about we focus on that?"

Sibeal took a deep breath and looked away from Sid. She opened a virtual workspace and dragged everyone's subjective into it, and then pulled in the results from the rock sample testing.

Living underground, they were all experts on rocks.

After a few seconds, Sibeal sighed. The results looked typical: mostly metamorphic rock, the mica schist that formed the bedrock under Manhattan. Some flakes of quartz and granite gneiss—the crystalline basement of the crust under the East Coast—and some ground-up glacial till.

"Wait, what's that?" Sid asked, dragging one of the test results to the top of the workspace.

Bunky and Shaky's avatars frowned, but Sibeal's eyes grew wide.

"Quasi-crystals," she said aloud, pulling up more samples into the center of the test-result world. "Do you see that?"

Shaky's avatar nodded. "What's that doing there?"

Sid looked up the definition: A quasiperiodic crystal is a structure that is ordered but not periodic.

"That's not even an icosahedrite," Bunky pointed out.

Sid shook his head. "What?"

Sibeal forwarded him some background data, but it was barely intelligible. "Quasi-crystals don't occur naturally—at least, not on Earth."

"The only ones in nature are from the Koryak Mountains in Russia," added Bunky. He was something of a rock historian. "And some in the New Guinea highlands. But all have extraterrestrial origin." In the pub he took a sip from his stout, leaving him a foamy mustache. He smiled. "What I mean is they're from meteorites."

Sibeal spun the model of the crystal structure around in space. "And these look natural, not lab-grown. There's residue of uranium." She popped their viewpoints back into normal space at the pub. "Bunky, can you contact underminers in cities where Wally's proxxi made stops, see if they can find any more of this?"

Bunky nodded.

Sid didn't quite understand, so he pulled up the tech sheets Sibeal had forwarded him.

A splinter following world events chimed in with a future prediction that had topped the ninety-percentile, "With Atopia joining the Alliance, it is only a matter of time before a kinetic attack is launched against Terra Nova unless it gives in to UN demands for weapons inspection . . ."

Something else was bothering him. The digital organism Sibeal had been complaining about, it shared some of the same digital fingerprints as the virus that infected and nearly destroyed Atopia.

Burrowing into his workspace to investigate, he shrugged off an attempt by someone to grab his primary subjective. Closing his virtual eyes, he sighed, relenting, deciding he'd better apologize to Sibeal for his rant earlier. She was right about that glass being odd. He opened a private space, a small meeting room with beanbags on the floors and walls covered in whiteboards.

But it wasn't Sibeal.

Vince materialized sitting in a beanbag across from Sid. He smiled. "Miss me?"

# 25

"BACK!" BROADCAST THE droid across a wide spectrum of audio and radio frequencies, its red and blue lights strobing at the crowd. A second droid was working the other side of the plaza, while a third and fourth rolled in and sprang into action, pushing back the street vendors and hawkers and robotic scavengers.

It wasn't easy clearing a landing space for a VTOL in the Lagos slums.

Bob stood still in the center of the square while the crowd dispersed, his head bowed. He wore a stained white robe and sandals, his dirty blond hair falling around his shoulders, merging with his beard. Passage through Assembler City was thankfully uneventful, just about the first thing that had gone to plan in this whole adventure. The drone he'd hidden in had passed by one automated transport and microwave array after another, eventually depositing him here in the outskirts of the Lagos mega-city.

A light mist began to fall, and the moisture triggered a phase change in the bio-plastics lining the alleyways and shop stalls. Like blooming flowers, walls and awnings spread against the coming rain.

Over the tops of the tin roofs and neon signs, the Spike—a glass tower a mile high—glittered between scudding clouds in the night sky, dominating the skyline of Lagos beside the greyed-out hundred-story Islamic business feminist complex. A point of light flashed from near the top of the Spike, and Bob watched it arcing through the murky air. The point of light grew into an African Union turbofan transport. A knife-point of light stabbed out from it, illuminating Bob in a cone of white in the middle of the now-cleared plaza.

Stepping back from the center, Bob gave the transport room to land. The blast from its exhaust blew a cloud of dust and scattered debris. Bob closed his eyes, but his mind was already away, his primary subjective jacked into a private Terra Novan communication channel. The moment he made a data connection with Terra Novan representatives, his body was flooded with their own synthetic reality technology.

Observing from a virtual point-of-view in a conference room at the apex of the Spike, Bob watched his body climb up and into the transport far below in the slums.

The relief of reaching a safe harbor was almost overwhelming. Bob felt like he was resurrected, been brought back to life after wandering the underworld. Somehow he managed to navigate his way out, past the tortured souls that remained trapped there. The past week was a blur. He felt different. Most of his external mind wasn't reconnected yet, and a lot of it might stay lost, but it wasn't just that.

After making a connection, he was instantly cordoned off, his presence isolated by thick security blankets. He hadn't spoken to anyone yet, and so Mohesha pinging him, asking if she could come and talk to him, felt like the start of his journey home. He'd done what Patricia asked. He made it to Terra Novan territory, and could tell Mohesha what he knew. Perhaps his part was done.

"We were afraid we had lost you," Mohesha said as soon as her virtual presence materialized in the room with him. She looked down through the windows at the transport. "We haven't been introduced, I'm—"

"I know who you are." Bob turned to face her, a slender, dark-skinned woman with close-cropped black hair and kind eyes. She was an old friend of Patricia Killiam, and was, in fact, a student of Patricia's more than fifty years before. Together they created the foundations for synthetic nervous systems, the foundation for both Atopia and Terra Nova.

Mohesha smiled. "You understand bringing you here is dangerous."

Given that I'm a hunted terrorist. Bob resisted the urge to defend himself.

The room was cool, their voices echoing through the empty room. It was a conference space designed for international meetings, forty chairs lining each side of a massive table ten feet across. The floor-to-ceiling glass window walls sloped outward. They were alone.

"Patricia told me to come."

"I know." Staring through the window, Mohesha's reflection hung side by side with Bob's. "Atopia has formally declared war, joined the Alliance with America."

"I had nothing to do with what happened in New York."

Mohesha spun mediaworlds into Bob's sensory frames, announcing the sighting of Robert Baxter in the Lagos slums. "It doesn't matter what you did or didn't do anymore. International courts have filed for your extradition, to Atopia of course. They claim you possess stolen information that threatens Alliance security."

Bob retreated from the window. "Not stolen, it was given to me." He sat down in one of the conference table chairs.

"By Patricia? This is Patricia's proxxi data?"

Bob nodded. He was holding the data cube Patricia gave him in the center of his systems, protecting it like an egg. It seemed another world and time when she gave it to him. It was a burden he'd be glad to be rid of.

"And you have it with you?"

Bob nodded. Leaning his elbows onto the table, he pressed his hands together and steepled his fingers. The data cube might be a burden, but he hesitated to just give it up. "I have it encrypted in the bio-electronics in my body."

"Good." Mohesha watched the transport arcing through the sky on its return, cradling within it the precious cargo of Bob's body. "One more thing."

Bob looked at her. "What?"

"Did you find Willy's body yet?"

# 26

"THIS PROVES IT!" screamed a newsworld anchor, his face apoplectic. "Robert Baxter is a Terra Novan spy, flying home to roost." In the background hung a three-dimensional image, the viewpoint flying around from all angles, of Bob climbing into the transport in the Lagos slums from the night before. "The Allies need to launch an immediate attack on Terra Nova before we get a repeat—"

Sid controlled the primary feed, and he switched to another newsworld.

"—with Atopia joining the Alliance, an era of peace stretches forward for humanity. In countries where their synthetic reality system has been successful, we're seeing the highest happiness indices that have ever—"

Sid switched worlds again.

"—they are trying to destabilize Atopian technology for their own gain." This time a square-jawed synthetic anchor, in a suit and tie with his hair neatly parted and his voice steady. "Granting asylum to Robert Baxter, while refusing UN weapons inspectors entry to their space power grid installation is not—"

Vince swiped away the mediaworlds with a phantom. "Enough. At least we know Bob is safe. Did you send out a message?"

Nodding, Sid sent a copy of his inquiries to the external Terra Novan offices. There was no response. "I still can't believe he made it." He must have one hell of a story to tell.

He was with Sibeal and Zoraster in the White Horse. It was their meeting place. On the other side of a fused augmented reality were Vince and Connors in the barn in the Louisiana bayou, sitting on peeling wooden chairs. Now that he knew where Bob ended up, Sid was able to retrace his path through parts of the accessible wikiworld. Sid bought bits and pieces of the data path that weren't publicly available. He'd already contacted the paramilitaries that had taken him up the Yoba River.

Connors stared at Sibeal through the augmented reality display. "Explain to me again these crystals you found?"

After some haggling, Vince had convinced Sid to allow her into the meeting. Understandably, Sid wasn't comfortable including in their discussions a member of the same police forces that were trying to hunt him down. He only allowed it on the condition that her memories of the discussion would be externally stored, where they could be wiped if needed.

The shared meeting space blossomed into a visualization of atomic orbitals, shared valence bonds, and crystalline structuring graphs. "Quasi-crystals don't occur naturally on Earth. The only ones found outside a lab were discovered in the Koryak Mountains and Indus Valley."

The viewpoint zoomed to sub-atomic detail, zeroing in on the wave pattern of a single electron. "At each point that Willy's proxxi stopped in the undergrounds of cities, we found traces of these same formations."

"Meaning either it was looking for them, or it implanted them there," Connors said.

Nodding, Sibeal dove into technical details about the resonance of spin between quarks in the crystals' sub-atomics and power dissipation curves from a surrounding matrix of uranium.

Sid had been researching the quasi-crystals for hours already. Deciding to take a break, he opened a private world to chat with

Vince. They morphed away from their physical bodies to sit down at another table in the White Horse, their conversation protected by a glittering security blanket. "So you're telling me you were possessed by a voodoo spirit?"

"I don't know, it all happened pretty fast. It felt the same as sharing sensory channels in a synthetic world." Vince smiled. "But, you know, some of us just can't help having fun no matter what we're doing."

"Figures you would be inhabited by . . . who was it? Papa Ougan, the voodoo spirit of boozing and womanizing?"

Vince laughed. "Yeah, that's what they say."

"And I see you're going all Stockholm syndrome." Sid motioned at the image of Connors, already up to her elbows in schematics with Sibeal. "The woman kidnaps you, loses you"—Sid checked the latest mediaworlds on the Phuture News meltdown—"about a trillion dollars, threatens you with jail, and you want to make her a part of our gang?"

"What can I say?" Vince laughed again. "I'll get it all back, and it wasn't personal. She's just doing her job. I respect that."

Sid shook his head in wonderment. "You're one special kind of guy."

Vince's smile faded. "Seriously, though. She's a straight shooter, wants to do the right thing, and more than anything, she wants to make her mark, prove herself. I think she could be a big asset."

"If you say so." Sid switched topics. "So you want details on where we tracked Willy's body?"

Vince nodded.

"It stopped at each of these cities in the continental United States"—the room faded into a view of the entire Earth, with New York, Chicago, and Washington highlighted—"and then moved on to Europe and the Middle East."

"Where did it end up?"

Sid spun the globe. "We think we saw traces in Kuala Lumpur and Jakarta, but that's where the trail ends."

"Anything else?"

There wasn't much else to go on. Something tweaked in the back of Sid's mind. "There was one other thing that didn't make sense, or at least, I couldn't fit it in."

Vince nudged him. "What?"

"This might seem ridiculous, but I was reading some of the religious texts you sent me—the ones Willy's proxxi was reading in the Commune in Montana."

"Been reading a lot of those myself. So what is it?"

"There was one phrase that I couldn't find any other reference to, something scrawled into the notes you sent me: The beginning of man, where time stops in a thousand tongues."

"That sounds like pretty standard Gnostic nonsense," Vince said after a pause. He frowned. "Wait a second. Where time stops . . ."

Sid looked at him. "What?"

"I met with that gangster Patricia told us to find."

"Sintil8?"

"Yeah, that's his stage name. Real name Mikhail Butorin. He gave me a copy of some Gnostic texts that he dug up in the Egyptian deserts a hundred years ago, the Book of Pobeptoc. There was a passage in there that popped out at me." He shared it with Sid. "*Wal lie body is where the flesh eaters live.*"

"That's just a translation coincidence," Sid said. "Or maybe Butorin is having a bit of fun with you. Doesn't he encourage his followers to eat their own flesh? That's one sick—"

"Where did you say the trail ended, Jakarta?"

Sid nodded.

"Where time stops," Vince whispered. He laughed, and then collapsed their private meeting space and grabbed everyone's attention from the lecture on quantum computing Sibeal was giving.

"Did you say some of those quasi-crystals were found in the wild up in the New Guinea highlands?"

Everyone stared at Vince.

Sibeal nodded. "Yeah, New Guinea. Why?"

SUNLIGHT STREAMED DOWN through the jungle canopy, and a lime-green parrot fluttered overhead. Pushing back the last of the foliage before the village, Vince peered in. Smoke rose from cooking fires between thatched huts, and children chased each other, squealing, while their mothers prepared sweet potatoes in stone-lined pits.

Vince was projecting himself into the village through the base station repeater that he dropped here months ago, just about the time Willy's body disappeared. It was when the future death threats were peaking, hunting him down, forcing him on a goose chase around the world to try to protect himself. This part of the world was still remote and wild; there were no networks, no wikiworld feeds, barely any technology beyond what humans had a thousand years ago. The perfect place to hide, it was still in a primal state . . . the beginning of man.

It was here that Vince had met the Yupno witch doctor, Nicky Nixons. The Yupno didn't perceive time in the same way the rest of the world did. They didn't just see it as going forward, but also as going backward, sideways and in circles . . . where time stops.

If it was primitive, it was also one of the most linguistically diverse places on earth. The New Guinea highlanders spoke a thousand tongues.

Vince remembered that it had seemed like Dr. Nicky Nixons was able to see his proxxi, Hotstuff, even though, without any smarticles in his system, it would have—*should have*—been impossible.

Hunched over one of the cooking fires, Vince saw a man, naked save for a loin skin, covered in chalky paint the witch doctors applied to those searching the spirit worlds. He was arranging sweet potatoes in the cooking pits. The villagers here wouldn't be able to sense Vince's virtual presence unless they were loaded with smarticles and connected to the base station repeater. Vince walked over and put a hand on the man's shoulder.

The man turned and looked up—and smiled.

"Hey, Mr. Indigo," said Willy's proxxi.

# 27

THE TURBOFAN TRANSPORT was on its way to Terra Nova.

Bob felt a swarm of medbots scouring his body as he lay in an emergency pod. The symbol of Terra Nova, a thick circle with a square cross through its center, was imprinted on the ceiling of the passenger compartment his body was in.

"This man you escaped with," Mohesha asked, "do you have any additional information?"

The priest had come further than Bob expected, all the way into Lagos. They said their goodbyes just before Bob initiated the contact sequence with Mohesha. Bob hesitated. The priest said he had enemies here. He didn't want to get his savior into any trouble.

"Just that he was a priest, and that he wasn't welcome in the AU." Bob spun some information packets with the priest's face into Mohesha's networks. He'd do his best to protect the priest if anything came up. He owed him.

Mohesha assimilated the data. "Ah, yes, we know him. A Bedouin shaman, but an advanced user of our technology. We don't see him as a threat, but politics in Africa are complicated." Mohesha stood next to Bob and put an arm on his shoulder. "Don't worry. I'll keep his identity between us."

Mohesha pinged Bob for location, and taking a deep breath, he released it to her. "You can relax, young man, you are with friends now. Come, let me show you more of what we're about." Mohesha took charge, and his primary viewpoint rocketed out from the top of the Spike, up and into the dark clouds. They looked down at an enhanced image of the plains surrounding Lagos.

She highlighted a circular area two miles in diameter, dotted with radio receiver dishes. "This is what Atopia is pushing for UN weapons inspectors to look at."

It was the microwave power array for Lagos, part of the space power grid that the African Union and Terra Nova pioneered. Bob was familiar with it: over a hundred satellites in LEO, each capable of transmitting hundreds of megawatts of power in line-of-sight microwave bursts.

Nearly two hundred years ago, the "old" world built dense networks of power transmission lines that stretched across America and Europe and China, but with the sharp rise in commodity metal prices, replicating this in Africa had been impossible. So they created the space power grid, becoming the leader in wireless power transmission.

"They're worried the power grid could be used as a directed energy weapon in a coming conflict," explained Mohesha. "But it's the basis of our economy, and we cannot consider demands to throttle or limit it."

Mohesha began spinning out one project after another into private worlds for Bob to see. Bob watched her Chief Science Officer credentials flash as each one opened. A massive tornado filled Bob's visual fields.

"The controlled vortex project can capture energy from the upper atmosphere," Mohesha explained, "and convert it into usable kinetic energy at ground level."

There were a dozen vortex installations across Africa. Promoted as terraforming projects to combat global warming, they generated vast energies. Anything that generated that much power could be used as a weapon, a new and terrifying Weather War weapon, he thought but didn't say.

Mohesha spun their viewpoint a hundred miles into space and highlighted a ring running under the western half of the African continent. "The supercollider, a project only the African Union has been able to realize."

It was on the drawing board for decades, the ultimate endgame in a series of high-energy physics experiments to probe the very nature of the fabric of the universe. A thousand miles in circumference, it ran beneath Lagos, toward southern Africa and then eastern Africa, and even ran under the Sahara desert to the north. It was the scientific triumph of the AU, and was only just operational.

"Patricia was a big supporter of many of these projects." Mohesha brought in views of other projects, the Arbitrarily Large Phased Array—ALPHA—a swarm of satellites that collected solar energy and beamed it down to Earth via the space power grid. "The supercollider, in particular, was the twin of Patricia's own Pacific Ocean Neutrino Detector." Mohesha paused. "Patricia shut down the POND just before the crisis. Do you know why?"

He shook his head. "No idea." Bob's attention sharpened—the POND data, the transmission from another universe. "I'll give everything I have to the Council." Not that he didn't trust Mohesha, but it might be wise to wait. "Patricia asked me to talk directly with them."

Mohesha paused before collapsing the display spaces. "Yes." She sighed. "I miss her. It is good you made it. You're the genetic embodiment of everything Patricia worked toward. You are her children, her pssi-kids. She is not gone, she is with you, in you."

Their viewpoint sailed across the ocean, and the crystal towers of Terra Nova glistened in the distance. Mohesha guided them in, circling the main tower complex. They materialized together, walking next to each other in a tropical garden of flowering red begonias and gladiolas. It was already dark, but the night garden was lit by the soft glow of aerial plankton.

Bob had questions of his own, things that he'd been waiting to ask. "You say you miss Patricia, but she said it was you who infected Atopia with the reality skin that nearly destroyed us." Mohesha had used Patricia's trust to gain access to Atopian networks. "You used her."

He stared at her. He wasn't sure if she'd try to deny it.

Mohesha's face turned to the floor. "It was the only way."

Bob waited for more, but she just walked ahead of him. "Half the reason my friends and I are being hunted is because they think Sid and I created that virus," he added after a few seconds.

She turned to him. "You think we should admit we attacked Atopia? That would be an automatic declaration of war. The uncertainty is all that's buying us time. Patricia was lost to us already. Now it's too late. There will be more bloodshed, and on a far larger scale than just Atopia."

"More bloodshed?" The skin on Bob's arms prickled. "What do you mean?"

Mohesha turned away and started walking again. She turned his attention to the sky, amplifying an image of the comet, its curved tail like a giant scythe aimed at the Earth. "The comet is decelerating too quickly. It was supposed to remain in an extra-lunar orbit."

Bob's systems assimilated the data she sent him. "But it's not going to hit Earth."

"Not yet, no." She emphasized *yet*.

"And you think this has something to do with Atopia? With Jimmy?"

She shrugged. "It's hard to say."

"Is this the destruction you see coming?" Bob jumped forward several steps to get even with Mohesha. "Is this the bloodshed?" There were ways a comet could be stopped. It was still on the far side of the sun, a hundred and fifty million miles away. He grabbed Mohesha, turning her to face him.

Her face remained impassive. "It might be best, as you said, to wait for the Council meeting." She pulled away and kept walking.

Bob stood still. He glanced at the enhanced image of the comet in the sky. It faded as Mohesha released it. "When can I reconnect with my friends?"

As soon as he made the connection with Mohesha, her networks had given him a status update. Sid had pinged Terra Nova with several requests. His friends were safe. Terra Nova hadn't responded to them yet, but they'd know that Bob was all right. The mediaworlds were in a frenzy with the images of him getting picked up already. Bob watched the probability of imminent kinetic attack against Terra Nova spike in his phuturing channels.

He was out of the frying pan and into the fire.

"As soon as your physical body is secured in Terra Nova, we'll let you talk to them. In the meantime, get some rest." Her face softened. "Soon you'll be free to roam your worlds with them again."

"And my proxxi, how long will it take to reconnect with him?"

Terra Novans had a strict approach to synthetic intelligences. You couldn't just create and destroy them here. Bringing one in required processing. In the desert, Bob decided to free Robert from his service, to abandon the use of a proxxi. The priest's lessons had sunk in. The only problem was that he was sure Robert wouldn't want to be freed, but that was another bridge for another day.

"It'll take a few days for the legal process to engage. You can still converse with him in a secure space, but his essence will be held in a holding world."

Bob nodded.

Mohesha paused. "I do have one question for you."

"What's that?"

"This data beacon from Patricia, did you share it with anyone else?"

Bob stared into her eyes. It wasn't a time to hide information, but something made him want to keep these cards close to his chest. "Nobody," he replied.

# 28

"CAN'T WE JUST cut off the connection to Terra Nova?" Sibeal asked.

The excitement of finding Willy's body—with Willy's proxxi—wore off fast. Now they were trying to figure out how to reconnect Willy's mind to Willy's body directly. Sibeal was sitting at the cooking fire in the New Guinea village, together with Sid and Vince. Connors was observing through an avatar, and Bunky and Shaky and the rest of the gang from the White Horse Pub were ghosting through Sibeal.

Before any of that, though, one thing needed to be cleared up.

Sitting next to Sibeal on the log by the fire, Sid turned to face her. "Are you still planning on turning him in for bounty?" A part of him had thought that they'd never find Willy's body, but all of a sudden everything had changed. He'd almost forgotten the reason why they'd struck a bargain, why Sibeal and her friends kidnapped him in the first place. Was the friendship routine just a sham? Just a scheme? In the background he was readying a systems attack that would disable the Midtown den. He waited for her answer.

She crinkled her nose. "Well, we didn't really find him."

Sid frowned. "What do you mean?" Was she trying to be clever?

"Vince found him. I mean, we couldn't take credit for someone else's work."

Sid relaxed his attack vectors. "Otherwise you would?"

Now she laughed. "Cool off, hot shot, of course we wouldn't. This is about more than just money now."

"Good."

"Good. Now can we work on Willy?" She began filling a shared workspace with Willy's brain's network connection topographies. "And you can let go of your sneak attacks." She smiled. "Do you think I didn't let you trap Zoraster that time?"

Sid laughed, shaking his head, and relaxed. He began highlighting paths on the connection diagrams. "Willy's mind is working inside there." He pointed at Willy's head, and Willy's proxxi smiled with it. "But it's routed through Terra Nova. If we cut the connection, his consciousness will remain stuck in his head without any sensory input." Full sensory deprivation was a fate worse than death.

Sibeal nodded. "So we need to open a channel to Terra Nova?"

"I'm trying." With mounting cyberattacks and an impending physical attack, Terra Nova kept only a few diplomatic connections open. The connection to Willy's head wasn't one of them.

"Maybe we could just stick a wire in there . . ." Sibeal waved a hand at the base of Willy's skull.

"Are you kidding? We'd need surgical isolation—"

"I *am* kidding." Sibeal looked at Vince and rolled her eyes. He smiled back.

A silent pause was punctuated by barking howler monkeys. For the moment they were stumped.

"Okay, Wally, time to tell us what happened," Vince said. "Why did you steal Willy's body?"

Willy's proxxi stared at the smoldering fire at the bottom of the cooking pit, his face smeared with Yupno warrior paint, caked around his forehead and into his hair. Taking a deep breath, he looked up at the gang.

"Jimmy Scadden is stealing peoples' souls inside the Atopian system."

Now Sid rolled his eyes. *Please, tell us something we don't know.* "And that's why you left, because you found out?"

Willy's proxxi nodded.

More silence while monkeys howled.

"That's just great," Sid said, throwing a sweet potato into the fire. *A whole lot of work for nothing.* But it wasn't nothing. They had finally found Willy's body. That was something. He picked up another potato.

"There's more." Willy's proxxi looked at Sid. "He's not crazy, not some psychopath. It's not Jimmy's fault. He's been infected—his mind breached—he's not in control."

Sid stopped mid-swing. "And you know who this person is?"

Wally shook his head. "I found out when Jimmy helped me re-program the Atopian perimeter. He gave me access to his personal conscious firewall subroutines. A communication leaked out."

"And that's when you left?" Vince asked.

"I had to. Whatever was controlling Jimmy, it knew I'd found out. It would have killed us."

"And what are these crystals you went and looked at?" asked Sibeal. Her research revealed that they interacted with neural potentials.

Wally smiled. "So you saw that. I found some embedded in the Atopian infrastructure. When Jimmy leaked the communication to me, it mapped back to a set of nodal points."

Sid tried to put it together. "So what, this is like a different version of synthetic reality technology?"

"If it is, it's far advanced of anything I've seen," Sibeal observed.

"Is this why they tried to destroy Atopia?" Sid frowned. Even if Jimmy was being controlled by someone else, sacrificing hundreds of thousands of lives aboard Atopia seemed a heavy price.

"I don't know." Wally shook his head. "I was just trying to protect Willy. When I saw Vince drop the repeater connection point here, it seemed about as far away as I could get." He looked away.

"Are you okay?" Sid asked. Willy's proxxi looked like he was going to cry.

Wally took a deep breath. "I'm not scared, not for me." He sniffled and smeared the war paint across his face with the back of one hand. "Have you talked to Willy? Is he okay? It's been so frustrating—he's right inside here"—he tapped his skull with one finger—"but I have no way of talking with him."

"Don't worry. Your brain activity looks normal." Sid had done an external scan. "Bob's at Terra Nova now. He'll get in touch and we'll be able to sort this out soon."

"I still don't understand why the Terra Novans wouldn't just try to isolate Jimmy," Sibeal said. "Why try to destroy the entire Atopian colony?"

Sid nodded. It seemed like overkill no matter which way he tried to look at it. Suspicious overkill. "We'd need to get a channel into Terra Nova—"

"That won't be a problem."

Everyone turned around.

Bob stood at the edge of the jungle, still in his white robe and sandals. "The Terra Novan Council is about to start. I suggest we look for answers there."

# 29

THE LIGHT CAME from within and without, the surface function of the meeting space like a stone worn smooth in the river
of time. The space was thought-plastic, molding itself around each
attendee. At the head of the table-concept was Tyrel, leader of the
Terra Novan Council. At his side was Mohesha, surrounded by a
halo of the other members of the Terra Novan leadership. Their
faces appeared both young and old at the same time, their features harmonizing with the thought patterns of the observer. In
the background, fleeting images shifted in dark forests, thoughts
and ideas and images spinning through the meta-cognition systems
of the assembled, each merging with the other through virtual-
synaptic connections that brought the separate parts into a single,
cohesive whole.

"You have many questions." Tyrel brought the meeting to order.
"As do we."

Willy was there, his virtual presence wedged between avatars
of Bob and Sid, with Sibeal and Vince flanking them. There wasn't
time for celebration at their reunion. The presence of Mikhail
Butorin hovered in a dark patch of the light. He smiled at Vince.

Tyrel formed an image of an oceanic platform. It was Atopian in
design, but looked nothing like Atopia itself. Its surface was angular,
jet black. A schematic of its capabilities sprung up around it. "Allied
battle platforms are encroaching on the African Union in physical

space. The deadline for allowing UN weapons inspectors access to the space power grid facilities has lapsed."

Connors wasn't invited. An agent of the Alliance was too risky to include, even one that appeared friendly. Back in the barn in Louisiana, as night fell, she was playing cards with Vince's proxxi by candlelight. Vince kept a splinter of himself watching over her.

Tyrel looked around the table. "The time to act is now, my friends."

"With all due respect," Vince said. "I'm still going to need some convincing of this 'friends' part. We've risked our lives to get here, and you're the ones that nearly killed us and our families when you infected Atopia with that reality skin. Seems to me you brought this on yourselves."

The battle platform gave way to a flood of situational data. "This fight is not of our choosing, but of necessity." He looked at Bob. "We need the information Patricia left you, and we need access to the data in Willy's body."

Bob stared at Tyrel. Patricia's instructions were to deliver the data she collected here, but had she known what they were up to? Who to trust? He shook his head. "With the greatest of respect, Vince is right. Before we share anything, you need to convince us that we're with friends." He glanced at Vince. "Explain why all this is *necessity*."

Data flowing into the sensory focal-point of the meeting slowed to a stop, went blank, and was replaced by pinpoints of light spreading up and down, left and right into infinity, ordered in irregular but repeating patterns.

"You've seen these crystals," Mohesha said, her presence rising to the center of their thought-space. "A complex alloy of metals that enables the stable flow of sub-atomic quantum states between neighboring atoms." Data was uploaded into the shared cognition of the meeting space. These quasi-crystals could hold information at quantum scale, transmit and transform the information.

"A computing device," Sibeal said. "One that can sense neural potentials."

"Yes." The matrix of pinpoints of light faded. "Self-replicating, difficult to distinguish from natural mineral."

"Unless you know what you're looking for." Sibeal caught Mohesha's attention. "Do you have anything to do with it?"

"We only recently discovered the crystals, but it confirms what we've suspected for some time."

"And that is?"

"A truth glimpsed by secret societies in the past." Tyrel took back the focal point. "Something we hadn't the means to understand until now. Now it is almost too late."

Bob pulled their attention to him. "Is this something from space?" Natural quasi-crystals were found in meteorites, and his first thought was the POND signal. Did Tyrel know about it? He hadn't shared the information yet.

"Possibly, but we think the crystals are ancient, regenerating from the deep past."

The mind's eye of the meeting space opened up into a field bordered by strange-looking trees, and giant animals with green skin stood eating ferns at the edges. None of the plants or animals looked recognizable, not of this Earth.

"We suspect there was a technological civilization of Earth before, two hundred and fifty million years ago, before the Great Permian Extinction that wiped out life for tens of millions of years."

The meeting space shifted to alien-looking bipedal humanoids, with mottled green skin, walking through soaring structures. The viewpoint retreated upward, revealing a city of skyscrapers twinkling beside an ocean. Bob stared. Somehow he'd seen it before.

"They developed systems similar to our synthetic reality technologies. We think this is convergent evolution, that biological and memetic evolution will push technological civilizations to produce synthetic reality systems in the same way that an eye will evolve over and over again. Like an eye, nervenets are evolutionary adaptations that allow organisms to see, to perceive the true fabric of reality."

The space around them grew dark.

"When their world ended," continued Tyrel, "their technology persisted, self-replicating, building itself into the fabric of the Earth. Like the wikiworld we use, it's been constantly recording. A memory of every human is contained in this machine, every person that ever existed, but apart from this function, it's been dormant."

"Dormant?" Bob said. "So it's woken up?"

"They've been waiting."

Bob waited. "For what?"

"For sentience to arise once again."

Silence.

"Why would it be waiting."

"Not it," Tyrel said slowly, "*they*."

"They?"

"Because their world did not just end, it was destroyed."

"So what are you saying? How does this relate to Jimmy?"

"Because he is evidence of the truth that has long been suspected." Tyrel returned the meeting space to the gardens on the surface of Terra Nova. "The Great Destroyer has returned."

# Part 3:

# Treachery

# 1

THE ORANGE GLOW of sunset faded behind bearded silhouettes of cypress trees lining the bayou. Fireflies began their mating dance as darkness fell, winking between the Spanish moss that draped into the waters, while a symphony of crickets and spring peepers kept rhythm with the wind that swayed the treetops.

Vince and Connors started a fire in the hard-packed earth under cover of the barn roof. There wasn't much they could do about heat signatures, but avoiding direct overhead visual observation was something.

"So what happened in the meeting?" Connors asked Vince again.

Vince knew she wasn't happy about being excluded, but then she couldn't do much about it. Now she wanted answers.

He slid another branch into the fire. It was muggy, but the heat would be soon replaced by a damp chill. Not only that, but they had to eat something. Strips of catfish sizzled on an improvised grill. Trying to avoid Connor's questions, Vince had gone fishing as soon as his primary subjective returned from the Terra Novan Council meeting. Standing knee-deep in the muck amid lily pads and cattails, he let some of his smarticles loose in the water. A fat catfish had swum obligingly into his hand within a few minutes, after he flitted into its mind and asked it to come.

What happened in the meeting? Vince wasn't sure how to answer this. The Terra Novans believed there was some ancient technology at work—*the nervenet*—similar to but more sophisticated than existing synthetic reality systems. They said that when Saint John sat in the cave on Patmos Island and wrote down the Apocalypse, he had connected to this old machine. What he wrote down wasn't as much a prediction, but a description of what had happened before, and what would happen again, like an echo.

Humans had been connecting into this nervenet for thousands of years, but it took a certain "society of mind" that only religious ascetics, who practiced meditation, managed to achieve. For the Terra Novans this explained why prophets described moving into other worlds, out-of-body-experiences, and talking to gods who were just imprints of ancient intelligences trapped in this nervenet.

They believed the release of the Atopian technology was the last straw that awoke this old machine, that this was why the crystals were appearing and replicating. Hundreds of millions of people connecting into virtual worlds triggered this tipping point with a burst of global neural activity. The old world and new were merging, the realities fusing, and Jimmy was the reincarnation of the Great Destroyer, the White Rider of legend. This was why they tried to destroy Atopia, to stop the release of pssi, to stop the unleashing of the Four Horsemen of the Apocalypse.

It felt insane.

*He* felt insane.

He'd been hoping—*praying*—when they contacted Terra Nova, that everything would sort itself out, that things would become clearer. Now things were less clear, more frightening whether he believed them or not. Either there was an ancient being let loose that was bent on destroying the Earth. Or, one of the most powerful groups in the world sincerely believed that the Apocalypse was underway and were ready to start a global war over it.

Those were his two options. Both were terrifying.

"There are some crazies operating out there, and we need to stop them," Vince finally answered. One way or the other, that was true.

"Tell me something I don't know." Connors slid a branch into the fire. "What, like terrorists? That was Robert Baxter who appeared in the forest in New Guinea, wasn't it? What was with the robe and sandals?"

Vince had forgotten that she was ghosting him in the forests of New Guinea when they found Willy's proxxi. Connors had seen Bob appear at the edge of the forest. Then again, the whole world knew that Bob was in Terra Nova. The mediaworlds were whipping into a frothy conspiracy fever over it. "Yeah, that was Bob. He was in the meeting." He sighed. "And this goes way beyond terrorists."

At the meeting, Vince had instantiated a private channel with Bob to say hello, but Bob barely acknowledged him. It wasn't like Bob. He'd changed. Something happened to the kid. Something bad.

Sid and Bob seemed to swallow the Terra Novan story. Then again, they were pssi-kids: they barely saw any difference between the real world and the imaginary ones they inhabited. If Sid woke up one morning as the Queen of England, he wouldn't be surprised—he'd just ask for a cup of tea. Bob wanted to get back on Atopia, rescue Nancy and his family away from any danger, and apart from that, he just wanted to make everyone happy. Sid was excited that there might be a new system of realities he could explore. Vince was the only voice of reason.

And he was faltering.

He felt like he was stuck in a mirror maze. Part of the problem was that he'd already been halfway there himself, reading secret codes into ancient manuscripts, half-believing that there was some fantastical explanation for the multi-headed Buddhas. But before this was a kind of intellectual game, good for chatting about over beers. Now it was laid out as fact.

Or, rather, someone was trying to convince him it was fact. Terra Nova could just be another sophisticated institution with a doomsday cult at its center, like countless others around the world—the Communes, even the Catholic Church itself.

"I need answers, but I can wait a bit." Connors poked at the catfish. "Are you okay?"

Vince smiled, his mind raging in the background. "Yeah, I'm fine. I think those are ready." He leaned forward with a clean wedge of plastic, and flicked one of the filets onto it. He inspected it. They were done. "Did you ever have anything weird happen to you, that you can't explain?" He deposited half of the catfish onto an improvised plate for Connors.

"Like what?"

"When I was a kid"—Vince took a tentative bite of the catfish, it was hot—"I was maybe twelve, and we were going on vacation with my family. My dad was driving, and I was dozing in the back with my cousins. But I swear to God, I could hear what they were going to say before they said it. And it wasn't a fluke, I could do it again and again by getting into this lucid dreaming state."

"That's amazing." Connors picked her fish up with her fingers and took a bite.

"What, the fish or my story?"

Connors' catfish fell apart, spilling onto her plate. She rolled her eyes at her own clumsiness. "That you were alive when people still drove cars."

"I'm being serious."

When they'd talked, Mikhail Butorin claimed he had supernatural powers that came and went, like clairvoyance, invisibility, and more. If Vince connected the dots—and took the Terra Novan explanation at face value—it meant Butorin had been connecting into this ancient nervenet, but just didn't know it. It sounded nuts.

"No, I've never experienced anything like that." Scooping the bits of fish up on her plate, Connors looked at Vince. Flickering firelight reflected on her face. "The more you tell me, the more I can help. What about those crystals? Is it some kind of alternate pssi technology?"

"Yes, that's exactly what they think it is."

"*They* being the Terra Novans?"

Vince nodded.

"And it's not theirs?"

He picked up another piece of catfish "Not that they said, anyway."

"But there are some kind of terrorists at work?"

He stared into her eyes. *Terrorists.* She always came back to this idea. She would think it was crazy if he said that Jimmy Scadden was the White Horseman of the Apocalypse, that ancient aliens were infiltrating Atopia. Even he thought it was crazy. "Something like that," he replied.

Sitting there with Connors, listening to the frogs chirping, everything felt surreally calm. Time was always something he'd wanted more of, but it could also be the enemy. It was time for action before he convinced himself out of what he needed to do. Emotions were one thing, and logic was another, but in the end, he had to do the right thing. And for Vince, there was only one option.

"I need you to take me into Washington, as your prisoner. I have information for Allied Command—I need to speak to their most senior person. Then I can tell you everything."

Connors frowned. "And just how do you propose to do that?"

Out of the darkness, beyond the doorway of the barn, a small bot appeared. Connors reached around to grab anything she could fight back with, but Vince held up one hand to calm her. "It's okay."

The bot dropped a pile of mechanical parts onto the grass and disappeared back into the darkness.

"These are the parts we need to fix the turbofan out front," Vince explained.

Connors rocked forward to her feet. "And you got these how?" She walked over and kneeled to inspect the parts.

"I still have some connections."

They collected the parts and walked out front, toward the downed turbofan.

"So can you get me in front of a senior Allied commander?" he asked. "Do you think you can do that? It's important." They reached the turbofan. Connors opened the access hatch and they both switched to low-light imaging in their optics systems.

"Maybe, but my last attempts to raise comms with my boss didn't work out too well."

"Try again."

Connors paused. "You have dangerous friends, Vince. I'm not sure all your connections and money can protect you anymore."

"These are dangerous times."

"I'm being serious. Are you sure you want to go to Washington?" She stuck her head inside the access panel.

Vince smiled. A few days ago, Connors had been in a rush to arrest him and bring him to Washington, and now he wanted to go and she was resisting taking him there. She was so driven to do the right thing. "Can you fix it?"

Connors grunted. "I think so." She pulled her head out. "You know what they're going to do to you if you go there? You know, right?"

Vince sighed and nodded.

"This is a national security issue now, not just some jumped-up white-collar crime. They're going to rip into you."

"I know." Vince looked up at the stars. Sooner or later you had to pick sides. "I'm going to tell them everything. Make the call."

"If you're thinking this will get you off the hook, get your Phuture News back—"

"That's not what's this is about." Vince looked down into Connor's eyes. "This is about doing the right thing."

She met his gaze. "Okay then." She leaned her head back through the access panel.

"And I want to get you somewhere safe," he whispered under his breath while her head was deep inside the drone. He glanced at the horizon, at the streak of the comet just rising, then looked up at the stars—but there was nowhere safe to go, not on this world, not anymore.

# 2

EIGHT SILVER CAPSULES hung motionless together, spaced out over a four-kilometer line. The gold and silver webs of city lights crept through nightshade far below. A burst of sunlight illuminated the curve of the Earth, the rising sun blossoming across seas and the wrinkles of snow-capped mountains. Retrorockets fired on the capsules, tiny soundless bursts that slowed them in tandem. One after another they dropped from space, glowing orange and then white as they tore into the upper reaches of the atmosphere.

Sid's display spaces lit up. "We've tripped the Alliance defenses. Wait for my signal."

On Himalayan mountaintops strung along the Chinese side, batteries of slingshot shield-effect and surface-to-air weapons systems powered up, zeroing in on the incoming threats. The first of them lit up, spreading a blanket of incendiary pellets in the path of the capsules. The pellets exploded and flamed into a wall of plasma.

Sid waited, watching the distance close. "Now!"

The capsules shed their blistering shells, and dozens of fragments rocketed out from each at random angles, hundreds of decoys that zigged and zagged on hard angles, spreading across thousands of cubic kilometers of space.

As one of the world's best players in tactical combat in the gameworlds, Sid had been given command of the infiltration. He'd never been involved in real combat, but there was barely any difference anymore between the real world and the gameworlds he dominated. When they were planning this, he'd insisted that they didn't have any better options, that he could execute this better than anyone else they had.

Now he was hoping he was right.

His mind spread out into the future, modeling the incoming flux of defensive strategies in hundreds of phutures that evolved and collapsed in fractions of seconds as their predictions came true or faltered. Latency delays between the battle zone and his meat-mind were too long, so he'd embedded an autonomous splinter of his mind into the attacking capsules. A very thin stream of perceptual data updated his primary consciousness several seconds after the fact.

Electromagnetic cloaking systems bent radio and visual wavelengths around the invaders, rendering them nearly invisible, while darknets descended to disrupt the informational spaces that linked this physical space to the cyber-worlds. Weaving and dodging, dozens of the decoys flamed out in the blazing defenses, but one and then another of them got through, slamming into the mountainsides and foothills of the Langtang Valley in the middle of the Himalayan plateau.

"We made it," sighed Sid's splinter to nobody else but itself. It had embedded its primary point-of-presence in the fragment-decoy in which Zoraster's body was encased.

Blasting its way several feet into the granite of the mountainside, the impact of landing imparted thousands of gees onto the capsule, but the core had remained intact. Sid began the rapid heating sequence, thawing Zoraster's frozen body while he powered up the bots and exoskeletons.

He fired the explosives to separate the exterior casing.

"Incoming," alerted another splinter of Sid's mind. On the tactical maps, hundreds of Alliance drones swarmed outward from their bases in the mountains, descending on the seismic signatures that the impacts created.

Railgun slugs tore into the side of the mountain above them.

Sid had to hurry. With a bang the exterior casing exploded away, opening the interior to the wind and snow of the Himalayan plateau they were still rolling across. His splinter was now totally cut off from the outside world as dense security blankets descended on this new theatre of war. In the outside world, he was filling the mediaworlds with propaganda, trying to create a fog of disinformation around the attack.

Nearly a second had passed since they'd hit the ground. The debris and snow was still settling while they rolled to a stop. Sid engaged the robotic surrogate housing him to begin constructing a local situational report. In his mind's eyes, the other Grilla units came online, and a tactical display began forming. Seven of them, all ex-commandos from Zoraster's old special-forces team, had made it through the gauntlet.

One was unaccounted for.

In overlaid display spaces, Sid watched each of the Grillas undergo the rapid thaw-and-heat cycles, their bodies coming back to life. He couldn't help thinking about resurrection, about the Resurrection. How much of the old texts were true—how to separate fact from fiction? Was Judgment Day coming? Would the unforgotten dead rise, springing from the ancient nervenet's memory banks?

Zoraster twitched as his body came back to life.

And would it be only humans?

The hollow thud of the railgun slugs grew louder. The Alliance defensive systems had located Sid and Zoraster's capsule, but they were already away, disappearing into the swirling snow. Behind them the capsule exploded in a crunching explosion.

Zoraster's meat-mind was coming back to groggy life as his exoskeleton marched him along the mountain ridge. He smiled a toothy grin at the drone Sid's mind hovered in. "You okay, kid?"

Sid laughed. "I'm not the frozen steak dinner. How are you feeling?"

"Not something I'd like to do every day, but okay." As a protection against the extreme accelerations, they'd put the Grilla commandos in deep-freeze. It was something they were engineered for. To the Alliance, this would all just look like a failed kinetic attack. "Everyone get through?"

Sid relayed the situational report into Zoraster's systems. Seven of the capsules carrying his Grilla commandos got through. One was still unaccounted for. Now it was listed as destroyed.

The Grilla sighed. "Damn it, Zane." He looked at Sid's drone. "He was a good friend."

Sid tried to find more information, but there wasn't any. All of Zoraster's old army buddies had volunteered for the mission, without asking any questions, when he put out the call. Now one of them was dead. They trudged through the ice and boulders in silence. The first stage was complete. There was a long hike ahead, over the spine of the Himalayas to the plains beyond, but so far, that was all Sid knew.

"Do you have any idea how we're going to get into Arunchel Pradesh?" Sid asked, texting the question quietly into Zoraster's secondary channels. Arunchel Pradesh—literally, the "land of the rising sun" in Sanskrit—was the location of the first Sino-Indian wars in the Himalayas over a hundred years before. It was also the flashpoint that started the Weather Wars.

It was now where Allied Command kept their main headquarters.

"We're heading into Nyingchi first," replied Zoraster.

Sid waited for him to expand on his plan, but the Grilla just trudged through the snow.

Glancing up at the towering peaks of the Himalayas, the splinter of Sid's mind hovering in the drone hoped that the Grilla *had* a plan.

# 3

"ALL IS LOST!" screamed Hezekiah. "And because of what? This boy?" He threw an accusing finger at Bob.

Isaiah placed himself in front of Bob, protecting him. "You are the King of Judah, you cast out the false idols. Yahweh will protect us."

Bob trembled, the scroll of papyrus balanced on his knees shaking. Night was falling, and the smoke from the cooking fires of the two hundred thousand Assyrian troops camping outside the walls of Jerusalem was drifting in, even into the royal palace.

Hezekiah scowled. "Where is this god you speak of?" He grabbed a smoldering pan of incense and threw it against the wall. The slaves cowered. "The twenty-four cities of Judah have been sacked. It was on this boy's words that you counseled me not to pay tribute to Sennacherib!"

"He will come," Bob heard himself saying, leaning forward to look the king directly in the eyes. "Yahweh will lay waste to the legions."

"Your head will be the first thing I will present to Sennacherib come the first light," growled Hezekiah, but already there were the screams of life being ripped from thousands of souls beyond the walls. Hezekiah's head turned to look through the billowing curtains into the screeching night, the expression on his face turning from anger to bewilderment, and then into fear.

◆◆◆

THE DREAMS WASHED from Bob's mind as he awoke. Australian aboriginals believed that man dreamed the world into existence. *What world am I dreaming of?*

Bob's mind flitted into the sensor systems of the transport in which his body was being smuggled. There were no humans aboard except for him and the priest, stowed below decks in a life-support crate. All around was the heaving blue of the oceans, the wind whipping the tips of waves into a froth that skidded across the sea's surface. He was in an automated oceanic tanker-transport, one of the thousands that mindlessly plowed the watery wilderness.

On Atopia, the ocean was Bob's friend, his playground. He tried mapping his tactile sense—his water sense—onto the sea's surface around the tanker, like he used to do at home, but now it felt alien, angry.

Nearly the only things that were alive out here—if that label could be applied—were the machines that roamed the waves, ferrying cargo back and forth to feed the seething mass of humans on the shores. Human biomass now exceeded all wild terrestrial biomass. Overhead in the skies, he could sense the turbofan transport networks, their insides filled with this same human biomass that they ingested and regurgitated at each stop. Dead seas, dead lands, and all creatures enslaved to the human project of pleasuring themselves.

The priest, his body in stasis in the pod next to Bob, was awake as well, and he opened a private communication channel. "Are you feeling ready for the coming fight?" he asked.

Bob mentally shook himself, waking himself up. Such dark thoughts, it wasn't like him. Then again, his body lay encased in a life-support unit at the bottom of an oceanic transport, an unwilling linchpin in a surreal global conflict. "Not really," Bob replied. "My mind is filled with such—"

"Fear and doubt is normal in such a situation."

In such a situation. "You were right." Right about the end of the world. Bob didn't entirely trust the Terra Novans, but everything Tyrel said seemed to make sense. Mohesha was the one to suggest that the priest come with him. She contacted the priest to debrief him, and he'd offered to continue on the journey with Bob. The priest was more comfortable with Terra Novan technology than he was, and Mohesha knew Bob trusted him. She knew this would be a rough road.

"The truth comes in many ways to those who seek it," replied the priest.

Both of them were immobile in the bottom of the transport, speaking through their minds. Bob had renounced Atopian technology—it was too dangerous to connect into it anymore. He was using Terra Novan tech now. Terra Novans didn't use proxxi, so Bob freed his, creating a set of corporations around the world that Robert could control to establish his identity as a legal person. He missed his old friend, and on this leg of the trip he was in total radio silence.

Once again he was cut off from the world, but now he was on a mission.

"We need you to return to Atopia," Tyrel had explained to Bob at the end of the Terra Novan Council meeting.

"Return to Atopia?" Where just days before this would have excited him, when Tyrel said it, his stomach had knotted up.

"You are the only one that might be able to get through to Jimmy Scadden. What's left of him in there still trusts you, even loves you. He spared you. You might be able to drive a wedge of uncertainty into his mind." Tyrel had paused. "Or obliterate him."

"Can't I try talking to him from here?" Bob had complained.

"You need to get inside the Atopian perimeter; it's the only way we can try to ensure the White Rider won't intercept you."

Bob had finally agreed.

But only as it gave him the chance to rescue his family, and to rescue Nancy. But he didn't know if he'd even be able to convince them to leave. Still, he had to try.

A part of Bob wished he'd managed to speak to Sid more after the meeting, but somehow there hadn't been time. To be honest, he hadn't made the time. To be honest, he didn't really want to talk.

At the meeting, they'd unpacked all the data that Patricia gave to him. It seemed to confirm what the Terra Novans were thinking, but the POND data was unexpected, and nobody had any idea what it meant, or if it was even relevant. Sid was still working on decoding it. The most critical information, though, had been what Willy's body had been carrying, the information on the identities of the other Horsemen.

It was this that had set the plan in motion.

The Terra Novans had given him nearly unfettered access to all their resources, the ability for him to summon their entire cyber-arsenal if needed. He was the critical node in the fight that had to get through, that might be able to cut the head from the snake.

"How much did Mohesha tell you?" Bob asked the priest. He wasn't sure what Mohesha had shared.

"Enough. We must decide for ourselves what to believe and what to cast out. The battle between the Sons of Light and the Sons of Darkness began long ago."

In his mind's eye, Bob saw a fly crawling on the strip-lighting embedded in the ceiling. The fly crawled around, its only concern finding its next meal, perhaps finding a mate. If he reached up to swat it, it would try to escape, realizing something was trying to kill it. It wouldn't understand what was trying to kill it. It would only understand that it had to run. Bob had a creeping sensation of the same thing.

Inside his mind, he burned to get back onto Atopia, to take his family and Nancy to safety. He couldn't fail again.

He was the only one who really knew Jimmy, the only one Jimmy might listen to, and he was the only one who knew the Atopian systems as well as Jimmy did. An image of Jimmy on the beach back at Nancy's thirteenth birthday party floated into his mind, that young trusting boy looking to Bob for help. Now he needed to use that trust, find the love for Bob that might still exist somewhere inside his old friend.

And use that love against him.

# 4

NANCY SURVEYED THE hall. It was filled with row upon row of young men and women, healthy young men and women—healthy save one respect. They weren't aware at all. They were cocooned in life-support units, white pods stacked along the length of the hall like eggs in a hive, ready to hatch. Attending drones hovered and buzzed between them.

The facility she was virtually inspecting was located in an office tower in the middle of San Francisco, but she was finding more of them in nearly every city. They were operated as infirmaries by Cognix Corporation, a spillover from the private health care systems it helped operate around the world.

In the cocoons were the disappeared, the people who'd become lost in the Atopian virtual reality system. They went in, but their awareness never came out. On Atopia, before launch, there were reports of this happening, but they'd been pushed aside. Nancy wished she had paid more attention. Only now did she understand the truth.

Jimmy was stealing souls.

*"Some report that over a million people are now among the disappeared,"* a *Boston Globe* reporter said in a mediaworld that Nancy watched in a corner of her mind. *"Inquiries at Cognix Corporation go unanswered, yet the FDA refuses to hold an inquest into the issue."*

There were rumors, reports, but nobody seemed too worried. It wasn't just that people were too busy to care, or too interested in their own selfish pursuits. They honestly didn't notice, or when they did, they'd forget. The highest rates of disappearances were in areas with the highest penetration of pssi, and there was a collective blind spot operating in the externally stored memories and meta-cognitions systems. The disappeared list Nancy was compiling correlated with people in influential positions. Jimmy was taking control.

Another newsworld caught Nancy's attention: *"UN commission reports happiness rates soaring around the world . . ."*

Something had to be done. She couldn't wait any more.

"ARE YOU CONTENT knowing Jimmy is taking Cognix away from you?" asked Nancy. Cognix was Herman Kesselring's baby. She turned to look out of the phase-shifting windows of the Cognix Board room onto the forests of Atopia more than a thousand feet below.

Kesselring's face flushed. "I am still the main shareholder. I've got nothing to fear from young Scadden."

"Is that why you hide up here all the time?" Kesselring had barely left the confines of the upper corporate office complex in weeks. "You're sure acting scared."

"Have you seen the stock price of Cognix?" Kesselring blustered. "We're on track to become the fourth-largest economy on the planet—"

"This isn't about money anymore, Mr. Kesselring. Do you know he's amassing a private psombie army?" She didn't need to specify who they were talking about.

"The body lend-lease program? That's not a private army—"

"Let's cut the bullshit right now, Herman."

That stopped Kesselring in his tracks. In the silence, Nancy stared out the window at the crescent of white sand beaches ringing the floating-island-nation-state, at the waves breaking over the frothy breakwaters. The beaches were empty, where before they'd been packed with tourists. They hadn't been coming here for the water, however, they'd been coming to experience pssi, and now that pssi was everywhere, the tourists were elsewhere. Nancy used to feel such peace when she looked out at this view—but now when she saw those waves, she always thought of Bob and wondered where he was.

"Aren't you part of the science team going to the Dallas Commune?" asked Kesselring, trying to shift topics.

The Commune outside of Dallas, Texas, under siege by American internal security forces, had been breached. It was the sister to the much better fortified Montana Commune. Atopia had been asked to send in its head technical team to do a forensic analysis of the Commune's systems. "I am. My main subjective is there now."

Kesselring drummed his fingers against the conference room table. Nancy could almost see the gears clicking in his head.

"How do you know you can keep anything secret from him?" he said finally.

"I don't, but then we're going to have to take some calculated risks if we're going to stand up to him." Implicit in this was the risk she was already taking. She didn't know that Jimmy didn't *already* own Kesselring. She was sure Jimmy was controlling the rest of the Board, starting with Dr. Granger, whose normally vapid expressions had become more sinister.

"We?" Kesselring smiled. "So now *we* are a 'we?'"

Nancy turned away from watching the waves to face Kesselring. "We are." She sent some data into Kesselring's networks, some of the information Bob gave her. Kesselring's eyes widened. "I need you to call a special, very private meeting of senior shareholders."

On an overlaid situational display, Nancy watched Alliance battle platforms converging on Terra Nova in the Southern Atlantic. She didn't reveal everything she knew about Jimmy. She kept secret that Jimmy had stolen Commander Rick Strong's wife. That needed to be used at the right moment.

Kesselring's mind raced through the data she gave him. "You received this from Patricia?"

Nancy nodded. Maybe she should attempt to contact Mohesha at Terra Nova. The other option was Bob, but that was far too risky. Jimmy would have sensors waiting to be tripped if she tried anything like that. Even here, she was keeping her memories of this meeting locked away inside the perimeter of Kesselring's private security blankets. Each part of her mind would have to start to work independently, like cells of an espionage network, each knowing the other existed, but not knowing where or what they were up to.

Not until it came time for them to come together.

AT THE SAME time, another part of Nancy's mind hovered at the peripheries of the Dallas Commune in the scrublands of Texas. Surrounding it on all sides were bipedal bots, the letters "FBI" stenciled on their sides. Overhead, in the clear blue sky, the Dallas Commune's mile-high electromagnetic shield of aerial plankton shimmered, pulsated, and then a gust of wind washed it away. There were four Communes in America, and all of them were under investigation. The Dallas location was the first whose perimeter had been breached.

"Good to go," came the all clear command.

In an instant, Nancy's point-of-view shot across the dirt roads and barns into the center of the Commune, inside the vestry of a small church. She eased her virtual presence inside, slowly materializing her virtual body onto a chair. Already a clouding of Atopian smarticles permeated the space. This Commune's Reverend was pouring himself a cup of tea.

"You realize it was futile to try and stop us getting inside," said Jimmy, draping himself across the Reverend's desk. Jimmy wasn't just projecting himself here virtually—he'd infected the body of one of the Commune's residents.

The Reverend finished preparing his tea and turned to Jimmy. "Do you need to inhabit my son's body?"

"Have to, and want to, are two different things." Jimmy smiled. "But what I do *need* is some information."

"I know what you are."

"It doesn't matter what you know anymore. Whatever is in there"—Jimmy pointed at the Reverend's head—"will soon be in here." He pointed at his own head.

"The Day of Judgment is soon coming—"

"Oh, I know, I know," Jimmy interrupted, his smile growing wider. "But your day of judgment has already arrived, and I don't think your God will help you now."

Jimmy slid into the Reverend's cognitive networks. The Reverend's cup of tea, halfway to his mouth for a sip, slid out of his fingers and tumbled to smash on the wooden floorboards. A wet stain spread around the Reverend's feet as his body shuddered at the invasion, his mind struggling to resist.

Nancy watched dispassionately. "Can I speak to you privately?"

Smiling back from the Reverend's face, Jimmy's eyes narrowed. "About what?" But he instantiated a series of dense security blankets around them.

"You and I have had our differences," said Nancy, "but we've known each other a long time. I think we want the same things."

"Do we indeed?"

In augmented space, Nancy watched Jimmy crack the Reverend's mind open like a nut, spilling its contents into a data bucket.

Nancy nodded. "Kesselring approached me today. He's worried you're gaining too much power, and he's convening a meeting of senior shareholders to limit your reach." It was a gamble. For security reasons she couldn't connect to the other splinters of her mind. She couldn't be sure.

Jimmy stopped disgorging the Reverend's mind. He looked at Nancy.

"Is that right?"

# 5

"COPY THAT, DCA, we're releasing control to you now," said Connors. Her networks handshaked with the capital city aerial routing system. Up ahead, the spike of the Washington Monument rose above an urban sprawl that spread, twinkling, to the horizon.

Four fighter drones rose up in formation around their turbofan to escort them in.

Vince's mind was still roiling. How was it possible that the old Russian, Mikhail Butorin, had dug up an ancient text that just happened to explain where to find Willy's body? It had been the critical clue that led them to him. And yet it came from a two-thousand-year-old manuscript found a hundred years ago, buried in the Egyptian desert. Was the text just random coincidence? Or had Butorin purposely lied? Any other conclusions stretched all believability.

All the things he was obsessing over—ancient carvings on buildings depicting what looked like alien creatures, the Voynich manuscript, images of Buddha with multiple arms and legs, even the Buddha carved from a meteorite—the Terra Novan hypothesis fit all these, but it felt too neat.

"Are you going to tell me why you need to speak to Allied Command?" Connors asked. "You're not going to be telling them some doomsday nonsense, are you?" She turned to him. "Can I trust you?"

"Yes, you can trust me." He was going to tell the truth, or at least, he was going to tell most of it.

The Mall hovered into view, that green strip of space in the middle of Washington that stretched from the Lincoln Memorial to the Capitol Building. Vince remembered family trips to the Smithsonian as a child. The memories were still vivid. For forty years he'd lived on Atopia, but he was still American, and this place held an aura that inspired him.

Why wait till now, though? His mind kept circling back. Why lay dormant for two hundred million years? If these beings existed, they had almost god-like power. Why would they be interested in us? Mindless destruction didn't make any sense.

The web of turbofan transports in the air grew denser. Below, Vince saw traffic moving like fish in a stream. He was overcome by the idea that he was watching the dying motions of a doomed world, the people going on with their lives as if anything mattered anymore, as if they were still alive.

But was it doomed?

The Potomac River snaked around the city into the distance, and their turbofan dropped down and followed it, accompanied by their drone escorts. It wouldn't be long until Vince was locked down.

"One thing." Vince touched Connors's arm. "I'd like to release Hotstuff. I don't know if I'm going to get out of this, and it's not fair for her to be stuck in some hellhole with me."

A part of her would always stay inside him, but he could release her core identity into one of his shell companies. Bob had already released his proxxi entirely. It felt like the right thing to do, but he needed Connors's help.

She looked at him, her expression unreadable.

Vince let go of her arm. "I know you could get into a lot of trouble—"

"Go ahead." Connors opened a channel for Vince to let Hotstuff out.

# 6

THE KEY TO creating convincing synthetic realities was attention to detail, and nobody was better at it than Atopian pssi-kids. And no pssi-kid was better than the legendary Sidney Horowitz. Sid laughed grimly at his own internal monologue. It was the same trash talking he used in the game worlds, but this was no game.

This was real.

The adrenaline felt like holding a mouthful of nails, but he wasn't in any physical danger. Zoraster was the one who was there physically, but looking at Zoraster, the big monkey looked remarkably calm. Zoraster smiled at the drone Sid was inhabiting.

"Is it working?"

"You wouldn't be standing there if it wasn't," Sid replied, projecting a smile.

This was a one-time shot. Hacking into a hardened military network wasn't something that you could do on the fly. Mikhail and the Ascetics gave them a collection of back-doors and exploits to get inside the military networks. They said they would work. Soon they'd find out.

The skirmish they started with Alliance forces was blossoming into a full-blown battle. Hundreds of incoming Alliance drones lit up Sid's situational maps. He hacked into everything he could, even distant command posts and orbiting satellites, burrowing into their sensors, subtly modifying them. Detecting stolen or wrecked systems was much easier than detecting small changes in data flow. The sensors were the eyes and ears of the robot attackers that created their reality, each one feeding into the main situational map of the enemy.

By controlling their reality, Sid controlled the battle and could destroy at will, but he had other goals.

It was a game of misdirection played out in milliseconds using optical and radio cloaking, alternately jamming and releasing communications while he slipped in false sensor readings. The attacking weapons systems just missed their marks as they aimed at shifting ghosts.

Sid launched cyberattacks at the same time as kinetic ones—defusing and exploding ordnance in transit, recognizing patterns that would be forming in the future, splitting the battle into alternate realities, and having the enemy attack itself in bursts of friendly fire. Both sides were layering reality filters with feints and decoys, and it was Sid's job to see through it and anchor a base reality for his team to fight through.

Sid helped the Grilla commandos dance through the raindrops of incoming fire without getting wet—or not too wet, anyway. He was purposely leaving gaps in their defenses. If the Allied forces decided the battle wasn't possible to win, they'd carpet-bomb the area. Zoraster's plan needed the Alliance to send in a transport to mop up, and that was what Sid was trying to engineer.

A nearby explosion rocked the drone Sid's main point-of-presence was riding in, blinding him. A tank-bot wheeled across the dusty ground, the air buzzing with shrapnel. It took aim.

"You okay, kid?" grunted Zoraster in a private comm channel.

The Grilla bounded from behind Sid's drone in two loping steps, grabbing and tossing the two-ton tank-bot into the air like a child's toy. Even a natural mountain gorilla could dead lift a ton, and a raging Grilla in an exoskeleton and battle armor was something fearsome to behold.

"Yeah, I'm—"

Before Sid could finish, another explosion fried his drone. His primary subjective dropped into dimensionless space for a fraction of a second while he latched onto another bot nearby. By the time his senses returned, the comm channels were filled with screams.

"Fall back!" Zoraster yelled across all frequencies.

Directly in front of Sid's new drone, one of their Grilla commandos was hit, his leg severed. Blood spurted from an artery. As Sid watched, transfixed, the coagulants in the Grilla's bloodstream kicked in, staunching the flow. At the same time, the Grilla's exoskeleton arm extended downward and clicked into the damaged leg structure.

Sid's situational map glowed red. The Alliance had designated it a kill zone. All kill decisions went to automatic, the attacking drones disengaging from their sensors and shifting into a frenzy. There were no humans here, just Grillas. Sid concentrated and threw an invisibility shield down around the injured commando.

"Norrece, you mobile?" Zoraster growled, bounding over and picking his friend up.

Norrece nodded, putting down one arm to support himself. He stood on the improvised leg his exoskeleton had reformed. They ran back under cover of their own drone support. A signal in Sid's situational display confirmed they'd achieved their goal. A transport was coming in.

"Now we do it my way," Sid said to Zoraster. "Drop your weapons."

Zoraster let go of Norrece, letting him run for cover. "What's next?"

The main Alliance drone force was already taking off to the south, chasing the retreating Grillas, but a swarm of them still circled overhead. Zoraster dropped his MD and dropped a utility belt of detonators and explosives.

"If we carry any weapons, it'll be harder to mask our presence," explained Sid. He had the transport on visual. It was dusting the horizon. He looked at Zoraster. "Come on, all of them."

Frowning, Zoraster reached into his body armor to pull out an old gunpowder-pistol and a knife. He dropped them into the dirt as well.

The transport grew in size until it was hovering above them, its exhaust blasting away the dirt beneath their feet. With a roar it descended, rocking on its landing gear while the whine of its electric turbofans cycled down.

The hatch opened.

"Stay still," Sid instructed. The Alliance wouldn't be expecting this. It was as much a technical feat as a magic trick of misdirection. He hardened the reality filters around them.

Bipedal bots climbed out of the transport, oblivious to the presence of Zoraster or Sid's drone in their midst. They began scavenging through the debris of the battle, looking for any scraps of machines that might be analyzed for data recovery.

Sid powered up the rotors on his drone and hovered, sending up a small cloud of dust. "Don't worry," he said to Zoraster. "Just continue straight on, slowly, no sudden movements."

Zoraster took a deep breath and walked through the knot of Alliance bots to the transport. He grabbed the rung of a ladder on the side and began climbing up. "You better be sure about this, kid."

Sid watched the Grilla disappear into the hatch of the transport, then he powered up his drone and followed.

# 7

THE ORANGE LIGHT of a sodium bulb on a solitary lamppost spread across the cracked concrete sidewalk. Bob floated, searching the blackness. He found what he was looking for in a cinder-block shack, its corrugated-tin roof hung aslant. Slivers of electric light shone through the cracks in its closed wooden shutters.

Bob heard voices within, raised voices. An argument.

He glided from the sidewalk to the side of the shack, across tufts of crabgrass littered with trash, and eased himself up to the door. Reaching forward he pushed it open. Inside, rust stains leaked down the walls onto metal shelves piled high with stacks of graying paper.

The argument stopped. All faces turned to the door.

Toothface, the one who'd captured Bob—*hunted him*—was sitting at a table. Across from him sat the gaunt-faced paramilitary who had guided Bob up the Yoba River. Two of his men sat on a couch against the far wall, dressed in stained fatigues, slouching with their rifles, smoking cigarettes.

Ignoring them, Bob crossed the room, directly toward Toothface. Bob's former guide jumped out of his seat, backing away, hesitating, but Bob didn't hesitate. A blade flashed in his hand, slicing through the air into Toothface's neck. The table and chairs clattered to the ground as Bob fell onto Toothface, urging the knife deeper, hot blood pooling beneath them onto the concrete.

◆◆◆

FREUD CALLED DREAMS the "royal road" into the unconscious, all the forbidden wishes you had but wished you didn't. Bob
wondered what wishes his dreams were yearning for, but this last
one wasn't hard to interpret.

Waking and sleep were becoming hopelessly intermixed while
he roamed virtual worlds of his own creation, his body trapped
in the life-support unit at the bottom of the oceanic transport. It
was refreshing to finally get outside his own mind, into a synthetic
external world. The Ascetics controlled this section of the darknet,
and the priest bartered to get access.

Squinting, Bob looked across breaking waves caressing a perfect
beach. He sat in the shade of palm trees that drooped to the surf,
thick with green coconuts. Digging his fingers into the hot sand, he
leaned back to stretch his legs. "So Sid's doing okay?"

"He's good, mate," Bunky replied, the underminer's avatar sat
beside him in the sand. "He helped Zoraster infiltrate Allied HQ."

"That's good," said the priest, pacing behind them. "The Red
Rider must be stopped."

"And Vince?"

Bunky scratched his neck. "Haven't gotten much from him, but
he's gone into Washington. It's all going to plan, if you can call
it that."

Bob's body had arrived at a deep-water connection point in
Rio de Janeiro. Bunky came in person to oversee the transfer
from one oceanic transport to the next. The underminers had
close connections with the transportation guilds. More than that,
though, Bunky was bringing underminers around the world to
the cause.

"So you've found these crystals everywhere?" Bob asked.

Bunky nodded. "Once you know what to look for, they're pretty easy to spot, spreading into the rock strata under the big cities like mold on cheese. Sibeal says it might explain how Atopia is expanding its computing infrastructure so quickly."

This had been something of a mystery. The computing infrastructure Atopia controlled didn't seem to add up to the exponential proliferation of virtual worlds that were spawning from it.

"So it's merging with Atopian pssi?"

Bunky shrugged. "Beyond me, mate."

"And these other underminer guilds, they're joining in?"

"Never thought of myself as an evangelist, but yeah, for the most part." Bunky flashed his broken-tooth grin. "Especially when I show them the stuff. They're digging it all out now, trying to slow the spread." An alert lit up in Bunky's workspace. "I can't stay in this world much longer."

They were connected in a darknet pleasure world, part of the Spice Routes that crisscrossed the underside of the multiverse. Bob heard children playing in the distance, laughing. He looked up the beach to see them splashing in the water.

"You're straight onto the Atopian territorial boundaries on this transport," Bunky added. "No idea what you're going to do then." He cocked his head and looked at Bob. "But that's why they're sending you, buddy. I guess you'll know."

Bob shook his head. "I hope so."

"Me too, mate, me too. Listen, I really have to run." He clapped Bob on the shoulder. "Good luck, and nice to meet you." Smiling, Bunky faded away, leaving Bob alone with the priest.

Bob watched dark shadows sweep across the ocean. He rose to his feet.

"What do you think?" Bob asked the priest. They began walking together, up the beach toward the children.

The priest hung his head. "It matters little what I think."

"That's the first time I've heard you say that."

"I think our quest is suicide." The priest looked into Bob's eyes. "But not to act is also suicide."

They walked in silence until they were near the children. No adults were in sight. One of them ran up to Bob, splashing through the water.

"What's your name?" Bob asked.

The young boy, dressed in swimming shorts and not more than seven or eight, looked into Bob's eyes. "You can call me what you like."

Bob reached down and ruffled the boy's hair. "That's a strange name. What are you doing here?"

"Whatever you want," replied the boy.

All of the children were staring at Bob. There were six of them, playing what looked like a game of tag. The thatched roofs of huts stood over the tops of sand dunes lining the beach.

Bob frowned. He checked their metatags. These were proxxids, simulated children derived from copyrights of real human DNA. They shouldn't be here. Not alone. They were supposed to be with their copyright owners. "Are your parents over there somewhere?" Bob waved a hand toward the huts.

The boy smiled. "No."

Bob's smile faded and dread seeped into his veins. "Then why are you here?" But he already knew.

The priest grabbed Bob's arm. "We should go."

"We're here for you," the boy replied to Bob. He reached to hold Bob's hand.

Bob hadn't dug into the structure of this world when they arrived. He'd been happy just to get out of his mind, but now he spun under the fabric of it—hundreds, no, thousands of children, all waiting to please. To pleasure. Bob shrugged off the priest, spinning to face him. "What is this?"

"You wanted a world to escape into, and this was the only one firewalled off deep enough to be safe."

Bob clenched his jaw, veins popping out in his neck. "Go play with your friends," he stuttered to the boy.

He'd heard rumors of these worlds. It was disgusting. Even in a virtual body, he felt like he was going to vomit, his skin crawling as he watched the children returning to their game.

"We need to go," the priest whispered. "The transport had left already. We're going to lose the connection to this world."

"And leave them here?"

"This is the only world they know," replied the priest. "They know no different."

Proxxids had emotions, if not much in the way of higher cognitive functioning. "We can't leave them."

The priest looked into Bob's eyes. "There's nothing we can do."

He looked at the children, playing again, unaware. There was something he could do.

They'd never know.

"Help me," said Bob to the priest. As the connection faded, Bob flexed his mind, reaching into the fabric of the world, down into its very core. Twisting, he began pulling it apart, ripping it out of the network. In the blink of an eye it ceased to exist, and so had the proxxids.

But then so did their suffering.

Or perhaps, so did Bob's.

# 8

SID WATCHED THE spider-bots hovering overhead, darting between hanging orchids while they spooled out high-tensile microfilaments behind them. They were weaving the structure of a protective shell between blossoming boughs in a thicket of tea trees, sending down a rain of white petals as they quivered the branches. Sid turned to look at Zoraster, busy unpacking his rifle and gear that had arrived via a delivery drone.

"You're being quiet. Anything wrong?"

"Wrong?" Zoraster grunted. "What could be wrong? I spent the worst years of my life fighting my way out of this place." His huge nostrils flared. "And now I risk my life to get back in."

Sid swiveled the bot he was inhabiting to get a view down the valley. He could just see Allied headquarters in a straight line-of-sight from their perch on the opposite wall of a valley. Arunchal, sandwiched between China and India, was still a strikingly beautiful place despite the wars that had gripped it for decades. Its valleys were filled with a kaleidoscope of lush tropical forests that rose into the Himalayas.

"Why did you volunteer to come, then?" Sid asked.

"Because I know this place better than anyone."

An iridescent blue butterfly fluttered past Sid. "And because you believe this apocalypse stuff?"

Throwing a bag of gear onto the ground, Zoraster shook his shaggy head. "Don't you?" He didn't look Sid's bot in the eye.

"All of that is human legend—you should try a mile in my shoes. Grillas have no past, no future, just a single generation damned into existence to fight a war we had no stake in. So excuse me if I don't get shivers when a ghost story about the end of humanity comes up."

Sid didn't say anything. For him, the Terra Novan's background data was convincing. Mohesha had almost decoded the way the quasi-crystals worked. The technology was advanced, but not that much more. For Sid, it was an opportunity to analyze a new system.

"You want to know why I'm here? What I believe in? Is that what you're asking?" continued Zoraster. "I fight for my friends. The Terra Novans are the only ones who've given equal human rights to Grillas. They believe this is happening, and I believe in them. It's as simple as that."

Sid nodded. He didn't need to believe Tyrel or not. Soon Sid would be inside this nervenet thing and could find out what it was for himself.

"Speaking of friends," Zoraster added, "your friend Bob didn't seem too friendly."

Sid had to agree. The Council meeting was the first and only time Sid had a chance to talk with Bob after they lost track of each other, but he'd been evasive. "Yeah, but that's not like him. He's usually the friendliest person you'll ever meet."

"If you say so," Zoraster grunted.

"He is." Sid buzzed his drone down to pick up the gun sight for Zoraster's rifle. "Even as a stoned surfer, he was an inspiration, doing things nobody else could do, always talking to people. But I introduced you and Sibeal at that meeting, and barely a peep. Something happened to him in that desert."

Sid tried talking to Bob about what happened in New York, if he knew anything about the pssi weapon that was unleashed, if he was mad at Sid for the synthetic-K. Bob said he didn't know anything. Sid asked about his escape across the desert, but Bob just mumbled about suffering and redemption. The only thing Bob said, after Tyrel dropped the bomb about the ancient nervenet, was, "Isn't the White Rider the savior in the Apocalypse?"

It was an odd comment, and one that worried Sid. Was Bob angry at him?

"Your friend is fine." Zoraster lifted his rifle onto a platform and began sighting down its barrel at Allied headquarters. "He just got a little knocked around. Not sure what he's going to do when he gets to the Atopian perimeter." Zoraster looked away from Allied headquarters and at Sid. "But then you're Atopians. You must have a trick or two up your sleeve."

Only just. There was a worryingly thin list of options, especially when Jimmy probably knew they'd be coming at him. Sid nodded without conviction.

Sid switched topics. "So Tyrel sent you to New York to get me?" He'd researched Zoraster since they met. In his way he was famous—he'd gone AWOL from Allied forces to rescue his mother, a non-uplifted gorilla, when she'd been scheduled for termination. He'd ended up seeking asylum in the African Union.

"You and Bob, yeah, but I messed that up." Zoraster laughed. "Sorry about roughing you up a little. Just wanted to see what made you tick." His smile disappeared. "By some miracle Bob got through, but I'm not going to be counting on miracles this time." He stared down the barrel of his rifle. It was a precision mass-driver.

"Do you really think you can get into this nervenet? Infect it?"

Sid nodded. "Yeah, I do. To start with we'll just track the topology, try to pick up network traffic. Then maybe we can slow them down a little."

Zoraster laughed. "We might be able to slow them down." He swiveled his head up to look into the sky, using one giant hand up to block the sun. Just at its edge, the comet's tail was becoming visible again. "But that freight train is on its own schedule."

Sid switched into a simulated viewpoint a hundred million miles away in space to have a look. The comet had swung around the sun and was heading for Earth. The Comet Catcher mission still hadn't figured out what was slowing the comet down more than it should be.

"Do you really think that's the plan?" The deceleration of the comet could just be violent out-gassing, and it was still only projected to swing just inside lunar orbit, but the problem was taking on ominous dimensions. "Not very elegant."

"Sometimes war isn't elegant," replied Zoraster. "Blunt trauma is my personal favorite. Simple and effective."

And more than one mass extinction in Earth's past was blamed on comet impacts.

Zoraster returned his gaze to the Allied headquarters. "Just one shot, that's all I need." He stared back down the rifle sight. "Payback time, you bastards."

*I guess he was the right choice for this mission.* "We're not killing anyone, right?" Sid confirmed. "Just injecting some of my hotwired smarticles."

"Not yet," Zoraster replied, his voice somewhere between grim and enthusiastic.

The idea was to suffuse trace quantities of nerve conduction particles into the target's biological matrix that would start leaking data back to Terra Nova. They were going to literally infect the head of Allied Command, and watch to see if any unusual network traffic connected with the crystal nodes they collected. The rifle Zoraster was fondling would accelerate a tiny payload, less than the width of a human hair, which would penetrate the walls of the compound and disintegrate itself on impact with the target and release its content.

"When you locate a Trojan infection, especially a virulent one like this"—Sid shared some more examples with Zoraster's meta-cognition systems—"it's best to isolate it, learn what it's doing. If you just wipe it out, it'll pop up somewhere else and be that much harder to find."

Zoraster assimilated Sid's examples. He smiled. "But eventually we wipe it out, yes?"

"I guess." Sid shrugged. His job was just to get into the network.

Overhead, the spider-bots were nearly finished. The tensile microfilaments bonded together, creating a gossamer shield that the optics and radio cloaking could spread across. Sid sighed with relief. He wasn't sure how much longer he could maintain the reality filter in place, spoofing the sensors of the Allied base. He started withdrawing his agents.

This whole time, he'd been listening to conversations inside headquarters, monitoring their movements. Sid switched to a visual overlay of the building, and the red outlines of people inside glowed within the three-dimensional frames of its walls.

"You did a good job back there, kid."

This was surprising enough that Sid withdrew his primary subjective to stare at Zoraster. "Huh?"

"On the drop down. I risked my team in the hands of some kid who'd only ever fought in gameworlds, but you did good."

Sid didn't expect this. "Thanks."

"The second I saw you, I didn't like you," continued Zoraster, "but we're friends now, right, kid?"

"Right," replied Sid.

"Good, because I only risk my neck for friends." Smiling, Zoraster pinged Sid to get the visual overlay for the building, and they both dove into the display. "That's the target?"

"Right." Sid highlighted the senior Allied Commander.

It was time.

Zoraster nodded and accessed the control systems of the rifle. "Are we go?"

Sid nodded.

Sounding like a hammer hitting a steel plate, the rifle fired. Its projectile, little more than a thousandth of an inch in diameter, shot across the valley at a velocity of several thousands of yards a second to pierce the wall of the Allied compound building like a hot needle through butter. Several feet short of the target, it disintegrated, spraying its payload of neuro-active smarticles onto the target. The building intrusion was detected, the self-healing walls and glass of the building registering an impact at the same time as external sensors picked up the shockwave outdoors, but with no apparent damage and no detected anomalies within the building, the alert threshold was filed as a low priority. No alarm sounded.

Exhaling with relief, Sid opened up the workspace designed to track the network activity. The display blinked then lit up like a fireworks show. "It's working," he whispered.

# 9

. . . TWO . . . THREE . . . FOUR . . .

Time.

. . . six . . . seven . . . eight . . .

Time.

. . . two . . . three . . . four . . .

Time.

Who am I? Vince, I'm Vince. Is this a game? No, it's not a game. Was it all a dream? That we can't be sure of. *How can we be sure of anything?*

. . . two . . . three . . . four . . .

Time.

. . . six . . . seven . . . eight . . .

Time. Time to take out the garbage.

In his mind's eye, Vince watched himself as a young boy, pulling trash bags out back of the old house on Bowen Street in Southie. It was dark, early November, and bitterly cold. "He needs to get a job!" his father shouted. "Don't yell," hissed his mother. "Vince doesn't fit in here, you know how he is . . ."

Vince dropped the bags on the street and leaned against the red brick wall in the shadows of the streetlights, lighting up a cigarette. It was only a few miles, yet an impossible distance, from there to the halls of MIT, a distance that would forever separate him from his father.

Looking up at the window, listening to them arguing, he yearned for the warm yellow glow of home.

"I'm sorry," he whispered.

*Nobody cares for you*, sang a voice in his head. *Nobody is waiting for you. This life was wasted, wasted on something that doesn't exist. The future is a ghost, Vincent . . .*

Colors washed in front of his eyes: greens, golds, shimmering reflections like God's oysters falling open before his eyes, spilling pearly tears. I wish I could close my eyes. Or open them. Please make this stop.

. . . two . . . three . . . four . . .

Please.

. . . six . . . seven . . . eight . . .

Stop.

"TICK TOCK, SAID the Ticktock man."

"Is someone there?"

No response.

I'm suffocating. Drowning in nothingness.

"Tick . . ."

"Please, is someone there?" Vince said again.

". . . tock."

"Tick tock, tick tock, you are the man of time, are you not, Mr. Indigo?" the voice said. "Or perhaps, the man out of time." The voice laughed.

"Sensory deprivation is banned," Vince whispered, "by all international treaties." He couldn't hear his own voice, but he knew he was talking.

"You'll have to take that up with the courts when you get out." The words flashed in his vision, a bright green that faded like the strobe of a flash. "Of course, that's if you remember, and you won't, because your memories are classified now. Allied property. You understand?"

It was indescribable relief to have something to focus on. "Yes," Vince replied.

"Good."

A soothing blackness fell across Vince's senses, the frayed edges of his mind curling together.

"Is that better?" said the voice.

"Yes."

The blackness fell away, replaced by the nothingness of the void. Vince felt himself falling.

"Tell us about the garbage," demanded the voice.

Calm, Vince told himself, you know the game. They wanted to access his memories, but they needed to understand the structure. His externally stored data used compression keys tuned to his earliest memories, ones that existed only inside of his gray matter. Ones only his own mind could extract.

"Yes, you know the game," said the voice, "so give us what we want."

They could hear him thinking. There was no escape. Think nothing.

"Try thinking nothing of this," said the voice.

And then came the pain. His body was on fire, his skin stripping away in molten chunks. He screamed. And then nothing.

"It leaves no marks, no trace, and no memories," menaced the voice. "You can cooperate or not, rot in this hole of your mind. It makes no difference to us."

"I will only talk to Colonel Kramer," stuttered Vince, his nerves stinging, his mind a point of nothing in a nothingness space.

"You are in no position to make demands. Tell us about the garbage."

Vince had to give them something. "It was the moment I decided I needed to leave home."

The soothing blackness returned.

"See, that wasn't so hard, was it?" In the background he sensed them using this reference point to begin unpacking some of his memories.

"I need to speak to Colonel Kramer," repeated Vince.

"Why?"

"Because there are leaks in your organization. I need to speak to him. Personally."

The voice considered this. "You know you cannot lie to us."

"Then you know I am speaking the truth. I came here of my own free will."

More silence, but the nothingness gave way to a gray fog. It became deeper, thicker, and then evaporated. Vince found himself sitting on a concrete floor in total darkness. Not total darkness. He could just see a slit of light coming into the solitary confinement cell through the food receptacle. He reached up to feel his face, laughing and crying at the same time. Leaning over, he curled into a ball on the ground.

CLICK, CLACK, CLICK, clack—steel balls on Colonel Kramer's desk circled through empty space before returning to hit the next one in an endless loop—click, clack, click, clack. Twelve-foot glass walls stood behind the desk, framing a gray and rainy view of one wall of the Pentagon from ground level. Leafless trees bent in a sudden gust. A squall of rain hammered down onto the sidewalk, soaking men and women in uniform as they hurried between buildings.

Colonel Kramer sat in his high-backed leather chair, facing away from Vince, staring through the window at the rain. "I'm a busy man, Mr. Indigo." The balls stopped motionless in the air.

Vince was sitting in a leather chair in front of the Colonel's desk, dressed in an orange jumpsuit, his hair disheveled and several days of stubble on his face. "This is worth your time."

There were no guards in the room. They weren't necessary. Vince's neural systems were under his captors' control.

The Colonel swung his chair around to face Vince. "So?"

Vince did his best to verify the metatags of whoever was appearing before his senses. What little network access they granted him seemed to confirm this was Colonel Kramer. There wasn't any way to be sure, but Vince had few options. "There's a plot against you." Vince held the Colonel's gaze.

Laughing, the Colonel replied, "I hope you have more than that. If I had a dollar for every plot—"

"The Terra Novans think Jimmy Scadden is some kind of reincarnation of the devil that's dragging the world into an apocalypse."

The Colonel stopped laughing. He was verifying the feedback loop into Vince's mind. He knew Vince was telling the truth. "That doesn't surprise me."

Vince frowned. "It doesn't?"

"Just more extremists." The Colonel shook his head. "What proof do you have?"

"I have information that Patricia Killiam gave to our group." Reaching inside himself, Vince unlocked a data vault containing a recording of what Patricia had given them. He sent it into the Colonel's systems.

"Interesting," the Colonel replied, analyzing the contents. "Tell me more."

"They think a computing matrix of crystals is forming under cities, connecting into an ancient machine. The Terra Novans have been studying it."

"An ancient machine?" The Colonel's eyebrows arched. "Have you seen these"—he paused—"*crystals*"—he drew out the word—"yourself?"

Vince stared out the window at the winking lights of the turbofan skyways hanging in a small patch of sky that was just visible. "No."

"So you want me to believe that there is some kind of alien technology—"

"Not alien," interrupted Vince, "just not human. And no, I'm not asking you to believe anything. I'm just telling you what the Terra Novans think."

The Colonel nodded. "And where is this leak?"

Vince shook his head. "I just know they think your organization is compromised at some level."

The Colonel finished assimilating the data Vince sent. "The neutrino detector data, this is new. What else do you know about this?"

"I have no idea, just what Patricia said. The Terra Novans have no idea either."

"Again, from aliens?" The Colonel smiled.

Vince said nothing, and didn't return the smile.

The Colonel asked one last question. "And William McIntyre. We know you were searching for his body at the Commune. Did you find him?"

Vince took a deep breath. "No." He shook his head. "No, we didn't."

# 10

"DO YOU BELIEVE in heaven and hell?" asked Sid.

Sid rotated the viewing lens of the bot he was inhabiting toward the Grilla. Zoraster was splayed out against the trunk of the tea tree in the middle of their enclosure, inspecting the fur on one of his arms.

"Goddamn bugs." Zoraster picked at his arm, his surprisingly dexterous fingers finding the offending six-legged creature, a brightly-colored beetle. He set it down and watched it scurry off. "Like the human Bible version of heaven and hell, you mean?"

Sid's bot nodded. "I guess."

"I've seen a lot of pain, kid, and I can tell you, plain and simple, suffering is hell." Zoraster rocked forward on his haunches and checked down the sight of the rifle again, looking at the Allied headquarters compound on the other side of the valley. "Whether it's physical, in your head, in this world, or the next—hell is wherever you find suffering."

Sid-bot didn't bother reminding Zoraster that he didn't need to keep doing a visual check. Sid was constantly monitoring the site. "So then a lack of suffering is heaven?"

Leaning against the tree, Zoraster grunted what Sid imagined was a laugh. "I didn't say that." He scratched under his exoskeleton. "I don't think there needs to be an opposite of hell, just a lack of suffering—so I think there's hell and not-hell."

"That's not very optimistic."

"You wouldn't be either if someone as messed up as humans designed you." Zoraster found another insect in his fur and, again, gently removed it to set it free. "Do I have a soul?" he asked rhetorically. "And if I do, did humans create it? On the balance, I'd prefer not to risk it."

Sid-bot balanced itself on one side to rotate its lower gimbals. "I like to think there's a heaven." A breeze ruffled the enclosure, shaking loose a flurry of white-and-yellow tea blossoms that gently settled around the gorilla and robot.

"If what Mohesha is saying is true," Zoraster ventured, "then you've got your heaven. A copy of every human mind that has existed is in that nervenet somewhere. Endless life and meeting of passed loved ones."

Pushing itself onto its other side, Sid-bot rotated its other gimbals. "Maybe." It stopped and de-focused its optical lens to stare into infinity. "But if it's possible that something exists, does it really matter whether it exists here or not? Whether we can actually see it?"

Zoraster frowned. "I don't follow."

"I mean, if there are an infinite number of universes, then if it's possible to imagine something, isn't it the same as actually existing somewhere?"

The Grilla rolled his eyes. "You have a messed up way of looking at things. Saying everything is true also makes nothing true. There need to be limits." Zoraster thumped the ground with one giant hand. "How's the signal doing?"

This splinter of Sid's mind was connected through a ground-based mesh network of insect-bots that stretched to the border of the African Union. It was low bandwidth, but information was steadily seeping back and forth.

Sid-bot checked the feed. "The network map is really starting to come together." The plan was working. They were tracking data flow through the crystal network.

"Good," grunted Zoraster. It was the first indication the plan was working. "So do you believe all this stuff Tyrel is saying?"

Sid-bot nodded, the gears in its neck whirring back and forth, and then wagged its head side to side. "It's hard to dispute the evidence—"

Zoraster interrupted him. "You Atopians just nearly wrecked yourselves fighting a giant storm that didn't exist. How can you be sure this isn't more of the same?"

"You're right, but we tested for that. There are too many proof points, too many interconnected instances. And in a way it didn't surprise me."

The Grilla frowned. "What didn't surprise you?"

"We've found life on Mars and Titan—our solar system is teeming with it—and one in five stars out there have planets in habitable orbits. There's got to be trillions of eyes staring back at us from out there, but not a single transmission or evidence of any kind?"

"Except for that POND signal," Zoraster noted.

"Yeah, except for that." Sid was still working around the clock on that, but nothing yet apart from a repeating nine-element sequence that hinted it was a warning signal. "So we've finally been contacted by other life, one way or the other. I'm relieved."

"Relieved? These things want to kill us."

"Maybe, but like they say, the devil you know is better than the devil you don't. Mohesha thinks nervenets are an example of convergent evolution, that any intelligent organism will eventually develop and integrate into their minds, just like they'd always develop eyes of some kind. I think she's right."

Zoraster sat in silence, absorbing this. "You're a strange kid."

Sid-bot affected the best smile it could. "Thanks." He shared more of the network diagram. "You can look at this nervenet like a virus that can infect both people and machines." The shared display, a geographic map of the world, crisscrossed with glowing lines.

"We're getting a peek at its command-and-control structure. Once we start to locate the nodal points, Mikhail and the Ascetics will hunt them down, begin exorcising them—"

Zoraster nodded. "And if Bob can cut the head off, we might have a chance of stopping it. Why don't we just kill anyone that's connected in this map?" He pointed at the nexus nodes that were already lighting up.

"People infected by the nervenet didn't do anything wrong."

The smile slid from Zoraster's face. "You're right." He rolled forward to get up onto his knees.

"I could do some cutting off right now," said Zoraster, leaning to stare down the barrel of the rifle sight. "Just one shot, and boom, no more head on this part of the snake."

The moment he uttered these words, the Allied compound disappeared in a brilliant flash. His internal systems only just protected his retinas in time to avoid being blinded. Sid-bot jumped up. The monitoring feed coming from the headquarters winked out, and a second later a shockwave ripped through their enclosure, shredding it in a thundering concussion.

"Zoraster, what the hell did you do?" messaged Sid-bot.

The roar was still reverberating through the valley, a mushroom cloud was climbing into the sky above the spot where the Allied buildings had been just seconds before. Shaking his head and coughing, Zoraster pushed himself up from the ground. Tea blossoms were swirling around them in a cloud of dust. "Didn't do anything," he groaned, holding his side. Something had hit him.

A swarm of attack drones rose from the roiling clouds on the other side of the valley. They headed directly for the spot where Sid and Zoraster were hiding.

"Zoraster!" pinged Sid-bot across all of the Grilla's emergency channels. "You gotta get moving!"

The whine of incoming fire rained down around them. Zoraster looked at the advancing drones, then back at Sid-bot and smiled. "Call me Furball, kid, and don't worry, I'll—"

The transmission cut.

SITTING IN THE White Horse Pub in UnderMidTown, Sid put his beer down. "Zoraster? Are you there?"

There was no response.

In a viewpoint from a weather satellite, hundreds of miles above India, a smudge of smoke spread across the Arunchal valley. An alert pinged Sid's networks, and he opened the channel, expecting to see Zoraster's face, but instead he found an image of an oceanic tanker.

Bob had arrived at the Atopian perimeter.

# 11

HIS CHALK SQUEAKED across the blackboard as Bob finished writing out the minimum critical parameters for fissile actinides. His hand ached. The board was filled with equations. With a flourish he underlined the result. The chalk snapped in his fingers, the broken end tumbling onto the threadbare Persian carpet of his study. He turned to his guest. "So, you see?"

A rakish man, his hair slicked back, leaned forward. His freshly pressed suit squeaked against the polished leather of the copper-studded wingback chair he slouched in. "Are you sure?"

Bob stared at the decimal point of his result. Just a mote of calcium carbonate stuck against the sheet of porcelain enamel of the blackboard, but it represented something that would change billions of lives. "Yes."

In an ornate mirror behind the man in the chair, Bob saw his reflection: an old man stared back at him, a fringe of white hair circling a balding head, bushy black eyebrows above thick jowls, and an unkempt suit. He dusted the chalk dust off the arms of his jacket.

There was a quiet rap on the door. "Would you like some tea?" came the muffled voice of his wife.

"No, Margrethe, but I think we might get some air," said Bob. "The children could still go and play in Tivoli, why don't you bring them out?"

Bob glanced at the man in the chair, who nodded. Outside the windows, fluttering yellow leaves fell from bare trees in a gust of wind. Winter was coming.

"Please bring our coats," Bob called out.

Getting up from the chair, the man walked close to the blackboard.

"I have to leave, Niels," said the man. "I need to tell Goering in person."

Bob nodded. "Margrethe!" he called out. "Could you please fetch Mr. Heisenberg's cases?"

BOB STARED ACROSS the Dead Man's Walk Desert, pulling down goggles to protect his eyes.

A voice echoed from a loudspeaker, ". . . three . . . two . . . one . . ."

The next instant, a blinding flash enveloped his senses and an intense heat burned into the flesh of his face. An orange fireball leapt into the sky on the distant plain, billowing up into a mushroom cloud. The air was eerily calm. Behind him Bob heard words in a language he hadn't heard spoken in thousands of years.

"I am become Death, the Destroyer of Worlds," said a voice in Sanskrit, just as the shockwave roared through their observation point.

"WE HAVE ARRIVED," an automated message announced, waking Bob up. He activated his somatic systems and groaned as he struggled upright. This was as far as the transport network could take them. From here he had to find his own way.

The dreams were more intense.

"They aren't just dreams," the priest told Bob when he spoke of them, "these are your past lives. As the nervenet grows stronger, the psychic fabric of the past is weaving itself into this world."

Memories of the dreams faded like morning fog under a rising sun. Bob only retained fleeting impressions of them. Nothing of the dreams remained in his inVerse, the recording of everything he ever saw or felt, and he couldn't find any trace of them in his meta-cognition systems.

Bob verified their location. They were in an off-shore docking complex, one the Ascetics assured him they controlled. For a short time they could mask his signature from any sensors. He was close now. Bob could feel it, the thrumming vibration of the Atopian multiverse just past the event horizon of his senses.

More than anything, he felt a craving to get back inside.

The priest was awake and sitting up in his opened bio-containment unit.

"We can go up top," Bob said to him, swinging his legs onto the floor.

Taking a moment for them both to stretch, Bob led the priest to the service ladder on the wall of the cargo bay. People weren't supposed to be in here, not awake. Soon it would be crawling with bots loading and uploading. Bob wanted to feed some fresh air into his lungs. Grabbing the first rung, he felt its cold metal. He clipped into the splinters that watched the world while he slept, leaving his body to climb by itself.

His mind exploded into the mediaworlds.

Green-scaled faces filled one visual display. *"Bioethics boards reconsider license of recombinant DNA manufacturer Remedica in the wake of discovery of a nest of human-lizard chimeras in Waco, Texas,"* said the splinter monitoring the story. *"Would you like more?"* Bob accepted, and a flood of images around the idea circled his mind; flying human bats and grotesque experiments gone wrong, self-assembling robotics fused with organic layers of living tissue, synthetic reality nervous systems tying it all together in the expanding eco-system of the Atopian stimulus.

*"Should we tell them?"* asked a newsworld in a splinter circling at the edges of Bob's awareness. He pulled it closer to his center. *"Why would we?"* was the answer. The object of discussion was a virtual world filled with synthetic beings, none of them aware that their world was simulated. The man that created it was posing as God to his creatures. He overrode controls forcing external awareness in digital organisms that could pass the Turing-threshold.

*"The Destroyer of Worlds is upon us,"* rang a shrill voice in another mediaworld. Bob shifted his attention to the ever-expanding sphere of the doomsday cults. *"The day of judgment is coming. Two thousand years ago the Kalachakra tantra predicted a future war where the forces of Shambala would arrive in flying ships to begin a new external cycle of time—"*

Bob disengaged from the mediaworlds. He stood on the deck of the transport, in the open for the first time in weeks. He clipped into his body to feel the cool wind and taste the sea air. He sensed Atopian smarticles, a dusting of them floating on the breeze from Atopia. His skin tingled. The priest stood beside him, his robe flapping in the breeze.

On the horizon Bob saw something, a glitter that stood out against the deep blue. The twinkling light was the reflection of the sun off the glass-walled farming towers of Atopia, less than five miles away. Nancy was there, his family was there.

All that stood in his way was Jimmy.

Bob turned to the priest. "Thank you for coming this far, without you . . ." He searched for words.

"It is not just for you that I have taken this journey." The priest held his arms wide. "But for all of God's creatures. We must stop this scourge."

They silently watched the waves.

"From here I go alone," said Bob. "If you can maintain the connection to Mohesha, make sure that the Terra Novan resources are available when we need them."

The priest nodded. "I will wait here."

Stripping out of the coveralls he wore in the hibernation pod, Bob prepared himself. His skin shimmered as his epithelial layers exuded a hydrophobic layer of protection against the water, while he began leaking perfluorocarbons into his lung tissue. Nodding at the priest, Bob dove headfirst from the platform into the frigid waters and began networking into depths.

These waters were his home.

# 12

JIMMY SCADDEN STARED at the ocean through a break between the trees. He stood in Herman Kesselring's private gardens at the apex of the farming tower and research centers—the highest point on Atopia, and one that Kesselring kept very private.

Jimmy had been summoned, in person.

"Why did you change the report?" Kesselring asked. He pulled the hood off the peregrine falcon sitting on his gloved hand and began feeding it raw meat.

They were in a grass field dotted with blooming purple heather, several hundred feet across, bordered by pines and yews. In augmented space, the real forests of Kesselring's private gardens stretched into the Austrian Alps of his home. Set back in the trees at the edge of the space was Kesselring's retreat, a wood-shingled, two-story chalet with white stucco walls.

"What report, Mr. Kesselring?" Jimmy stood straight, his hands clasped behind his back. "I thought you called me up here to discuss details of the operation."

Kesselring continued feeding his bird. "The report presented at the board meeting, with the information Colonel Kramer extracted from Mr. Indigo."

Jimmy frowned and glanced back at the break in the trees. "What do you mean?"

"The original report had details about you being responsible for the disappearance of Commander Strong's wife and other Atopians." Kesselring didn't look up as he said this, but stared into the eyes of his falcon, giving it another chunk of bloody meat that it gobbled back.

Jimmy's full attention swung to Kesselring. "Where did you hear that?"

"I think you forget who built this place, the resources and connections I have."

Jimmy looked at the ground. "They were just lies, fabrications by the extremists to try and destabilize the Alliance. I thought that spreading them further would only serve their goals. The Alliance gave us interim command of their forces for the operation against Terra Nova—"

"I know, Jimmy," interrupted Kesselring. The entire Allied Command staff in Arunchal Pradesh had been killed in a surprise attack. The Alliance had captured a Grilla, Zoraster, in connection with it, and Sidney Horowitz was implicated. It had pushed the Alliance into declaring war on the AU, confirming Jimmy's terrorist theories. "My problem is that you lied to me."

A whirring noise came from the direction of Kesselring's chalet, and a swarm of ornithopter bots rose into the sky, darting and weaving. The falcon saw them and its head twitched to the side, flexing its claws into the leather glove covering Kesselring's hand.

"I don't know what you mean, sir." Jimmy shifted from one foot to the other, his head down. "You've been like a father to me, even more since Patricia passed. I can't tell you how grateful I am—"

A bell chimed and Jimmy glanced into the augmented space of the Alps, at a church spire that climbed over the trees in a village nestled high above.

"I think it's time, Mr. Scadden, that we dispense with the charade." Kesselring looked at Jimmy, who stopped shifting and looked up to return his gaze. "Do you know anything about fal-conry?" In the background, Kesselring tensed his phantoms, moni-toring the data flow around Jimmy's networks.

"Not really, no."

Lifting his arm, Kesselring whistled and set the falcon free. With two quick and powerful beats of its wings, it lifted up and soared across the grass, then sailed into the sky to chase the ornithopters.

"Raptors are not pets," Kesselring explained, his eyes following the bird. "They are non-affectionate animals. Do you know what this means?"

Saying nothing, Jimmy shook his head. Wheeling overhead, the falcon shrieked as it caught the first robot, pinned it in its talons and dropped to the ground.

"It means they have no ability to deal with dominant or submis-sive roles. There is no love, no aim to please, just an opportunistic understanding that the falconer affords it the easiest source of food and protection. It's a matter of convenience, not love."

The falcon took several stabs at the robot with its beak. Kesselring whistled, and the falcon hopped toward him and then took to the air, the robot still in its grip. It landed back on Kesselring's gloved hand, the bot clutched in the talons of one foot.

"When it comes down to it," continued Kesselring, reaching to take the small bot from the bird's grip. He presented it with another morsel of red flesh. "At most, it's a matter of trust: the bird trusts the falconer not to steal its food and to provide protection, and the falconer trusts the bird to hunt and return when called." He lifted his hand and set the falcon free again. "Now which one of us is which?"

Jimmy unclasped his hands from behind his back. His face hard-ened. "Isn't this what you wanted, Herman?" He lifted his hands, palms up. "Terra Nova laid down, the world at your feet? Happi-ness indices are at an all-time high, the populations of the world lulled into a pssi-induced coma while it funnels money into your accounts. Don't tell me you did this for truth and beauty."

"These disappearances are becoming problematic—"

"Did you imagine this would be trouble free? There are a lot of people—governments, corporations—that don't like what's happening. Don't tell me that you didn't think sacrificing a few lives would be necessary to save billions."

"And Nancy has come to me with concerns," Kesselring said, "details of a private psombie army, promises of eternal life."

Jimmy nodded. "So this is coming from Nancy?"

Kesselring shook his head. "Not entirely, but we have concerns."

"These are not just empty promises," said Jimmy. "We are on the verge of that promised land that we started all this for, leading the world toward Atopia, the world without borders that has no end."

The falcon screeched in the sky, trapping another flying bot.

Kesselring stood still. "That Patricia and I started this for, not you."

"And now she is gone, and here you and I stand." Jimmy dropped his arms.

Kesselring paused. While they were talking, Jimmy added layers around this reality, sectioning it off from the multiverse. Kesselring's agents fought for position, but it was difficult to resist Jimmy's strength. Kesselring was cut off from the outside world now.

"Let's speak plainly." Kesselring stood and faced Jimmy. "I am ready to allow your"—he searched for the right words—"indulgences, and to fully protect and support you with my resources, as long as these indulgences serve our common interest. In return, you share with me what you're doing."

They watched each other while scenarios played out in the background. Kesselring could feel Jimmy's networks probing, feinting, as they sized each other up, their private display spaces filled with timelines that spread out from this nexus point.

"Agreed," Jimmy said finally.

Their networks exchanged access and safeguard requests. Kesselring nodded. "And find Robert Baxter, will you? This is getting embarrassing."

Jimmy nodded and smiled. "The final battle has begun, Herman, you should be proud of what you've achieved. You will soon be getting everything you deserve." He turned and walked toward the trees, disappearing into them and toward the access tunnel to go below.

Kesselring waited until he felt Jimmy's presence gone, and then initiated a sweep, cleansing the area. The falcon squawked in the grass, busy ripping the guts of the second bot it had captured. He ignored it and reached out with one of his phantom limbs to open an invisible door. It swung open into blackness, and Nancy stepped through, closing the tunnel behind her.

"You see?" she said. "Do you believe me now?"

# 13

HUMMING TO HIMSELF, Bunky flexed his motor cortex, feeling the thrum of his digger bots eating their way into the bedrock. After weeks of talking with underminers around the world, he was happy to get back to work. Thankfully, Sibeal and the glasscutters handled ongoing communications with the other groups, leaving him to get back to what he was really good at—digging.

It was a busy week, trying to juggle his contract work while working with Sibeal to search out and remove as much of the mystery crystal as possible. He offered to drop the contracts, but she insisted he keep them, saying they needed to maintain normalcy to keep their cover.

He didn't mind. He liked being busy, and it helped keep him from wondering what happened to Zoraster. They hadn't heard anything from the big monkey since they lost contact with him. Everyone feared the worst.

"What's shakin', Shaky?" he messaged to his partner who controlled the other half of their fleet of diggers. Shaky was two blocks west of him. They were both five hundred feet below Times Square.

"I'm drier than a witch's tit, mate," Shaky replied. It was the end of the day, or at least the end of the work day. He forwarded an image of a stallion charging across a grassy plain.

"Yes, I think it's time for a beer at the White Horse, my friend."

"One beer?!"

"Oh dear, did I say beer?" Bunky smiled. "I meant beers, my good man. Set those borer bots into a cross-grid . . ." He stopped mid-sentence and frowned. *What the hell is that?*

"What did you say, mate? The signal cut off. Hurry up, I'm thirsty!"

Bunky checked his networks. Bringing his awareness back into the pod of his construction mechanoid, he flicked the manual control switch for their largest tunnel-boring machine. It didn't respond. Was it offline? He began running through a checklist.

"Hey, Bunk," Shaky said, "I just lost contact with some of my diggers up three and four shafts."

"Give me a sec."

Out of the corner of an eye Bunky saw something, and reflexively he lifted one of his mechanoid's arms. The next instant he was knocked backward as one of his pipe runners came flailing out of the darkness into him. Regaining his senses, he turned on all the lights in the tunnel, then leaned over to pick up the bot that smashed into him.

Before he could grab it, the bot wriggled around and shot straight at his head again.

He gripped the small bot in his mechanoid hand, having barely caught it before it would have brained him. It took him an instant to process. *A malfunction?* No, not a malfunction. The bot squirmed in his grip. *This thing wants to kill me.* "Shaky!" yelled Bunky. "Get the hell out of there!"

He crushed the bot and threw it aside.

His entire network of bots dropped from his network. An explosion lit up the tunnel behind him. He logged into the city sensors, and his jaw dropped. The giant boring machine, thirty feet across and half a football field long, reversed direction and was charging back up the tunnel toward them, heading directly for the Midtown den.

"RUN!" he screamed to Shaky as he turned and began sprinting his mechanoid into the blackness.

THE SEAS OF the south Atlantic were calm. The Alliance battle platform, its smooth black surface designed to cloak it from both kinetics and electromagnetics, was quiet on the outside, but inside, its slingshot systems were cycling up. Just over the horizon, ten miles away, the glass towers of Terra Nova glistened. A series of small panels, each no thicker than a man's arm, opened up across the mile-wide surface of the platform.

Even cloaked, this raised alarms on Terra Nova.

The battle platform's slingshots began unloading, the off-center rotating platform weapons hidden below spitting out thousands of incendiary pellets at several miles per second. The surface of the platform erupted in an inferno of super-heated plasma shockwaves. The ocean around the platform boiled. Three seconds later the island of Terra Nova was immersed in a miles-wide fireball, its own shield weapons staving off the initial attack.

"SIBEAL, DO YOU notice anything odd?" Sid asked, sitting in the White Horse.

Bunky and Shaky were supposed to be back for a pint soon, but he'd lost contact with them.

"What do you mean, odd?"

"There haven't been any security alerts in the past two hours."

"I hadn't noticed." She flashed a part of her mind over his data. "Yeah, I see what you mean."

It wasn't that anything was wrong, just an absence of something being wrong—an anomaly. Not getting any security alerts had been soothing for a half an hour, but after an hour it became unusual. When two hours passed, Sid became downright suspicious. He began digging into the sensor logs, but then looked up. Something was roaring down one of the main arteries toward the den. Nothing was showing up on the sensors.

Sid grabbed Sibeal's arm, pulling her away from the table just as Bunky's mechanoid launched out of the darkness of the main tunnel, jumping to crash into the opposite wall just beside the pub.

At almost the same moment Shaky came skidding out of another tunnel. "Out of the way!" he yelled as the rock wall behind him crashed down and the boring machine launched itself into space and into the opposite wall. Slabs of rock rained down into the lower levels. The screaming began as people scrambled to get away.

Opening his eyes, Sid found himself face to face with Shaky. He had somehow cradled Sid and Sibeal beneath his mechanoid, protecting them. Grunting, Shaky began to lift himself up, a shower of rock and debris sliding off his back. The rotors of the borer were still going at full speed and it began grinding into the far wall, slowly dragging itself away as it ate into the rock.

An overlaid display opened in Sid's optic channels. "You need to see this," said Vicious, Sid's proxxi. Reports flooded in about mass arrests. Sid watched as the underground den in Rio they worked with erupted in flames. An orbital view of the South Atlantic showed Alliance platforms opening fire on Terra Nova. In Montana the protective shell of the Commune lit up as it was attacked by drones.

A coordinated global attack was underway.

The Ascetics were under assault by police forces across America. Mikhail Butorin chimed in with a report. Sibeal locked into Sid's workspace and they began plotting escape routes while setting secondary communication channels with their partners.

"Don't bother," said a voice from the gaping hole in the wall above them. From the darkness, an army of black-uniformed troops in body armor poured into the den. Their faces were covered by smooth black masks. One of them stood motionless in the middle while the rest flowed around him, and addressed Sid. "It's been a long time, my friend."

Sid stared at the masked face. "Do I know you?" he asked. Then the featureless mask morphed into a face that Sid recognized. Fear jangled his fingertips. He pushed Sibeal behind him. "What do you want?"

Jimmy smiled at Sid. One of his splinters was inhabiting the psombie trooper that stared down at them.

"You never were much for social ritual, were you, Sid?" Jimmy's psombie jumped down and stepped across the ragged pile of rocks onto the patio of the White Horse. "Maybe a nice, *hi, how are you? It's been a long time, my friend.*"

"Are we friends, Jimmy?" Sid asked, backing away with Sibeal behind him. He was projecting escape routes into the future, but as fast he could create new scenarios, Jimmy cut them down and overpowered him. Sid was used to fighting in the gameworlds where he was swift and brave. Now his skin prickled at the naked danger. His hands shook.

Jimmy nodded. "I thought we were."

"Then why did you almost just kill me?" Sid looked around the den. The psombie troops were collecting the survivors. There were crushed bodies under the rocks.

"Not my choice," Jimmy said, shrugging, "not anymore. This is an Alliance military operation. After what happened in Arunchal—"

"We didn't do that," Sid interrupted. Was this the same Jimmy he knew and grew up with? The meeting on Terra Nova flooded his mind. *Am I face to face with some ancient evil?* He looked into Jimmy's eyes, but sensed nothing, just a blank emotional wall.

"Then come with me and prove it." Jimmy edged closer. "Your Grilla friend has been very uncooperative."

Sibeal pulled Sid aside. "You have Zoraster?"

"We do," admitted Jimmy, coming another step closer.

"I know you think you're the fastest gun in the network," Jimmy laughed. "In fact, it's one of the reasons I always liked you. But you can't win this fight."

"Then why don't you come get me," Sid said more bravely than he felt. He still had a few tricks up his sleeve. The other psombie guards formed a circle around them. He might be able to take out one or two.

Jimmy backed up a step and sighed. "We can do this the hard way, or the easy way." A new wave of psombie troops appeared at the gaping hole in the rock wall.

Sid's shoulders slumped. Better to wait for another moment. He could use some more time to probe the networks of the psombies, see if he could hack into Jimmy's connection. Maybe it was an opportunity. "Okay, we'll come." He started a private network with Sibeal.

"Good." Jimmy crossed the last few steps between. "I need to know where Bob is."

Sid shrugged. "I don't know."

"I know you know," sighed Jimmy. "And I know I can't hack into your networks remotely. But there are other ways."

Sid backed up, but there was nowhere to go. Psombie guards grabbed them from behind.

"And more important . . ." Jimmy paused, leaning down to pick up a shard of shattered glass.

"What?"

Jimmy held the sliver of glass up to Sid's eye. "Where's Willy, Sid?"

# 14

FAITH WASN'T SOMETHING that came easily to Vince. He had it once, but it had been ripped from him, replaced with a need to control. Sitting alone in his cell, Vince knew it was this that drove him to build Phuture News—his desire to control, a futile attempt to hold destiny in his hands.

But in the end, his creation had controlled him. He had robbed himself of his own freedom.

Trapped in a jail cell, he felt free for the first time in years. All he had left was faith now. It was a funny thing, to feel free in a jail. He smiled and pulled a woolen blanket around his shoulders, then settled into the metal cot.

There was nothing to do but wait.

After cooperating and giving them his information, Colonel Kramer transferred him into the minimum-security brig at the Anacostia-Bolling base just across the Potomac from the Pentagon. Vince bargained each bit of freedom—for a shave, for a shower, for a cell with a tiny view of blue sky—for every new piece of information.

Soon enough they'd discover the lies, but that wasn't in Vince's control.

Not anymore.

He did everything he could. His struggle to believe the Terra Novan story had been replaced by the simple idea of doing the right thing. In his mind, that meant sticking up for people close to you, so he carried out his end of the plan Sid and Bob laid out.

The network map of the *nervenet* that they recovered from Willy's proxxi indicated that a senior member of the Alliance military command in Arunchal Pradesh was another nodal point, just like Jimmy. So Sid and Zoraster snuck into Arunchal to infect this nodal point with their own virus. Vince came to Washington to unload the information that Terra Nova discovered this ancient machine. If they were right, then Sid would see the network of crystals light up as the information passed from Colonel Kramer to his senior staff, and from there into the nervenet. He hoped it worked.

And if it didn't, then he'd just alerted the Alliance of a dangerous new doomsday cult. Either way, there wasn't much more he could do.

Closing his eyes, Vince drifted off. His mind went back to the voodoo ceremony, to the night on the shores of Lake Pontchartrain. In his mind he saw the hulking figure that had risen out of the fires with a star pattern burning in its forehead. Half asleep, Vince opened his eyes. The presence from the fires on Ponchartrain was standing in his cell next to him. Vince wasn't surprised. He smiled. "Bob," he whispered. "Is that you?"

The figure moved toward the door, and, silently, it slid open. Swinging his legs off the cot to stand, Vince followed his rescuer out and down the hallway. Other detainees were in their cells, but they all looked away. Vince followed in a dream. At each checkpoint, the guards opened the doors and looked away at just the right moments—chatting to a colleague, dropping a coffee, everyone looking at anything but Vince. Like a ghost he slipped out of the building until he was standing outside next to a dumpster.

Vince woke to find himself standing alone in the alleyway.

He'd thought it was a dream.

Hotstuff stood in front of him, her glowing virtual presence in sharp contrast to the dingy alley. Blond hair fell in waves over her black sweater. "How the hell did you get out here?"

Vince blinked and looked up. The sky was clear and blue, but the air was freezing cold. He shivered. "I don't know." No alarms were raised. It was quiet.

"Let's just get out of here." Forwarding a set of phutures into Vince's networks, Hotstuff constructed a set of escape routes. They might not own Phuture News anymore, but they had enough back-doors to last a lifetime.

Wiping the diagrams from his workspaces, Vince shook his head. "No." He plotted paths to the Federal detention center.

"Seriously?" Hotstuff shook her head in disbelief, but she was already following him out of the alleyway onto a tree-lined street, turning left toward the center of Washington. She frowned at his orange jumpsuit. "At least let's get you into something a little more fashionable."

"COME ON, LET'S go."

Connors looked up. "Vince?"

He smiled. "Time to get going."

But she didn't budge from the cot she was sitting on. The cell looked a lot like the one Vince had been in; rough concrete walls, folding metal cot, gray steel bars. Detention wasn't the most imaginative of businesses.

Connors frowned. "What do you mean, time to get going? Why are you here?"

"They've released us," Vince replied. "Come on." He smiled and held out his hand. "Before they change their minds."

Connors hesitated but then rocked forward onto her feet. She didn't take his offered hand.

Vince dropped his hand and began leading the way. "Don't talk to anyone," he instructed. "Just follow me, strict orders."

They walked out of the cell block hallway, out past the guard at the desk who just happened to be holding the door open and talking to his wife in a virtual space as they passed. Outside the cellblock section, the rooms were filled with desks, federal agents busy filing reports, standing chatting at coffee machines, all of them looking away from Connors and Vince as they walked past.

"I heard you cooperated," Connors said, following quickly on Vince's heels. "I'm glad you did. I told them everything, every detail, about how you asked to come here and give yourself up."

Vince jogged down the stairs, glancing up at Connors as he turned to the next flight. "Good."

"I was worried you sided with the terrorists," continued Connors. The newsworlds were flooded with stories about the attack in Arunchal and the capture of the Grilla linking this all back to Sid and Bob and Terra Nova. "I'm so relieved you kept your head and weren't so wrapped up in it that you couldn't see the truth."

"And what's that?" Vince asked as he banged open the doors to the ground floor. They walked outside.

"How dangerous these religious extremists are."

Vince walked without saying anything.

"Hey, slow down." Connors grabbed his arms and swung him around. "What's the hurry? Where are we going?"

"I just want to get out of here," replied Vince. "You can understand that, can't you?" He tried to reach for her, but she backed away.

"They didn't release us, did they?"

Pedestrians slid by, sidestepping them as if they weren't there, and a wind kicked up, driving wet leaves past their feet.

"We need to go." Vince turned and kept walking.

Connors paused but then ran after him. "You don't really believe all that stuff, do you?"

Vince said nothing.

"Thoughts can be viruses," she continued. "You know that, don't you? Virulent memes can rip through thought-space, half-truths and deceptions can destroy just as violently as kinetics. It almost destroyed Atopia, and now you're stuck in it again. Why can't you see it?"

Alarms began sounding. "We need to go."

"I can't come with you."

"You can't stay here. They'll think you were a part of this."

The wind whipped up again, sending leaves spinning into the air. They were hiding between the lines of perception in this reality, but the lines were blurring. The base finally noticed Vince had disappeared from his cell, and it wouldn't be long till they saw Connors was gone as well. The authorities had all the information they needed. This time the directives going out to the enforcement branches wouldn't be to capture, but that dangerous terrorists had escaped, shoot to kill.

Connors weighed her options. "And where on Earth were you thinking of trying to take me?"

Grabbing her hand, Vince angled them into a fresh slice of the future. "Someplace safe."

# 15

"JIMMY, HEY JIMMY!" Bob called out.

There was no response.

Hesitating, Bob looked at the lollipop trees and chocolate chip moon of the Little Great Little, and then walked into the thunderfall, a wall of sensory white noise. It enveloped him, crushing his senses, and he edged forward, afraid, but also determined. He knew this was where Jimmy hid.

The thunderfall fell away and his senses returned. Behind was a cave, and Jimmy sat in a corner, his eyes cast down, surrounded by his play creatures and guarded by his proxxi Samson, who stared at Bob.

"Jimmy, hey, I didn't know," Bob pleaded. He was replaying sections of his inVerse, going over every interaction—*every word*—he had with Jimmy when they were growing up. This scene had been just after Nancy's thirteenth birthday party. "I'm sorry."

"Leave us alone," Samson growled.

Bob allowed a respectful pause. Jimmy was crying.

"I was just trying to help." Bob moved a little closer, and Samson grew a little larger. "Listen, stuff like this happens all the time, they'll forget in a week."

Jimmy's face twisted. "It doesn't happen to you! And no they won't!" He wiped his tears away and didn't look Bob in the eye.

Back then, Bob had just tried setting Jimmy up with Cynthia, a girl Jimmy had a crush on. The results were disastrous. Bob had suggested that Jimmy should take Cynthia into Jimmy's private worlds, where he was doing research for Solomon House, but somehow Cynthia discovered a very private world—one where Jimmy tortured little creatures. It also contained some private memories where Jimmy's mother was ridiculing him.

Cynthia copied it all and broadcast it to the other pssi-kids. It was cruel fun, and now all the pssi-kids were making fun of Jimmy—whole worlds constructed for the sole purpose of mocking him. Jimmy was awkward, never quite understanding how to interact with the other kids. With Bob's encouragement, this party had marked the first time Jimmy opened up a little, and now all this had happened.

It was a disaster.

"Hey, I'm not perfect either," said Bob. Even as he said it he realized how it must sound. Bob was popular, everyone wanted to be his friend. He sighed. "But I'll tell you something, just between you and me."

Jimmy sniffled, still staring at the floor, but Samson retreated a pace.

Bob took a step closer. "I lose my temper. I yell at my brother all the time. I feel bad, but I can't help it sometimes."

Wiping back more tears, Jimmy took a deep breath. "Oh yeah?"

"Yeah." Bob took another step toward Jimmy and sat down, cross-legged. "We all have stuff about us we can't control."

"Everybody hates me," sniffled Jimmy, his face snotty, eyes bloodshot. More tears streamed down his face.

"Jimmy," said Bob softly. "Hey, Jimmy . . ."

The scared little boy looked back at Bob. "What?"

"Not everybody."

SPITTING OUT A mouthful of water, Bob stopped to swim in place, regaining control of his body from autopilot. The glittering farm towers of Atopia hung in the sky before him. It wasn't much farther now. Already he was at the outermost edges of the kelp forest, their air-filled hold-fast bladders sitting like fat green goblins in the rolling swells. He reached out and grabbed one to rest.

His body had been fit as an Olympian's when he left Atopia, but the trek across the desert drained and damaged him. Even so, swimming these few miles wasn't much of a challenge. The cold water was draining his reserves, but the hydrophobic shell covering his skin was doing its job. Leaving his body in low-power autopilot swim mode, eking every fraction of fluid-dynamic efficiency it could, he plotted paths through the waves and current and stayed away from drone patrols.

The sensor networks of Atopia were keyed to cyber and mechanical-kinetic intrusions on the wide-angle side, and pathogenic and microbiologicals from a small-angle view. Macrobiologicals were lower on the threat scales. He maintained a small alternate reality clipped around himself as he swam, a cloaking filter that would be enough to keep any alerts below the thresholds for escalation. As powerful as Jimmy was, Sid and Bob had been his equals, even surpassing him in some areas.

This was Bob's house, too.

Moving up and down in the swells, holding onto the gas bladder, Bob took a deep breath and closed his eyes, opening them to take in the blue cathedral of the sky overhead. Cirrus clouds streaked the heavens above. He felt the familiar surge of the surf pounding on the beaches like an old heartbeat—*not far away now*—and he was reconnecting with his friends in the water, the smarticle-infused phytoplankton, the fish, the sharks.

He was thinking about what Tyrel had said in the Terra Novan Council meeting.

This thing they were facing, if it was all-powerful, it would have just risen up and destroyed them. Whatever it was, it wasn't supernatural, it was of this world. It needed their technology to do whatever it was trying to do. Otherwise, it would have just done whatever it wanted. It was a virus that was infiltrating their social and technical networks, but it still needed them.

And if it was something that needed, then it was also something that had weaknesses.

But what were they?

But the more essential question, and one the Terra Novans weren't able to answer, was why was it doing whatever it was doing? Did it want to subjugate humans, make them suffer, hold them in thrall? Or did it just want to destroy? Bob shook his head. He was anthropomorphizing, trying to apply human desires and traits onto this thing. They really had no idea what this thing was. Did it even really *want* something? If it was just an echo, then it was just repeating a pattern. There might be no conscious intent. The apocalypse legends all talked about a day of judgment, but why would this thing want to judge us?

He looked up at the looming towers of Atopia. He had to figure it out.

Soon.

Releasing the gas bladder, Bob set his body into swim-mode again and left it to pick its way through the thickening kelp. He was close enough to start projecting some private network tunnels. He had all of Terra Nova's resources, funneled through the darknets, at his disposal when the time came. Once opened, though, he wouldn't have long to make his attack before those connections were found and choked off.

He could use some inside help. He was close enough now.

SEAGULLS YELPED UNDER wet skies framed by white chalk cliffs. The portal of Durdle Door stood above the beach. Bob leaned down to pick up his red plastic bucket, then ran toward the girl with blond hair who was turning over rocks in a tidal pool.

"Nancy!" he squeaked in a tiny voice. He was only four in this secret world.

She looked up, her eyes growing wide as her primary subjective filled the placeholder they each always left for each other here. "Bob? Is that you?"

"It's me." He closed the last few feet, splashing through the shallow water. He offered his bucket for the squirming crab she held daintily between two fingers.

She dropped it into the bucket and leaned in to hug him. "What are you doing here? Are you still on Terra Nova? I'm terrified, they've started a kinetic attack. I'm trying to get Kesselring to call it off."

Bob hugged her back. "No, I'm not there."

Releasing him, she leaned back to look in his eyes. "Good."

"I'm here."

"What?" She frowned. "Here?"

"Atopia."

She backed up. "Bob, it's too dangerous. I unpacked your data beacon. We're trying to contain Jimmy. We have supporters inside."

Lightning lit up the clouds in the distance. It was always storming in this world now.

"And that's why I need your help."

Nancy wiped her small hands against the frilly edge of her polka-dot one-piece, nodding. Their networks merged in the background, the familiar sensation of their phantoms and synthetic bodies feeling each other close.

"Isn't this touching?"

Nancy and Bob spun toward the voice.

◆◆◆

"YOU KNOW I never trusted you, Nancy." Jimmy towered above them. "And Bob, did you really think you could just waltz in here?" He danced a half-step, mocking them.

Bob looked at Nancy. "Run." He initiated the tunnel linking Atopia and Terra Nova, and unleashed the first barrage. The sky turned to fire, their childhood world exploding into flames.

Jimmy laughed.

But Bob didn't run.

He watched.

# 16

NANCY TRIED TO hold her mind on the beach as long as she could, but the splinter snapped off. Bob closed the connection. The last thing she saw was young Bob's face fade from her visual channels. He didn't look scared.

And that scared her.

But she didn't have long to dwell.

Already Jimmy's networks were swarming hers, overriding her automated defenses. Her physical body was in the labs of Farm Tower Two, just below the Solomon House. She was going over some research notes with one of her staff. "We're going to have to look at this again later," she heard herself saying, just as psombie guards slammed open the doors.

Someone screamed, glass crashing to the floor, as the guards shoved people aside and advanced toward Nancy. She reached into synthetic space with her phantoms, worming her way into the psombies' controls to click them off. One by one, each of the attacking guards dropped like a sack of potatoes to the floor. Horrified faces turned toward Nancy as she sprinted out.

Escaping wouldn't ordinarily have been that easy, but Jimmy was distracted, busy protecting himself. A vortex opened in the shared mindspace of Atopia, a virtual black hole that was ripping the fabric of pssi-space apart. Bob was the Trojan who penetrated

Atopia's perimeter. He opened a tunnel straight to Terra Nova and unleashed their entire cyber-arsenal against Jimmy.

Running through the corridors, Nancy flooded the realities around her with security blankets while she keyed into Kesselring's networks. His face floated into her displays.

"I've locked down Solomon House," Kesselring said immediately. "Come up top to my level, we'll coordinate from here."

Nancy nodded and clicked off, watching a protective corridor open up and lead into the upper levels. Safe for the moment, she let her primary presence slide off into the hundreds of splinters her distributed consciousness was monitoring at key locations around the globe.

In a spasm, the world had erupted.

She watched the protective dome of the Commune in Montana blaze as Allied forces attacked. The battle platforms hammered the defenses of Terra Nova in a hundred-mile perimeter that stretched into the stratosphere above the southern Atlantic. Psombie armies flooded city centers around the world.

In counter-attack, the Ascetics launched offensives in Manila, Hong Kong, and Sao Paulo, but it wasn't much.

In Boston, Nancy was ghosting through a bot stationed in Faneuil Hall market. She watched a man leaning over to inspect a basket of tomatoes. He picked up one of them, turning it over, while all around him rained small weapons fire in a battle between the Irish Ascetics and local police forces. The stall behind him burst into flames while he smiled and put the tomato in a bag. The person standing next to him exploded in a mist of red. The man reached down to select another tomato.

The reality blackout was almost complete in metropolitan areas.

Anyone that had pssi installed in their nervous systems, nearly half the planet now, was having evidence of the conflict erased from their realities. A reality filter spanning the globe connected most of it into a world where none of it was happening. Half of the world was being destroyed while the other half didn't even notice.

The physical world was just the tip of the iceberg. In millions of virtual worlds connected to Atopia, the battle had also begun. Some worlds just winked out of existence, others tried to resist, and some fought back. The struggle for existence had begun.

Nancy ran down the corridor and jumped into a service elevator. Kesselring's complex was on the upper level. She stared at the manual controls, and then reached out and pushed a mid-level address.

She'd been saving one last wild card.

# 17

PULLING HIS FEET underneath him, Bob stood, feeling his feet sink into the sand. He raised himself out of the water and splashed the last few steps to dry land. A couple on beach towels looked at him, and he waved them away. "Get out of here!" he yelled, but all along the beach the screaming had already begun as the drones descended.

A projection of Jimmy materialized in front of him. "Come back for a little surfing, Bob? Have a nice swim?"

"Just hold on." Bob staggered forward. The swim weakened him more than he thought it would. He leaned over to get his breath, slicking the water off his body. "I just want to talk."

"So talk."

It was the moment of truth. Would Jimmy just kill him? It was a possibility. Even with the swarming attack Bob unleashed into the informational structure of Atopia, Jimmy could destroy this section of Atopia with an untargeted kinetic bombardment. Overwhelmingly blunt, but it would get the job done. Bob waited, holding his breath.

"I'm not going to kill you, Bob." Jimmy's projection frowned. "What, are they telling you I'm some kind of monster?"

Bob slowed his breathing. Jimmy might just be buying time. Bob's surprise attack ripped the Atopian networks wide open, far more than Bob anticipated. Bob and Jimmy stood facing each other on the beach, but they were also grappling in the background, reality shattering from reality, as they tried to insert themselves into each other's networks. The hyperspaces around them blazed. Bob stayed silent.

Jimmy laughed. "Come on, you don't believe in monsters, do you? I've heard the fairy tales Terra Nova is spinning about me."

Bob stood up straight. "I don't know. I don't even know who I'm talking to."

Jimmy stopped laughing. "They tried to destroy us, Bob. They would have killed you, Nancy, everyone here. Based on what? Some religious fable about the end of days? Religious extremism is a dangerous thing, and they're about as extreme as they come."

Already Bob's attacks in the cyber-infrastructure were slowing. The tide was turning. Nancy was in Farm Tower Two. His parents were in their habitat. In a splinter Bob watched Commander Rick Strong's face in the Atopian Command center. His team had isolated most of the viral threads Bob let loose. The Commander was always a big believer in boots in the mud, of the need to keep low-tech solutions on hand. His reserve platoon of his staff, humans with their minds sealed from pssi-space, were on their way to the beach.

Bob began planning escape routes, pinging their networks.

"Who do you think this is?" Jimmy thumped his chest and threw his arms wide. "This is me, Jimmy. We grew up together. And don't think I don't appreciate everything you did for me. It's the only reason you're standing here. You know that, don't you?"

Bob didn't respond. It had been a little too easy to swim in undetected.

Jimmy grimaced. "And I know I have weaknesses, things that I do . . ." He paused. "And yes, I am taking control of this place, but am I any worse? What do you want me to say?"

Bob stared at him. "Explain the crystals."

"I have no idea." Jimmy let his hands fall, slapping his thighs. "How about asking your Terra Novan friends? They seem to know a lot about them."

Bob didn't have much time. If he rushed, he could make it, grab Nancy and his parents, get them onto the passenger cannon with him. He'd taken control of enough of the Atopian systems to burrow a path through. He could just make it. He lurched forward but stopped himself.

"Go ahead." Jimmy moved to one side. "Go and get her. I won't stop you."

"Bob?" said another voice, one Bob hadn't heard in a long time.

He turned. It was his father. His image materialized on the beach next to them.

"Your mother and I just got a message to meet you at the passenger cannon. What are you doing?" His dad frowned and looked at the water still dripping off him. "Were you surfing?"

"Go and get them," Jimmy offered again. He stepped back further, even clearing a path through the digital infrastructure.

"Bob, stop whatever you're doing." His dad was angry. "Be responsible for once in your life. Stop this."

Bob watched a swarm of bots gathering overhead. It wasn't just Jimmy, but the entire Atopian Defense Forces Command Center was bringing its weight to bear. They'd been surprised, but had quickly regrouped. Bob's window of opportunity was closing.

"It doesn't matter," continued Bob's dad, his face contorting. "I don't understand what you've been doing, where you've been, I don't care. I'm sorry for anything I did. Please just stop."

Jimmy stood beside Bob's father. "You should listen to him."

"Dad, I'm sorry, I can't . . ."

"You can't blame yourself for what happened to your brother." Bob's dad started crying. "It wasn't your fault."

"It wasn't your fault," echoed Jimmy.

Bob took a step forward, but then stopped again. In his mind's eye he could see Nancy rushing along the corridors high in Farm Tower Two. He could still make it. *Not your fault.* His father's words reverberated in his brain. *Be responsible.* Bob stared up at Farm Tower Two, its glass walls shining before him.

He could save his own heart, but he would be breaking a million others.

He stepped backward.

*Don't do it*, insisted the voice in Bob's head. He struggled inside. *Get Nancy, get Mom and Dad, get out of here.* We can't do that. There's a way we can stop Jimmy. *But you can't leave them, you can't fail again.* We won't fail. This will work. If we stop Jimmy, then we save everyone. *But what if you're wrong?*

Jimmy shook his head. "You know this is hopeless."

"Bob, stop, please," begged Bob's father. "Take responsibility, stop this."

Tears in his eyes, Bob retreated another step toward the water. "I can't. And I am."

Bob took one last look at his dad, then up at Farm Tower Two. "I'm so sorry," he whispered, turning to walk and then run back into the water.

Jimmy's projection smiled. "There's nowhere to go."

Already splashing knee-deep, Bob said, "I know," and dove headfirst into a wave.

# 18

AN ORBITAL VIEW of the southern Atlantic filled the room, centered on the glittering sphere of the Terra Novan perimeter. Alliance battle platforms encircled it, each highlighted in their own red spheres, and each ringed by battleships. A dusting of red dots orbited above it all, drones weaving in and out, testing the defenses. The display pulsed in time, morphing alternate scenarios the Command team analyzed and modified in real time.

The sudden appearance of Robert Baxter, launching a Terra Novan offensive inside their perimeter, had thrown Commander Strong's Atopian defensive team into disarray, but his staff regained control quickly. It was already contained with minimal system losses. He was proud that they reacted so well. It was their first real test.

The inside attack was a surprise to his team, but the Commander wasn't surprised. Looking at the main battle display, it was clear Terra Nova wouldn't be able to withstand them much longer. He couldn't blame them for fighting back, but it just emphasized the need to neutralize them as quickly as possible.

The attack on Alliance headquarters in Arunchal had been the final straw. Atopia had been petitioning the United Nations Security Council for international backing to legally remove the leadership of Terra Nova through use of force. The petition was finally granted after the Arunchal attack, giving the Alliance legal grounds to assemble and attack Terra Nova.

Due to mutual protection treaties, attacking Terra Nova would be taken as a declaration of war against the African Union. For months the United Nations had been trying to get weapons inspectors into the African Union, to look at the space power grid. The weapons inspectors were also working to understand the extent that Terra Nova had infected systems worldwide, just as they'd almost destroyed and killed hundreds of thousands of people on Atopia with their reality virus. Terra Nova was spreading dangerous lies, tipping the world toward destruction.

It was now Commander Strong's job to remove this threat.

"Commander, I need to speak to you."

He blinked, tearing his attention away from his displays. Nancy Killiam stood in front of him.

"I don't know how you got in here," said Commander Strong, glancing at her, "but you need to go, *right now.*" Most of his mind was plugged into the battle in the Southern Atlantic. He stood in the middle of the battle projection that spanned the room. He stared at the image of the Terra Novan platform displayed in the center.

"I'm here in person," she replied. "I need to talk to you."

He hadn't checked her metatags. *So she physically breached the Command entrance.* Without looking at her, he shook his head. "You know this is not a good time," he answered, but he could guess why. A thread of his mind was following Bob as he tried to escape on the beaches below. "I know you and Bob are close, Nancy, but there's nothing I can do."

Almost right away, Jimmy had taken over the Terra Novan intrusion into their networks. He specifically asked if he could handle Bob himself. The Commander agreed. He understood. Jimmy and Bob were childhood friends. Jimmy had to try to reason with his friend.

His guards had already grabbed Nancy and were pulling her to the door. "It's about your wife," she cried out.

Even in the middle of all this, Commander Strong still kept a good chunk of himself with his wife Cindy, her body in stasis in their apartment. Several months ago she committed what the doctors called "reality suicide"—she was one of the first *disappeared*, people who went into the multiverse of pssi worlds and never returned.

The Commander distilled his attention into the room. He held one hand up to stop the guards, halfway out the door. "What about her?"

"Privately." Nancy shook the guards off. "And this is about Patricia, too."

There was no reason he should listen to her, but he had the greatest of respect for her great-aunt, Patricia Killiam, even after what happened. Nancy was many things—stubborn, obsessive— but she also never wasted his time. That commanded his respect. In a snap decision, he opened a private channel. His primary view-point shifted into a white room. They sat face to face, opposite each other across a small rectangular table.

Nancy cut straight to the point. "Jimmy is the one who stole your wife's mind."

Commander Strong stared at her. Of course she would do anything, say anything right now. Desperate people did desperate things. "That's a very serious accusation."

He felt sorry for her, but lies wouldn't help.

And yet.

Nancy forwarded the data beacon Bob sent her, details that Patricia Killiam had left: evidence implicating Jimmy in the deaths of his own parents, dozens of disappearances, even the death of Patricia herself. The most damning, though, was evidence that Jimmy stole his wife Cindy's mind, taken her away to gain control over him.

He assimilated the data. "I've seen most of this before." Jimmy had presented the data recovered from Patricia Killiam at the last Council meeting when they received approval to attack Terra Nova.

"Not all of it."

She was right. Jimmy had hidden the parts incriminating him. The Commander recognized the digital authentication of Patricia. He verified it with his old keys. It was from Patricia. "What do you want, Nancy? If you knew about this, why did you wait?"

"I had to be sure." Nancy tried raising Kesselring, opening a channel together with Rick, but Kesselring didn't answer the ping. "Kesselring is together with me." She shared her rendering of the meeting Kesselring had with Jimmy, when he'd confronted him.

Veins popped out in Rick's neck. "If you and Kesselring were discussing this, you should have come to me . . ."

"I needed to wait."

Until now, she didn't have to add. They were about to crack the Terra Novan defenses.

"I can't prove it more than this," she added breathlessly, "but have I ever lied to you?"

Rick stared at the data. He'd always been a gut thinker, and the things that happened with Patricia Killiam hadn't made any sense to him on a gut level.

In the splinter of his mind that was always with his wife, he looked down into her face.

Hell, he thought, is not a place where you burn, but a place where you are frozen—frozen in time, alive and never dying, immobile with your thoughts and regrets. The more you struggle to get out, the more the thoughts dig into you, pulling you deeper. Rick had been living in a frozen hell for the past six months. None of it had made sense.

Until now.

# 19

"THE GIRL FROM Ipanema"—Sid was sure that was the muzak being played in the passenger cannon waiting area. This waiting room would normally be packed with businesspeople and tourists, but it was empty. Something was going on in the city, but Sid was disconnected from the networks. Holographic ads played across the wall of palm trees and people winning money in casinos, promises of the womb of warmth and security. He was sitting next to Sibeal, facing Bunky and Shaky seated across from them, surrounded by psombie guards in their black body armor.

"Where are we going?" Sid asked, looking at the guard nearest to him. It seemed like he was the squad leader, but it was hard to tell. They didn't talk, didn't make any noise at all except the whisper of the metallic fabric of their uniforms as they merged around each other in a fluid, non-human gait.

Of course there was no response.

The psombie guards' faces were covered in a reflective black shell, and Sid doubted they even used their own eyes to see. They were just nodes in a network. Tiny ornithopter bots hovered everywhere they moved, coordinating the activity, bees hovering around their mobile hive.

Sid wondered what the owners of these bodies were doing right now. They were still thinking, using the brains inside of these heads, but they were off in virtual gameworlds, or perhaps living in another version of New York, living out a fantasy life with a girlfriend that jilted them or some other situation they weren't able to come to grips with. Whatever it was, it was enticing enough to lease their bodies to Cognix Corporation. He wanted to get up and shake them awake, ask them if they knew what they were doing, but even if he did, it wouldn't make any difference.

The public didn't care anymore. Everyone was too wrapped up in pleasing themselves, which was exactly what the plan had been all along.

Sid could guess where they were going. Atopia was well within the launch energy of the passenger cannon. Everything was resting on Bob being able to get inside, and get inside of Jimmy's head. If he did, ironically, it might even be a good thing they were being shipped there right now.

A low vibration hummed through their seats, and a two-tone chime sounded. Their passenger pod was here.

"First time I'm getting on one of these," Shaky said as they all stood. "Will it make me sick? I'm not good with zero gravity."

"We got more serious things right now," said Bunky, his face grim.

Shaky looked at him. "You're the one sitting beside me, mate. Have you ever seen someone vomit in low gravity?"

The waiting area doors slid open, revealing the passenger cannon pod interior of nondescript gray walls with thick g-seats in creamy fake leather. Sid waited for instructions to be fed into his displays, but instead their psombie minders stood back and away from them.

And then something amazing happened: one of them spoke.

"You are free to go," said the one Sid had imagined as the leader.

Turning on their heels, the psombies marched off, trailing their beebot entourage.

Sid was speechless. He glanced at Bunky and Shaky and Sibeal while "The Girl from Ipanema" played on in the background.

"Did you . . . what did you do?" stuttered Bunky. He took a step toward the exit, but then reconsidered.

Sid shook his head. "It wasn't—"

"Come on!" commanded a voice from inside the pod.

Sid turned to look inside the passenger cannon pod. He nearly fell over backwards.

It was Nancy, or at least, a synthetic space projection of her. "Hurry up," she insisted, motioning for them to get inside.

He checked the encrypted metatags of the projection inside the pod. It was Nancy in front of them, or someone that had stolen all of Nancy's authentication. She sent him details of a flight plan. "It's okay, she's a friend," Sid said, making a decision. He pulled Sibeal through the doors. Bunky and Shaky followed.

Sid was busy reconnecting his network feeds. His meta-cognition systems flooded with images of battles raging outside. A lot had happened since they were captured. The world had erupted around them.

"Hurry," Nancy urged as they seated themselves and clipped in their webbing restraints. "Commander Strong and Kesselring are with us now."

"Did Bob make it through?" asked Sid.

Nancy's projection shook its head. "He's here, but it's not that easy." She opened a connection.

A splinter opened in Sid's mind, and he saw an ocean. It was a view from just offshore of Atopia. Someone was in the water. "He's swimming?" Sid said incredulously. It was Bob, churning through the surf, cutting under a wave as he pulled away from the beach.

The passenger pod jolted and began accelerating, pinning the passengers back into their seats.

"Uh, guys, don't mean to spoil your reunion," Bunky said from the seats behind Sid. "But where exactly are we going?"

Sid networked them into the display that was tracking Bob, and then uploaded the flight plan. "We're going to the only place that's still safe," he replied.

"At least for now," added Nancy.

"And where's that?" grunted Bunky.

Sid's face squeezed into a grimace under the growing acceleration. "You'll see."

With a muffled roar, the pod exited the cannon, launching into the air. In an instant it was enveloped in a layer of plasma that cut off the data connection. It would burn off in a few seconds as the pod cleared the first tens of miles of the atmosphere, arcing on a ballistic trajectory toward Montana.

"OH GOD," WAS the last thing Nancy heard from inside the pod. It was Shaky, trying to hold down his lunch.

Nancy smiled and shook her head, then retreated her primary perspective back into her physical body on Atopia. After talking with Commander Strong, she'd made it back to the service elevator. It was already on its way up to the top level, past the Solomon House to Kesselring's retreat.

The elevator pinged to the top level. The door slid open.

Nancy expected to be greeted by the rolling green fields and trees of Kesselring's private gardens, ready to start planning the final stages of removing Jimmy from Atopia's networks and halting the attacks underway. Instead, she found blackened earth, still burning.

Jimmy stood in the middle of it all with a falcon on his arm.

# 20

NATURAL HUMANS HAVE two systems for making decisions—the fast-thinking emotional gut reaction, and the slow-thinking logical process. When it comes to decision making, slow-thinking generally comes up with better results, but it is the fast-thinking that makes us human—quick responses that follow the path of least resistance, the potential pain of losing greater than the promise of gaining something else. The human mind is biased and flawed, but in a systematic way.

Humans are irrational, but predictable, and Bob was counting on it.

He was just past the edge of the swells and swimming toward deeper water, filling his lungs with the rest of the perfluorocarbons, networking into the water to find his old friends. He hoped they were still there. Below in the depths, a great white shark turned with a flick of its tail and swam upward into the kelp.

Incoming pings from his mother and father hit his networks, but Bob ignored them. He had to focus. After diving in the water, he lost track of Nancy. He couldn't pick up her signature anywhere. The last he saw, she was in the Tower Two elevator on the way to the upper levels. Kesselring was inside with them, she'd been able to tell him that much. He hoped they had enough to hold out until he could finish.

Cutting through the water, he saw his family's habitat in the distance, the deck of his old room just visible. He remembered how

Nancy came and cleaned his place up one day when he was out surfing, the frustration he felt when he came home to find his comfortable and carefully arranged mess tidied up. He wished he could come home to that clean room now, be frustrated with her perfection, but the mess of his life was his own alone now.

The white shark breached the surface beside him, exploding up out of the water, and Bob grabbed its dorsal fin, holding on tight as it dove back down again.

"Sacrifice," said the priest, his projection riding shotgun with Bob into the depths, his robes flowing in the rush of the water, "is the only way to salvation."

Bob nodded. "Don't take this the wrong way," he replied, communicating through sub-vocal channels, "but I need to do this alone."

In seconds, Bob reached the undersea ledge of Atopia, fifty feet down. Through glass window-walls, he watched people flash by, sitting in their apartments, none of them aware of what was going on. The avatar of the priest nodded at Bob and let go, disappearing in a rush of bubbles as Bob reached the edge of the ledge at over a hundred feet. The blue-black of the abyss opened beyond, and Bob urged the shark down into it.

He still couldn't reach Nancy. There was too much interference in the networks. In the deeper water the smarticle concentration fell off rapidly, reducing bandwidth that could pass through its mesh, but even so, Bob could feel another presence.

"Sid, is that you?"

"I'm here, buddy," came the reply.

The pressure was building, and Bob urged the last bubbles of air from his lungs. The oxygen he'd stored in the perfluorocarbons would keep him going for at least ten minutes. *That should be enough time.*

"You're on your way to the Commune?" Bob messaged. The light from the surface was waning as he dove deeper. Sid sent some information—his passenger pod was over halfway through its journey, sixty miles above Minnesota and arcing downward. "Yeah, we're almost there."

The cold was intense. Bob shivered. "Good."

LOOKING OUT OF the window of the passenger pod, Sid craned his neck to try and get a view of the Pacific Ocean, where Atopia was, where Bob was. The curve of the Earth was covered in swirls of clouds. "Where are you going?" he asked, but he already knew. Following the external sensors on Atopia, he watched Bob's body, still clinging to the shark, now three hundred feet down.

"I need to get down to the main trunk," Bob replied after a pause.

There were external access airlocks built into the length of Atopia. They had manual controls. Bob must be heading for one near the computing core of Atopia, down below the fusion reactor, five hundred feet below the surface.

Sid shared the data feed with Sibeal and Bunky and Shaky. "You sure you want to do that, buddy?"

He watched Bob dive ever deeper.

BOB DIDN'T REPLY. Jimmy had to know where he was going, but in the confusion of the initial attack Bob disabled the deepwater kinetic defenses. A part of him knew he was going to do this all along. He amplified his visual system, adjusting for the low-light conditions. The shark slowed and the deep-sea pressure hull of Atopia loomed out of the blackness. Bob released the shark and swam the last few feet, grabbing onto a handhold to steady himself.

"You've been a good friend, Sid," said Bob, twisting the external release mechanism. The cold and pressure were slowly shutting down his biological systems. "Can you do one thing for me?"

"Anything, buddy, you name it."

"Take care of Nancy—promise me you won't let anything happen to her." The door to the underwater airlock opened. He hesitated, but there wasn't much oxygen left in his system. His cells were dying already.

"Of course I will," he heard Sid reply, now a faint signal.

Bob swam into the airlock and punched the button to close the door. Pumps banged loudly, pumping air into the chamber. Bob put out a hand to steady himself against the wall, and then leaned over to retch out the perfluorocarbons as the water pumped out below his knees.

"What are you doing down here?" Jimmy's projection sat cross-legged on the floor of the airlock.

Bob gasped for air. "They've stopped the attack. I just want to talk to you." Standing up, Bob pulled a metal tab from his swimming trunks and began unscrewing an access panel.

"Just a temporary hiccup," Jimmy replied, smiling. "And we were talking, but you swam away."

Bob finished unscrewing the panel and reached in to pull out a mass of optical wiring. This was as close to the routing core of Atopia as he could get.

Jimmy watched Bob. "You know, these chambers can be used for more than just pressurizing."

There was no way he could get anyone or anything down there quickly enough to stop Bob from doing whatever he was doing. The pumps fired up again and a hissing noise began.

Bob found the photonic transducer array. Closing his eyes, he ripped open a cut on his index finger with the metal tab and pressed the cut onto the transducer, sending a flood of smarticles from his bloodstream onto it. He coagulated the blood, forming a hard connection to the machine. He was connected directly into the core now. Even Jimmy wouldn't be able to track everything. He started flooding the networks.

The noise of the pumps increased in frequency. The air pressure in the chamber was dropping. "Stop it." Jimmy's projection stood up and walked next to Bob. "Don't make me do this."

Bob wheezed. "I'm not making you do anything." He felt Jimmy's networks trying to stem the flow of information gushing from him into the core.

"Stop it," insisted Jimmy again, banging one hand against the wall of the airlock.

Bob was trying to contain it, but his cellular membranes began shredding in the sudden and massive decompression. He doubled over, coughing, keeping one hand on the transducer while the other came up to his mouth. He brought it away. It was covered in blood.

"Bob!" Jimmy yelled, his eyes growing wide. "Stop!"

Bob's internal organs began rupturing, and blood ran out of his nose and ears. It was nearing vacuum in the chamber. Still he kept his finger on the photonic array. His body sagged against the wall.

"STOP IT!" Jimmy screamed, but he was now screaming at himself. Nobody else was left in the chamber.

Trailing a streak of red against the wall, Bob's body slid down to slump into a pool of its own blood.

# 21

SID PULLED THE restraints of his seat, his knuckles white on balled fists. The image of Bob's inert body lingered in the shared display of the passenger pod. Tears streaked down Sid's face. The only sound was the low hum of the pod's life support system recycling the air.

Sibeal reached into the display with a phantom and clicked it off, then reached with her real hands to hold Sid's. She encouraged him to release the webbing tabs.

Shaking his head, Sid muttered, "Why did he do that?"

"I don't know," whispered Sibeal.

"Jimmy didn't need to kill him." Sid clenched his teeth and looked at Sibeal. "He could have just left him unconscious. Why did he have to kill him?"

She shook her head. "I don't know."

"And why didn't Bob try to stop him?" Sid mumbled. "He could have hacked the controls. He didn't even try . . ."

"Ah, sorry," said a quiet voice from the back of the pod. It was Shaky. "But how do we even know that just really happened? Maybe it was a fake."

Sid began breathing again in shallow breaths. "It seemed real enough to me. None of the connection streams ever switched, it was continuous"—he analyzed the data they received—"and the encryption tags were intact."

Shaky shrugged. "Even so, you Atopians . . ."

"I don't know, is the answer." It wasn't something Sid could analyze, wasn't something he could crunch the numbers on.

Shaky shrank back into his seat. "Sorry."

The pod cut through space in silence while Sid ran through the connection mechanics again and again, searching for any evidence of tampering.

"Hey."

Sid glanced over his shoulder while the bulk of his mind focused on the analyzing and replaying the scene of Bob's death over and over again. Bunky was reaching forward in his seat to reach out and touch Sid's arm.

"Look, I know this is a shock," continued Bunky, "but there was no good reason why Jimmy wouldn't have killed Bob."

Sibeal turned around. "Bunky this isn't—"

"Let me finish." Bunky held up a hand. "We might have to accept this at face value."

"You don't understand." Sid's voice was ragged.

"No, I don't. So tell me."

"Bob was the only one that ever stood up for Jimmy, protected him. We grew up together."

"So you were mates as sprogs, then?"

It took Sid a second to decode what he meant. Sprog—cockney for child. "Yeah."

"Sometimes mates kill mates in war, mate." Bunky gripped Sid's shoulder. "I know. I was in the British Army when the Troubles rose up again in Ireland. It was why I left."

Shaky frowned. "I didn't know that."

Bunky nodded. "Yeah, and if you want to make whatever he sacrificed himself for to be worth it, you need to get a grip, right now."

Sid said nothing. The muscles in his jaw flexed.

"Or do I need to remind you," continued Bunky, "that we're in a thirty-foot long capsule,"—he checked the altimeter reading—"forty miles in space above enemy territory, in the middle of a war, traveling at six thousand miles an hour straight into an enemy blockade."

The Commune wasn't just a Luddite ashram. Its founding fathers, some of the richest people in America, had foreseen a day like this. It had been built with a final battle in mind. There was a fortress under those farms. While it might be safe on the inside, the problem was that Allied forces had encircled it—the Commune's perimeter was now an enforced no-fly zone.

Nancy knew this, and must have had a plan, but since comms were cut off for twenty seconds in the plasma burst of launch, they hadn't been able to contact her. They were heading straight into this mess at nearly two miles a second. The heat shield of the capsule was already heating above a thousand degrees as they reentered the thicker layers of the atmosphere. Their chairs swiveled around to take the g-forces in the opposite direction.

"This Nancy girl that Bob spoke of, to take care of—that's the same one that bundled us into this thing?" Bunky asked.

Sid nodded. "Yes."

"Try her again—seems the first order of business would be making sure she's all right."

Sid tried again. "I have been." Jimmy was steadily regaining control of the Atopian ecosystem, driving out the Terra Novan tunnel Bob wedged into its perimeter. Sid's connections were shutting down.

"I think the first order of business," Sibeal interrupted, "would be making sure we're not blown to bits by the Allies *or* the Commune."

"We should be okay. Did you check the flight plan?" Sid summoned the details Nancy gave them. They had to assume Nancy had a plan. He noticed that Commander Strong had authorized Allied tags for their capsule. He pointed this out to Sibeal. "That should let us straight through, at least until it's too late to stop us reaching the perimeter. And I assume she contacted the Commune to tell them we're coming."

From here, they had no way to communicate with the Commune directly.

Sibeal shook her head as the g-forces of re-entry squeezed her back into her seat. "Assume she contacted them?" The acceleration was piling up, much more than at launch. Their trajectory was taking a steep dive into the Commune.

"And we better hope that those Allied tags are still good."

The pod ripped down through the atmosphere, blazing a bright tail behind it as the comet rose over the curved horizon. Holding their breath, they breached the Allied no-fly zone. Sid spun a viewpoint out into the surrounding area. The Allied attack on the Commune had stopped. Everything in the Allied networks indicated a stand-down status. *What happened? Why'd they stop?* The auto-rotating blades of the pod popped out, shifting their capsule from a ballistic into an aerodynamic flight path. It began decelerating hard again, squeezing them into their aerogel seats. They neared the Commune's shield.

Sid detached from his body to watch from the outside. Like a helicopter, the pod hovered just at the edge of the aerial plankton dome a mile and a half in the air. Then, like magic, an opening appeared underneath them. The plankton parted to allow them through.

"We're in!" Sid exclaimed inside the capsule.

Flight plans uploaded from the Commune into the pod's controller, and it slid through the air to land upright on its landing gear, in a field a few hundred yards from a barn on the outskirts of the Commune village. Two people in a horse-driven buggy were coming their way along a dirt road.

Unstrapping himself, Sid motioned for the rest of them to do the same. "Seems we have a welcome party."

Sid had never been inside the Commune. He wondered what would happen next. The door to the pod slid open just as the buggy arrived. Sid took a deep breath. "Hello, thanks for letting us in, my name—"

One of the men hopped down from the buggy. "I know what your name is," he said, his face obscured by a large black hat. Sibeal stuck her head out from behind Sid.

"But," said Vince, taking off his hat, "I don't believe I've been introduced to your friends."

# 22

*SO THIS IS what it feels like to be dead.*

Bob pulled back the blinds hanging on the window of his old room and peered out. After his external meta-cognition systems rebooted, he flitted his primary viewpoint into his family's habitat, one of the few above-ground living quarters on Atopia that sprouted up out of the water just offshore, attached to one of the mass driver legs. The seas were calm, gently rolling, with nothing to hint at the titanic events that had just taken place beneath its surface.

*I just died.*

*And yet.*

*Here I am.*

He looked at his hands, turning them over. He'd inhabited countless virtual bodies before now, but this instance took on a special significance. Now he had no physical body to return to. Did he feel different? Yes. Like a ship that had thrown off its anchor, his mind felt at sea, drifting—but free. There was no meat-mind holding him back, no dead weight.

He laughed grimly at his own joke.

*But how to tell if "me" remained "me"?*

Mind uploading wasn't proven, and "mind uploading" wasn't even the proper term. They still couldn't copy all of the intricacies of the live brain, but just the external and internal signaling. He was now a black box that mimicked the original in nearly every detail, with "nearly" being the operative word. People had died and kept their externally stored minds active, but the jury was still out whether these were still "people"—no legal courts would uphold the idea. So even if Bob was still Bob, he was technically no longer a person.

Bob walked upstairs and looked around the kitchen. It was empty. A part of him wished his parents were here, but more of him was glad they weren't. In some corner of his mind he thought that if someone had to tell his mother that he was dead, it would be best that he told her himself. He laughed again, sad now. Dying seemed to have a strange effect on the mind.

Being dead would take some getting used to.

Almost against his will, he moved across the entranceway to the door to his brother's old room. His brother had been dead for more than six years, after committing suicide. *And ultimately so did I.* Funny how that worked out. The door slid open, and everything was where it always was. Their mother hadn't touched a thing in the room since Martin died. She probably wouldn't touch anything in Bob's room now. He wondered if this habitat was on its way to becoming a mausoleum.

Perhaps it already was.

Gliding away, he climbed the stairs, out onto the rooftop terrace.

Outside the sky was still blue, the sun still shining, and the beaches of Atopia stood where they always had, just beyond the booming surf. The world always felt unreal to Bob, but before he'd been able to lay his hand on a table, pinch himself when he needed, but not anymore. The dream of existence felt like it had swallowed him.

Through all of life, thought Bob, death was our closest companion. It was always there, just a misstep away, patiently waiting, and always, in the end, winning and bringing us back into its arms—but no more. That constant companion was gone now. Death had become him. Bob breathed deeply, realizing even as he did it that he'd already taken his last one. He didn't need to breath anymore, but didn't have the luxury of long reflection either. He had a job to do.

His gambit had worked.

Letting his physical body be killed had drawn Jimmy in close, the human part of Jimmy's mind going frantic, separating itself from the other. Jimmy didn't want to kill Bob, not the human part of him. Bob had been counting on it, and with Jimmy's guard down he found a crack into Jimmy's inner networks.

Bob had one more trip to complete: a journey into Jimmy's mind.

His view of the shining towers of Atopia, above the green forests and surging ocean swells, gave way to a voluminous, bright corridor. Not really a corridor, but a long set of huge rooms, connected by archways. At the far end Bob could see Jimmy arguing with another projection of himself, their voices echoing through the hallways.

Bob walked toward them.

Sky-blue frescos of angels and cherubs adorned twenty-foot ceilings bordered in gold carvings. Dark-framed oil paintings of uniformed men on horseback hung across one side of the walls. The other side was floor-to-ceiling lead glass windows that looked onto manicured gardens surrounding a long reflecting pool. Sunlight streamed in between purple drapes tied back with gold sashes.

The place smelled stale. Elaborate furniture was scattered everywhere, much of it filled with sleeping creatures. Bob recognized them, the playmates of Jimmy's childhood, the ones he once met in Jimmy's hiding place under the sensory thunderfall. Jimmy sat behind a polished cherry desk set with an antique globe on it. Sitting on the desk was another version of Jimmy. The two of them were deep in discussion. They hadn't noticed Bob yet.

*So this is what the inside of Jimmy's head looks like.* That voice we all had in our heads, now Bob saw Jimmy's inner voice, incarnate and sitting on the desk. Or perhaps behind it? *One of the two.* Whether this was some psychosis of Jimmy's, or an invasive intelligence, was an open question, but either way he had to be stopped.

Bob couldn't help feeling intrusive. He was in the innermost sanctum of Jimmy's being, past all the protective barriers. *Intruding.* He felt like he wanted to apologize, but resisted. *He just tried to kill me.* He should have felt angry, vengeful, but he didn't. Looking at Jimmy's face, still unaware Bob was here, he only felt sorry for him.

Everyone had weaknesses. Bob knew Jimmy's, had long known them ever since he'd watched Jimmy pick the legs off insects in the topside forests when they were kids. Jimmy had hidden it as they grew older, but now Bob felt like he'd failed Jimmy as well.

"He forced us, we had no choice," said the Jimmy sitting on the desk. The seated Jimmy had his face in his hands.

One of the creatures stirred, noticing Bob, and Jimmy-on-the-desk turned around. His dark eyes flashed, but any evidence of surprise was replaced with a cruel smile. "See, no harm done. Here's our friend." He patted the other Jimmy on the shoulder.

Bob's feelings of sympathy evaporated in the naked malice he felt filling the room. He might have cheated death, but this Jimmy might kill him again. "I'm no friend of yours," he said to Jimmy-on-the-desk.

"How cliché," mocked Jimmy-on-the-desk. "Sacrificing yourself for the sins of man."

The seated Jimmy looked up. His face registered genuine surprise. "Bob?"

All of the creatures had awoken. Some of them approached, but Jimmy-on-the-desk held up a hand, easing them back from obstructing Bob.

"Not everybody hates you, Jimmy," Bob said, easing closer. He forwarded some private memories he had, of their talks, the times under the thunderfall—all the memories he shared with Jimmy, ones only Bob would have.

"Hate us?" laughed Jimmy-on-the-desk. He spread his arms wide. "The world loves us." Smirking, he nodded at Bob. "And you can call me James, I'm Jimmy's better half. I know you talk to yourself sometimes too. Come join the party."

"I'm nothing like you," Bob said to James.

James smiled. "You'd be surprised."

Bob kept approaching the desk. "The more important question is, do you love yourself, what you're doing?" he said to Jimmy.

James laughed again, louder. "This is ridiculous." He laughed, but in the background Bob felt him testing the networks, trying to find the hole that was allowing Bob to be inside their mind.

"What was it you wanted to talk about?" Jimmy asked. "On the beach, you said you wanted to talk."

"We have no time for this," James insisted. Now he stood and blocked Bob.

The network traffic in Jimmy's cognition systems became frenzied as James tried to force him out, but Bob had driven a splinter deep into Jimmy's mind. The creatures began to converge, but now Jimmy held up his hand, forcing them back. They hung in a menacing circle around Bob.

"This thing"—Bob pointed at James—"is not a part of you. It's preying on you to get what it wants."

James confronted Bob, was just inches from his face. "Lies, just lies to try and confuse us."

The frustration at how difficult it would be to remove Bob's connection was becoming apparent. James grimaced. Just bringing more force to bear wouldn't solve it. He couldn't just destroy Jimmy's mind. It was where he existed as well.

"I'm not lying, Jimmy," Bob said. "Did I ever lie to you?"

"I've always been a part of you." James tried pulling Jimmy's attention away from Bob. "He's the one that hurt you, made people laugh at you. Do you remember? I'm the one who protected you."

"I KNOW YOU have weaknesses, Jimmy." Bob ignored James. "We all do. This thing knew yours, exploited them. God knows the world is a horrible place, and a lot of people deserve punishment, but you need to let *them* go." *Them*, the disappeared, the ones Jimmy trapped within the pssi-system.

"Let them go?" James was working himself into a fervor. "After what they've done?"

Bob knew James needed Jimmy to agree to block out Bob, but Jimmy wasn't cooperating.

Bob pointed at James. "He is not a part of you, Jimmy."

"Who's made you strong?" insisted James, his face distending, staring at Jimmy. "We've done this together."

Bob shook his head. "He's killed everyone who loved you. He killed your parents, killed Patricia."

"Lies, all lies!" yelled James, now a grotesque caricature of Jimmy, a monster that towered over the room.

Jimmy cried out. "My parents abandoned me—"

"No, they didn't." Bob forwarded copies of the data Patricia Killiam collected before she died. "This thing lured them away and killed them."

With Bob this far inside their shared mindspace, James had no way of intercepting or adulterating the data. "He's just trying to trick you, trying to make you weak—"

"Patricia loved you, and this thing killed her, too."

"She was an old woman," James insisted, "she gave up, she had no will to live."

Bob paused to let Jimmy analyze the data. "And I loved you, too, Jimmy. I still do."

"He doesn't love you," growled James, fire burning in his eyes. The creatures encircling Bob morphed into monsters with fangs and claws menacing.

Bob looked straight into Jimmy's eyes. "And now it's killed me, too."

"Lies!" James screamed. "He's being clever. He let himself die, he swam down there, trapped himself. Get rid of him, Jimmy, we have no time for this. Get rid of him!"

But the little boy Bob had once known, tears streaming his face, stared at the monster towering over him. "No," Jimmy said quietly.

# 23

SID LEANED BACK in his rocking chair and looked into the sky. It was snowing, or at least it was snowing on the outside. High above his head the Commune's shield deflected the snowflakes, sending them skidding and tumbling across the sky. It seemed like they were in a giant inverted snow globe, the snow churning and dancing outside while the real world inside it watched.

He was sitting on the covered front deck of the Reverend's church, the floorboards creaking as he rocked back and forth. Vince and Connors sat on a bench beside him. The Reverend leaned against the railing in front of Sid. A man and woman in a buggy, pulled by two horses, clip-clopped past, the man tipping his hat at Sid. Nodding and smiling, Sid waved back.

"So the attacks stopped?" the Reverend asked Tyrel.

Mohesha nodded, her projection appearing with Tyrel's just beside the Reverend on the deck. "Yes, Commander Strong called a halt to the operation. Beyond that we have no information."

"Good." The Reverend bowed his head and glanced at Sid. "Perhaps young Robert Baxter succeeded in his efforts, as great as the cost was."

It was midday. Even through the snow, Sid saw the tops of the mountains ringing the Commune. To say this place was a fortress was an understatement. It had a near unlimited supply of energy tapped from the magmatic upwelling below, matched with a continuous flow of fresh water from underground aquifers fed in from the mountains.

Using Sid's network diagrams, the Ascetics had neutralized more than a dozen people identified as nodal points, infected by whatever was flowing through the crystal networks. Everything now rested on what was happening inside Atopia. Sid stopped rocking and leaned forward in his chair. "Did we manage to get in touch with Nancy or Kesselring?" Still nothing from Nancy since she initiated contact with them in the pod.

In fact, nothing at all had come out of Atopia in the past hour. The Atopian reality blackout meant that half of the world was unaware, but governments of the Alliance were clamoring for information. The viral skin that infected Atopia not so long ago was still fresh in people's minds.

"No." Tyrel shook his head. "And the access keys to the Terra Novan systems that we gave to Robert Baxter are still active."

Out of the corner of his eye, Sid saw the couple in the buggy disappear into the mouth of an access tunnel that led underground. The Commune had opened them when the first attack awakened the sleeping behemoth of the Commune's defensive systems. The smoking remains of Allied drones were scattered high in the hills around them. Above ground was only a small part of the Commune's infrastructure. The larger part of it stretched below, in the networks of tunnels that stretched under the granite shields of the mountains. This place could withstand a direct nuclear strike.

Sid let out a long sigh. "I'll see what I can do about that." He was the most familiar with Bob's networks and systems. It would be like bringing a part of him home, if he could find anything. "Do we still have any connections into Atopia?"

Mohesha shook her head. "Nothing."

Sid hoped Nancy and Commander Strong had the situation under control, but the longer this information blackout persisted, the more worried he was.

"Do you know where Willy's body is?" Mohesha asked after a pause.

Sid looked to his right, at Willy and Brigitte nestled together. Willy shook his head.

"No, we don't know where Willy is," replied the Reverend. The people in the Commune were serious about keeping their privacy, and the Reverend had had enough of his grandson being used as a pawn in this game.

Mohesha frowned. "Are you sure?"

Tyrel raised his hand. "If he says they do not know, they do not know." In the projection from Terra Nova, Mohesha narrowed her eyes, but didn't push the point.

"Sidney, if you could please look into—"

Tyrel was interrupted by a high-priority broadcast. In an alternate display an image of Jimmy Scadden appeared.

"To our friends and allies, we apologize for the disruption in communications. We would like to reassure our partners that everything is in order and under control." The viewpoint panned back to reveal the Boardroom of Cognix Corporation at the apex of Atopia. Conspicuously absent was Commander Strong, but Kesselring was there, smiling vacantly. "We discovered internal spies working with Terra Nova, and had to suspend operations pending an investigation."

"I am happy to report that we have apprehended the suspects." The viewpoint zoomed in on Jimmy's face. "With the removal of Commander Strong, Mr. Kesselring and the rest of the Board have placed me in direct command of Allied forces. Operations against Terra Nova and its agents will resume."

Sid's splinter network watched the Allied platforms powering up their weapons systems in the southern Atlantic. Jimmy's broadcast continued on in the background.

His heart sank. What had happened to Nancy?

"Ladies and gentlemen, we are going to have to speak at a later date," said Tyrel.

"Shouldn't we get underground?" Willy asked Sid, leaning over to put a hand on his shoulder.

"Not quite yet." He looked at Willy and squinted.

"Why?"

Sid frowned at Willy. Why was it that Jimmy was still so intent on finding Willy? By now he must have known that Sid and his friends had gotten the information from him. And Mohesha just asked the same thing. Were they missing something? Sid had extracted all the data available, but maybe he should look at it again.

"What?" Willy was getting uncomfortable with Sid still staring at him. "You're freaking me out a little."

"Would it be all right if I checked your body again, see if we missed anything?"

Willy shrugged. "I guess."

Brigitte giggled. "I've already been over every inch."

Sid smiled. "With your permission of course."

"Of course," Brigitte replied.

Alarms sounded.

# 24

OLYMPIA ONASSIS AWOKE with a start. It had been months since she had seen anyone else as she wandered alone across the world, trapped within the Atopian pssi-system she installed in her brain. Her mind had unglued, terror and despair replacing the anger and unhappiness that filled her life before. She traveled the world—on the turbofan transport network, on the passenger cannons—but everywhere, the world she created was empty of people.

Eventually she came home, to the little house in Brooklyn where she grew up. Her mother still lived there, or at least, she did in the real world. Olympia wasn't sure what world she was in, but whatever it was, it gave her some small comfort to know she might be in the same space as her mother. Each night she would get into the small single bed of her childhood, still in the same room overlooking the oak tree in the Schmidt's house next door.

And each morning she would awake alone in the world.

This morning, though, something woke her up. A noise. *There it was again.* Not just a noise, but a human voice singing. Olympia pulled off her bedcovers, her heart in her throat. Of course she'd heard human voices in her lonely travels—in recorded films, old newsworld broadcasts that she spent most of her days watching— but this voice sounded like her mother.

Pulling open the door to her room, she almost fell to her knees.

"Olympia?" said her mother, recoiling slightly, holding a basket of laundry. "What are you doing here?" She frowned. "Where have you been? I stopped at your place and found your cat. He looked like he was starving so I—"

But before she could finish the sentence, Olympia jumped and hugged her. Her mother dropped the laundry and, ever so slowly, reached around to hug her daughter back. "Are you okay?"

"I love you," gasped Olympia. She felt something brush her leg. Looking down, she found her cat, Mr. Tweedles, staring up at her and purring. "Mr. Tweedles!" Olympia leaned down and picked him up, squeezing him into the hug with her mother.

Her mother stopped protesting and hugged her back.

Opening her eyes, Olympia looked out the large bay windows on the front of the house. Through her tears she could see someone on the front lawn, looking at the house. A young man seemed to be staring at her, and he looked familiar.

CINDY STRONG WOKE up with tears in her eyes, still dreaming of her proxxid children. She had wanted to let them go, yearned to release them, but felt compelled to stay, felt the need to stay by their sides as they aged and died before her eyes. It felt like being trapped in a dream. She wanted to get back to her husband, Commander Rick Strong, but always she had been drawn back in, the needs of the proxxids outweighing her own.

She found herself staring at a ceiling, lying on her back. With some effort, she lifted herself up onto her elbows. Looking around, she blinked. It was her apartment, the one she shared with her husband. Her mind had been ripped from the endless replay of the small cottage on Martha's Vineyard where she lived with her proxxid children.

Where was her husband? Why was she lying in a stasis pod? What happened?

"Rick?" she whispered, her throat dry, and then again and louder, "Rick?!"

"Jimmy's taken him."

Cindy turned her head. Sitting on her couch was Bob.

"Or *something* has taken him," Bob continued, his expression grim. "I need your help."

"WHAT ARE YOU doing?" roared James, still towering over Jimmy.

"Letting them go," Jimmy replied.

All around them, the palace crumbled. Cobwebs of cracks ran through the marble walls as they disintegrated, chunks of plaster falling from above. The creatures ran away, the purple curtains bursting into flames, pouring billowing black smoke into the frescoed ceilings.

In the middle of it all stood Bob, staring at Jimmy and James as they fought.

"We need them," screamed James, "they feed us."

"I think that they"—Jimmy held up his hands—"feed you."

He ripped his hands down, and in the same motion, the walls of the palace came away, tearing its reality to shreds. In its place appeared a world from Jimmy's inVerse, a synthetic-space projection of a different palace, a Spanish palace. The three of them were now standing in the middle of an open courtyard under a deep blue sky, surrounded by a three-story terracotta palazzo. The walls were decorated with intricate murals inlaid with tiny blue, white, and gold tiles. A baby played between potted ferns next to a pool filled with colorful koi fish. A fountain bubbled water into the pond, while dragonflies buzzed at the water's edge.

"How much of this is a lie?" Jimmy demanded, facing James.

The baby by the pool was Jimmy, and his mother walked over to pick him up. She walked back to the table where she was sitting together with Jimmy's father and another couple, guests of her parents. They were having coffee. Jimmy's mother sat him down on her lap and gripped him tight. "Who's my little stinker?" she growled into his face, shaking him.

The exchange could have been affectionate, but in this rendering Jimmy's mother looked threatening, gripping Jimmy too tight, her eyes menacing.

Jimmy was transfixed as he watched. "Is this a lie?" he demanded again.

"A lie?" James swept his hand across the scene, pulling it apart. "All of life is a lie, Jimmy."

Bob was weakening. In the background, James methodically tore through the Atopian networks, rooting out any threads of Bob, erasing any trace of him. He was disappearing from the realities he lodged himself into. Bob fought back, enlisting the help of the disappeared that were awakening, asking them to hide little pieces of him. They were connected into Jimmy's mind, and some of them were fighting back, but James was powerful. James was killing Bob again.

In the melee, James took control of the military networks. In a splinter of his mind, Bob saw James's face plastered across the mediaworlds, preaching calm and control while he ranted and raved on the inside. World after world fell away around the three of them, flashes of New York, of Big Ben in London, of places Jimmy and James had trapped souls. And at each stop, more were released.

"You want to release them?" cried James in frustration. "Then release all of them, all of them can witness the end."

# 25

"THERE ARE NO such things as coincidences," Connors said. "That's the first rule."

Sid was looking at the information in Willy's body again. He instantiated a private space to talk with Connors, to get her input as a professional investigator. Mohesha was the one who interpreted the information they got out of Willy's body. Sid hadn't involved himself too deeply out of respect for her seniority and skill. Maybe that was a mistake. Mohesha had given them the first clues to hacking into the machine, but Jimmy was still looking for Willy, and now so was Mohesha.

*Why?* They must have missed something.

Connors created a diagram of her investigative procedures on the wall of their workspace. "And you need to look at all your background material. It all needs to make sense, to be coherent."

Vince was with them. "And I want to know why we haven't been able to speak to any of these *creatures* in the old machine, if it exists. If the bad guys are here, where are the good guys?"

Sid hadn't thought of that. "Maybe they're already helping and you just don't know it."

The attacks against the Commune had resumed. In a splinter of his mind, Sid watched a white-hot sheet of plasma burning high over the farm buildings outside. Gobs of it began raining down as the Commune's dome started to fail in places. The falling plasma ignited the wooden buildings into flames, and then, like the wall of an aquarium shattering, the dome burst. Even through a hundred feet of bedrock Sid heard the thunderous impact that destroyed the ground level of the Commune. A part of Sid was helping in the defense, hacking into the Alliance networks outside, but it was a losing battle.

They were in the underground complex, open caverns with bio-luminescent ceilings that glowed blue. The buildings below were nothing like above, rectangular bio-plastic cubicles stacked to the ceilings. Sid and his friends were corralled into a string of buildings directly underneath the Church. Bunky and Shaky were much happier being underground. They'd already gone off to inspect the digging gear.

"So you really want to take this apocalyptic text literally?" Connors asked, looking at Sid and Vince.

They both nodded.

"The legend is true somehow," Vince replied.

Connors rolled her eyes.

"Or," Vince added quickly, "whoever is orchestrating this thinks it is. Either way, there should be Four Horsemen out there."

"Good point." Connors looked at a diagram hanging in space between them. "So if that's true, in the analysis, there are two outliers and one big problem."

"What's the big problem?" Sid asked.

"If we're fighting the Four Horsemen, who are they?"

Sid pulled up a network map. "Jimmy's the center pivot."

He pointed out the main trunks of data exchange on the nervenet. Most of them routed through either Atopia or Terra Nova, the two competing platforms, but the vast majority centered on the large cloud around the connection point of Atopia.

The Ascetics had neutralized smaller infections, but the large ones, three huge clouds on the network maps, were too diffuse to single out individual people. The big problem was that there were only three large end-point clouds; one around Atopia, one around Allied Command, and one around DAD—the agricultural contractor for the Department of Defense.

"There before me was a white horse, and he rode out as a conqueror bent on conquest," Vince said, quoting from the sixth verse of Revelations. "The White Rider."

"That's one," Connors said, pointing to the large cloud of data connection points around Atopia. This cloud of activity was at least twice as large as any of the others. They all assumed, by now, that this was Jimmy Scadden. The implication being that he was a kind of anti-Christ. Sid had argued that most historians viewed the White Rider as the savior, not the destroyer, but this was a matter of interpretation.

Connors pointed at another nexus point, this one a clouding of connection around Allied Command. "And there you have the second rider."

"A fiery red one, its rider given the power to take peace from the Earth," said Vince, again quoting Revelations. "Yes, sounds like a military reference."

Connors traced her finger along to the third nexus. "And at DAD we have the third one."

Vince nodded. "A black horse, holding a pair of scales—the agricultural contractor for the department of defense—DAD—famine and pestilence, makes sense to me."

"That's three." Connors held up three fingers. "So where's the fourth?"

Sid shrugged. "There isn't one."

"I think the fourth is more of a metaphor for what happens next." Vince accessed more of the Revelations text. "Before me was a pale horse, its rider was Death. They didn't even give him a color."

"Actually, they did," pointed out Sid. "They translated as 'pale' from the original ancient Greek of 'chloros,' which could also be translated as light green."

Vince shrugged. "Okay, so the Green Rider. I don't recall seeing anything referencing green." He began running searches anyway.

Sid turned to Connors. "So you think we're missing a node?"

"If you think the Apocalypse is literal for what's happening out there, then you're missing one." She paused. "It wouldn't make sense that one of them is a metaphor."

All of the other network traffic was routed through Terra Nova and Atopia. Sid began breaking the traffic down, seeing if he could get any more detail on it.

Connors left him to it and returned to her analysis. "And the two outliers that don't fit are that POND message, and the hint about where to find Willy's body."

Vince nodded. "Keep going."

"There's no way that a mysterious message from another universe shows up right when all this starts to go haywire." She took a deep breath. "And that hint for finding Willy's body, appearing in a two thousand year old text?"

Vince wagged his head. "So if it's not real—"

"—then someone faked it." Sid completed the thought for Vince. "Or it's just a coincidence."

Connors held up a finger. "But there are no coincidences. That's the first rule." She brought up a new workspace with Mikhail and the Ascetics on it. "So the Willy hint came from Mikhail. How much of that network traffic goes through the darknets? Maybe that POND message was meant to throw us off track?"

"So you're saying the fourth horseman is in the Ascetics? Mikhail?"

Connors nodded. "It would make sense, wouldn't it?" She took a deep breath. "In any investigation, you need to step back, usually it's staring you right in the face." Connors took a literal step back. "Who's at the center of all this?"

They stared at each other.

"We're at the center," said Sid after a pause, and then after more consideration. "Bob's at the center."

Connors nodded. "Okay, so in these two outliers—the POND message and the ancient clue about Willy—have you applied everything you know about all of yourselves to them?"

Sid shook his head. He hadn't. It seemed like a long shot, but he started running processes, pattern matching everything in their own backgrounds and histories. He also grabbed everything he had on Bob, which was a lot. They'd lived their entire lives together. He had petabytes of Bob.

# 26

BOB SHOULD HAVE left, should have escaped to protect himself, but Jimmy was starting to lose the battle. James was too well entrenched.

So Bob stayed, enlisting the hundreds and then thousands of people who were released from James's control in the fight. Bob sensed another presence fighting with him. It was the priest, helping support Bob at the fringes. One world crashed into the next. And then as suddenly as it had started, it stopped.

Through the sensory whitewash of a thunderfall, Bob regained his senses, the splintered parts of his psyche reintegrating in one place. He found himself standing in the cave that Jimmy used to hide in. Jimmy was sitting on the floor with his proxxi, Samson.

A fearsome monster, clawed and fanged, lurked in the corner.

"It was never my mother," screamed Jimmy at the monster. "It was always you!"

"I am you," snarled the monster.

"Did you kill them?"

"Why would you care?" The monster came out from the shadows. It was a distorted version of Jimmy, its skin flaking, hands curled into claws, teeth protruding. "We killed them, Jimmy, you and I together."

Jimmy shook his head, but he knew the truth. "You used me, just like you used them."

"And it made us strong." The monster edged closer to Jimmy.

Despite his struggle to hide parts of himself, Bob was disappearing from existence. James was wiping him out. The image of Jimmy and James faded before his senses.

"I can destroy you," whispered Jimmy. He stood up to the monster. "Because I can destroy myself."

In a mind-collapsing thunder, the world around Bob buckled.

# 27

FROM A HUNDRED MILLION miles away, the dot of light that was the Earth flickered and dimmed, then grew lighter and darker by turns as the space power grid echoed energy back and forth from one terrestrial power web to another. The bright pinpoint of light that was the battle in the South Atlantic flared and then went dark.

"Whoa!" Sid exclaimed. "Did you guys feel that?" A massive spike in network traffic exploded from Atopia. It lit up the entire multiverse in a wide-spectrum pulse, even creeping below the bombardment assaulting the surface level of the Commune.

Then everything went silent.

The thunder above stopped.

Sid's main subjective was still in the private space with Vince and Connors, sifting through the masses of pattern matching. Nothing new was coming up. The disruption pulled his attention back into the underground cavern.

Sid looked at Willy. "What happened?"

"The attack stopped again."

"And?" That was obvious, but what had stopped it?

"I don't know," replied Willy.

Sid's mind jumped from one splinter to another. The Allied forces outside the Commune were standing down again. Energy surged in massive waves back and forth through the space power grid, microwave radiation that was bouncing through the hundreds of power grid satellites in low earth orbit, down to transmitter arrays and back again. Ground potentials around the world spiked. The communication networks filled with noise.

From what he could sense, the attack against Terra Nova had stopped again as well. Tyrel and Mohesha were sending connection signals. He tried to latch onto them, but the heaving electrical interference from the space power grid was too much, saturating even ground-based systems.

Vicious, Sid's proxxi, materialized in the underground cavern. Sid expected an update on what was going on outside, but he grabbed his attention on a private channel, back to the pattern-matching algorithms running in the background. "You need to see this."

Sid shook his head. "The attacks just stopped. We need find out what happened on Atopia." Everything was emanating from there.

"This is more important." Vicious plugged a data feed into Sid's mind.

The world shimmered and reformed.

Sid found himself standing in a steaming jungle filled with alien-looking plants. Green monsters with spiny dorsal fins lumbered toward him. In the next instant he watched a mushroom cloud rising into the air over corrugated tin shacks, and a moment later he was watching Assyrian troops amassing outside Jerusalem. His head filled with figures and dates, streams of nearly unconnected meta-data. "What is this?"

"The contents of the POND message."

His proxxi slowed down the data stream. Sid was now standing next to Bob in Battery Park in New York. A huge Nazi flag draped down the side of one of the old World Trade Center buildings.

"I applied one of the old time-cloaking encryptions you and Bob used to play with as kids."

He and Bob used to play games, hiding worlds from their friends, interlacing them in time over the top of the ones they were in. Places that were there but not there at the same time. The information they were seeing was Bob's own sensory data, like thousands of gameworld simulations, but these were streams from Bob's metacognition systems. It was like Bob had lived hundreds of lives.

"Any guess what this means?" Sid asked. The data had to be corrupted somehow, cross-connected on Atopia, or from Bob carrying the data beacon.

"I already checked all that."

Sid tried to make sense of it. "So Bob sent himself a message encoded in neutrinos? From another universe?"

His proxxi shrugged. "I don't know what to say."

Sid brought up some simulations of possible ways to create neutrino bursts. The entire Earth was bathed in the signal that Patricia picked up, a signal that must have literally been sprayed across the cosmos.

Just receiving the message was a stretch with existing technology. Creating it required energy on unimaginable scales, larger than even a supernova. How was it possible? And if Bob sent himself a message somehow, then why wouldn't he have told them?

Unless he didn't know himself.

Sid needed to get more eyes on this. Vince and Connors were still in the cavern, trying to establish the connection to Terra Nova. Sid pinged Vince, dragging his attention back into the private space. Vince accepted.

But before Sid could say anything Vince blurted out, "Sid! We have a message from Bob!"

Sid blinked. "How, uh," he stuttered. "How did you know?"

Vince's eyes were wide. "Didn't you hear me? We got a message from Bob. He's not dead." He grimaced. "I mean, not exactly dead." He shook his head. "Just look on the main display." Bob was connecting into them, his projection already appearing in the cave. "Don't you want to say hello?"

Vicious was already handling the introductions through Sid's body in the cave. Bob smiled and started to explain what happened, but Sid resisted.

"You need to see this." Sid pulled Vince's attention to what he'd found.

Vince's expression turned from excitement to confusion. "Bob sent the POND message? Why didn't he tell us?"

"Maybe he didn't know about it himself," ventured Sid, trying to make sense of it. "Should we ask him?"

Vince hesitated as well. "Maybe you should explain to me what's in the POND message."

Sid was still sifting through it himself. Not all of it was Bob's sensory encoding. Some of it was instructions, some of it network diagrams. He couldn't make sense of much of it yet, but one consistent message came through. He forwarded this part of the message to Vince.

In the cavern, Bob was explaining how he had to sacrifice his physical body to get close to Jimmy, how he let Jimmy kill his physical body to force a wedge into Jimmy's mind. Jimmy was gone. With the truth revealed, he destroyed the other side of himself. Bob now had control of all the Allied weapons systems.

"So Bob killed himself?" Vince said to Sid. In augmented space, the message that Bob had sent himself in the POND transmission sat in highlighted bold text in front of both Sid and Vince: **Don't let me kill myself.**

Sid nodded. Some of the network diagrams in the POND message looked familiar. They matched what they found inside of Willy's body. He began to see what he couldn't let himself see before. "That network traffic between Jimmy and Bob on Atopia, I'd discounted it before as an artifact of the volume of traffic going through Atopia."

Vince understood what Sid was saying. "So the fourth nexus point was inside Atopia."

Back in the cavern, Vicious asked Bob about Nancy, about his family. His face impassive, Bob replied that James wiped them out, erased their minds, destroyed any traces of them in the networks.

Vince slumped into a chair in the private workspace, squeezing the heels of his hands against his temples. "Usually chloros translates as pale, as in the pale rider, and like you said it also means pale green."

Sid waited for him to finish his thought.

"But there's also another meaning of chloros."

"What's that?" asked Sid with a mounting sense of dread.

"Chloros can also be translated as recently dead."

Sid stared at Bob. "There was another translation for that ancient text where you found the clue for Willy. In ancient Greek, Pobeptoc could be literally translated as Robert."

"The Book of Robert," said Vince quietly. "So the Fourth Horseman . . ." He didn't finish his words.

They both stared into Bob's smiling face.

"So Bob is Death," whispered Sid.

# 28

SMOKE WAS STILL rising from the blasted top levels of Atopia where Kesselring's private gardens once stood. The charred remains of Kesselring's retreat stood at one end, but at the other was a single copse of green trees that remained intact, a small patch of green against the blue of the seas and skies beyond.

Bob sat next to Nancy, holding her hand. Her face was blank.

The priest stood in front of Bob. "Give Tyrel back control of the weapons systems."

Bob still had full systems access to Terra Novan resources, even access to all of Mikhail's darknets, and now, with Jimmy gone, he'd taken over control of Allied networks as well. He held the world in his hands.

Looking at Nancy's blank face, Bob felt rage rising up inside him. "Should I?" She was gone. Bob was sitting next to her body, but it was an empty shell. James had erased her mind and any traces of her in the networks. Bob's mother and father, as well.

He'd failed them.

"We are not here to inflict more suffering, but to reduce it, ease it," replied the priest, his long robes flowing in the wind. When the network pyrotechnics had cleared after Jimmy destroyed himself, the priest appeared. He had never been far. "And the longer you hold them, the more they will fear. We don't need the weapons systems."

The green trees at the edge of the destruction swayed in the breeze. Nancy sat with her hands in her lap.

"Is it gone?" Maybe Jimmy had destroyed himself, but whatever had infected him, was it gone as well?

"No."

"Then how do we stop it?"

"Do you want to stop it," asked the priest, "or do you want to stop the suffering?"

"Nancy?" Bob squeezed her hand. "Nancy!" he yelled, shaking her.

There was no glimmer of recognition in her eyes. No connection in the hyperspaces surrounding them. Just a blank mindspace filled by her body.

Why did I run? *I could have saved her.* The rage of self-loathing rose in the back of Bob's mind. Why was it that he could protect everyone but the ones he loved?

"They're awakening now, all of them," said the priest.

"All of them?" choked Bob between his tears. "Not just the disappeared?"

The priest nodded.

"Give back the weapons," insisted the priest. "We don't need them."

"Why should I?" Bob snarled from gritted teeth.

"Because"—the priest paused and laid a hand on Bob's head—"there are better ways to stop the suffering."

# 29

"YOU SURE YOU'RE okay?" Sid asked Bob.

Bob's main subjective was already in a meeting with Tyrel and Mohesha as they tried to coordinate a stand-down of the Allied forces and African Union forces. Sid received a message from Zoraster. He was safe. A splinter of Bob's mind walked together with Sid and Vince and Willy up the service tunnel toward the central bunker to meet the Reverend. The rest of their gang went ahead, leaving them an opportunity to catch up.

Sid checked and rechecked, querying Bob's cognition frameworks while Willy and Vince made small talk. He had to make sure this was Bob. So far every test returned a positive result. His friend had cheated death. He felt ridiculous for coming to the conclusion that Bob was the Fourth Horseman when all seemed lost.

In a flash, it all was over.

"Guys, you can stop," laughed Bob, "it's me."

Vince and Sid hadn't disclosed what they thought they'd discovered to anyone yet. Too much was happening, and anyway, Bob had released all the weapons systems back to Allied and Terra Novan control. Terra Nova was badly damaged, as was Atopia. Mohesha and Tyrel had enough to handle without throwing something else onto the plate, something that didn't seem to have any bearing.

Even so, with both sides standing down, everything under control, something didn't feel right. What had they missed? The pieces just didn't seem to fit. Then again, as Zoraster told him, war wasn't neat. It was messy. Maybe Sid just had to let it go.

While it had been a happy shock to find Bob standing in front of them, walking and talking, that was only because Sid assumed that all of Bob's cognition systems would have perished with him. Having his dead friend returned to life wasn't that all that surprising. The line between physical and digital had long since been blurred for Sid. Talking to the resurrected version of Bob didn't faze him.

Sid contacted his own mother on Atopia the second normalized channels had opened. She scolded him, told him what a scare it was seeing him on the newsworlds. He told her it was a mistake. The relief that he felt, knowing his family was okay, was intense. He couldn't imagine what Bob had to be feeling. "I'm sorry about Nancy, about your mother and father," Sid said to Bob.

Bob kicked some gravel along the floor of the tunnel. "Me too."

Talking to his dead friend might not disturb him, but Sid was worried. He knew Bob could lash out. Sid was tensed up, waiting for the explosion, waiting for Bob to process what had happened. Sid waited for the screams and tears and anger.

But there was nothing.

This was definitely an instantiated Bob he was talking to, all the background checks proved it beyond a doubt, but he was barely registering any emotions. Had something happened in the cross-over?

Bob's projection shrugged its shoulders when Vince sympathized about his parents being killed.

"Sometimes sacrifices have to be made," said Bob, looking at Vince. "For the greater good, you know?"

Vince opened a private channel to Sid. "This is creeping me out."

"Me too," replied Sid.

"Maybe he's just shell-shocked," Vince suggested.

"Maybe." Sid wasn't convinced. Bob's face looked sad, withdrawn. It both was and wasn't the Bob he knew.

"Should we bring up the POND data?"

Sid took a deep breath. They hadn't had the time to bring this up yet. When they decoded the POND signal, Terra Nova and the Commune had been on the edge of destruction, in a final fight for existence. In almost the next instant, it was over, the fight was won, and an intense flurry of activity started to gain control over the situation. What was in the POND message was mysterious, but it was hardly mission critical.

Or was it?

"We need to tell him," Sid replied. "Maybe he can answer the mystery, and it's his own sensory streams in the POND data. He'll be able to decode what's in there way faster than me."

"And you're not worried that his main message to himself was, *Don't let me kill myself*?"

In the background, all over the world, the disappeared were reawakening. It was messy. People were awakening not just in their stasis pods, but in virtual worlds and in augmented space, coming to their senses to find themselves walking the streets like ghosts outside of their bodies.

"Of course I'm worried," Sid replied. "But we shouldn't wait. Bob can help us."

Vince shrugged.

Dropping from their private conversation, Sid put an arm on Bob's shoulder. "We decoded the POND signal." He forwarded the decryption tags to Bob. "I don't know what to make of it, but it seems like you sent yourself a message." Sid watched his friend's face carefully.

Bob accepted the key. His face creased up. "This is my own sensory data, what in the heck?"

So Bob didn't know. "I don't know, buddy, we were hoping—"
But Sid was cut off midsentence.

"Sidney?"

It was a familiar voice, but one Sid hadn't heard in years. It pinged long forgotten memories. "One second," he said to Vince and Bob as he shifted his primary subjective to have a look.

In a newly formed world, in their old family home back in Hoboken, New Jersey, Sid's grandmother stood before him. He'd never even been there before. His grandmother had visited them once on Atopia, when he was four, just before she'd died. She motioned for him to sit down.

"Grandma?"

"Sit down, Sidney, it's time to eat," she insisted, waving a spoon at him. She was cooking.

Sid obeyed and sat at the kitchen table. He began testing the metatags of the world he was in, but there were none. His mother appeared through the living room door.

"Sid," said his mother, "what are you doing here?" She pointed behind her. "Did you see in the living room?" There were more people in there. He recognized his grandfather, and through a portal from this world to another, he could see more, all connected together in a string that stretched back in time.

"Vince," Sid called out in alarm, bringing his mind back into the corridor. "I just—" He wasn't sure what to say.

"I just met my mother," said Vince, stopping walking in the corridor and staring at Sid. "She died forty years ago. What the hell is happening?"

"They're being released." It was Bob speaking. Sid and Vince turned to him. "All of them, they're being released."

"Who?"

"Everyone."

Sid grabbed Bob's shoulders. "Every *who*?"

"Every human, everyone who reached the threshold of self-aware intelligence."

And in an instant Sid understood. His splinter network spread out from his grandmother's kitchen, back through the portals and into the other worlds connected to it. Each generation of his family had come back to life, each one of them seeing just the generation or two that it knew. Parts of their cognition and memories were resurrected. Enough for them to be aware, but not fully cognizant. Vince grabbed Sid's hand and shared what was happening inside his networks.

It was the same thing.

"Who's that?" asked Sid's grandmother.

Sid looked up into the corner of her kitchen. It was an image of Bob, but not the Bob walking with him in the corridor, nor the version of Bob talking with Tyrel and Mohesha. It was Bob on the top level of Atopia, sitting with Nancy. A man in flowing robes stood before them.

"That's my friend Bob, Grandma," Sid replied.

But if that was Bob, who was walking with him in the corridor? He checked and rechecked the metatags. "Bob, what the hell's going on? Is that one of your splinters?" Sid directed Bob's attention to the image of him on the rooftop of Atopia. "And who's that you're talking to?"

For the first time since Bob's return, his face registered something more than mild emotion. "I think we've got a problem, Sid."

"No kidding."

Sid sensed both the Terra Novan and Atopian synthetic reality systems flaring in a massive spike of activity. Behind it all, the space power grid continued to cycle back and forth. It wasn't damping down, but intensifying.

"That's me, too," Bob replied after a pause. "Another copy of me. It must have happened when I died."

This was getting worse and worse. "And who's that you're talking to?" Sid asked again.

"The priest."

"Who?"

"The priest," Bob repeated. "Mohesha told you about him, didn't she? Didn't I mention him?"

Sid shook his head. "No, you didn't." He tried raising Mohesha on a private channel, but there was no response. Global communication systems were overloading. A sinking feeling settled into Sid's gut. He began pinging his friends, and the sinking feeling solidified into a hard ball of fear.

What was happening to Vince and Sid seemed to be happening to everyone with whom he could get in touch.

Tens of billions of human minds were being resurrected somehow, each of them in places they remembered, speaking their own language, everything translated and intermediated by the Terra Novan and Atopian synthetic reality platforms. All the other synthetic worlds were being displaced by these new realities.

And all of them were watching Bob on the roof of the Atopian towers.

"Sid?"

"Yeah?" He turned to face Bob.

"I've had a look at the POND data."

Sid didn't need to ask Bob what was happening. He knew what was happening. It was happening everywhere, in every time, and to everyone.

"And?"

"I think something very bad is about to happen."

# 30

BOB LOOKED DOWN at the farming towers of Atopia, a thousand feet of steel and glass reflecting the blue of the ocean around them. He squeezed Nancy's hand again. It felt like he was holding a dead fish.

Jimmy had released the disappeared, and in a flood, James had released everyone else. In his mind's eyes, Bob saw them, the millions and then billions of minds that were being recreated, their awarenesses blossoming back into the multiverse. He looked into Nancy's eyes beside him. She smiled vacantly.

The knuckles of his hand holding Nancy's were white. She flinched.

"Life is suffering," said the priest, looking to the horizon.

Bob's mind flashed. A man impaled on a pike in a medieval battle, red and white banners flapping in the breeze; a woman sitting by a garbage heap, haggling for the price of her child with a group of men; a slave pushing his hands up between the floorboards of a ship, its sails heaving in the mid-Atlantic; a hulking Grilla, its eyes glazed over in a drug-induced stupor in a ghetto; the imprint of the digital slaves, the synthetic intelligences that he'd help create inside of the virtual worlds of Atopia. These and countless other impressions crowded his mind.

"But not all life is suffering."

In another mind he saw a different world, a world without humans. This mind soared above green forests and plains filled with buffalo and seas singing with whales.

"Humans are not evil by nature. The evil is in what causes the suffering, the desire and attachment of the mind." The priest paused. "Intelligence is the root of attachment. Intelligence is the evil."

Bob closed his eyes.

The priest kneeled in front of Bob. "There is a path to the cessation of suffering."

"Yes," whispered Bob.

He had no physical form here anymore. One universe was as real as the next now. The vastness was suffocating.

"All of reality is created, it is both as real and not real, everything and nothing." The priest cupped Bob's chin, trying to get him to raise his head. "How many worlds have you already created and destroyed?"

"Hundreds, thousands . . ." mumbled Bob, keeping his head down, keeping his eyes closed.

"All things that come to be, come to an end," said the priest. "Everything tends to disorder until a reordering is due."

Bob felt Nancy's dead hand in his.

This suffering was too great.

# 31

SID AND VINCE sprinted the two hundred feet up the access tunnel to the main chamber. There wasn't much time. Bob ran with them. Like everyone else, their display spaces were forced onto the image of Bob sitting on the bench next to Nancy, the priest kneeling in front of them. The wind whistled through the trees, carrying smudges of smoke that still rose from the burnt grass around them.

The entire present and past of the planet watched—ten billion humans, ten times that many resurrected humans, and at least as many sentient non-human creatures. Whatever languages they spoke, everything was being intermediated so they could understand. All were focused on Bob and the priest.

The priest squeezed Bob's hand. "Do you want to end this suffering?"

Bob's head was down. A tear streaked down his face from eyes squeezed shut. "Yes," he replied.

The split copy of Bob stood in the middle of Sid and Vince, staring at himself on the roof of Atopia. "No," he whispered.

Sid glanced at him. His psyche must have split when he died, and a part of him—his anger and fear—stayed with the priest on Atopia. The rest of him was here in the Commune. Sid was desperately trying to help Bob reconnect with himself, but Bob didn't want to speak with Bob anymore. Sid worried that the priest might use Bob's connections to launch an attack, but all the weapons were dormant. In fact, all of the weapons were disabled.

But it wasn't the weapons he was after.

The oscillations in the space power grid weren't just reverberations, not just echoes of the struggle for power in Atopia. The space power grid was steadily cycling power from around the planet, redirecting the energy into the capacitive storage grid outside of Lagos. The only thing connected to this was a supercollider. Mohesha was working to regain control of it, but this had been an afterthought.

Until now.

Sid pulled Vince back in their private workspace. "Have you ever heard of a vacuum meta-stability event?" The supercollider was designed to test extremely high-energy physics, creating miniature black holes, studying the very fabric of space-time. He pulled a graphic, a curved line down with a dip and then a lower dip in it.

Vince shook his head.

"A meta-stability event is an idea that the fabric of our universe is not in its lowest possible energy state." He pointed at the first dip in the graph. "But that we're in a dip, a local minimum." He pointed at another dip in the curve, this one a saddle point lower down. "The problem is that there might be a lower dip nearby." Between the dips was a small hill.

Vince frowned at him. "Get to the point, please?"

"The problem is that if a part of space—even a teeny, tiny part—manages to get over the energy gap and tunnel through it"—he highlighted the small rise, opening a small gap underneath it from one dip to the other—"then all of this universe will leak out into the other one."

Vince stared at the small gap between the dips. "And you could use this supercollider to do that?"

"Maybe." Sid didn't know. It was just a theory. You could create miniature black holes with the collider, but they winked out as energy dissipated over their event horizons. He couldn't see any other threat that made sense. Sid urgently messaged Tyrel at Terra Nova, telling them they had to destroy the collider somehow. A ping returned. They had already come to the same conclusion.

Vince and Sid stared at the graph in front of them. Bob was with them as well.

Sid turned to Bob, pulling him aside to sit on a packing crate. "You have to get in there, Bob."

The mediaworlds roared as they watched the scene playing out on the roof of Atopia. People were questioning the synthetic realities connecting them to their old family, wondering how the system had glitched. Most of them were upset that whatever alternate reality they'd burrowed into had been disrupted.

Very few understood that Judgment was being passed.

On the roof of Atopia, Bob opened his bloodshot eyes. "Make it end."

# 32

BOB SAT ON the crate and stared at Sid while his mind raced through the POND data. It was like he was having a conversation with himself, a self that had lived a hundred lives in a hundred different worlds. There was never any ancient civilization, at least, not one on Earth. It was all just a ploy, a feint to keep their attention elsewhere. Finally, all the pieces fell together. It all fit.

It was always him.

Bob was the fourth nexus. He was the Fourth Horseman. He was Death. And if Bob was Death, then the priest was the Destroyer. Jimmy had just been a pawn in a struggle that stretched across worlds. The priest had used Jimmy, preying on his weaknesses but also using his strengths, and in the same way the priest had used Bob. Used his ability to inspire trust, his emotive intelligence, to gain access at all levels. As if in a game of chess, Bob was moved into the center of events, the priest sacrificing one piece to win the prize.

The other side of the coin was Bob's anger, his willingness to capitulate to others to solve his problems, his desire to hide behind the pain. He remembered the desert now, when he opened his mind to the priest, let him inside. He should have known. *He did know.* And yet he wanted someone else to take responsibility. To save him. To stop the suffering.

The priest had never been real, not in the physical world. It was an echo that had infected Bob, co-opted him. Reviewing the sensory stream from the POND data, it was something that was happening again and again, not just in this world, but in all worlds. Bob was never forced. He always invited the Destroyer in, and he always chose the end.

But, perhaps, not all was lost yet.

Bob was trying to connect into himself, but his other self wasn't responding. When he died, the priest split Bob's psyche, schisming off the parts it didn't need. Or perhaps he'd done it to himself. His angry self was sitting on top of Atopia, holding Nancy's hand, wishing for destruction.

Bob made one last push to get through to himself. To his relief, his other self relented for just a moment, and in the next instant he was sitting on the roof of Atopia, staring into the Destroyer's black eyes. The priest smiled and released Bob's hand, then stood and walked away.

Grabbing himself, he dragged both parts of him down to his family's habitat.

"Stop this!" he said to himself. His emotional side glared at him from across their breakfast table.

"It's too late," the other Bob replied. "You had your chance on the beach. I said to stop, to save her, to save them, but you wouldn't."

"You need to make it stop."

"So now you want to stop."

A seagull sailed by, angling away on the breeze. The slow roll of the swells and setting sun gave the impression of a lazy end to the day. On the other side of the world, the collider powered up.

Less than three minutes remained.

Bob shook his head. "I don't want to."

"You have to."

"Why?"

"You can't kill all these people."

"I'm not killing them." Emotional Bob laughed. "They're already dead. We haven't been alive since Martin killed himself six years ago.

Getting high, playing games, we're as bad as they are." He waved an arm at the waiting billions. "We don't even exist here anymore." Both sides of Bob felt the awful void.

Bob stared at himself. "Do you know about the POND data?" He forwarded copies of Sid's data streams. "The priest used us."

Angry Bob laughed. "Maybe we used him."

A wave crashed on the shore. Bob watched himself assimilating their past lives. He paused. It was a moment for truth. Had he pushed his brother over the edge to commit suicide? He looked himself in the eye. "You mean your suffering must end."

Bob gritted his teeth. "Our suffering."

"You know he took them away. Your priest, he's the one that took Nancy and Mom and Dad." Bob hesitated. "Even our brother."

"Did he? Are you sure? And anyway," said Bob, looking at himself and smiling, "if that POND data is true, then Sid and Nancy and everyone here is somewhere else as well. What does it matter if we end this one reality? The game here is lost."

He was right.

The fragments of the POND signal, streams of Bob's memories from other universes, contained snippets of conversations with Sid with Nancy in other similar but different places.

*Two minutes now*, came a warning from Sid. Two minutes until the supercollider could fire.

"This doesn't need to be over," Bob said to himself.

"What do you mean?"

Bob forwarded the details of a technical schematic contained in the POND message.

Both of him nodded. He might be angry, but he wasn't entirely unreasonable.

"We haven't much time."

# 33

"MOM, THERE'S SOMEONE I want you to meet," said Vince, holding Connors's hand, pulling her attention into the world he was in.

His mother was watching an ancient cathode-ray television set, sitting in the living room of their old house on Bolton Street in South Boston. It wasn't really a house. It was the ground level apartment of a triplex, but to Vince it was always home. He wondered how detailed this world was. If he walked outside, would he see the old neighborhood—three-level brick walk-ups with trees struggling up through cracked concrete, beat-up cars lining both sides of the street, his old friends Nick and Tony sitting on the stoop next door?

And was it all just a simulation?

Vince's mother perked up, straightening her hair. "Oh my, it's been a long time since you introduced me to anyone." She leaned forward in her chair to get up.

Vince smiled. "It has been, Mom. It really has been."

"This isn't really the time," hissed Connors under her breath. She was talking to her own dead mother in an alternate world when he jerked her aside.

*Ninety seconds.*

"This is exactly the time," soothed Vince. "Bring your mother. We're going up on the mountain."

Vince secured a private spot in the wikiworld, on top of a mountain next to the Commune. The view eastward was pristine, and the sensor resolution made it feel like you were there, staring at the stars in the night sky. Vince had seen himself in the streams in the POND data. He'd seen himself through Bob's eyes, a different version of himself, but still recognizable, living out there, somewhere else in some time and space. He'd also seen Connors. With him.

Connors started up a private world to talk, but Vince dismissed it with a flick of a phantom. "There's nothing we can do." Bob was gone. Vince felt that strange sense of freedom he'd felt in the jail cell. "I don't know what's going to happen, maybe nothing, maybe everything."

But in his heart he knew.

From the corner of his eye, back in the cavern, he saw Zephyr smile at him. Vince smiled back. Zephyr stood holding hands with Willy and Brigitte and the Reverend. They were praying. Sid was sitting on a crate, talking to his own family.

Vince returned his attention to his mother. "This is Sheila, Mom." It was the first time he'd used Connors's first name.

His mother tottered forward, her smile and eyes wide. "It's a pleasure." She looked at Vince. "Did he mention my name's Sheila, too?" She laughed.

Connors smiled and glanced at Vince. "No, he didn't." She had her own mother in tow, pulling her from her own world, their realities merging. "Mom, this is Mrs. Indigo, Vince's mother."

*Thirty seconds.*

"Come on," said Vince, "there's somewhere I want take all of you." Extending his phantoms, he grabbed their attentional matrices and brought them up to the top of the mountain.

The stars spread like a carpet of diamonds above their heads.

"Vince, this is so nice," said his mom, uncomprehending, but the reconstruction of her mind trusting like a child's.

Hotstuff stood with them, and Vince's mother looked at her and smiled. "Who's this?" she asked.

"That's a friend," replied Vince.

Hotstuff winked at Vince, then smiled at his mother.

Thank you, Vince mouthed silently to Hotstuff. She knew what he was thinking anyway. For the first time, Vince wondered what she was thinking. He reached out and embraced her with his phantoms while reaching down to take Connors' hand and squeeze it. "Can I ask you something?"

"What's that?" Connors whispered.

*Only seconds now.*

"Can I kiss you?"

# 34

A PULSE OF protons was born, a tiny cloud of millions of hydrogen nuclei stripped down to their cores of three quarks glued together by the strong interaction force. In the intense magnetic field into which they were birthed, their combined magnetic charge accelerated them, pushing them around the thousand-mile circumference of the supercollider. Inside the protons, strong nuclear forces were orders of magnitude stronger than the electromagnetic or weak nuclear forces, each of these orders of magnitude stronger than gravity. Since the birth of this universe, this arrangement was how it had always been, but soon, it would be no more.

Around and around the collider the protons flew, their magnetic fields accelerating them ever faster. First, to ninety-nine percent of the speed of light. Time slowed down as their masses started growing exponentially. Onward toward the ultimate barrier they were pushed, to point-one percent, then to point-zero-zero-zero-one percent of the speed of light. Lights of cities around the world dimmed as the space power grid soaked up their energy and directed it into the collider.

The magnetic fields containing them shifted slightly, peeling off a few protons on each pass into a slightly different path, a path shared with a stream of protons traveling in the opposite direction.

And then it happened.

The smeared wave function of one proton lined up perfectly with a proton heading in the opposite direction. Their collision unleashed a density of energy not seen since a billionth of a billionth of a second after the birth of this universe at the edge of its creation. The burst of energy tunneled the combined proton's wave function through the fabric of space, pushing it into a lower vacuum-energy state.

The collapse began.

On the mountaintop in Montana, Vince leaned down to kiss Sheila Connors. Vince's mother was looking at the comet just rising above the horizon. "It's beautiful," she said in the instant that the wave front of the expanding lower-energy vacuum-state bubble destroyed them.

The bubble expanded at the speed of light.

In half a hundredth of a second, a fraction of the blink of an eye, the planet Earth was gone. For nearly nine minutes, the crew of the Comet Catcher mission, their space habitat a hundred million miles away, were the only humans remaining in the universe.

Five hundred and forty seconds after the initiation of the collapse, they too were gone.

At the initiation of the bubble, Bob had inserted information about himself into the collapse sequence. Contained in the POND data had been instructions describing how to encode information onto the surface of the space-time nucleation bubble that the meta-stability event would initiate. This universe would collapse, but a new one would reform, carrying with it an echo of the past. That echo would be Bob's memories, thrown out in patterns of high-energy neutrinos across the fabric of the multiverse.

The bubble was destroying this universe, converting it into another.

All the pain and suffering of the Earth had come to an end.

And within the bubble, all was calm.

# Epilogue

BOB STARED AT the Great Seawall of New Amsterdam at the edge of Battery Park. It was the first time he had seen it with his own naked, natural eyes. If this place wasn't still the financial capital of the world, they would have given up and moved to Manhattan by now. All the way up to Canal Street was at sea level now, guarded by an immense system of dikes and seawalls. Money was holding back the sea, but time was a thief and soon would steal it all.

"We need to wait a little bit longer." Sid slapped Bob on the back. "The glasscutters need to verify us in person."

The night was gray as the lights of the city lit up the sky, the concrete and metal and glass of the city the same color as the sky and the sea, all of it indistinct from the other in a precipitation that was neither rain nor mist, but something shifting in between.

He let a splinter sweep above the bay, sailing over the top of the Monument de Libertad, ringed by her own skirt of concrete that kept out the rising seas. Spinning further out to sea, he turned his point-of-view to look back at the twinkling city, extending his viewpoint far as he could see. Greater Sophia-Lisbon stretched down most of the east coast of the Republic of States, a hundred million people crowded into one unending metropolis.

They said the meek would inherit the Earth, but nobody had said anything about the kind of state it would be in when it was time for handover. The wind pushed a break in the clouds, revealing the faint twinkle of brave stars that tried to shine down on Gotham.

"Do you ever wonder why?"

Bob snapped his attention back into his body and looked at a man in a gray raincoat, with a hydrophobic shell, sitting on a park bench. The falling mist of rain danced away from him in a veil as the man looked toward the bay. That's odd. No identity popped up in Bob's identity algorithms. "Why what?" asked Bob.

The man looked into Bob's eyes, smiling. "A hundred billion stars in this Milky Way galaxy, and a hundred billion more galaxies just like it. Life fills every available crack in this solar system, and most stars have planets—maybe a quarter of them with planets similar to Earth."

"And yet?" Bob was still trying to get an identity.

"And yet not a peep from anyone out there. Do you ever wonder why?"

Except for the POND data, thought Bob, remembering the mysterious signal from a supposedly extraterrestrial source that Patricia had detected with her Pacific Ocean Neutrino Detector. Perhaps they should release information about it. It might even change the world from the downward spiral it was in, if the world realized that someone else was out there. But first they needed to decode it. That's what Patricia had told them. What was inside the message might be as important as the message itself.

Bob shook his head, feeling weight bearing down. He was the wrong person for this.

The man was still smiling at Bob. "No? You never wonder? You look like you do."

Bob sensed that something had gone terribly wrong. In his mind the Sea Wall before them opened up and the irresistible force of the black ocean beyond came swarming through, swallowing them and everything in its path, sweeping the world away. The vision pulled the breath out of him and he had to lean on the bench the man was sitting on.

The man reached for Bob to steady him. "Sometimes, to look out there, we need to look inside."

The man looked familiar, but Bob's internal systems were sure he'd never seen his face before. Bob sent splinters shooting out into the multiverse, looking for a recognition point, for any identity associated with his strange visitor. Still nothing. Bob regained his balance and tried to string out the conversation to buy time. "I don't think about it much."

The man retreated and smiled. "You should."

Then, like a thunderbolt, it came: *the priest*. Who on Earth was the priest? Bob was inundated by a flood of information, images, and memories that began flowing into his meta-cognition systems. The POND data was unlocked by a time-cloaking encryption that he and Sid used to play with as kids. In this flood of decrypted information came the answer to his question: *The priest is the Destroyer.*

"We can go." Sid grabbed Bob's arm. "We've been vetted. The glasscutters have seen us."

Bob shrugged Sid off. "One second." In the background he was processing the memories of a world that had just ended. One that he'd destroyed.

Sid craned his neck to look around Bob. "Who's that you're talking to?"

Bob's eyes grew wide as he understood.

Why hadn't humans detected any signs of other intelligent beings out there? Fermi's paradox. Trillions upon trillions of worlds, and all evidence pointing to life being endemic, but no other signs of intelligence, no other signs of other technological beings out there? Why?

Now Bob knew why.

Because there was nobody else out there.

Intelligent civilizations didn't just fizzle out or tend to destroy themselves. They were purposely stamped out, erased by the Great Destroyer, the wrecker of worlds. Synthetic-reality technology was a convergent evolutionary point that all intelligent creatures tended to create. Creation of perfect sensory reality opened a tunnel to the underlying nature of reality, the fabric that underpinned the web of universes. Nervenet technology opened a tunnel that could be traveled, letting the Destroyer cross the threshold.

He tried to make sense of the POND stream. If the multiverse was an infinite series of universes, then why struggle? If everything happened an infinite number of times, then everything would happen, and nothing had any meaning. The answer was obvious: Because it wasn't infinite. The choices that were made reverberated, forcing some realities to coalesce and become stronger, while others faded away.

The man sitting on the bench—the priest, the Destroyer—smiled at Bob. "So now you see?"

Bob looked at the priest. "Yes, I see."

"Good," said the priest. "So now we begin."

# Glossary of Terms

**Atopia**
An independent, sovereign city-state that is a floating platform in the Pacific Ocean, about 2 miles across and reaching more than five hundred feet into the depths of the ocean, home to half a million Atopians. It is the largest platform in the Bensalem group of platforms that are first recognized as sovereign nations by the United Nations in the mid-twenty-first century. These are high-tech retreats where the world's wealthy come to escape the crush and clutter of a packed and polluted Earth. *Cognix* funded the development of *Atopia* as a capital project, as well as to gain their own regulatory environment to proceed with the development of *pssi technology* and clinical trials that would have been difficult or impossible elsewhere.

**Cognix (Corporation)**
This is the leading technology company of the mid- to late-twenty-first century that rises to dominate the "*synthetic reality* and intelligence" market. The founder, Herman Kesselring, uses his amassed fortune to fund the construction of *Atopia* and the *pssi project*.

**Distributed consciousness**
This isn't really "*distributed consciousness*" but a simulation of this, using "*splinters*" that allow a user to send a version of themselves to be at an event or investigate something without needing to actually be there physically.

### Infinixx (Corporation)
This is an Atopian start-up (*Atopia* is like a new Silicon Valley where entrepreneurs flock to develop new *synthetic-reality* applications) that is using the *pssi platform* to create "*distributed consciousness*," which is targeted as the top business productivity app for *Cognix*.

### Phantoms
*Phantoms* is a contraction of "phantom limbs" and in the context of *pssi* refers to additional fingers or hands or limbs that are created in purely virtual spaces that the user can control using their adapted motor control centers. Just as when a person has a limb amputated and can learn to operate a robotic arm by reusing other packets of neurons (using the principle of neuroplasticity), using *pssi*, a person can learn to control a dozen or more purely virtual "fingers" that can operate workspace in synthetic spaces. Many Atopians, and more specifically *pssi-kids*, grow dozens of *phantoms*.

### Phuture
Where the future is the singular outcome of this universe in the next moment of time that your mind finds itself in, a *phuture* is a "possible future" and just one of a set of any possible future universes this timeline may slide into (and that your mind might find itself dragged into). A *phuture* could be simply regarded as a probabilistic event that either happens or does not happen, or they could be equally regarded as real alternate universes that sprout out from the present moment of time. This is based on the "nearly infinite multiverse" model of multiple universes and timelines that many physicists think is how the world may work.

## Phuture News Network

A twenty-four-hour news network, but instead of dealing with news of today, it reports on the news of the *phuture*. It delivers high-probability news stories that haven't happened yet, with a particular focus on celebrity (e.g., "Tomorrow morning, a famous celebrity will die in a plane crash"). *Phuture News* is used not just to passively watch what will happen to the outside world, but to predict what happens in people's immediate environment (e.g., friends, family, work, etc. . . .). Combined with *pssi*, people on *Atopia* don't just read about possible future events, they actually experience them as they begin to live even further in the worlds of tomorrow.

## Proxxi

In the *pssi-technology* platform, a *proxxi* is the digital alter-ego of the user that is a synthetic intelligence construct based on the cognitive models of the user, and that, importantly, retains a sensory recording of everything the user has ever seen, touch, heard, tasted, etc. . . . (a more-than-memory recording of their memories). The *proxxi* is the entity that helps the user navigate pssi space, hopping from one *synthetic reality* to another, even allowing other people to enter their owner's sensory streams (equivalent to "ghosting" into someone else's body) or allowing other people to totally take over someone's body. Importantly, the *proxxi* can walk and talk with the user's body when the user is away, physically protecting the body, and also coordinate hand-over of the body when another user occupies it. A user can commingle, or combine, their subjective reality with the reality experienced by their *proxxi*. For Atopians, a *proxxi* is a direct stand-in for its user, accorded the same respect and identity as the user themselves. Under the *pssi* protocols, users can only assign one *proxxi*, but they often create multiple sub-proxxi to attend multiple events at once. *Proxxi* are also the entities responsible for creating "*splinters*," which are parts of the *proxxi* that are splintered off to attend or review events or appointments. This becomes a cultural convention—sending a *proxxi* is a full stand-in for a person for an important event, but only sending a *splinter* means this is less important. The full attention of the a person is termed the "primary subjective" and it is rare that a person's primary subjective would be in only one place at one time, even more rarely within their own body.

## Psombie

A *psombie* is when a human's body is occupied by a machine intelligence that has nothing to do with the person (i.e., their body is not left in the control of their *proxxi* or even a *splinter*, and they have no subjective sensory stream coming from their body that they can tap into), often when a person leases or lends their body to perform work when they don't need it—or in the event they are incarcerated for crimes, their minds will be disconnected from their bodies, and their minds imprisoned while their bodies are used to help in farming or cleaning during the sentence period. On *Atopia*, *psombies* occupy and run the vertical farming complexes as well as cleaning the property.

## pssi

This term is purposely uncapitalized because it is so commonly used)—acronym for "poly-synthetic sensory interface." This is a platform of technologies that enables an absolutely perfect *synthetic reality*—a perfect sensory reconstruction of sight, sound touch, smell, taste, plus a range of 20-plus other senses. For example, the sense of touch by itself is made up of five senses—tactile, kinesthetic (the position and motion of limbs), sense of temperature, sense of skin being penetrated, and the proprioceptive sense of things being a part of our bodies.

The *pssi technology* platform accomplishes this by intercepting and transducing afferent (from sense organs to brain) and efferent (from brain to glands and muscle) nerve signals using *smarticles* embedded in the body, turning the mind into a "brain in a box" that can either be presented wholly *synthetic reality* or a mix of reality and augmented reality. Critical in this technology platform is the ability, when *pssi* is installed in the nervous systems of a host, to control the motor functions of the body, enabling a *proxxi* to control and protect the body of the user while the user is in synthetic space and/or protect the body in the event of any danger whatsoever.

*Pssi* enables the user to directly plug his or her mind into the informational flow of the multiverse, filtered and aided by their *proxxi*. It also enables the user to create *phantoms* (additional fingers and hands in virtual spaces, directly attached to their neural system) as well as to remap their sensory system—for instance, to remap your skin to the surface of the water when surfing, or to trigger the hair in your back to stock trades so you can "feel" the stock market.

**Pssi-kid**

The first generation of children born on *Atopia* who grow up with the *pssi stimulus* embedded in their nervous systems from birth. They are a part of the final clinic-trials phase of *pssi* as a medical device. *Cognix* Corporation carried out these trials on *Atopia* as they wouldn't have been able to receive approval for this, and many other trials, in any other jurisdiction. *Pssi-kids* grow up seeing very little difference between this world and purely synthetic worlds.

**Slingshot**

An off-center rotating platform weapon that can sling thousands of pellets a second, at speeds of up to several miles-per-second, at incoming targets—sort of like a souped-up Gatling gun/rail gun combination. This is based on real research—imagine dropping a ball bearing into an empty beer can, and then holding the can at its base and wobbling the can around in concentric off-center rotations. The ball bearing would rapidly accelerate around the circumference of the inside of the can at high speed for very little motion or effort on your part. That's the idea, but on a much larger scale. *Atopia* uses batteries of *slingshot*, as well as a mass driver cannon (that doubles as a passenger transport) and a range of drones and other weapons systems to defend its physical assets.

### Smarticle

These "smart particles" are the physical basis of the *pssi-technology* platform, nano-scale devices (about the size of a virus) that enter into and suffuse through the body of a host, automatically latching themselves along the axons of nerve cells. They derive their power from the heat of the body. Once in place, they create a sensor-communication-transduction network within the neural systems of the host, communicating and modifying nerve signals in real time. A user can typically install a *smarticle* network within his or her body by simply drinking a glass of water containing trillions of the invisible-to-the-eye devices. They are so small they can also float in the air, buffeted and held aloft by Brownian motion of air—on *Atopia*, the entire environment, air, water, etc., is infused with *smarticles*.

### Splinters

Synthetic intelligence meta-cognition constructs, which are like simulated versions of "you" (packed with as much of a user's memories and cognitive models as needed) that are sent out to investigate something or monitor an event. These *splinters* report back to the user in highly compressed user-specific sensory and memetic constructs understandable only to the user who owns the *splinter*. Imagine your best friend winking at you when someone enters a party—based on your unique shared memories and knowledge of each other, that wink—which contains only a single bit of information—forms the basis for a huge amount of conveyed information. A *splinter* is like this best friend, a shared memory version of you with whom you can send out and communicate.

## Synthetic reality

An older term for virtual reality that actually takes the concept further. Rather than being virtually there, a *synthetic reality* can be actually and completely there, with full physical sensation, yet created wholly within an intangible environment—it could be thought of as "virtual reality 2.0." Importantly, it does not need to totally replace reality, but can often be used to create an augmented reality or seamless bridges from reality to augmented reality to wholly virtual reality—the term encompasses all these modes.

# Acknowledgements

I'd like to thank my beta readers (and I'm sorry if I don't have all your surnames!) Dennis, Adi Sagi, Alan Shearer, Alison Hidge, Ann Christy, Justin Killam, Antoinette, Ashley, Austin McConnell, Stephen, Alex Henriksson, Bill Derb, Bill Mather, Amber, Bruce Keener, Pamela Deering, Lance Barnett, Craig Haseler, Chris Wojdak, Chrissie, Cody Parks, Dave Edmonds, Dan Norko, Esther Fraser, Scott, Alistair Gellan, Haydn Virtue, Dan, Jae Lee, Jennifer, Jon, Josh Brandoff, Joy Lu, Julie Schmidt, Allan Tierning, Ken Zufall, Lowell, Laura, Tationna Lowe, Fern Marburg, Michel, Marcus Brito, Meg Born, Chee, Olesea, Patty Gee, Phil Grave, Portia Gillespie, Justin, Rachel Wills, Loretta, Rob Linx, Rob, Sara Dieros, Josh Saliba, Shabnam Perry, Steve Siracusan, Adam, Sheila Conners, Aaron Smith, Lori Travers, Clayton, Josh, Tomas Classon, and Tom Power.

# About the Author

*Matthew Mather, 2013*

After earning a degree in electrical engineering, Matthew Mather started his professional career at the McGill Center for Intelligent Machines. He went on to found one of the world's first tactile feedback companies, which became the world leader in its field, as well as creating an award-winning brain training video game. In between, he's worked on a variety of start-ups, everything from computational nanotechnology to electronic health records, weather prediction systems to genomics, and even social intelligence research. In 2009, he began a different journey, returning to the original inspiration for his technology career—all the long nights spent as a child and teenager reading the great masters of science fiction. He decided to write a sci-fi novel of his own, and the result was *The Atopia Chronicles*. He divides his time between Montreal, Canada, and Charlotte, NC.